Cleaning Up

© 2013 Paul Connor-Kearns

Published by Muswell Press Ltd.

ISBN 978-0-9572136-3-0

A CIP record of this book is available from The British Library.

Design by Bewick Abel Thompson
Cover by Barney Beech
Printed and bound by Shortrun Press Ltd, Sowton Industrial Estate, Bittern Road, Exeter, 7LW EX2

Muswell Press Ltd.
www.muswell-press.co.uk

PAUL CONNOR-KEARNS

cleaning up

MUSWELL PRESS LTD

For my Dad, Dennis, see you further on down the road.
To my wife, Juliet, keep walking by my side.

WINTER

JANUARY

PC Darrin May was out riding a lone patrol, driving north on the Orbital. It was the quiet time of the day, a bit of commercial traffic and some solo mums who'd dropped the kiddies off and were up for a bit of 'get it out of the way' shopping. He took the next turn off the motorway and ran down towards the High Street with no particular intention in mind, just happy to be a presence in the centre of the town. He did a slow lap of the outdoor market but there were still more traders there than shoppers out and about on this bright, cold day. It was way too early for any action. The shoplifters would still be at home warming up their sticky fingers.

He cut up to the Barrington Estate and it was more of the same thing there, single mums and a couple of teenage boys self-consciously draped over their low-slung bicycles. He pulled over and scoped the kids just to keep in practice, nothing doing though. They were a little too old for school and he couldn't nick them for just malingering. He stayed parked up for ten minutes or so and then made a leisurely loop back towards the newish shopping centre. All was quiet on the centre's pedestrian mall too.

Darrin was hungry, it was just shading past eleven and it was time for a pit stop. He left the Centre turned into Dangar Street and parked in front of Mr Aziz's shop.

Mr Aziz was nowhere to be seen, his youngest girl, the ever demure Shaista, was serving behind the counter. She had to be, what, in her late teens now, maybe twenty at tops. Drop dead gorgeous in her traditional clobber. It would be a short visit then, if the old man had been in there it would have been a twenty minute job at least. Mr Aziz was the font of all Leeside knowledge, some of it worth keeping, the rest of it just filling in the time. Still, clocking Shaista was always a bonus, that caramel skin and shy smile.

He grabbed a samosa and a big bar of chocolate. As he handed over the dosh Trish crackled out something over the radio about the Community Centre that he didn't quite catch. He had been distracted by the lightest of touches between them as Shaista had handed him the change. He knew that it was all mind play though, she was a good Muslim girl and he was smart enough not to try and start something that wouldn't be finished. He quickly ate the food in the car and then asked Trish to repeat the message. She told him that they'd had a tip off about the incident that he'd attended over the weekend, Barnesy and big Chev were following it up. Nice one, he thought, the chance of a collar.

It had been nothing much really, just low-level grit in the ointment stuff. A group of lads had left a burning wheelie bin pushed up against the car park fence of the Community Centre. He and Travers had pulled the bin away and then radioed in the fireys. Calling them in was standard procedure but, given the scale of the fire, a complete waste of time and resources. They could have sorted it with a couple of buckets but, rules were rules, and Travers, the rigid fucker, ate them up with a fork and spoon.

A couple of minutes later Trish contacted him again, a little archly this time. What time was he coming in for lunch? It was an innocuous sounding query but one that was loaded with meaning. Trish was one of the lads and, as he had recently discovered, definitely one of the girls. They'd had a leery fumble towards the fag end of a heavy session just before the Christmas holidays. It was nothing, just an itch that they had both wanted to scratch. She still played with him though, that arch tone, the purse of her lips and the cocked eyebrow, pleasant reminders of that night together. They both knew that it could happen again. The right time, the right place and the right amount of Stella and whiskey chasers.

He whistled as he arced down towards the bypass, an old tune that his mum sometimes sang to his somewhat reticent, always slightly embarrassed old man. His fingers lightly drummed the wheel as he sung out the melody, *sweet, sweet, the memories you gave to me*. Darrin thought of Shaista's smile and the taste of Trish's heavy breasts - sweet indeed.

The cold wind whipped across Tommy's face, it was a northerly for sure, all self respecting brass monkeys would be tucked up inside, nice and warm. He'd been later than he'd planned in getting away from the Centre, as a few of the lads had been reluctant to let the evening wind down to its natural conclusion. It was a compliment of sorts but a bleeding nuisance too.

He turned the corner and went into his old man's street which was a hunkering row of uniform terraces. Most of the houses had the lights on, probably telly and a couple of cans with the missus. A soft glow came from inside his old man's place; Mick in the lounge room with his newspaper and fags. He turned into the short pathway that led to the front door and gave his usual rap, one slow, two quick, done with plenty of heft to it. He heard the radio dim followed by a mutter, probably Mick's back giving him a bit of grief as he stood up from the chair. A shadow moved across the lamplight and Mick came straight to and smoothly opened first the vestibule then the front door. Tommy registered again the now noticeable angle between their eye lines, there had to be a good three or four inches difference. Mick gave him a brief salutation and, with an impatient jerk of the head, hastened for them to get back inside to the warmth of the gas fire.

'Bloody perishing out there lad - get that bloody door shut.'

He's in a good mood, Tommy thought, there was that familiar hint of mischief in his baby blues.

After a day completely alone the old man was more than up for a chat. For the next hour they trotted out the usual gallery of rogues; the rapacious bankers, the multinationals, the old right, the new left who are actually the new right and, of course, the nanny state. All lacerated, skewered and kebabed from the comfort of their armchairs. Catharsis and company for the old man and, for him, the pleasure of shared time.

Tommy had to ration his visits though, the old man's world had become substantially smaller in the years since his retirement, but age had not made Mick any the less intense and the old fucker could be wearing. Tommy preferred to walk on the sunny side of the street - life was too short to be permanently pissed off with it all.

Eventually the conversation wound down, the old man ragging his scalp through his thinning thatch and yawning. Tommy too was starting to feel the length of the day and it was an early one again tomorrow.

'Time for the feather eh son - what you got on then?'

'I'm doing the literacy stuff in the morning.'

Mick tutted at that and flicked his chin up at the ceiling, there was still a bit of petrol left in the tank then.

'Literacy, literacy! What happened to the bloody schools eh? God help us, a nation of bloody ignoramuses we are.'

Tommy let the fire peter out - no more coal. His Dad had

a slurp of his cold tea and took a couple of leisurely puffs on his fag.

'I bumped into Dougy May on the Hill yesterday, down near the butchers there. He told me there'd been some shit down your place last week. His lad attended it, he said.'

'Yeah, wasn't much really. A couple of lads burned a wheelie bin round the back there.'

His Dad tutted again, 'not that much that, yer reckon son?'

Tommy breathed deeply, pressing down the irritation.

'They were gone by the time the cops arrived - it would be some of the local lads, no doubt.'

'Mum and Dad eh, I ask yer, what are they bloody well doing?'

Tommy slapped his thighs and stood up quickly, feeling a hint of a sharp pain in his left knee as he did so. He'd pushed the skipping a bit in his last training session.

He smiled down at his father. 'I don't know Dad - modern times eh?'

His dad nodded.

'Aye yer right son, modern bloody times.'

Tommy turned towards the door.

'Alright Dad, I'm gone, you down watching the band to-morra?'

'Aye, I'm having it - just for a couple mind.'

'Might see you in there then.'

'Alright son - later.'

'You too - have a good kip.'

He saw himself out and retraced his steps back to the Centre to grab his car. The wind was at his back this time, still fucking cold but at least it was giving him a push.

He grabbed the Corolla and drove on back to his gaff,

which was down near the heart of the city. There were a few late nighters meandering through the streets, not that many though, it was still too early in the week for the party people. Tommy parked in the back alley behind his flat noting that next door's four-wheeler was partially blocking his gate. He'd have to have a word with that tosser, sooner rather than later. He squeezed through the gap and roughly opened the gate then walked on through the small back yard and on up the steep wooden steps to the flat.

He thought about firing up the computer but he was too tired to get horny. He undressed and went straight to his pit. He glanced at the illuminated alarm clock next to his single bed, seven hours kip, he thought, just enough.

Pasquale's Mum had left as he was eating his breakfast, bustling her way on out with her familiar smooth fast efficiency, eager to get to work. She'd done her usual thing of watching him sort out his back pack for school and she'd reminded him to take what was left of last night's tea for lunch. He gazed out of the kitchen window at a small square of blue sky. What to do, what to do? he thought. She'd be pissed off with him if he didn't go in, that was a given, but he could ride that out, she always caved in in the end.

So, the first decision of the day had to be made - stay or go? Who was he kidding? He'd already made his mind up. Stay home for a while and chill, then on out to catch up with Matty and Junior some time before lunch. He'd get round to M's place for a smoke and a laugh and then they'd probably have a wander down the shopping centre, see who else was knocking around. Anyway, first up, he had time to kill. A bit of Xbox to kick the day off, that would do. He had none of the hard core at his place, she'd put the mockers on that, no fucking chance, were there. He'd have to wait till he got down to M's for the proper stuff.

He pulled off his trainers and dragged a cushion onto the floor. He sat down in front of the sofa and kicked the game up. His hands worked quickly, his bottom lip pushed out to form a little inner tube of concentration as he made his way through the maze. Pasquale was working hard, collecting up the ammunition and taking out the enemy, one by one.

Tommy was down at the Centre nice and early, much nearer eight than nine. Old Alf had beaten him in but by no more than a couple of minutes and he was still busy flicking the lights on in the kindergarten room. Alf turned at the noise as Tommy walked in through the Centre's double swing doors. He gave Tommy a cheery wave then immediately turned to continue finishing off the room, systematically tidying up the desks and chairs. The old bloke loved being of use and being seen to be of use.

He made his way to the back of the building, on to the little office that he shared with Corrine, which was the home of the Centre's youth service. He made a pot of strong coffee and then sat down at his desk. He fired up the computer and systematically read through the emails answering what he needed to and consigning the rest to the virtual bin.

The literacy class would be kicking off in half an hour. The class was aimed at local 18-25 year olds who'd tumbled through the cracks in their passage through the education system. They'd started off with eight enlisted students but had lost three of those within the first month. To their ever lasting credit the remaining five were doggedly hanging on. Joyce,

Rasheed and Wes were the hard core. In every week and always ready to go. Both Joyce and Rasheed had job interviews coming up and Wes was looking at doing a Graphic Design course at the local college. He had talent too our Wes, and a fair bit of grit. Tommy reckoned Wes was on the up.

Toni and Bones were the two somewhat looser cannons that made up the rest of the group. Toni was a good looking young woman whose flirting skills were light years ahead of her literacy ones. Good old Bones was the class joker, a cheeky little red-headed fucker who lived on the Coleshaw estate with his Gran. Bones had plans, a lot of them. He was blessed with enough energy to light up a small town but he had a lot of difficulty with focus and concentration. Tommy gave him leeway as long as he didn't pull too much of his energy and time away from the others.

As the weeks passed by he and the class had established a rhythm, one that worked for them as individuals and for the class as a whole. A light handed steer and words of encouragement for Joyce, Wes and Rasheed; mild indulgence of Toni's coquettish preening, which was usually focussed on Wes and himself, and plenty of one-on-one and banter with Bones. He tried to work to a plan with Bones but usually had to tear up the script and just think on his feet - the little fucker made him earn his money alright.

Today there were no real dramas and a minimum of fuss, and that was enough to call it a win. At the end of the session the class broke up quickly and headed off to their different points on the compass. With the exception of Bones, they all had places to go and things to do. For them the Centre was a means to an end and nothing more.

Bones always hung around for a while after the class finished, sharing scally tales with him of life on the Coleshaw, pumping plenty of techni-colour into the drab monochrome reality. Tommy knew a few of the boys that Bones was hanging with, some of them already into the drug dealing and thieving, the usual shit, all of it worryingly underpinned by the feckless rejection of aspiration. Bones was only a beat away from diving right in. His pedigree was chequered at best. Dad, nobody knew who and where the fuck he was and the lad's mum had been a user for decades, she'd OD'd when Bones was still at primary school. Only a naturally sunny disposition and an iron-willed matriarch for a gran sustained a thin membrane of protection between him and a slide into the worst of all the bullshit.

They went through the same old, same old, macho bollocks. Bones telling him about some scrape he'd got in with one of the kids from the Barrington at the weekend. It was tedious, but it was his job and Tommy saw it as a half arsed attempt by the kid at a scrabble towards common ground and an exploration of his yet to be fully formed sense of what it was to be a man.

'Don't try to be a tough guy Bones,' he had told him, again, 'try and be a decent one.'

Bones would take the advice with laughable cod seriousness; a couple of beats of faux introspection and then the grin was back on.

'Yeah, yeah, I see it Tommy. But, Tommy. He was asking for it man. I mean, what would you have done like?'

Hunger and restlessness finally saw Bones bugger off home. He now had half an hour to kill before the start of the staff meeting and he used the time to walk up to the corner shop for a paper. The paper was the price of walking into the shop, that and ten minutes listening to Mr Aziz give it to the council, national politicians and some of the local kids. He was as predictable as old Mick in his tub thumping. Luckily, just a couple of minutes into the old fella's circumlocutory diatribe, Jamal - Mr. Aziz's eldest son, came into the shop and that quickly helped to change the focus. Jamal was a light breeze compared to his old man.

For Tommy, walking into the shop would always trigger an indulgent memory of Noora. He and Noora had had a very discreet thing a long, long time ago. Fear of discovery and its repercussions had heightened and coloured the already considerable erotic charge between them. He was pretty sure that Jamal had been aware of it and probably Sohail, the other son, too. But, a little surprisingly, they'd kept their counsel, which was probably due to the force of personality of both their older sister and their father.

Before they'd found the resolve to make a serious commitment, he'd made his choice to leave his home town. They hadn't stayed in touch. There had not even been the pretence of it - she was pissed off and hurt by his decision and had made no bones about what she wanted and by the time he'd got back she'd gone. She was now living in Newcastle with her done-well Asian solicitor husband and everything that they once had now belonged up stream in the past.

On his return to the Centre he went straight to the meeting room. Even though he was a little early most of the staff were already in there. Pauline, the Centre manger, was up on her feet, busy circling the tables, divvying up the minutes and what looked like a pleasingly short agenda. She was emitting her usual vibe, an egalitarian good cheer offset by a barely hidden, tight-eyed worry. Tommy knew that her tension was a product of her ongoing struggle to ensure the financial health and viability of the Centre and, a consequence of her unyielding, unconditional love and practical support of a son who battled with a combination of mental health problems and an unhelpful fondness for Class A drugs. Tommy was staggered at her stamina and her tolerance of the foibles of both her son and of humanity in general. In his opinion, Pauline Hughes was a minor-league urban saint.

Sonny the youth team street worker had popped in for this particular staff meeting as he sometimes did. Sonny, who had become a bona fide mate, was well…sunny. An always welcome source of respite from the meetings' frequent bursts of ponderous worthiness.

Sonny took the empty seat next to his. His missus was expecting their first born and they chatted briefly about that and then they moved on quickly to a spate of muggings that had flared up on the Barrington Estate. The Barrington was a colossal shithole, a peripherally located mini town with the ambience and crumbling infrastructure of a dystopian, sweat-soaked nightmare.

Pauline called the meeting to order as Geoff, the Centre's coach driver ambled into the room mumbling slightly red-faced apologies for his tardiness. Nobody was that mithered, the Centre had yet to embrace anything within sniffing distance of the 'corporate' model and thank fucking Christ for that.

They did the round the table thing and the talkers took the opportunity to talk and the rest did a quick, cursory pass the parcel. Tommy spoke a little about the literacy group and the need for some new sports equipment which brought a slight frown of worry from Pauline so he didn't press on it. He thought about mentioning next week's 'safe rave' at the Centre but he didn't want to open that particular can of worms either. Too many people were prepared to share their opinion on it and in this instance he was soliciting brevity not a talk-a-thon. His mind drifted as the staff continued round the table. He'd get down to the Crown later on. Catch up with the old man for a couple then maybe pop into Piccolos to round the night off. He corralled Sonny after the meeting to see if he was up for it but Sonny declined the invitation

'Like to bro, but, you know, Estelle. She likes having me home, now it's getting close.'

Tommy had been back for well over a year and he was still struggling to find regular playmates. Years spent away had seen all the old gang inevitably paired up and settled down. A couple of them had moved away though nobody had gone as far as he had. Twenty years was a long, long time.

These, he knew, had been predictable drifts in a place that was still a rough facsimile of what he had gladly left behind. Now here he was, back again; older, single, still jumping the hoops, still trying to stay solid and rolling on. Despite the passing of the years he remained ambivalently set apart from his birthplace. Sometimes, he could taste the loneliness in his throat. That was a feeling that a few beers could never quite wash away.

Darrin had hung around the station for a little more time than was his usual inclination. He was nursing a hangover that had left every cell of his body feeling dried out, frazzled and frayed. He got away with it for a while up until Thommo, the gnarled Welsh desk sergeant, had flicked a querulous eyebrow his way that was followed by a pointed glance in the direction of the reception's wall clock.

He had a couple of follow ups to do, a young mum who had had her letter box vandalised and an old lady whose purse had been snatched in one of the supermarket car parks. The old lady's description of her assailants didn't bode well for an early collar; a pair of hoodies, low-rise denim jeans, one black youth, one white. The old girl was shaken though, she'd held on tightly to her bag making them work for it and she'd taken a tumble and banged up her knee. Turned out she wasn't one of the 'flog em and hang em' brigade and she had even displayed a degree of compassion for the perpetrators that had made him feel like throttling the little fuckers. If he got the collar maybe he would put a little bit of hurt on them.

The mum was quite a tidy piece, she had a good idea who the culprits were and when she told him the names he realised that the kids' families were known to him. He'd go up and have a word later although he knew that it would probably be as effective as plaiting sea mist. Still, it was good to have the chat, let the pricks know that they didn't have carte-blanche.

He got back to the station to do the paperwork and to engage in some routinely unsubtle banter with Trish and Big Chev about last night's shenanigans in The Ship. His hangover was just about on the ebb and the next blow out was already being planned. They'd start at The Ship, have a few in The Moor Hen then end up in Piccolos, the late night place just off the High Street that was owned by a pair of shirt lifters.

The crew had to cherry pick the pubs they frequented, if there was enough of them it didn't really matter but any small groups had to plan ahead and use a bit of common sense, they were known after all, and not everybody in town had the plod on their Christmas card list. He pencilled himself in with the caveat that he'd get down to the old man's gym for a work out first. Boozy benders had put the start of a belly on him over the Christmas and New Year and his dad hadn't let that go without comment. There were plenty of examples of the Ghost of Christmas Future knocking around the station and, besides, what self respecting bird didn't like the look and feel of a well toned six-pack.

He had been teamed up with one of the experienced detectives to do some door knocking about the muggings on the Barrington. A couple of the incidents had been nasty - much more assault and battery than anything else. They had pulled up at the estate's dingy looking row of shops and their arrival was sullenly scoped by a group of Barra' boys who were hanging out near the entrance of the launderette.

By the time they'd climbed out of the car most of the kids had turned their backs, the lads slightly raising their voices in order to share their limited command of the English language with them. The D was an old lag with a rep for business-like toughness and he didn't even bother looking over in their direction. He made a point of eyeballing a couple of the young 'uns and his challenge had elicited laughter from the group. Darrin felt his face colour and the tension rise in his back and shoulders, but he didn't push it. He caught up with the D in a few long-legged strides. Later, he thought, later.

Pasquale had got into school today - no problem. He'd got there because his mum had dropped him off at the fuckin' school gates. He'd landed back home at around eleven last night. He'd sent her a text about seven but had ignored her subsequent responses, eventually turning the mobile off just to get her out of his head. He'd been smoking with Matt and

Junior pretty much all of the afternoon and for most of the evening too. He was well battered. They had headed out for a kebab, too skint to score any more weed and then they had gone back to M's for some more Grand Theft Auto. Matty only had the third one but he was talking up being at the front of the queue to buy the new one.

She'd gone ballistic when he made it home, coming out of the lounge room at him like a bat out of hell. She'd caught up with him just as he'd placed his foot on the first of the stairs. She must have been sat there in the dark and silence waiting for him, fucking mad she was. At first he thought she was going to hit him, that was something she hadn't done for years and he was surprised at his reaction to her anger. He'd instinctively pulled back from her with a jolt of fear. But, as usual, her concern had outweighed her anger and, after a lengthy bollocking, she'd made them both toast before insisting that he go up to bed.

Now here he was, stuck in this fucking dump of a school. Apart from the late morning history lesson with O'Donnell he'd been bored absolutely shitless. He'd always liked Donno, a big bluff Glaswegian, who effortlessly handled the kids whilst bringing the subject alive. Last year, Pasquale had done a project for him on Scott's South Pole expedition and he had been given the best marks in the class. He'd really pulled that out of the bag - writing the assignment as a diary illuminated with sketches. O'Donnell had been that impressed that he'd taken it off to show the other teachers, some of whom had shown it to their own kids. He'd been a fucking star for the rest of that week. Today was a monumental drag but at least the fit girls in the class were a distraction and there were more than a few of them to perv at.

21

Anyway, he'd be out of here next year right enough. He, M and Junior had a plan to make some readies. The three of them were putting down some rhymes together. They were always up for it but they often ended up too blasted to really get it together and whatever they tried was usually lost in a fit of giggles and piss taking. They nailed it sometimes though - for real. He'd keep it low key for the next few days at least until she cooled down. She'd come round, she always did. After all, she was his mum.

Tommy's old man was at the bar when he walked into the Crown, holding court with a small gaggle of his cronies in attendance. Mick may have been physically diminished but, in his cups, he was as verbally robust as he'd ever been. A break in the juke box roar gave him the gist of the conversation.

'Free trade, free trade,' Mick opined, 'what's so fucking free about it. Bending over for t' rich and powerful they mean… fucking wankers.'

Yep he'd heard that one before - plenty of times. He agreed with it too but he wasn't in the mood for the splenetics, not just yet. Mick's Think Tank nodded along in easy unison; Nev, an easy going beta male who was an old mate of his dad's from the Union days, Teddy Black, a ruddy faced scowler who only smiled on public holidays and Danny 'Drink' Gorman who looked plastered enough to nod along in agreement to Pol Pot.

He stuck his name up on the board and fed some coins into the jukebox, wryly noting that none of his selections had been penned after the turn of the millennium.

Just as he finished his choices there was bit of a commotion behind him at the tight entry doors of the pub. A few youngish scallies had rolled in. They were travelling abroad by the look of them, down here from either the Coleshaw or the Barrington. They were loud enough, with plenty of piss and vinegar, but they were also savvy enough to tread a little lightly. The Crown had plenty of old school in it, ever ready to defend its shop worn honour.

There was a middle-aged guy with the crew, somewhat incongruous compared to his younger mates; nice clobber, a nifty pork pie hat, untrimmed sidies that were worn a little long and sharp, shrewd eyes that gave the pub the once over with a look that was as light and unobtrusive as a zephyr. He gave one of the lads, a slightly mad-eyed fucker with full feminine lips a twenty and nodded him towards the bar. Tommy briefly locked eyes with the stranger and the guy smiled at him, a pleasant, no sweat grin that set off a dim distant echo of memory.

Nugget Dawson came up behind him and tapped him on the shoulder - it was his turn on the pool. Tonight he was in the mood for it and well on form and he kept the table for a good hour. The old man had sent a pint his way and he'd reciprocated. The stranger and the shell suits had had a drink and fucked off, probably gone down into town looking for action that they would probably find.

His old man had quietened down by the time Tommy made his way to meet him at the end of the bar. Nev gave him an easy smile and Danny burbled a greeting and proffered a warm, clammy handshake. Ted Black had left the crew which suited him fine, Tommy found his company to be as refreshing and palatable as a bucket of slops.

His Dad pulled him slightly to one side just a little way from the others. 'Yer clock that bloke, came in here before, with the young uns?'

He nodded, 'yeah, I did, and?'

'Gypsy Keith, Keithy Dalton - you remember him from bloody way back now?'

He did and the name still fitted the face. Tommy nodded at his old man

'Thought you would, with that bloody memory of yours. Haven't seen that fucker for nearly twenty years,' Mick said, 'he's not changed no doubt. Trouble, he is.'

His old man was right about that, Keith Dalton; a connected drug dealer, fence, a card skimmer, a sometime bare knuckled fighter back in his youth and a reputed procurer of young kids. He had a colourful CV alright did Keithy. Tommy remembered that Dalton had gone away some time ago for a two year stretch, sent down for glassing some guy in that poxy old pub near the central railway station. But that had to be a fair time ago now. He'd have a chat with Sonny about it next time they caught up. Keithy might be clocking on a bit to be involved with the street stuff. But, given the company he was still keeping, who knows?

Tommy got a text around half ten. Chris and Jimbo were in Piccolos. Did he fancy it? It was only a ten-minute cab ride away. The bar was home to a mixed straight and gay crowd - what passed for the city's bohemia. And there was always more than a smattering of talent in there. He had a quick one with the old man and told him of his of plans.

'Piccolos,' Mick vented, 'bloody Piccolos, a bloody wine bar! Ten bob millionaires and over priced piss.'

Mick wouldn't be joining him then. 'Be careful in there Tom,' Nev offered, 'you don't want to have one of those el-o-el- a- la Lola - moments.'

They had a good laugh at that, although it crossed Tommy's

mind that a few of the Piccolo trannies were convincing enough to have turned plenty of heads in the Crown. He kept that thought to himself, there were audiences and there were audiences.

The cab quickly arrived, the driver calling out his name as he walked in through the doors. He necked his Guinness with a couple of hungry gulps and made his way out. As he did so he overheard Danny commenting to his old man.

'He's reight your lad Mick in't he…sorted like.' From Danny 'Drink' Gorman there was no higher compliment.

Darrin's dad had worked him hard on the pads for nearly half an hour and then the crew had worked him over with pints and chasers in the cop friendly boozers around the centre of town, and down along the rough holes on Argylle Street. At Trish's suggestion they had ended up at Piccolos. She seemed to love hanging out with gay boys and the drag queens. He'd only been in there with her the one time before, just after their festive shag and he had spent an arse clenching hour making sure that the shirt lifters weren't checking him out. She'd disconcerted him further by telling him in front of a couple of her gay mates that she was a queer man in a woman's body - the three of them laughing uproariously at his ill concealed discomfort. All in all it had not exactly been conducive to a relaxing night out.

He was glad that he had given it another go though. It had been more of a mixed crowd last night, the place packed but refreshingly good humoured. He had to admit there was some quality skirt in there too. Barnesy had teased him a little about going over to chat with a couple of drag queens and he'd held Barnesy's eyes a little longer than usual to let him know that it would be wise to drop it. Turned out that Ged Keegan, who was in the bar when they had arrived, knew the 'girls' in question and Ged had silently took Barnesy at his word and ambled over to chew the fat with the gaudy pair. That move had left Barnesy a little querulous and wide-eyed - rocking the skinny, bandy legged fucker's world right enough. Keegan had leant in close to the pair to make himself heard over the babble that bounced off the low ceiling of the bar. A nudge, a wink and that irritating thing he sometimes did whenever the crew were out on the piss - twisting his closed hand in front of his nose along with a pursed lip look in Darrin and Barnesy's direction had set the pair off. The two of them laughing like a pair of drains, as lady like as a pair of old school tag-team wrestlers. Keegan, according to Trish, was mates with the owners; a couple of blokes that had previously owned a 'celebrity' hair and beauty salon down near the city's coach station. Darrin never knew where he was with that ham-hocked fucker, who didn't need to be chatting up a couple of drag queens to be disconcerting. Keegan had been a detective, a very successful one at that, for twenty plus years now. The brass gave him plenty of leash and he had the rep of a one man wrecking crew - plenty of beef yet very light on his feet. A formidable fucker was Ged, always comfortable in his own skin, seemingly relaxed and easy going but with the unmistakeable purr of a big engine. Darrin had to work hard at just appearing to be himself whenever the big man was around.

He'd also caught a glimpse of Tommy Cochrane. Tommy was still looking good, chilled and at ease, out and about with a couple of his mates. His dad still mentioned Tommy now and again. The old man had known the Cochranes since Tommy was a nipper. He was thinning a little on top but yeah, he looked good, colour in his face and plenty of size in his shoulders and chest, it looked like he still had plenty under the hood too. Trish had broken the train of thought - his pencil sketches of handy, capable middle-aged men. She'd grabbed his arm and swayed into him, pulling him into the circle to make him listen to another one of Choppy's slightly off colour jokes.

Come one o'clock and he had been more than ready to pull the plug. He was working tomorrow and starting to flag after a long day and a busy week. Barnesy was on next day's early shift and he needed no persuading in joining him to make tracks and they had left the joint together. Darrin was hungry and the kebab shop on the High Street was just around the corner from the bar, but there was too much of a queue in there to justify the wait. He'd do a couple of those mini pizzas when he got home.

They made their way up to the top end of the street, dodging through the still surging hordes of the marauding piss heads. They walked up the incline to the Maria that was parked across the middle of the road making sure that there would be no through traffic. It was pedestrians only on the Golden half-mile of the town's boozy epicentre on both Friday and Saturday nights.

Travers, Sarge Collins and Jolika were guarding the van. The three of them had drawn short straw duty tonight. Out of politeness and comradeship, he and Barnesy chewed the fat with them for a little while and Jolika had given him a couple of nice smiles, which made him forget about the mini pizzas for a while. Apparently, it had been a relatively quiet night, which explained why the three of them looked so chilled out. There had been one dust up in the nearest taxi rank but the taxi marshalls had pretty much nipped that in the bud. Although, as Travers pointed out, the marshalls themselves could be cause for plenty of concern. It was too cold to be hanging around. His feet were starting to numb and they said their good nights and made their way back to the nearest rank. A couple of blowsy, pissed up girls were already in the queue and the marshalls briefly interrupted their wit and repartee with the lasses to gave them their due nods of recognition and respect.

It was an Asian bloke who picked them up, a young guy playing some noisy beats per minute. Darrin asked him to turn it down and the young guy did, not mithered at all by the request. The three men shared silence and the melded fug of sweat and a little too much after-shave as they smoothly drove away from the roiling blather of the city centre.

Tommy had no plans for the weekend and that was just fine, if it cleared up maybe he'd take a trip over the tops to catch up with Wayne. If not he'd relax and have a people free day, maybe go down Doug May's gym later on and have a workout with the old goat. He'd seen Dougy's young lad clocking him last night. He'd thought about going over for a chat but young Daz was with a gaggle of plod and they'd stood out like a turd in a spa with their un-groovy haircuts and try hard denims. He knew Big Ged from the old days, Tommy reckoned that DS Keegan had to be up in his mid fifties by now. He had been a wild one had Ged, with plenty of rep for being handy on the cobbles. There was a time when the big man could have gone either way but being a copper seemed to be enough of a valve for his particular energies. Keegan had seen him early in the piece and tipped him a wink. Tommy didn't bother going over for a chat though, underneath the bristling bonhomie Keegan was heavy company and it would be too much like shop talk.

Jimbo had insisted that they engage with a table full of obviously married women. He'd indulged him and one of the ladies had been obviously interested. She was nice on the eye but he didn't fancy being somebody's cheap frisson for the night. She backed off quickly, so no fuss either way. He liked the crowd in Piccolos and the relaxed good will and expansive cheer reminded him of some of the bars that he frequented with Bonnie during his time in the very gay friendly bars of inner-city Sydney. There was some prudent muscle on the door, a couple of polite bouncers that maintained a friendly but rigorous door policy. It was enough to keep the numb nuts and thrill seeking gawpers away.

He'd had some fun watching Jimbo at work. His mate slipping through the gears with his well honed patter, the lad fully engrossed in the game. Jimbo was forty five going on twenty two, incorrigible, unsinkable and daft as a brush.

The chat with the ladies had made his mind wander onto his current 'hobby'- the trawling of internet dating sites. He'd vowed to stay off the computer over this weekend, although he knew that it was a promise that he was likely to break. What was once a (too) easy way to kill time and assuage the loneliness was now beginning to shade into 'must do' addiction. He was spending hours cruising dating sites of the down-market variety, engaging in virtual chat with strangers, cock out of his pants whilst sitting at the keyboard. His mind had even started to go there whilst he was at work too. Tommy knew that he was tumbling towards risky behaviour.

So, he stoically resolved, breakfast, and then he'd get stuck into some housework. An hour later and he was done and it had just started to rain. He glanced at the computer and then, with a reproachful snort, he made his way into the bedroom to grab his gym gear. Dougy would sort him out, he was better than bromide that grizzled old sod.

It had been a toss weekend. Mum had kept him on the leash for the full duration. The only concession that she'd allowed him was the Xbox and he'd had to play it up in his fucking room. He was up there for hours whilst she played her dopey tunes in the lounge, sitting there on the sofa hogging the phone, busy doing nothing other than chatting at excruciating length with her girlfriends.

Pasquale had no credit on his mobile either so he couldn't text the boys to find out what was going on. He thought about knocking hers off and getting a message to M or Junior, he knew that there was going to be a party down on the Barrington tonight. In his ongoing frustration he'd toyed again with the notion of leaving home, luxuriating in the thought of being able to do exactly what he wanted to do when he wanted to do it. But, he couldn't really think past the act of leaving, and, if he pushed it, he felt a kind of vertigo, spinning out with the uncertainty of it. He was more than anxious about that uncertainty, in fact it scared him shitless.

Matty had talked about getting a place of his own. The prick was starting to make some real spends now too, muling smoke for the bigger lads on the estate. He'd shown them a fan of twenties over at his place, M had to have been carrying about four ton there at least. The older boys were moving smoke, crack and ice and, according to M, there was plenty of it to be moved. Matt loved to talk about the older boys being 'mobbed up' but you never knew with him what was bullshit and what was real. He could say both within the same sentence. But he and Junior couldn't mask the fact that they were impressed and whenever he thought about it he felt giddy with the possibilities that such money would give him.

She ordered in a pizza on the Saturday night and then cooked him his favourite meal on Sunday afternoon. They watched a movie together in the evening and they'd even had a bit of a laugh together. Fuck it he'd go in to school tomorrow - keep the peace.

Tommy had taken the old man over the tops for lunch on the Sunday. Pub grub washed down with a couple of pints. His old man was eating like a bird these days, a couple of tastes of the steak pud, a few chips and a desultory stab at the vegetables - Mick had never been that big on his greens. Tommy was as hungry as a horse after his workout with Dougy and he cleaned up the old man's plate too - Mick watching on with a fond, tolerant amusement.

His dad wanted a cig' after the meal so they went outside and sat on the bench that was just to the left of the entrance of the pub.

'Ta for that son, nice grub that. It's a bloody grand day eh?'

'Yeah it's a good-un alright Mick, nary a cloud in the sky.'

His dad turned and smiled at that. 'Pity there's not more of them. You going to go back then son, get out of this bloody shithole?'

His old man hadn't mentioned that for a while and Tommy was taken off guard by it - surprised by the lack of context. It was a conversation that they had been having on and off for the last twenty odd years.

'Probably Mick, probably, no rush at the moment though, I reckon.'

His dad jutted his jaw, he removed a non existent flake of

tobacco from his lower lip then took another tug on his gasper.

'Don't let it slip away son. I know you've got the job here now but, bloody hell.'

Tommy didn't reply, they both knew why he was still here.

They passed a few quiet moments together. His Dad smoked down the fag, crushed the dimp underfoot then stiffly scooped down to pick it up off the floor.

'Fancy another then Dad?'

'You alright for the driving like?'

'On top of all that grub, no problem.'

'Bugger it then son eh - why not?'

Tommy did the honours and took their beers back on outside. He handed the old man his and they sat and drank in an easy silence, the pair of them gazing over at the wide valley that unfolded to the south of the pub, taking in the view of the variegated greens and the stone walls that latticed the near and distant hills.

Not too bad, Tommy thought, for a shithole.

For Darrin and the crew Saturday had been a bit of a shocker. A couple of lads had been caught shoplifting from the grocers, which was down near the canal on Dyke Road. The shopkeeper had nailed the pair whilst in the act, re-obtained the goods and had given them a well deserved boot up the arse for their troubles. The store doubled up as a takeaway curry joint, and the owner's cousin and nephew had been out the back cooking up in the kitchen. They'd heard the ruckus and had rushed out to help send the shoplifters packing.

Unfortunately, the dipshits had not been duly chastened by their experience and, an hour or so later, they'd returned. But, there was about twenty of them this time. They'd steamed into the shop and had systematically started to wreck the joint. Hasty calls by one of the three amigos had rallied the local Asian community and soon it was on for young and old. The raiding party had scattered when the cavalry had quickly started to arrive. Grown men tooled up with bats and bars were a little out of their purview. A couple of the vandals had been grabbed, smacked around a bit and then handed over to the coppers. But, there had been ripples from the event, later that evening an Asian schoolboy was knocked unconscious just a couple of streets away from the shop then, later still, a wheelie bin had been set on fire on the edge of Leeside and that had been underpinned with some Stone Age apocalyptic dancing and chimpanzee arm waving. It was more than intimidating enough to scare the shit out of some of the local residents and provocative enough to further anger plenty of others.

Word it was that a group of lads from the Coleshaw, a gang of black and white united in their wanton idiocy. The area was cordoned off until the wee hours of the next day and community leaders had been brought in quickly to dampen down the aggro. It was a right royal pain in the arse, exacerbated by the usual Saturday night shenanigans in the town, which included a mass brawl in Beckhams, the plastic city-centre wine bar with the subtle hint of a plumber's arm pit, and a sexual assault in a side street down near the theatre.

When he got back to the station he was told by Sarge Thomas that there had been another mugging on the Barrington and he'd be up there with a D straight after tomorrow's footy match.

If anything the game at the Shed would be a relative balm after the Saturday shit storm, it ran like clockwork these days. True, the modern day reign of peace was occasionally punctuated by the odd group of visiting knuckle draggers who'd made the trip to the game by car. Such interlopers were often pre-determinedly set on trawling the local pubs with the purpose of sharing some of their opinions with the locals. They came looking for a fight and they always seemed to find one, so maybe some blokes just enjoyed getting filled in.

He had the coming Monday off. Roll the fuck on.

Pasquale had managed a full week at school, well half a week really, as he had bailed out on all of the afternoons apart from the Monday. He knew plenty of the other kids there well enough, in fact, he'd been to primary school with most of them. One or two had been friendly with him but most of the others had kept a bit of distance like he had the pox or something. In the afternoons he'd made his way on down to M's on the Barrington usually via the game store in the precinct. The new GTA was out this weekend and, this Saturday, M was adamant that he would be at the front of the queue.

He'd had a puff with M and Junior and then they'd gone down to the estate for a chat with the slightly older lads who usually hung out around the shops. The local boys tolerated their presence with a belligerent amusement, the three of them posed no kind of threat and, thankfully, all the Barra boys knew, at least by reputation, Junior's older brother Wes. So, they were not likely to give them too much shit, not while Junior was around anyway.

Wes was probably coming out of nick early in the New Year. Junior respected his older brother but that respect was tinged with obvious concern around the homecoming. Wes always brought a shitload of trouble home for Junior, his mum and his sisters to deal with. Junior didn't want to go back to it.

After a few minutes of back and forth M had been pulled away by the older boys and they were engaged in a tight circled straight faced conversation. Matt managing to shut the fuck up for at least two minutes, the odd 'sorted' and 'cool' coming from him, M revelling in being seen with the big boys. He'd waved away the offer of more smoke when they got back to M's place. He didn't want to be red eyed and shuffling when his mum got back from work. It was OK between them, at the moment. M hadn't been mithered by it; he'd met his mum and was always careful around her. Besides, him knocking it back meant more for him and Junior.

A couple of kids at the school had mentioned this Friday's alcohol-free music night down at the Centre. He knew a few of the girls who were regulars down there and they were well tidy. But, he didn't think that the three of them would bother to go, the Centre had way too many rules and restrictions, and the workers there - Sonny and the others - had a reputation for not taking any shit.

They'd probably get down the precinct for a while and, if Matt's mum was out on one of her benders, they'd hang out there later on. Last summer she'd been gone for a full week and he'd been bunkered down at M's for most of it. Maybe Tish and Sharyn would be at the precinct. Tish had let him cop a feel just a couple of weeks ago. She was tasty but a little too sure of herself. Knowing amusement in her eyes whenever she gave him the once over.

Monday was a write off. Darrin was knackered after the weekend's shenanigans and only managed to crawl out of his pit at midday. He did a quick reheat of a takeaway that he'd picked up last night and then chilled out on the couch for most of the afternoon. He intermittently toyed with the idea of making an impromptu visit to his mum's for an evening nosh up but that would mean the tedious trade off of a couple of hours of having to listen to and tolerate his parent's low level bickering. His dad would definitely be home this evening, he didn't usually open the gym on Monday nights unless some of his boys were competing, whereupon it was on six nights and six mornings. The reality was that the gym was the only place that the old man was truly happy, the rest of life just a test of his old man's patience.

He'd watched a box set DVD for a couple of hours, one that he'd picked up last week. It was a Sci-fi which wasn't his normal bag, but Barnsey and Johnny Jones had raved about it so he'd given it a bash. A couple of episodes in and he was completely hooked. Humanity trashed by machines that they'd created. Darrin got off on the irony of that all right. He was quickly drawn into humanity's epic battle for survival too; the survivors' desperation, lines drawn, all that *backs up against the wall* stuff. Bit like last Saturday night, he thought, but with better special effects and better looking birds.

Yesterday, he'd accompanied one of the female detectives up to the Barrington to door knock about the latest mugging. The victim was still in hospital, a broken jaw and three teeth and seven quid the lighter for the experience. The victim couldn't remember anything but he thought that there were at least two attackers and one of them was 'a big black lad'. Most of the locals had remained tight lipped and resentful in the face of their questions and he had admired the detective's patience as they'd made the rounds. He'd felt like belting more than a few of the ungrateful, po-faced fuckers.

At the end of the first disc he forced himself through some

press-ups and sit ups in his cramped lounge room. He'd give his parents a miss. He decided the DVD would provide all the company he needed.

For Tommy, the week had rolled by as lightly and as drama free as a fluffy white cloud. Thankfully, there had been no great fallout from Saturday's ruckus on the Leeside, which had surprised him a little, although the weather had been wet and cold, which was usually good news for the local crime stats. Pauline had pulled him in on Wednesday to ask him to help her with a new funding bid that she was putting together. It was the 'Building Communities' programme, run through the auspices of the Lottery. Tommy smiled to himself at that bit of information. Mick hated the Lottery, to him it was just another pipe dream for the masses. Mick reckoned you had more chance of getting struck twice by lightning than you had of winning the fucking thing!

Tommy had pledged to help her, although writing out funding bids were definitely not his thing. He could do it if he had to though, no sweat, he was actually more than competent at that side of the job and, at the moment, Pauline was visibly drowning not waving. Mired in the constant grind of ensuring the long term viability of the Centre and making sure that it was operating at a level that she thought would meet the community's needs. She was chuffed at his pledge to help and they had chilled out together briefly, sharing some of her slightly over brewed green tea and their youthful travelling tales.

He knew that she saw him as a bit of a kindred spirit. He wasn't sure about that but did nothing to dissuade her from the notion. Partly out of pragmatism, as it was a boat that didn't need rocking, and partly because he liked and respected her.

He'd stopped at Aziz's on the way home to pick up some provisions. The prices in there were twenty percent up compared to the ever-handy Tesco's but he would rather pay the mark up than put more money into those fucker's bulging coffers. Today, Jamal was in the shop busily restocking the shelves, accompanied by Shaista who chastely smiled at his approach from behind the counter. Jamal told him whilst nimbly unpacking some jars of Nescafe, that 'our Noora' would be down for a visit in just a couple of week's time, she was down with the kids for a few days. Jamal's news had knocked him off balance and he was surprised that his heart had skipped a beat. Jamal finished off a couple more boxes and told him to wait as he went off into the living area behind the counter. He came back with a big grin flourishing a glossy photo which he held at arms length like it was the fucking Koh-i-noor and belonged on a plumped up velvet cushion. Tommy took the proffered picture, it was a current shot of Noora and her family, taken at some collar and tie do. She looked great, as self possessed as ever and that smile of hers - Jesus.

Sonny popped in to see him the next day and they chatted for a while about tomorrow's rave. Sonny had his ear to the ground with the local Asian community and he definitely gave the workplace more of a rainbow coalition quality which always looked good in the Centre's publicity material. Big Lottery are you looking? Sunil was an old Leeside boy; his parents had been living on the estate for most of Tommy's lifetime. Sonny had been given the word that there were still some rumblings about Saturday's incidents and that some of the younger bucks were still talking about taking some kind of affirmative action. Luckily, the older guys in the community were holding sway, as they usually did, and any half-arsed retaliation was being held at bay.

They moved the conversation on to some of the 'at risk' kids that Sonny worked with. In Sonny's role as a street youth worker, containment and damage control was the order of the day. Sonny was well aware that some of the younger boys on the town's estates were getting into the periphery of the harder drugs scene. He told Tommy a couple of names that were now on his furrowed brow list; a kid called Matthew Marshall whose mum had been on the skid for years and a Floyd Alexander, a tall, skinny, wide shouldered black kid whose brother had once been a noise on the local scene before he'd predictably tripped over his pecker through a combination of greed and reaching beyond his grasp. The pair had been implicated in a couple of assaults down at the precinct and they were heading quickly down the slippery slope to Shitville.

Sonny shrugged his shoulders, with a show of resignation that Tommy knew Sonny did not really feel.

'You know what the problem with these kids is Tommy?' He did, they had said it to each other many times before. 'They have no bugger to look up to, right Sonny?'

'We are as that little boy with his finger in the dyke Tom.'

'Ah well Sonny, as long as the dyke don't mind.'

Sonny always laughed at his shitty jokes; big guffaws and a finger wagging mock reproach.

So, Matthew and his mate, Floyd, were out there, two baleful, restless clouds drifting away from the succour of any kind of safety net. The silly little pricks.

Sonny left him with a promise that he would be down at the Centre early tonight to help him move the tables for the rave. Thank fuck, the extra hands were always more than welcome. That evening, Sonny's concerns with the two boys had quickly manifested themselves in a tawdry example of universal synchronicity. The evening's 'safe rave' had gone well, as it usually did, plenty of local and not so local kids taking advantage to chill out and have some fun. The mood was lively but relatively relaxed given the amount of hormones bouncing off the walls. He and Sonny played the avuncular muscle, Corrine and Pauline gave that presence some female balance and a couple of local worthies bolstered the adult ranks by giving up their time as volunteers. MC Lipz, aka Terry Lipscombe, a good natured, fresh faced middle class kid who preferred the less salubrious side of town, was up there on the dismountable stage spinning the tunes.

At about half ten Tommy went outside for some fresh air and to get away from the mind numbing music for a while. There was a few kids out there, some paired off couples who were chewing hungrily on each others faces and a small group of the lads that he regularly took to the gym on a Wednesday. He had a bit of banter with them for a while until he was distracted by a trio of boys wheeling their low slung bikes across the car park. They were slowly meandering towards the pool of light and the open double doors of the basketball court that housed the rave, loudly calling out to each other as they did so. Tommy was pretty sure that he didn't know them and he unthinkingly edged away from the gym lads a yard or two, just to give himself a bit of separation and room. The musketeers pulled up a few yards in front of him, the carrot top in the trio called out to the group that he'd been talking to. The boys nodded back and a couple of them greeted two of the boys by their names - Junior and M.

The couples had taken a break from their snogging and were now looking over in the newcomers' direction. Tommy felt a bit of tension creep into his shoulders.

Only kids, he reassured himself - chill. He knew the black kid, Floyd. He used to come down to play basketball a while back - damn fine player too, as quick and evasive as an eel. The other two he didn't know; a good looking shrimp who was hanging back slightly and the red head who, he assumed, would be Matthew Marshall.

They'd been smoking, no doubt about it, red-eyed and movements that were slightly dulled. There was that tell tale tic of delay in their reactions, body and mind not quite in sync. The red head looked a little wired too, ants in his pants, lots of energy and a restless jaw.

'Can we cum in then?' The red head said to him, his eyes not quite meeting his own - still a lad after all.

Tommy appraised the request for all of two seconds.

He shook his head at them.

'No lads, sorry. We're wrapping it up in half an hour.'

The red head half turned and spat on the floor and the other two looked everywhere but at Tommy. Tommy now sensed the restlessness of the group of gym boys, their unease probably laced with some feral anticipation of a possible confrontation.

'Go on eh,' the kid said, 'you don't finish till eleven.' The little fucker even made a show of looking at his over-sized watch.

He gave them the bottom line this time, leaving no room for any debate.

'The answer is still no, you're all ripped. That's not part of the deal here.'

The other two looked at him, he met both their stares, there was no real challenge in either one of them.

Ginger wasn't ready to let it go though.

'Go on, you're community aren't yer - a youth service and we're fucking youth, aren't we?'

The kid was revving up, both literally and metaphorically, his pale hands gripping and ungripping the handles of his bike.

Tommy caught a movement out of the corner of his eye, a shadow that broke up the light which pooled out from the gym doors.

Sonny spoke up from behind him - his voice firm and steady, no chuckles in it at all. 'Evening lads, venturing further afield tonight, are we?' Sonny had stepped around him standing slightly to the front of his right shoulder. M ran the spiel by Sonny. It was more a request than a demand though.

'Sorry lads, Tommy is the main man here, he's just told you the rules, as I am telling you them now. You're all welcome here when you're straight, that's if you're still interested when you're straight.'

'But Sonny, we are straight, honest mate we are!' Young Matthew was on the slide now - any belligerence was gone.

'Bullshit Matt - next time eh?' Sonny good-natured, still friendly.

M let it go with a slump of the shoulders and the other two turned their bikes away with a couple of 'see yers' to Sonny and the lads. M broke away last and gave Tommy one more bristled look followed by a hawk and spit.

'See yer Sonny.'

With that M took off too, calling out after his mates as he rode away.

'Wait up yer fuckers - let's ride then, get out of this gay, manky shithole.'

M cackled at his own humour the other two looking back

at him, grinning appreciatively at their rapidly approaching comrade.

Sonny placed his left hand on his shoulder, 'you coming back in then Tommy?'

'Yeah Son, in a couple of minutes like.'

Tommy took a deep breath and looked up at what few of the stars the urban lights allowed in. The couples resumed their famished courtships and a couple of the gym boys looked at him, but made no comment. He felt his anger start to recede and gazed up again at the night sky. He realised he could just about make out Orion, now flipped over in the night sky compared to the last time that he'd made a point of looking at it. It was only a fleeting glimpse, as a large band of cloud cut across the constellation's attenuated glistening. He turned and went back inside, greeted by the bump and grind of Rihanna. Pauline and Corrine enthusiastically leading a few of the girls and a couple of the braver lads in a raunchy line dance. He had to laugh.

M was as good as his word. Up, out of bed and off down the precinct early in the afternoon. Junior and Matt were standing patiently in the queue, lined up for the brand new GTA. M had handed over the eighty quid to Junior who had the necessary fake ID, and made for a convincing eighteen. Besides, not many shop assistants were up to taking on Junior's dead eyed stare.

The store was well packed, buzzing with noise and fidgety anticipation - all the gamers with their itchy trigger fingers. He left the boys to get on with it whilst he chilled out checking out the display of second-hand and new mobiles. He was trying to swing a Blackberry from his mum but she kept on stonewalling him. His birthday was coming up soon and he'd work on it again - she'd fold. Ten minutes of browsing and Junior and M had been served, the pair of them sauntering away from the counter, shit eating grins plastered over their faces; GTA and Red Dead Redemption - fuckin' ace.

No hanging around the precinct today, straight back to M's and into it. He kicked their arses as per usual - he was the Xbox king. He'd got a pass for the day from his mum, a trade off for his school attendance and he stayed at M's till midnight. Eight hours straight, rotating the game between the three of them with the vanquished booted off to take his place on the grubby, battered sofa. He was on for most of the duration, only a stand down to get a bite to eat. He was the fucking champion alright.

Pasquale was quiet, up on his on tippy toes when he got back home to the flat. His nose twitched at the familiar week-end smells. She'd been cleaning; carpet shampoo and furniture polish in the lounge, and that lemon scented stuff that he liked the smell of in the bathroom. She'd heard the door and called out to him from her bedroom. He let her know that it was just him.

The next day he was up before midday. She asked him if he fancied a trip to Aunty Bet's but he binned it as politely as he could. It was boring as fuck, all that catching up with family shit. He wolfed down his cereal and toast and as soon as he could he headed off back to M's. Junior had beaten him to it by just a few minutes and he and M were already into the game. Pasquale gave out advice and abuse from the sofa, his upper body playing the moves, his fingers tensing and relaxing as M and Junior let loose at both their wins and their losses. By the time they'd wrapped it up they had played for nearly twelve hours and she was back in bed when he returned home. She'd left some of his auntie's trifle in the fridge for him. This time she didn't even wake up.

Sarge Thomas had asked him if he fancied some plain clothes duty working on the muggings for the rest of the week and he was on it in a flash. Up on the Barrington paired up with good old Steve Morris, sitting out the shift in Mozzer's cramped, battered and slightly humming Honda. He always enjoyed Mozzer's company, Moz knew the game and he could be a laugh too. He had to be kicking 50 and, despite his rep as a dogged and capable investigator, had somehow avoided promotion over the duration of his twenty plus years in the service.

They shared plenty of silence for the first half an hour of the watch and then, with a grunt of anticipation and a couple of warm up swallows, Moz had whipped out some foul smelling cheese and pickle butties and smilingly offered him one. Darrin took it because he was just about ready to chew off his arm. They tasted OK and ingesting it made the smell in the car a little more bearable.

'So, you what do you reckon then Moz, all this shit goin on?' He nodded down towards the flats.

'Definitely be locals Dazzler - take your pick. We have a cast of fucking hundreds living round here.'

'Arseholes eh, doing that kind of damage - for next to fuck all too.'

'Aye, there's no excuse right enough, living in a dump never makes it right. You know son I wasn't always a leafy suburb man meself. Got brought up on the Coleshaw and it was never that easy down there, even back in the supposed good old days.'

'True, I hear it was always a bit rum like.'

'Yeah too right, fuckin' rum indeed, all the great unwashed dumped together. Plenty of hard cases and a few drop kick families, even back then. Not this kind of stuff though. Most people worked and the community kept an eye out for its own and didn't bother calling on the plod that much either.'

'Old school eh Moz?'

'Yeah young un, old school alright. Gone now though, voices in the fucking wilderness all that stuff.'

They chewed on another round of his redoubtable butties for a few more minutes then Moz produced a flask and poured them each a cup of dark brown tea. Drinking it felt like somebody had dropped a concrete slab into his guts.

After necking his brew and letting go a couple of farts a clearly satisfied Moz did a little shimmy with his belly and then opened up the driver's door.

'Come on then young fella, let's get some sunshine under our belts, have a chat with the fucking peasants.'

Darrin glanced up at the sky that the morning cloud was starting to break up a little. True enough, he thought, the sun makes no exception even with a dump like the Barrington.

Tommy had had a couple of drinks with Jimbo on the Monday night, they'd shared a bit of nostalgia that was peppered with updates on Jim's colourful love life. Tommy had alluded to his internet trawlings but had played it down - not ready to share it with Jim, despite his friend's relaxed, open attitude around all things sexual.

He'd been on the laptop last night till nearly two in the morning, engaging in a feverish 'chat' with some Tex Mex bird in Houston, pretending that he was about to hit the States for his holidays. Two o'clock in the fucking morning, all for a glorified wank. He must be fucking mad.

A friend had once told him that any, 'out of balance' behaviour emanated from a need that was not being met. He could see that there was an obvious truth to that but he still hadn't got to grips with what now felt like a compulsion. What was driving it? Mid life crisis, vicarious thrills, a biological imperative, a sop to boredom and loneliness, all of the above and probably more. He vowed, again, to pull the plug on it and immediately, again, doubted his will to do so. Anyway, the bottom line was that the night had left him tired and slightly irritable and he hadn't engaged with either the literacy group or the afternoon's post-school gym class with his usual enthusiasm.

Sonny had given him a buzz in the afternoon to talk about one of the three lads that had turned up on the previous Friday night. That morning the kid's mum had called Sonny to express her concerns about, well, everything really. She'd asked Sonny about getting her boy some extra tuition for the basics as the kid was now rarely in school and was starting to fall well behind. Sonny had told her about the Centre's literacy programme. It was all one-on-one, relatively intense but designed to meet the kids' specific needs and abilities. She'd booked in to see him tomorrow lunch-time.

'Don't know if you remember her Tom, the mum - Donna Edwards?'

He didn't.

'Yeah, probably not. Bit younger than you, then again eh, who isn't.'

Tommy told him to fuck off and Sonny laughed loud enough for him to take the phone an inch or two away from his ear.

'She's a looker Tom - single as well.'

'Yeah, yeah, thanks Sonny, just what I need like, a single mum with a son sliding off the rails.'

'Ah well you like a challenge don't yer Tommy?'

'OK Cupid, I'll give her the once over, if you're that concerned about me.'

'Do that Tommy - if nowt else you can look at the menu can't yer?'

After the conversation, his mind wandered back to the three boys last Friday. He was still slightly annoyed with his own anger bubbling up like that but, that was offset by the disrespect in that little fucker M's behaviour. The quiet boy, Pasquale, had, at first glance, looked bright enough. No doubt there would be a story for her to tell tomorrow, the usual vale of tears stuff. He sighed and threw his pencil down on his desk. His mind strayed back to Jessica, the hot little Mexican chick that he had dallied with last night. He looked at his computer and for a few moments his dark passenger was there, tapping on the window and asking if he could come out to play. Instead, he quickly stood up from his chair. Pauline he thought, funding, get on with your fucking job. Some green tea would partially deflect that particular thirst.

His mum had told him about her plan for him to do some school stuff down at the Community Centre when she had got home from work on Tuesday. He'd felt a surge of pulsating anger at her, the fucking interfering cow! She'd been busy in the kitchen, talking at him through the kitchen door as he was parked on the sofa half watching some dull arse, stupid quiz show on the telly. When she'd given him the bottom line he'd jumped quickly up to his feet and he'd had the urge to boot the glass topped coffee table straight through the fucking box. He'd stopped himself but she'd clocked his anger and an uneasy silence had settled between them for more than a little while.

He'd taken his time thinking through all the permutations, then he'd laid the usual dance on her; why? What's the point? He could find a job, school was boring, the teachers were toss, he'd heard from the other kids that the Centre sucked and the programme was rubbish, a waste of time. There was half an hour or so of back and forth, but she wasn't budging. She even laid a new trip on him this time, if he wanted to stay here with her he would have to go to the lessons - non negotiable.

He'd feigned the pain but smiled inwardly - that might even work for him somehow. He'd waited a few beats and then he let her have his big smile. 'OK Mum I'll do it for you.' She'd looked at him through the doorway, the reflex of a half-smile that dropped quickly away, followed by an exasperated prolonged rasping stiff fingered comb of her wavy hair. She was well pissed off with him.

'It's not for me Pasquale, is it? I've got my qualifications, it's for you son, for you.' Her face had sagged just a little and she had turned slowly back towards the food that was cooking on the gas stove.

Pasquale felt something gnaw deep inside - she'd looked so…old.

FEBRUARY

Donna Edwards came in to see him right on the dot at one o'clock, obviously taking the time to do so on her lunch break. Sonny had not been overstating it, she was a peach alright, only a couple of inches shorter than him in her respectable but stylish heels. She had mid-brown skin with a dusting of freckles across her nose and cheeks, a full mouth and nice cheekbones. She was kitted out in a tailored suit that still showed enough legs for his mind to keep heading north. Damn, she was fine.

She offered him her hand in greeting, smooth-skinned, long tapered fingers and nicely manicured nails. He liked her voice too, soft with just a bit of husky sing-song in it. She was sunshine with the birds all-a-singing.

Tommy willed himself into the work zone and ushered her to the nearest chair. She sat down lightly and demurely crossed those long legs, her body just slightly turned away from his. She cut to the chase straight off, obviously on the clock and obviously concerned for her little Prince. She gave him the lowdown, surprisingly open enough to share a little bit of personal stuff with him too. The old man had fucked off when the kid was still toddling leaving her well and truly in it. She'd struggled working various shit, lowest rung type jobs; she'd gone to college in the evenings whereupon she had completed an accountancy degree. With the qualification, she'd scored a good job with a nearby local authority, which had afforded her and the boy a decent lifestyle. The kid had started to drift in the last couple of years, she said.

He was bright but with no focus, the usual adolescent angst coupled with a questionable taste in friends. The boy would listen, tell her what he thought she wanted to hear then do exactly what he wanted to do. To Tommy that sounded like the modus operandi of plenty of grown men, not just adolescent spin out boys, but he kept that particular nugget to himself.

He listened intently to her story with his mind taking a couple of brief detours to speculate what it would have been like to have met her in different circumstances.

Once she finished he gave her the details of the pretty much standard no frills package that the programme offered. To start with the kid was pencilled in for twice a week one-on-one sessions. He'd get in touch with the school and he'd let Sonny know what was going on too.

After she left, he stared out of the long window that was above his desk, it allowed him the oft needed balm of a view of a presently mottled unshifting sky.

Donna Edwards, he mused, a bloody peach.

Well, he and Moz had cracked the case of the century - an anonymous phone call tipping them off to a pair of likely lads for the spate of muggings on the Barrington. Both of the toe rags known petty crims whose idea of paradise was unlimited Special Brew, a state of the art pair of trainers and a fifty inch flat screen TV set up to go in a greased up, marijuana saturated lounge room.

They'd found cash cards and a rake of IDs in one of the bozo's bedrooms and, even better, they had an eye witness to one of the attacks, a doughty old pensioner who had the misfortune to be residing in the same postcode.

Mozzer Morris was embedded in the interrogation room chatting with the bright spark who'd kept the cards in his bedroom, his mate a few walls away cooling his heels off in one of the holding cells.

They were young, unemployed, bereft of aspiration; one black, one white. Mozzer had christened the pair Sammy and Dean. After an hour or so Mozzer came out of the 'hard questions' room and gave him the lowdown near the new drinks machine that was in the ground floor corridor. Moz had a piece of what looked like puff pastry on his left cheek and was fishing out some shrapnel to get himself a fizzy drink.

'Daryl (Sammy) has flipped over son. Somewhat surprisingly, according to his version of events, Scott (Dean) was the main protagonist, Daryl himself, just a reluctant, near innocent bystander. I'll have the drink then swap them over. Scott will be chuffed to bits when he hears Daryl's version of events. No honour amongst dick-cheese scum, is there son?'

With a grunt Moz leaned over to liberate his can of Coke and then duck walked with, what was for him, a degree of jauntiness back on to the interview room.

Fucking Rat Pack alright, Darrin thought. He spent the next half hour walking through the station telling as many bods as he could find about the collar - it was a result.

His mum had asked him if he'd wanted her to accompany him to the Community Centre but he had said no. They'd left the house together and she had offered him a lift in her sparkling new Elantra. Normally he wouldn't have thought twice - he loved that car as much as she did - but he wanted the walk, he'd had a crap sleep, tossing and turning thinking about it. His head felt musty and he could do with the time alone too.

From their place it was only a mile or so to the Centre and he zigzagged through the quiet back streets in order to get there on time. It was all pretty quiet at this time of the day, late starters heading off to work, a few oldies with their shopping bags trying to beat the rush, some dog walkers and a solitary jogger. He cut through onto the canal path stepping to the side into the longish grass so that he could squeeze past a line of silent men whose fishing rods almost reached to the other side of the canal. If M had been with him he would probably have made some smart-arsed remark. He was daft enough to mouth off to grown men even when there was a real chance that he would have been thrown head first into the canal's dank, scummy water.

Pasquale ambled up the path to the arched dark-stoned bridge that had once acted as a boundary between two boroughs that no longer existed, and then he made a diagonal on across the bleak looking empty park with its lattice of bird nests that were now in plain view, exposed to the elements in the tough looking branches of the bone naked birch trees.

He knew that the trees were birch because his mum had often spent many of their hours together engaged in the naming of things; trees, birds, cars, styles of architecture. All those times they'd spent together, he thought, just the two of them, either out driving in one of her spotless small cars, or out and about on foot. He had enjoyed it most of the time. Occasionally he'd wished that she would just shut the fuck up and let him enjoy his own thoughts. She was crazy about learning, to her it was the potential cure for everything and now that childhood had gone and here he was hanging on to school by his fingertips, off to meet a stranger for some more of the naming of things.

The Centre was buzzing when he arrived, lots of silver haired ladies and a few old blokes milling around in the reception area and some kiddies being sung to by a couple of birds in a partially glassed oblong room that was almost directly opposite the reception desk.

The fossil on the reception gave him a beady once over as he mumbled his name and the reason for his presence. The bloke warmed up a little when he finished telling him who he was and why he was there and he gave him directions with a crinkling of his eyes and a smile that Pasquale couldn't help but reciprocate.

'Go on then lad,' the old man made a little shooing motion at him with his right hand, 'Tommy won't bite yer.'

The room was out of the back of the building, on past the kiddies' room, then down a tight dog-legged corridor that led on to a battered, cheap looking door with the slightly peeling words youth service stuck on it.

Pasquale knocked lightly, heard a cough inside and then knocked again, a little harder this time. At that, a strong sounding baritone told him to come in. He stepped inside and the guy swivelled around from his computer. His eyes widened slightly. It was the youth worker who had stopped them from getting into the dance, but the bloke stood up and gave him a warm smile and proffered a meaty, square shaped hand. He was a pretty big fucker, maybe only slightly taller than average but big in the shoulders and chest. His hand was warm and the shake was firm but not a bone crusher.

Thankfully there was minimal of the getting to know you bullshit, the guy (Tommy) asked him what he thought he needed help with, then showed him a piece of paper on which was typed what Tommy called a study plan.

'Not cast in stone though,' Tommy told him, 'we'll play it by ear, to a degree. See how you go. Sonny tells me that you're a bright kid with plenty of potential. That true then?'

He nodded and just about held the guy's eyes as he did so.

Despite himself, he'd felt a swell of pride at that. He liked Sonny and the guy had said it in a way that made him feel good about himself - not with the underlying anxiety of affirmation that he always sensed with his mum.

'Mind the music while we work?' Tommy asked with a nod to the computer speakers.

'Fine,' he said with a shrug of his shoulders although it did sound a little toss.

'David Bowie,' Tommy said, 'heard of him?'

He hadn't.

Tommy laughed a little but Pasquale couldn't work out why.

'OK then bro, let's kick off with me reading and you writing down what I say, alright?'

That didn't sound too hard and it wasn't. They worked together for an hour straight through, Tommy humming along at times to the stereo warbling. Finally, Tommy rang the bell on it without any fanfare or notice.

'Good work Pasquale, Sonny was right, it's not a lack of brains that has landed you in here, is it?'

He didn't know what to say to that. Tommy let him off the hook with a friendly pat on the shoulder.

'See you in a couple of days son - stay well. Get your arse off to school then.'

For the rest of the week he managed both the Centre and

school much to M's scorn when the three of them had finally met up at M's house on the Friday. He riposted with giving M a good arse kicking on the Xbox. Usually he held back a little bit, letting him think he was better at it than was the case. But this time he gave it to him. After a couple of hours of getting smashed M threw his console at the wall and had given him a look, which caused Junior and himself to dissolve into laughter. That shut the fucker up for a while, good and proper. M went off and sulked for a spell but soon came back to the game. He couldn't bear to be alone for more than five minutes. As they played, M gave both Pasquale and Junior some initially half-hearted and then full bore exhortations, all the ill feeling well and truly gone. That was one good thing about M, he never held on to it for too long.

Although he won again, he gave it up to let Junior take the next game. M hopped back on, giving him a half-smile in recognition of his gesture. That was cool, he'd made his point and, what the hell, he thought, as he stretched out on the sofa and lit up a rasper. They were his mates.

It was a flat week at work after the high of the Sammy and Dean case. Darrin had been assigned foot patrol with Johno. That with a bit of desk duty interspersed with some rigorous workouts at the old man's sweat-box gym made up the rhythm of his week.

A DI Bowden from the Drug Squad had come to the station from the city headquarters and had prepped the crew about the upsurge in the manufacture and use of ice. It was a drug that had swamped the conurbation over the last few months; massively addictive, cheap and easy to produce, twelve times the high of sex and six times the high of cocaine.

'In my case that would be twenty times the high of sex,' said Mozzer, which had them all rolling in the aisles for a good while until an amused Sarge Thomas benignly cracked the whip.

DI Bowden dived back in. Darrin noted that he'd barely cracked a smile at the crew's reaction to Mozzer's funny. Then Bowden went on, about the downward spiral for the users, the 'inevitable law of diminishing returns,' ie more and more of the shit needed for the same effect - a drug dealer's wet dream. Increasing addiction, till the brain was fried to the point of being null and void. It was like shooting fish in a barrel for the pushers and they always had fresh meat to prey on; the young, the impressionable and the disaffected.

Word was that some of the old firm who had bossed the city for the last thirty years or so had started moving it around and they wouldn't be bothering to do that without a very good yield for both their investment and risk. The Drug Squad was operating towards the top end of the pyramid and they, the foot soldiers, would keep their eye on the bottom feeders in the industry, principally the dealers and their customer base up on the estates.

'It's a crisis waiting to happen,' said the Inspector, 'this drug ripped the heart out of loads of communities in the States.'

He looked around the room with a gravity that pre-empted any more glib funnies.

'Let's get the breaks on it, nice and early lads and lasses.'

At the break he chatted about it with Mozzer and a few of the other plods whilst they were hanging out in the canteen. The young end was fired up at the prospect of the battle. Mozzer had raised a sceptical eyebrow at him as Darrin enthused about getting stuck into it.

'Lopping off a few branches won't get rid of the tree.' Mozzer stated with a flat firmness.

Johno asked him what he meant and Moz snorted at him.

'War on drugs - it's about as real as Luke Skywalker waving his fucking light sabre at Darth Vader that is.'

Mozzer looked around the table and snorted again at the lack of comeback. He lifted his head towards the canteen counter and smiled. 'Sweet time - they've got the trifle on today.' Moz swung his gut away from the table, nimbly rose to his feet and made his way over towards the food counter.

Tommy had taken the Friday off and the luxury of a long weekend stretched out in front of him. Earlier in the week he had called his mate Lee who was living down in the smoke and after a brief catch up chat had arranged a stay with Lee and his missus. He caught the first train south just after lunch and he was glad that he'd bothered to reserve a seat. It was packed just like everywhere else in this fucking country.

He was still adjusting to that, nearly eighteen months back and the country still felt like a fucking anthill. He liked travelling the trains though, it had always soothed him and train travel was very much part of the warp and weft of his growing up.

Tommy's old man had worked for twenty years on the railways, ensconced in the upstairs offices of the substantial, soot covered, Gothic redbrick of the city's central station. Not that this train was anything like the powerful, belching, lurch, roar and rattle of the steam trains of his boyhood. It was almost silent, high speed with nary a ripple as it bulleted on to its destination. He'd brought some sounds with him and a decent mag, to read to help fill the time and, this time, he had brought his own butties too. Previously, he'd made the mistake of getting on board hungry and unprepared and Virgin had well and truly burnt a hole in his pocket.

A mixed race woman got on board just as the train was about to pull away from the platform. He glanced at her and she gave him a little smile, which warmed him up almost as much as Donna Edwards had. He let his mind wander over that notion for a while, bit of a non-starter though with the boy and all. A step-dad to a malcontent teenager, surely a busman's holiday and Donna didn't seem like the casual, no strings attached type. If he kicked it off with her he would have to commit himself, again.

The journey was over in a twinkle, just over two hours and they were pulling in to Euston. It was just coming up to three o'clock so it was not yet bedlam time on the tube, but it was still pretty busy down there and he was thankful that he was travelling light. That leg of the journey was not quite one of Dante's Circles of Hell, but five days a week of it would have to be close enough. His body percolated in the humid netherworld as he let his eyes wander around the carriage; students with iPods, a couple of tired looking African blokes and some slightly frazzled mums with mercifully placated children. A young French couple smilingly canoodled with each other, oblivious to their surroundings. He thought of that old Joni Mitchell song as he discreetly watched them, 'amour mama, not cheap display.' He changed lines then made his way back up to what passed for fresh air. He rode a few stops on a washed out local train and got off at Deptford, which had been Lee's home for well over a decade now.

Lee was waiting for him at the station entrance down

on the High Street and they gave each other a hearty bear hug, which lifted Lee onto his toes. He was still as skinny as a lat, but now with a hint of belly under the baggy shirt. His friend had never been big on exercise - making music, playing chess, drinking red wine and a loving indulgence of his extroverted partner, these were the things that rang Lee Murphy's bell.

They had last caught up at the previous Christmas break, Lee had undertaken his regular, usually solitary, flying visit to the old folks' home that housed his mum and had crashed on his sofa for a couple of nights before taking his leave to join Bern who was nestled at her parents' place somewhere down in the Norfolk boondocks.

The two of them chatted happily as they walked back to the couple's one bedroom gaff, which was located in a nearby warren of council flats.

Lee asked him how Mick was going.

'Hanging on really Lee,' he told him.

'It's just piss, vinegar and stubbornness that makes the old fart reach for his slippers in the morning.'

Lee had come round to the old man's for a feed the day after Boxing Day and Tommy had clocked instantly that Mick's deterioration had been as much of a shock to Lee as it had been to him. Lee had hid it well enough just as he had done the year or so before. Tommy had replayed that dreadful moment many times, Mick answering the door and the shocking, face slap awfulness of the immediate realisation that Mick was already running his last lap.

He'd been away from the UK for over eight years and he hadn't seen the old man for that length of time. Eight years! His staying away had been a mixture of choice and circumstances, his friends had tried to prepare him for it; Jimbo telling him more than once that his dad 'was not quite the same.' His monthly telephone chats with the old man hadn't given anything of the decline away. But, his old man was now wizened and frail, a goblin like version of the prime Mick. Tommy had quickly adjusted because, well he had to and because Mick was definitely still Mick, irrespective of the physical decline.

Lee had his own travails to deal with. His mum was in the middle of her own private hell in dealing with Alzheimer's. Tommy took a lot of comfort from the fact that his old man was fully firing mentally. To him, that was a sizeable mercy.

Bernie was out and about this evening, down at some community women's thing over in deepest, darkest Greenwich. They settled down in the flat's small kitchen and, as was their custom, opened up a bottle of red. Lee and Bern had spent a lot of the last couple of months in the recording studio and Lee immediately played Tommy some of their new music. It was the usual wash of swirling guitars and synthetic percussion, underpinning Bern's soulful voice and occasional freestyle warblings and yelps which always reminded him of a more tuneful version of Yoko. A couple of the tracks had a nice Asian feel to them. Lee, in particular, was eclectic and esoteric in his musical tastes and a mate of theirs had taken the music off in a new direction with some tasty tabla drumming.

They talked cursorily about life up north. Lee had never been that interested about the old crowd. It was yesterday's chip wrapper as far as he was concerned.

In their youth, Lee hadn't even been on the fringes of the in-crowd, whereas he had been a face, courtesy of sport and, in his opinion, a slightly inflated reputation for toughness. They'd been the two brightest boys in the class, right through primary school up until their successful university applications. Both pioneers of further education in their respective families, both of them raised on a pedestal by their kin because of it, and both resented for the fact by some of those same people. They had grown up in a row of two bedroom terraces - their family homes just three doors apart. A love of T-Rex, Bowie and Roxy Music had cemented their filial bonds. The music had offered them glimpses into another much more exotic world. The taste of the promise of the other had helped them through the drudge of those grey, winter days.

On Bern's return they were heading off to Lewisham to watch a band that a couple of their mates played in. The gig, as another custom had it, would be followed by a probable detour for a curry on the way back to the flat. Deptford had a couple of good Indian restaurants, but Friday night on the High Street could be disconcertingly heavy and if there was one thing that Lee didn't do it was heavy.

Bernie got back in about eight, a swirl of hastily applied red lipstick topped off tonight with a pill box leopard skin hat. She went for a kind of layered dress sense these days, which did a reasonable job of hiding her growing portliness. Bern shared Lee's anathema of physical exercise but not his Jack Spratt genes.

It was good to spend time with them, Bern telling him about the various projects that she, Lee and various friends had on the boil. Lee chipping in to correct her at the times whenever she gap-filled with a blatant if innocuous non-fact.

The band that night were a jazz blues combo, the kind of

stuff that Bern particularly liked and they had pulled her up on stage for a version of Strange Fruit. She'd got lost in it, eyes closed, right armed raised, her fingers slowly turning in the shadows beyond the spotlight. Lee looked on at her, a proud, slightly bashful smile playing on his lips. At the end of the band's set the crowd cleared pronto, as if a stink bomb had been dropped in the room and the band went quickly and quietly about the business of packing up their gear. The guitarist was a dark haired Cornish guy with quick eyes who had been a paramour of Bern's some time before she and Lee had started doing the twist together. He'd come came over for a brief chat with them, something about the possibility of doing a benefit together next month somewhere down Peckham way.

They had grabbed a takeaway on the way down to the mini-cab office, a couple of pissed blokes gave him the hairy eyeball when they'd walked into the crummy waiting room. Tommy ignored it, engagement with drunken strangers hadn't rung his bell for a long time and Lee and Bern weren't really into rolling around on the cobbles. Now if Jimbo had been with him? He shook it off - who cares.

Luckily, the drunks' cab arrived within thirty seconds of the three of them sitting down. One of the guys had made a point of turning round on the way out and he'd held the gaze until the guy had broken away to make his exit into the sulphur lit night. Lee had clocked him ramping up the testosterone but he didn't make any comment, Lee knew that part of him too. Bern was miles away, distractedly humming one of their new tunes. She preferred to live her life in a happy bubble, although that was a kind of coping mechanism because, in reality, she never really missed a beat. No more than a minute passed and it was their turn to catch a ride. A rangy silent guy in a turban drove the three of them back to Deptford.

Bern hit the sack as soon as they got back. She had ladies soccer in the morning. Tommy had seen her play a few times before, she spent most of the game giggling and talking to team mates and opponents alike.

He and Lee stayed up until the small hours. Lee asked him with a diffident dip of the head what his plans for the future were.

'Don't know yet Lee,' he told him, 'I'll stay with the old man for as long as it takes.' His voice trailed off and they remained silent for a moment or two.

'Not missing it over there then Tommy; the sunshine, the beaches the big expanse, less bullshit, maybe?'

Tommy appraised his friend with a smile, he was a shrewd little bastard our Lee.

'Yeah I do. But, you know bud, there is nobody that I really care about over there and, for that matter, nobody there who really cares about me.'

'Sometimes people matter more than the place, eh Tommy?'

Tommy nodded in agreement, but he'd told Lee an approximation of the truth. There was still somebody there that he cared for - more than cared for really.

'You two never made it to Sydney did yer?' He said, just for the sake of making some noise.

Lee shook his head ruefully, 'getting her out of Deptford and Greenwich is hard enough Tom.'

Tommy laughed and they had a refill for the road. Lee dug out the first Roxy Music album, which he found to be almost unlistenable. Lee supplied some levity with a more than passable impression of Ferry's affected warble. Fuck, he had once thought the band the epitome of exotic cool. There you go, so much for all our yesterdays! As for Ferry's voice, he and Lee had cracked up a couple of times, like two teenagers giddily sharing a joint.

All that time had gone, he thought and, tonight, he didn't mind that fact at all.

Darrin had lucked out so far with the drug op, he'd been hoping for a pair up with Moz or even that stone faced fucker Clarke. But, no, no go, Johno and Jolika were given the nod instead. He'd badgered Sarge Thomas about it but to no fucking avail.

'Not my decision son, don't take it personal like. They like to rotate you anyway, sort out the potential diamonds from the turds.' Thomas laughed loudly at his own mordant wit. There was no gilding the lily with that Taff prick.

'Anyway PC May, there's plenty else for you to do in't there? It's not the only bloody movie showin' you know. There's still plenty of patrol to be done, the desk and bringing me cups of tea…speaking of which, there's a lad now, you know how I like it.'

And that was it, end of discussion and an outline of his next few weeks in a nutshell. He bitched about it until the crew started to get sick of him. Even good old indulgent Trish started to put a swerve on him and look in the other direction. He took the frustration out on the bags and pads at his old man's gym - pistoning away at them in a mute fury until he had nothing left.

He'd got a collar towards the end of the week, some scrote

caught nicking from the pound shop and he's given the guy a quick dig in the kidneys on the way back to the car. Debbie Roach had clocked it but let it go, her silence as they headed back to the station was everything that he needed to know. He saw Mozzer a couple of times at change over, but all was quiet at the moment.

He'd asked Moz how Jolika was going just for the sake of talking about the op.

'Yeah - good, patient she is, unlike you son, that is for fucking definite. Can't get her to have a go at the cheese and pickle butties though.'

Darrin laughed and Moz patted him on the shoulder.

'Don't worry son, this shit is going nowhere. Heads will roll and new ones will replace them, just like the fucking Medusa it is.'

Crumbs of fucking comfort, he thought. That night he'd got himself trashed and Johno and Clarkey had to pull him away from some civilian who'd made a half-hearted grab of Trish's arse. With a gentle but persistent persuasion they had shepherded him into a taxi and Johno had climbed in with him to make sure that he had got all the way home.

Big Ged had approached him the next day as he was on his way back from the canteen, deliberately blocking his passage in the narrow corridor. Ged had been in the bar last night but had kept his distance when it had all kicked off.

The big man held his hand up and then leaned into him a little, giving Darrin a whiff of mints and something else that had a lot more fire to it. Keegan didn't drop his hand when Darrin came to a dead halt in front of him. He kept it up and lightly placed his thick index finger against Darrin's solar plexus. He could hear Keegan's breath whistling through his nose. It was all a bit too close and personal.

'You need to chill out a bit young Dazzler. Kicking up too much dust you are.'

The big man was smiling but the eyes held no comfort.

'I heard you're pissed off about not being asked to climb into a suit. But, well, that's just fucking tough that is. We all serve our time here son. Team play that's what we're about, accepting the status quo. You're not Wyatt Earp lad. Getting into it with a civilian in a boozer - now that is fucking stupid - right?'

The big man shook his head at him in disgust.

Keegan had slightly increased the pressure on his solar plexus just to underscore his point. His heart was racing but he held the gaze.

'Right son?' Keegan wanted a response from him.

'Okay Sarge - sorted.'

Ged Keegan nodded at him amicably enough.

'You're a good-un young Daz. That's what I get told anyways. Just stay with the program son - don't fuck it up, alright?'

Darrin assented and Keegan amiably stood aside to let him move on towards the station's lifts.

The next day on he was feeling notably more chilled and he even engaged with Debbie a little bit more than was their norm. Debbie with her interminable stories about her youngest son, an eight year old who had Asperger's, she kept the whole of the fucking station abreast of that.

It was a nice day at least, getting up towards spring now and he managed to persuade her to let him drive up to the butty van that was always up near the ressies. He grabbed them two teas then parked the car so that he could gaze down towards the urban spread, which poured down from the hills onto the western plain that was a thousand feet below. It was even warm enough today for a bit of heat shimmer, the big radio telescope doing a little dance in the distance. February, he thought, fucking nuts that is.

The radio crackled - Trish's voice came over, a purse snatch just off the High Street. A fast fifteen minute drive and they were there back down amongst the thick of it.

Tommy had caught the six o'clock train back up north on the Monday morning, he was a little tired with the early start to the day but felt mentally refreshed with the change of scene. It had been a stroll round Greenwich and a movie on Saturday and a kick around at the local park with Lee and Bern's bohemian buddies on the Sunday. The football was good-natured and excruciatingly non competitive. Jimbo would have been apoplectic with it all; no mazy dribbles, no pathological reluctance to pass the ball and no scything tackles on display. A couple of the crew had come back to the flat including a comely but married blonde who seemed to get off on his banter a little bit more than what was the norm.

Before he had left on the Monday, Lee had met him in the kitchen and they'd said their goodbyes. Lee would be back up in a month or so to see his Mum and he had rebooked the standing reservation on Tommy's couch. Lee always made the point of asking even though the arrangement between them was a given.

His good mood followed him on through the day and even the paperwork and the filing momentarily held no tedium for him.

The kid had come in for his one-on-one at eleven. He'd

even got there a little bit early today. He handed Tommy the exercise that Tommy had given out to him last week. He had wanted the kid to focus on somebody in his life who had taught him something that he had really enjoyed learning. The kid had written a piece about a bloke called Kim, a friend of his mum's, who, when he was eight years old, had shown him how to make origami. The kid was a little embarrassed at the disclosure and it took some courage for him to tell it, but he was visibly comforted by Tommy's words of support and encouragement. The story was pretty well written too. Fuck knows why the kid had ended up here. Regardless, he'd keep the safety net out for as long as the kid needed it.

The day was unseasonably warm and he was amazed when a bumble bee nudged against the office window a few times. Still, they were forecasting snow for the upcoming weekend so it wasn't knotted hankie time just yet.

He popped up to old man Aziz's in his lunch break. When he turned the corner to the shop the first thing that he noticed was an expensive car, a late model Beamer no less that was parked right outside the store. Instinctively, he knew that it would be Noora and he unconsciously lengthened his stride as he walked towards the shop. He even felt the stirring of tumescence at the thought of seeing her again - rolling back the years alright.

Tommy forcefully opened the door and there she was, an urban, desert rose if ever there was one. Noora! She, Jamal and her father turned towards him as he stepped into the store. Her smile magnetized him as it always had and Jamal and Mr Aziz quickly receded into the background as they always did.

'Hello Noora.' Keeping it in check in front of her brother

and the old man.

'Tommy!' That smooth voice of hers, educated and elegant, time folded in on itself.

Then there was a movement at the back of the shop, and a chubby faced boy of about seven or eight appeared. He trotted up to her and began tugging on her sleeve.

'Mum, Mum can I have a drink now Mum?' He implored, jiggling from foot to foot with impatience as he did so.

Her focus immediately switched to the boy, 'ask your Grandfather Sanjeev, this is his home - remember.'

'Poppy, can I, please, please Poppy?'

Mr Aziz nodded with all the gravitas of his decorous elder statesman benevolence.

'Of course my boy and take one for your sister too Sanj.'

The phone rang behind the counter and Jamal nimbly turned to pick it up.

'Dad for you - suppliers,' Jamal then guided Sanjeev to the living area at the back of the shop.

He looked at her again and they both smiled and he gave her the once over; nice jewellery, tailored pants, manicured fingers - long and elegant and, he remembered, very dextrous too.

'You look well Tommy - never thought I'd bump into you in here after all this time.'

She bowed forward slightly and clapped her hands together with pleasure, a mannerism of hers that he had always enjoyed.

He nodded at her, 'yeah well more through necessity than design I guess…and you?'

The word divorce leapt hopefully into his mind.

'Only a quick visit I'm afraid, Raj has been offered a job in

Vancouver - he has family there.'

He swallowed, 'Vancouver, my dad went there. Nice city by all accounts. Soon?'

'Next month if he gets confirmation, his cousin has law firm contacts there. He's busy negotiating a contract.'

'Soon enough then.'

She nodded and he held her eyes a little longer than was probably appropriate, obviously causing her a little discomfort this time.

A girl's voice called out from the back of the shop, she was upset - Sanjeev not sharing as he should. She tutted with annoyance at the boy.

'I'd better go Tommy, sort them out.' She gave him a little 'what can you do' shrug.

He held out his hand and that was that, a brief touch and then she turned and quickly walked away.

Tommy was slightly dazed by their encounter and he had left the shop without buying anything. He took time out for ten minutes or so on a bench in the little park not far from the Community Centre and his thoughts ping-ponged around without any focus, clarity or conclusion. An old lady pushed a trolley full of midday shopping through his eye-line and she turned to him and wished him a good afternoon. He nodded back and returned her warm smile. Fuck it, he thought, it's all about choices and dealing with their consequences, no more, no fucking less. He'd go back and do some work on that funding application and maybe Jimbo would be up for a drink or two a little later on.

Pasquale, M and Junior spent the Friday up on the Coleshaw, it had been a warm day but as soon as the low sun started to

dip towards the horizon the temperature had quickly started to drop and they'd rode their bikes in looping circles just
to keep warm, their chatter clouding their collective breath
over their three heads. Junior's brother Wes was now getting out as early as December and M's mum had a new bloke,
somebody who had a job according to M. He and Junior
shared an amused glance at that bit of news but they'd kept
their mouths shut.

He wanted to tell them about the literacy stuff but he
knew they'd just take the piss. He was enjoying it. It was
much, much better than school with its dumb-ass rules and
smart-ass kids who didn't know when to leave you alone. His
mum was pleased too and yesterday she'd bought him some
new trainers, mint they were and they got the thumbs up
from the boys too. M never wanted to be a step behind and
he told them that he'd blag a pair over the weekend.

Some of the older boys were hanging out just up the road,
engrossed in flirting and talking bullshit with a gaggle of
girls. M had engaged with the crew briefly and then returned
to him and Junior with a package tucked into the top of his
jeans under his zipped up top. He pulled up just past them
and quickly put the package into his back pack. 'Got to take
this down to the Barrington, fancy it?'

He and Junior were up for it. Why not, there was fuck all
happening up here.

'Whose down there then M, who yer running it to?' Junior asked.

'Bazzer.'

'Who?' Junior asked, 'you mean Bazzer Dougan like?'

'Yeah that's right, him.'

Junior shook his head, 'no way, fuck M, he's a nutter he is.

Even our Wes warned me off him.'

M shrugged his shoulders and one of the older guys from up the street, Dwayne, called out for M to get his arse in gear.

Just as M was about to take off, a maroon Jag pulled into the street then slowed down and pulled up right next to them.

A middle aged guy with long sideburns slid down the window and called out to M.

'Alright son - keeping out of trouble then are yer?'

He was all bright and breezy, very familiar too.

M dutifully cycled the few yards over to the driver's window and nodded his head at the stranger. The guy was no stranger to M though, otherwise he would have told him to fuck off.

The guy looked around M to him and Junior, 'whose yer mates then sonny boy? Be a good un', do the introductions for us.'

'Er right, this is Junior and this here is P like.'

'Pee as in piss, is it son?' The guy giving him a level look - no smile.

Pasquale felt himself colour.

'No, no, it's Pasquale.'

'Pasquale eh, spaghetti head are yer son?'

He let that go, he hadn't heard that one since primary school.

The man waved them to come over to the car, his steady light blue eyes moving over the boys as they approached.

Pasquale noted that the guy seemed to be a lot more focused on him than Junior.

'You one of those red-hot Latin Romeos are yer son?'

Pasquale shook his head. He didn't know what the fuck

the guy was on about - like he was tripping or something - fucking weird.

'Ah well, maybe you will be one day.'

The guy sniffed loudly and peered at the throng down the road, then had a little smile at the scene that was all to himself.

'See you later then boys - it's been a blast.'

He gave a cheery little roll of the hand, put the car smoothly into drive and drove the fifty or so yards down the road to the older boys, whereupon he stopped again.

Pasquale clocked the plates - GYP01.

'Whose that then M?' he asked.

'Dunno, some business bloke like, knows Dwayne and them like. His mum's just around the corner, in Sycamore.'

M wheeled away - not interested in talking about it, 'you two coming then or what?'

Fuck it, Pasquale thought, it was getting cold. He rode part of the way down, then turned off to go home. He knew Junior wouldn't be heading all the way down to the Barrington either. If Junior said that Dougan was a nutter then that was what he surely was.

SPRING

MARCH

The following week the job had started to pick up for Darrin. Moz had seconded him in for an early morning raid on the Barrington estate. The target was a grubby two bed-roomed flat that was home to a long known minor league drug dealer by the name of Sean Manning. Sean's CV showed a clear pattern alternating between relatively brief visits to the Job Centre and lengthy stays at Her Majesty's.

Five thirty in the cold morning and they hit the joint hard, half a dozen of the local plod and a smooth looking detective by the name of Young who was a DS in the drug squad. A dog handler and his pooch, a long eared spaniel by the name of Eric were also there, Eric brought in to sniff out all of Sean's little hidey holes.

Manning took the early morning call with remarkable equanimity, considering, blinking benignly at them as they systematically tipped the joint over. His present missus didn't take the intrusion quite as well though, a volley of expletives that was curtailed by a hissed 'shut the fuck up' from Manning himself. Jolika led her off to the kitchen with a soothing smile, whilst Eric and his moustachioed handler came on through to do the business in the lounge room.

Apart from some smoke and a couple of creatively assembled, state of the art bongs they drew a total fucking blank, which pissed the Drug Squad guy off no end. Moz gave the plods who'd taken the collar the nod to leave and a hastily track-suited Sean was led off to an unmarked car.

His bit of paperwork around the raid took him a little

longer than should have been the case, as their temporary proximity in the main office gave him a chance to chat Jolika up a bit.

She was an ambitious one too was our Jolika and at length they talked about their career options, the possibility of them moving on to something like Serious Organised Crime Agency down the track. He'd already toyed with that idea for quite a while although he knew that would mean a move away from home. She was cool was Jolika, a level-headed young woman with tasty looking curves, which the unflattering uniform did nothing to hide. She had given up a couple of polite giggles at his careworn banter. Johno was sat at a nearby desk and he had rolled his eyes a couple of times at his bullshit.

He asked her what she did for 'fun' - pushing it a little.

'Ah you know Darrin, the usual; keep fit, lots of shopping, salsa when I can.

That caught his attention, 'salsa?'

'Yeah, they do lessons at the Cricket Club you know up near Bridgewater there. We've been doing it for a couple of years now, party first Saturday in the month, this Saturday as it happens.'

He noted the 'we' but didn't ask the question. He kept his look bright and breezy - Mr. Happy Chappy.

'You should give it a go Darrin - you look pretty light on your feet, for a white guy.'

'Hey cheeky - I'll report you to the Board for that.'

He mulled it over.

'Hmmm, can't do this Thursday but might pop down on the Saturday - that sounds good, I'm having it.'

She nodded at him with a smile. 'It's a great way to unwind, lots of fun. It's like a different world especially for up here, believe you me.'

Darrin nodded, he believed her. In his mind he was already there.

Tommy lay in his bed and reproached himself as he replayed the incident. He should have handled it better - no excuses - but, there again.

He'd caught up with Jimbo and they'd decided on a few beers at his place with a takeaway and a DVD - all well and good. This had necessitated a bit of a hike as Jimbo, who had just moved across town to a nice little two bedroom place down Rosetta Park way, still shopped at the DVD store that was near his old gaff.

After a protracted debate they'd compromised on the director's cut of Apocalypse Now something they'd first watched together nearly thirty years ago.

It was just after tea time when they arrived at the shop and it was busyish with only one girl serving behind the counter. He grabbed the movie and Jimbo's card then joined the queue whilst Jim hit the offy for a six-pack.

A couple of youngish guys, a mixed race kid and his white mate, were being served by the girl and it appeared that they were neither feeling nor giving out the love. They were irritated at having to wait a few minutes before getting served. Terse commands to the girl; no please, no thanks, no kiss my arse.

The girl was flustered and trying hard to keep both her cool and her manners. Sod's law did its thing and she dropped the disc onto the floor as she was trying to press it down into the case.

The mouthy one of the pair didn't like that, tuts and hisses from him and a roll of the eyes from his mate.

Loudly and stridently, the guy berated her for her clumsiness. 'Not having that now bitch.'

She told him it was the only available copy.

He hissed at her in exasperation.

'Clean it then. Clean it, for fuck's sake.'

He half turned and gave a 'what can you do' shake of the head to the unsettled queue.

His mate sniggered and shifted his weight from foot to foot.

Tommy reached past the middle-aged woman who was standing between him and the pair and tapped the charmer on the shoulder. The guy spun round, scowled down at the woman then he realised that it was Tommy who had touched him.

'What the fuck yer doin man? Keep those fucking hands to yerself like.'

Tommy smiled straight at him - goading the fucker.

'Manners.' He said, with a thrust of his jaw.

'What?' What you fucking say?'

'I said, mind your fucking manners. The girl is just doing her job.'

He saw Jimbo arrive back at the door - the usual Speedy Gonzalez with him.

The other bozo had turned around to face him too.

'Stay the fuck out of it man,' he said.

Tommy looked at him then put his eyes back on the mouthy one.

He saw doubt there - anger - but a little bit of uncertainty too.

Pride won out though - inevitably.

'Wanna take it further then man - fancy it do yer?' the young guy said throwing his arms out wide then slapping them against his sides.

Tommy didn't even think about it, he pointed to the door. 'Let's go tosspot.'

The young guy hurried out of the store, his mate loping a couple of strides behind him.

Tommy followed them past the wide eyed girl at the counter, aware of Jimbo's presence, already just behind his shoulder.

The pair were ready, waiting a little off the steps that led up to the doors of the store.

Tommy didn't bother with any more pre-amble. He'd had enough fucking blather, he took the steps quickly and grabbed the mouth by the shirt front and began to shake him. He brought up his right hand and forced his fist into the guy's throat and jaw, kneading the knuckles into his neck. Tommy marched him backwards walking through the ineffectual slaps and pushes at his shoulders and chest, backing him up against a wooden slatted fence, hearing the wood pop slightly with the combined weight of their bodies. He felt enraged and he couldn't believe how physically weak the guy was - it was as if he was scragging a kid, a mis-match. The young guy was bug-eyed now, frightened.

Seeing the fear made his anger recede slightly and Tommy let go of the guy's jacket and threw him back at the fence.

The young guy reassembled his clothes and a little of his dignity and then made another mistake. 'You fucking white cunt you,' he spat out at him.

Tommy leapt at him and grabbed him again with his left

hand and this time he popped him with his right. A short cross that travelled no more than a foot yet had enough on it to put him down. As he fell, Tommy's left hand guided him gently down to the pavement. He didn't want the fucker banging his head on the hard surface. Tommy put his knees across his chest and rubbed the side of his head into the cold asphalt.

'A fucking racist too, eh cunt?' A plume of his saliva flecked the guy's cheek.

He gave it to him for a few more seconds, grounding his left ear into the unyielding surface. Tommy kept his weight on the guy's chest and looked around for Jimbo. Jimbo had the guy's mate in a scrappy half nelson; the beers were resting safely on the hood of a nearby car.

Ten seconds or so of more, stressing the point, face grinding, and then Tommy pushed himself up. He looked down at his chastened adversary, who made no attempt to get to his feet, coming back at Tommy, this time only with silence and a look of rancorous defeat. Jimbo spun the other guy around and then let him go, and the young bloke stumbled back towards the steps of the DVD store and ended up on his haunches in a kind of jittery crouch. Jimbo deftly swiped the beers up from their resting place and they headed off around the corner to their car. One of the guys shouted out something after them but, if it was a threat, it sounded as hollow as a politician's promise.

It had taken him a couple of hours to come back down and he had found it impossible to focus on the movie. He'd wanted to talk it out of his system, even rave a little bit really and Jimbo was willing to patiently listen to his hyper-intense musings and recollections. Tommy felt as naked and raw as a newborn, riding on the rush that the exchange had given him.

Now it was past two am and he was still awake - preoccupied with it but without any of the high. He saw how it could have all gone wrong, a knife, maybe even a gun - and bingo. But, what the fuck could you do? Stand back and say and do nothing, just let it happen? Mick would have disowned him and right enough too.

Pasquale was keeping it together - he'd requested that his visits to Tommy be upped to three a week and that had taken her on the hop alright - speechless and wide-eyed for a couple of beats. He'd been to school every day too, although he'd skipped sports on Wednesday, and well, as far as Friday afternoon went - no fucking chance. Junior was picking it up a bit too in his school attendance. And he was back to playing some basketball on Tuesdays and Thursdays down at the Centre.

No change from M though, out both times when he'd called around to see him on the Barrington. He'd eventually caught up with him at the shopping centre late Friday afternoon.

It was getting a little bit warmer and the days were noticeably starting to lengthen. It was still light round about teatime. Tommy had recently mentioned something about the spring just a couple of days ago. Equinox had been the word that Tommy had used. He liked the sound of it and had got Tommy to spell it out for him. Equinox - equal day and night all over the Earth - bit fucking mind blowing really.

When they had met up M had slyly shown them the huge wad of cash that he was carrying, telling them that the food was on him. The money was like a permanent fucking accessory with M now - the fucker was going to need his own security guards. There must have been nearly a grand in the bundle and even Junior, the king of cool, had let out a little whistle.

M's phone rang just as they were about to take off for the pizza.

'Yeah Baz- yeah, with a couple of mates now like. Tomorra yeah, yeah what time. OK down the Quays eh, yeah, yeah fuck, nice one. No, no, it's no problem, sorted.'

M had pulled well away but he was a regular fog horn they hadn't missed a word of his end of the conversation.

M pocketed his phone and came back with a big, self-satisfied smile plastered all over his freckled mug.

'Quays eh?' Junior said, 'bit posh for you that M?'

M did a laughable 'business is business' face then pulled away from them again.

'Come on fuck heads,' he bellowed, 'let's get some food, I'm fucking starving.'

Junior and Pasquale exchanged a look. It wasn't like M to keep any kind of secret from the two of them. They followed him, both pedalling hard, their stomachs growling in anticipation.

The upshot of the dawn raid? Sean Manning had given them nothing and he was bailed out for the smoke and the drug paraphernalia. Moz was pissed off about it, insistent that they had gone in too early and too hard, bemoaning the Drug Squad intel'.

'Fucking jokers they are, don't know their arses from their bloody elbows.'

86

Darrin deferred to Mozzer's experience although he had enjoyed the experience if not the outcome of the raid.

'What's next yer reckon then Moz?'

'You watch, it will be lots more of the bloody same son; surveillance, lots of constipation inducing man hours and then somebody drops the bloody dime.'

He caught Darrin's puzzled expression.

'Informing that is, you bloody peasant,' exasperated with his ignorance.

'It will probably be mundane,' Moz went on, 'you know, the way we crack it - not bloody CSI, not even Starsky and Hutch.'

Moz shook his head at him again.

'No comprendez eh young Daz? Another cultural reference passes you by - fuck me dead.'

Darrin let it go and put the shitty mood down to the fact that Mozzer had not yet topped up the blood sugar levels. He was a renowned cranky fucker when unfed.

That was it for the moment then, more wait and see. He had the weekend off, a piss up Friday, fry up Saturday, then the gym and then salsa. See what that new adventure brings.

Tommy drove up to the tops on the Saturday, parked off near the butty van and took the gentle and then steep incline up to the highest, or was it the second highest, reservoir in the land. He had a few butties in his backpack and a newspaper for a read if it wasn't too cold when he got up there. It was reasonably busy but, thankfully, not the bloody High Street. The people he passed were both open faced and relaxed, a cheery salutation received and given with pretty much every passing. It was only a half an hour climb up to the res' and he was pleased at the spring in his step and the lack of shortness of puff in getting up there. He found a sunny spot that also had the necessary wind break of a dry stone wall. It allowed him to sit down and enjoy the tranquillity; some much needed time out watching the shadows of the clouds scud across the hills.

He took a few deep breaths and gazed into the mid-distance, his eyes fixing on a hawk that hovered patiently over the rugged tussocks of grass that lay to the south side of the water. His mind turned over the events earlier in the week - he was finding them hard to shake off.

Truth was he'd enjoyed it; the adrenalin, the anger, the fuck it use of his strength. It was in him, the taste for it offset, thankfully, with plenty of self-control. The rage was a family heirloom; present in his grandfathers, his uncles and his dad, passed on down to him through the DNA. Such displays of aggression had been part of his passage of rites, omnipresent in the culture into which he'd been born.

When he had arrived in Sydney back in the late eighties, he'd been amazed at the lack of agro there, at how chilled were the minor, everyday interactions. You walked down the street and nobody was giving out de-rigueur challenging stares. Nobody displayed the over emphasised 'don't fuck with me pal' shoulder rolling swagger of his home. It had taken him a few months to adjust to but it was all part of a 'going native' process that he had readily embraced. He was happy to shed that skin, maintaining the facade just took up too much energy.

He'd been back eighteen months and it looked like the osmosis had been put in reverse. Chilled Tommy was now just another sun-soaked memory.

He wondered how the boys from the Centre would have viewed the agro at the DVD store. They would have probably eaten it up with a fork and spoon. He pictured Bones laughingly throwing his, 'be decent not tough' mantra back in his face.

Out of the corner of his eye the hawk plummeted and after a few moments in the grass, came back up with a mouse pinned in its talons - the little fella's back legs cycling away in futile struggle. Instinct, he thought pure bloody instinct. Nature, as Mick would say, red in tooth and claw.

Tommy picked himself up and made his way back to the car. He went down to the bookies to meet up with Mick. They'd have a short stroll and a couple of pints.

Darrin had enjoyed the salsa night right enough - it had been a blur of Latin rhythms and a permanently busy dance floor. The dancing was sexy, if, to his eye, a little complex looking. He'd put his hand up for the beginners' lesson, which kicked off the night. After that he stood around and watched as the instructor, a tasty South American bird, took the intermediates through their paces whilst a little Cuban bloke, who was as loose as a goose and as lithe as a cat, did the same with the advanced mob. Jolika was in the advanced class and when she moved she was as smooth and supple as water running over stones - very tasty.

She joined him after the class, bringing a tall, good looking dark haired guy over with her. He was advanced class too - and, he had to admit, a pretty good mover.

She introduced him as Stuart. Stuart slipped his left hand around her waist and then offered him the other, making the statement right enough.

'Hi Darrin, what do you think then, like it?'

'Yeah, yeah I do, very, very er good. How long you two been at it then?'

Stuart looked down at Jolika.

'Couple of years now eh babe?'

'Almost three for me, I started just before you, remember? I asked you to dance.'

She tapped him on the chest and both revelled in the memory for a while – so, nothing doing there for our Dazzer.

He kept the smile on his dial.

'Ah well - that's great. Maybe I'll be as good as you guys some day.'

A new song kicked off, booming out from the speakers that were located with the mixing desk at the far end of the room. Jolika grabbed his hand and insisted that he danced with her.

Darrin instinctively looked over at Stuart who smiled and jerked his head towards the dance floor. Jolika laughed, 'come on Northern boy, it's not the school disco, you don't need his bloody permission. You'll be right for this one, a nice slow beat - easy to keep the four-four time.'

She encouraged him all the way through, counting out the beat for him and, with a little concentration he managed to keep on it, only cocking up when he tried a simple turn. Whenever he went astray Jolika quickly guided him back to the beat again, as patient as a mum with her toddler.

'You're alright you are PC May - not bad at all - lots of potential.' She said that with her little chirp of a giggle that made him yearn, again, for Stuart's absence.

When the song ended she bowed to him and gave him a little round of applause. Darrin walked off the floor with a

Cheshire cat grin and a smiling Stuart gave him a brotherly thumbs up.

She spent the next two hours dragging her salsa mates over to get him up to dance and he even plucked it up enough to ask the instructor for a whirl.

He left the gig with Jolika and Stuart just after one in the morning; slightly high, sweat soaked and sober. She'd been right - it was a different world.

He'd spent the Saturday night at home with his mum, M hadn't been picking up and Junior was down with some bug. They'd had dinner together and talked about a planned holiday later on in the year. She had friends with a farmhouse down near Seville. Pasquale had been there a few times but he didn't fancy it all this year and he tentatively suggested that she go alone - after all, he'd be sixteen by then.

They chatted about Tommy and the literacy tutoring. She was chuffed that he was doing well and asked him a couple of questions about Tommy himself and that made him feel a little uncomfortable. He speculated as if to whether she fancied him, he supposed that was possible. It had been years since he had seen her with a man. He hadn't warmed to any of them really apart from Kim, who was, as far as he knew, still somewhere in South America. Just the two of them, that was the way it was and the way it always had been. He was straining at the leash though, literacy classes or no literacy classes. He'd even contemplated fucking off to London last year but fear and doubt had stopped him from doing it. He'd told her his plans to go, just to get a reaction and he had seen her fear. He hadn't mentioned it again, it was all a little too much.

He drew a blank with M again the next day and Junior

was still laid up, so he semi-reluctantly agreed to head over to Ben and Carole's place for lunch. They were long-term friends of his mum's and part of the Spain crew. They had a son who was a year or two younger than him, Andy. Andy had cerebral palsy, day after day all twisted up in that electric chair of his, using up masses of energy with that mangled voice of his just to make himself understood. Pasquale liked Andy, he liked his good cheer and his determination and Andy wasn't above giving his oldies a bit of shit either - playing the poor me card whenever he felt he needed it. Pasquale always found a degree of patience with Andy that he didn't find with others. Andy didn't try to hide his affection for him either - he was beyond feigned cool. Spending time with him always made him think about what it would have been like to have a younger brother or even a little sister. Be easier in some ways, he concluded, she might give him more space then, she'd have somebody else to worry about.

He hadn't had a smoke all weekend and on the Monday morning, he'd woken up feeling fresh and curiously optimistic. He'd even beaten her down to the kitchen to make his sandwiches and she gave him a little look about that, pleased and kind of curious at the same time. He swung his bag onto his shoulder as he headed out of the door. Tommy then school, he thought - sorted.

Tommy had spent a fair bit of time with the old man over the weekend and was glad of the break by the time he got back to his flat on the Sunday evening. One good thing though had come from it. He'd persuaded the old fart to have a weekend at the races with the boys from the Crown. His old man loved the nags and Mick was a daily, week in week out student of the form. More importantly, a change of scene would be good for him. The old man had prevaricated and had even become a little pissed off with him when he had pressed it. But he'd eventually listened and Mick had handed over the necessary readies to Paul, the Crown's landlord, when they'd popped down the pub for the Sunday lunch. Again, the old man had pushed most of the food to the side of his plate. Tommy didn't comment, he'd badgered him enough this weekend.

He was now laid out on the sofa watching some telly for a change. It was a documentary on Mallory and the conquering of Everest. He found it to be both compelling and irritating at the same time. The notion of 'conquering' a mountain he found laughable and he speculated as to what Bonnie's family would have thought about that. Probably, just more confirmation for them that white fellas are intrinsically fucked up.

There was the class thing too. Mallory and his mate were toffs through and through with the raft of assumptions and entitlement that went with it. Tommy had long moved away from class as a primary badge of identification, years away from Britain could do that to you. Those long years away and the seminal experience of being in a relationship with a woman who was from a race of people who, for generations, had suffered the privations of poverty, racism, dispossession, forced relocation and ongoing discrimination. The British working class and its burgeoning underclass would never have to confront that kind of reality. In comparison, they didn't know what fucking hardship was.

On the box, a contemporary version of Mallory and Lee, (the programme adopting a 'following in their footsteps' shtick), were being filmed trudging their way to the top of the king of mountains. The climb was a freezing, oxygen deprived, snail paced crawl, which looked about as thrilling and pleasure-filled as dipping your head into a bucket of snot. When they had realised that Mallory wouldn't be coming back, England's establishment had given him a huge memorial service in Westminster Abbey. The service was a blue blood gathering of the great and powerful, one of the last hurrahs of the dying empire.

After it finished Tommy flicked the TV off, he fired up the laptop and had a two hour steamy chat with some bird in Watford who was almost young enough to be his daughter. Fuck it, he thought, sometimes it felt good to take a stroll in the gutter.

It had been freezing all week in the run up to the spring. An icy eastern wind had taken hold, more than cold enough to help keep the peace around the shops and the estates - everybody was tucked up inside their homes with their three bar heaters on, all was nice and quiet.

For once, Darrin wasn't minding the lull too much, although he was still regularly pestering a tolerant Moz about getting a gig on the on-going op, which had seemingly stalled with the meagre pickings that had been garnered from Manning's arrest. It looked like Moz had been proven right.

He'd seen Jolika on the change over and told her of his plans to get down to the dance lesson this Thursday. Johno had overheard him and it was all round the fucking station by lunch the next day. They had given him the usual crap about sequins and being a poofter. The numbskulls wouldn't be saying that if they'd been there last Saturday, it had been wall to wall, tasty tush. He kept that to himself though, he didn't want it to become a gawping policemans' ball and he thought that Jolika would be doing likewise, which made him briefly contemplate why she'd invited him in the first place. Nice bloke Stuart, he thought, a damn pity though.

Mid-week he had tea at his folks' place, his dad had spent most of the time behind the paper, his mum good naturedly wittering on about his sister's kids, which, in his opinion, was the best thing to happen to the family for years. The young 'uns took a little of the rough edge off the old man and they fed his mum's incessant need to be a mother. He was grateful to get off that particular hook. The old lady certainly had an awful lot of love to give.

After the meal he chatted briefly with the old man. The old boy was more than a little preoccupied with the future of his gym. The possibility of local authority cut-backs was now being given open slather in the media. His dad had built up a lot of good favour over the last thirty years but, as the old man, said these were 'different times,' and he was finding it hard to get the numbers down there.

Dougy didn't mind sharing his analyses of the problem with him.

'Fucking lazy this new lot yer know - too much given to 'em for nowt. Hope there's not a war in the next few years, cos these fuckers won't know which way to point the bloody rifle!'

The old lady had chided him for the profanities and the old man had grunted a reflex, 'sorry love.'

The old man had a point though, you'd have to bribe a lot of the kids to get them anywhere near a gym and then probably the only way they would make it through the doors would be with the support of a rake of social workers who were being employed through some fucking community scheme.

'You know what the problem is son. They get their arses wiped and they've got next to bugger all to look forward to.'

That rang a vague echo in his head, something Mick Cochrane had said to him when Darrin had first started drinking in the local boozers. It had been a few years ago now, well before he joined the plod. There had been a long and heated debate at the bar about the state of the nation's wayward youth. Mick had turned to him and breathed whiskey and Guinness fumes in his face, a fierce glitter in those intense eyes of his. 'You know what the trouble is with the young people lad? They have nobody to look up to!'

Darrin shared the memory with his folks, the old man had snapped his paper and given him his industrial strength withering look.

'Well that's bloody Mick for you, he'd have a political argument about opening a packet of bloody biscuits. Bloody prophet of doom, he is.'

Darrin looked over at his mum who gave him a little raise of the eyebrows. He made with his excuses and got ready to go. She folded up a pile of his washing that had been sitting on the dining room table and with a few deft movements placed it all in his gym bag.

His dad asked him if he was popping down the gym tomorrow.

With a hesitation that he tried but failed to hide Darrin told the old man that he had something else on.

'On the arm are yer then son?'

'Aye, summat like that,' he replied.

His mum gave him one of her slightly cow-eyed smiles, no doubt planning the bloody wedding invites. Darrin buried his irritation at the pair of them and made for the door.

It had been freezing all week and it felt like life outside of school, the Centre and Tommy had contracted to almost nothing. Junior had got in touch late on Thursday to let him know he was back in circulation and that he too hadn't heard anything from M.

That evening Pasquale cycled down to M's place, opened the front gate and wheeled his bike to the scratched up front door. There were no lights on and nobody home, he turned away, taking note of the brimming plastic bag that was propped up at the side of the house full of empties of Special Brew and a cask of wine. As he trudged back to M's front gate the fat guy from next door was carefully parking his shit-box out in front of M's house. The man wheezed his way out of the driver's seat and gave Pasquale a bit of hairy eyeball then a watery smile of recognition.

'After Matthew are yer lad?'

Fuck, the guy had a loud voice.

He nodded a yes.

'Not seen him all week - Mum was in there last night, with that new bloke of hers. He's from down Langford they reckon.'

'Hmm OK - right.' He mumbled back.

'Got a job apparently!'

Pasquale looked quickly up at the fat man.

The guy looked at him and laughed, loudly.

'The bloke lad, not bloody Matthew or his mum - bloody hell!'

Pasquale grimaced a half smile at the fat fucker's merriment, the big man chortling happily as he waddled towards his brightly lit home.

He cycled away and returned straight home, his mum had made a shepherd's pie and, with a little effort, he pushed M to the back of his mind.

He called Junior a little later on and told him about his unsuccessful visit, but Junior didn't offer any comment or speculation. He could picture his friend shrugging his shoulders - one of Junior's stock 'what can yer do?' mannerisms.

They agreed to go down to the Community Centre tomorrow - no M meant that they'd probably be straight and be straight in too and, besides, he was Tommy's star pupil. Maybe Stella would be there, she'd been giving him a couple of looks at school and she was well tasty.

Tommy had finished his part of the Building Communities funding application early Friday morning and dropped it off to Pauline just before lunch.

'What do you reckon to the chances then Pauline?'

'No better than fifty-fifty I'd say Thomas, we have the advantage of the track record but given the bloody voracious Olympics - it's no better than that I'm afraid.'

Tommy snorted softly. 'People do love their circuses don't they?'

Pauline nodded, it was an old chestnut of theirs, one that they were happy to regularly trot out and play with. Pauline had lived in Amsterdam for much of her twenties and while she was there she had had involved in the city's radical fringe politics. She'd shown him a batch of old photos at last year's summer get together at her place; Pauline with dyed

spiky hair and some fetching, if out there apparel. In most
of the pictures she was pictured arm in arm with an intense
looking bearded boyfriend who'd been a political prisoner in
Chile. Pauline had spent almost a decade hanging out with
anarchists, living in squats, having regular dust ups with the
Amsterdam rozzers and producing a radical newsletter - the
Great Leap Forward. She laughed whenever they touched
upon it, but her eyes always took on a certain light too. Red
until she's dead our Pauline, he thought, old school radical.

'You down at the 'rave' tonight then Pauline?'

'I wouldn't miss it for the world Thomas, particularly if
you promise to get up for Beyonce again.'

He laughed and coloured slightly.

'Still got it eh Pauline?'

'Well you have something Thomas - that's for sure.'

They swapped some cursory info about his dad and he
asked her about the grandkids and her daughter in London.
She only had the one son, he was a real gone kid with drug
induced mental health issues. Apparently, the kid was as bol-
shie in his personality and politics as his mum and as bright as
both his parents but he'd missed out on their inherent stabil-
ity. The boy had been a long-term struggle that had almost
scuppered her marriage. Luckily, Den, Pauline's old man,
was as stolid as Gibraltar and as dependable as the phases of
the moon and they had made it through - just.

Her phone rang, crashing heavily into the conversation. It
was one of the local politicians, somebody she courted on a
regular basis. He nodded a goodbye and skipped back to his
office.

He had a bit of time to kill, he hadn't been up to Aziz's
since he'd seen Noora and he could do with a walk. He

thought of Noora and she was transmogrified, maybe with a slightly indecent haste, into Donna. Hmmm, he thought, maybe that was a sign of things to come? The kid though, he reminded himself, as wobbly as a shopping trolley wheel and a mummy's boy under all that street-cred' posturing. His shoes lying in that vestibule! Tommy thought that despite the growing trust that was developing between the two of them, such a move would be about as welcome to the kid as a dose of mercury poisoning. Still, he rationalised, Pasquale could use such an experience to learn a valuable lesson or two about compromise and sharing and he could take his time finding out what she tasted like under that musky perfume of hers.

Tommy picked up his coat and made his way out to the shop.

Sunday and the weather had changed - it had to be at least ten degrees warmer than the day before, maybe they were in for an earlyish spring after all. It was a game day today but, thankfully, a pretty low-key one. Today's opponents were a newly promoted, provincial city team with a relatively small following whose supporters had no real rep' for thuggery and mayhem. It proved to be an easy win for City too, which kept the local knuckle draggers placated. Darrin still couldn't get his head around the intensity of the fans and whenever he bothered to look at them he found the contorted faces and the vituperative bile that came from the terraces more than a little disconcerting. Grown men, many of them in their forties and beyond, apoplectic because a linesman hadn't flagged for offside, it was fucking wacked alright.

'It's just tribalism son,' was Moz's analysis when he'd

mentioned the primal shit to him. For once, he thought, Moz was being overly kind to the morons. To Darrin, it was more like feeding time at the zoo.

It was all quiet back at the station, just a couple of drunks who'd taken advantage of the nice weather by getting hammered in a beer garden and, to lower the tone further, a recidivist wife beater. Sarge Thomas was obviously a little bored behind the desk.

'Nice and quiet eh Sarge?'

'Aye lad - they're still paying us the same money though. A missing persons has come in. A young lad from the Barrington,' Sarge picked up the paperwork, 'a Matthew Marshall, you heard of him?'

Darrin hadn't. That must have been the mother that he'd passed by coming back in to the station from the game; red eyed, a nice enough figure but plenty of hard miles on the clock - obviously a boozer, probably more.

'Been gone a week apparently.'

'A week - Jesus!'

Sarge shrugged.

'She must have been busy, eh boyo?'

'Aye - fucking busy alright.'

'She doesn't reckon him as a runaway but, you never know, he could be somewhere down in London eating a burger and chips with a new uncle mind.'

Darrin flinched at the image.

'Anyway it's out there now - summat might turn up.'

And it did - word came out when he was back out on patrol with Johno - a body found in a skip, partially hidden under a tarp', out on the north western edges of the city. He was discovered by a crew of builders who'd been idle during the cold snap - a cursory ID and it looked like it was the Marshall kid. Trish and Johnno were off to do the door knock with the mother - a short straw job if ever there was one.

Confirmation came through just before he was ready to clock off, it was him alright, the poor little bastard. Suspected foul play- he hadn't climbed in there for a kip, had he? Autopsy reports would tell them more. Maybe he'd get in on this one.

Pasquale had heard the news about M while he was still at school, a big, gangly kid whose name he could never remember told him during the lunch break. He didn't believe it but, straight away, his legs felt wobbly and he felt his breathing change, quick and shallow in his chest. He immediately tried Junior's phone but there was no pick up from him.

His mum confirmed it later that day she'd heard it on the local radio and also from one of the women at her work who lived in the next street to M. It would be all over the Barrington like a fucking forest fire.

Pasquale was numbed - he didn't know what he felt and he didn't know what he should feel.

His mum tried to give him a hug when she came home but he blocked it, he didn't want to be touched at all. She ordered in a pizza but he only managed a slice, he went up to his room early and lay on his bed in the dark, his eyes following the car lights that slowly swept across the ceiling.

At three in the morning he got up, tiptoed downstairs, grabbed his bicycle and rode through the silent back streets over to M's home.

He stopped on the far side of the road and looked at M's place. All the house lights in the street were off, nobody was up. The fat man's car was parked outside of his own house this time. Pasquale pushed his bike over to the car and took the driver's rear view mirror off with a savage snap kick, it clattered away and came to rest a couple of yards in front of the car. He leaned his bike against the driver's door, walked up to where the mirror lay, picked it up and tossed it into the fat man's garden. He got back on his bike and made the return journey home. He fell asleep pretty much as soon as he hit the pillow; still dressed, exhausted and feeling indescribably empty.

The kid had turned up on the Monday but had missed the Wednesday session. Tommy decided to leave it till Friday and see whether he turned up then, by rights he should have been on to the school but he'd cut the kid a bit of slack.

Sonny had rung him the day before and let him know about Matthew Marshall. According to Sonny preliminary tests had shown alcohol, smoke and methamphetamine in the boy's system and it looked like an overdose but he hadn't jumped in the skip by himself. He was a pretty big kid for his age too, so there had to be at least a couple of adults involved. Tommy hung up, exhaled loudly then quickly stood and did some laps of the room. He was feeling slightly burned by the news.

He talked to his dad about it that night. They were nice and warm in the heat and glow of the lounge room gas fire.

Mick was quiet for a while, stroking his chin and looking into the distance.

'What was he like this kid?'

'Didn't really know him Dad, he had plenty of energy, full of piss and vinegar. Not that likeable really but, you know, not exactly been dealt the best of hands either.'

'Cops got anything?'

'Not heard owt, they're trying to back-track but the mum is all over the place. He'd been gone at least a week.'

His dad flicked his eyebrows at that and slowly shook his head.

'Let's hope they get the fuckers then Tom.'

'Yeah - let's hope they do.'

Tommy called both Donna and the school on Friday when Pasquale failed to show. He also got onto Sonny to see if he could track him down to have a word.

Donna told him that she had let him stay home, he wondered if that was for the best but he kept it to himself.

'Funerals on a Tuesday,' he told her, 'they had a whip round for the mum at some of the locals.'

'You going?' he asked.

'Pasquale wants to; I said I'd go along. You?'

'No, no I barely knew him. Sonny will probably be there.'

'On the 21st eh!' he said.

'Sorry?'

'Oh yeah, sorry Donna, The 21st of March, the funeral. It's the first day of the spring, you know, the equinox.'

'Oh yes,' she said, a little flatly, 'I suppose.'

He'd wished he kept that interesting gem to himself - portents and meaning in fucking everything and nothing.

They said a quick goodbye and Tommy stood for a while and gazed out of the office at nothing in particular.

RIP Matthew Marshall, he thought.

Jimbo called him after lunch - Piccolos again tonight, did he fancy it? He did - slaves to the fucking rhythm.

APRIL

Moz had joined him in the canteen on the Friday. Darrin was sat alone finishing off his brew while cheerily humming one of the tunes that he'd danced along to last night. He still wasn't that caught up by the music - but he kept coming away from it feeling plenty of bounce. He'd even had a crack at the intermediates last week, at the smiling behest of Rosa the Venezuelan instructor.

Moz had swerved his way towards him through a couple of busy tables. He plopped down a tray loaded with a plate full of a particularly anaemic looking lasagne, a wagon wheel for afters and one of the foul little trifles that the canteen often divvied up, usually towards the end of the week - all in all fucking disgusting. Little wonder the fat fucker was larding around three stone of excess.

Mozzer shunned any conversation, tucking straight into the lasagne. Darrin tried to look elsewhere whilst Moz dispatched the fodder. Five minutes of robotic shovelling and the main meal was gone. Moz leaned back in his chair let out a belch and reached for his napkin to give his face a cursory wipe, smearing a little bit of overdone white sauce up and onto his left temple.

Moz gave Darrin the once over - now ready to share whatever he had.

'Got something for yer PC May, should untwist those jocks of yours a bit. Tell yer what, let me rip into this trifle and then I'll give it to yer.'

Darrin felt his leg drumming impatiently as the fat man

wolfed down the trifle: three mouthfuls and it was all gone.
Moz yawned and this time gave out another more ostenta-
tious belch, which caused a trio of plain clothes who were
sat on the next table to turn around and look at him with
looks of both amusement and wrinkle nosed disgust.

'Go on then Moz - spill it - I'll have Sarge Thomas up my
arse if I don't crack on.'

Moz leaned forward slightly. 'I've drawn the kid who was
found in the skip - fancy being my wing man on it?'

That was well worth the waiting.

'Sure, sure - count me in Moz, Jolika on it too?'

Moz cocked a knowing eyebrow and gave him a little
shake of the head.

Yeah, yeah, Errol Flynn, she'll be on it too - Super's up-
ping the numbers on the drug squad op. The ice found in
the kid shows the probable link to the hottest ticket in town
and the kid being found rotting in a skip is not good for the
Super's beloved PR like - is it?'

It wasn't, even in a big ugly metropolis like this, the kid's
death had caused the ripples of unease and concern amongst
the community. Big media coverage in the first few days - the
local politicians being seen to be on it, strutting their shiny-
arsed, self-aware, self-promoting shit.

'Yeah, yeah, suppose.' Darrin didn't give a fuck about the
local politicians, the local media, the Super or his precious
public relations.

'When do we kick off then Moz?'

'You can get suited and booted tomorra young Dazzler.
We need to get an overview on the recent adventures of
young Matthew - if we can.'

Moz finger-nailed the food from under his temple and

examined the evidence. Thankfully, he chose to wipe it onto his crumpled napkin.

'The youth worker - Sonny Rasheed, you know him?'

Darrin did, Sonny was a smart, lively Asian guy with a big smile.

'He's bringing in two of the kid's homies,' Moz made the inverted commas sign, 'in this afternoon, see what they know. We've had the word that they were out and about with him on the Friday. The mum saw him for half an hour or so Saturday lunch and then, a big fat nothing.'

'They got a time of death yet?' Darrin asked.

'Early Sunday morning apparently – decomp' was slowed down a fair bit by that cold snap.'

'No responses of note from the stuff in the paper then?'

'No - we've drawn a blank son. We have a fair bit of work to do.'

Darrin cleared up his stuff and left Moz to the confectionary. Energy pulsated through his legs. About fucking time, he was more than up for this.

Later that day, they had chatted for a frustrating, silence-filled two hours with Matthew's mates but in the end they had drawn fuck all of any help from either one of them. Yes they were with him on the Friday and that was pretty much that. Sonny had tried to push and prompt the pair as much as possible. But they had proven to be the two half-smart monkeys. The Italian looking kid managed to be a mixture of diffidence and defiance whilst Junior, at the grand old age of sixteen, came across all world-weary and jaded.

He'd had a brief chat with Sonny in the reception.

'Sorry about that Constable, I think they are still coming to terms with it - big shock for both of them.'

'Might prevent them from using themselves though eh?' It came out a bit more blunt than Darrin had intended.

Sonny looked at him a little sharply then gave him a little half nod.

'Maybe - or they may even go the other way, who knows?'

'You think they might know more than they're saying then?'

Sonny thought about that for a little while and intimated his ambivalence with a tilting of his right hand.

'Not sure to be honest, M was the one on the fringes of the scene but I don't think those two are really. Looks like Matthew was all alone on this one.'

'Yeah he was all alone alright – that's for fucking sure.'

Sonny gave him another little look, followed by a friendly clap on the shoulder.

'See you later then Constable.'

'OK Sonny, it's Darrin by the way, Darrin May.'

Sonny gave him that cloud-bursting grin of his. 'Yeah nice one - PC Darrin May eh. OK then Darrin - later.'

Pasquale's heart had been racing for what seemed like ages after they'd left the station, Junior had bidden him a curt farewell in the station car park and he'd made his way back home alone. Sonny had offered him a lift but he knocked it back, he didn't want to talk about it anymore - he'd had a gutful of it.

He'd kept it together during the funeral though, unlike M's mum who had blubbered like a baby all the way through. His mum had put his arm around him and he had let her keep it there, grateful for the comfort that it had given him. He couldn't remember anything the vicar had said - it was just the usual empty Bible bollocks. All he'd taken in was a rheumy-eyed old guy opening and closing his mouth. They had finished the service with this song, which M and his mum had supposedly loved. It was some bird warbling her way through an Eminem rap - 'it's not so bad', she reckoned. It had caught him on the hop as he had never heard M talk about the song, he liked the feel of it right enough even if he didn't kick in with the sentiments, coz it was fucking bad, in fact it felt fucking terrible.

He and Junior had met up on the sly during the week when Sonny had told them about the impending visit to the cop-shop. They had decided not to tell the cops about the phone call. During the interview the cops had asked them if M had owned a mobile - so that meant that they didn't have it and somebody had to have taken it off him. Matty loved that fuckin' phone.

They hadn't discussed why they shouldn't tell the cops about the call but Pasquale knew that they were in agreement on it. There was no way that M would have blabbed to the cops about something like that - and that was that. But, when he thought about it, he knew that there was more to their decision, something a lot more basic than any kind of principled show of solidarity with a now dead friend. The very thought of mentioning Bazzer Dougan's name in any kind of proximity to M's death filled him with a numbing fear and he knew Junior well enough to know that he was frightened of the mad fucker too and Junior did not frighten easily. Besides, it was an overdose, that silly dumb bastard and his fucking drugs.

His mum mentioned the literacy stuff with Tommy and he mumbled a promise to get down to both the Centre and the school, and with his promise she had let it drop. He thought about going down the shopping centre for a while but decided he couldn't be arsed. He You-tubed the song that they had played for M and he played it maybe a dozen times, speculating idly as he did so about his father - gone when he was one year old and now with a new family, somewhere in Japan of all fucking places. His mum had encouraged him to go out there but he hadn't felt like seeing him or his half brother and sister. Maybe one day, he thought, he'd go out there and get one of those cool looking Samurai swords.

The following day Junior texted him about a party that was on not far from his place, his mum was a bit resistant to him going at first but she quickly relented, pleased that he had at least told her about it. One of her girlfriends had called earlier and a group of them were heading out for a meal and then a club - looked like his mum was ready for some fun too.

Pasquale met Junior just around the corner from the off licence in Abercrombie Street and Junior went in and scored two bottles of vodka. Junior had done some removal work for one of his uncles that morning and he'd scored fifty for his sweat.

Junior had flashed the fake ID but old man Sohail would have probably served him without it - no questions ever asked by that money hungry fucker.

Junior had told him that Stella would be there at the do and that there would be plenty of other talent there too and he was bang on. The placed was packed. Mum and Dad had gone off to Portugal for a fortnight - paaaarty. Junior found some coke in the fridge and divvied up the vodka. Some of the older boys who were slouching around in the kitchen were talking about a cage fighting night that was being held at the Expo some time next month. Junior was pretty keen to go and his birthday was coming up soon. Maybe his mum would divvy up the readies. He necked the vodka quickly and had a couple of smokes on top and the night had passed by in a blur. He managed to get close to Stella a couple of times when they were both dancing but he couldn't bring himself to make the move. Around midnight he was puking his guts up in the garden, a couple of the girls going back inside the house in disgust at the sound of his retching. Junior was on guard, keeping a distant eye on him from the kitchen door.

After an half an hour or so he managed to get himself upright and he made his escape around the side of house feeling a lot more sober and shivering like a wet, whipped dog. Thankfully, he was back home in ten minutes, his mum was still out with her mates and the house was quiet and dark on his return.

Tommy and Jimbo had pulled the pin well before midnight. Jimbo had the kids tomorrow and he was picking them up early from the mum's for a planned trip to the zoo. Looking around the bar Tommy had had the distinct notion that the two of them were creeping up close to becoming the oldest swingers in town. Just to keep in his hand Jimbo had engaged in some desultory chatting up of a brace of merry divorcees but it was all pitter-patter really. Anyway, Jimbo had just started a tentative thing with a single mum, from the Coleshaw of all fucking places! He hadn't bothered giving an opinion when Jimbo told him that one. Jimbo loved firing down a marker for reasons that Tommy had never been able to fully understand. He usually chose to observe it all from a distance and marvelled at his friend's long recognised bounce-backability. As a friend, Jimbo asked for fuck all from him apart from companionship, banter and the opportunity for disclosure and, when it mattered, he knew that Jimbo would be there for him in a flash.

He was still wired when he got home and he fired up the laptop.

Some bird from Las Vegas did a little cam show for him. She was as horny as fuck.

Saturday was bright and sunny and, after a sluggish start to the day, he got himself down to the plaza to do some clothes shopping. First up a pair of shoes, then he'd take a trip into Debenhams and look for some lightweight trousers and a couple of short-sleeved shirts for the summer.

Tommy had almost literally bumped into her, getting a little jog of excitement at her unexpected presence, taking in the smell of her perfume as her breasts had crushed, albeit very briefly, against his chest.

She had given a little start and a breathed curse, quickly followed by recognition and one of her wide smiles, the warmth of which instantly made him forget about the Ben Sherman display.

They laughed at each other.

'Hands full I see,' he said.

'Hmmm, couple of tops for me and some shorts and t-shirts for Pasquale. Hope he likes them.'

Tommy nodded at that, 'well yeah, let's hope so.'

They chewed the fat a little about the boy's reaction to Matthew's death.

'Let's hope he's OK for Monday - he's a bright boy and he's doing well - catching up quickly.' Tommy said.

'Hmmm think I might have to drag him there, he's moping the days away. It's understandable I suppose.'

'He should be OK Donna, just takes time eh?'

He looked at her intently and whilst he did he wasn't thinking about the boy at all. Maybe Jimbo had inspired him.

'Fancy a drink some time Donna?'

She coloured, slightly dipped her head and looked back up at him. He wouldn't say she was exactly coy but a smile was playing around those lush lips of hers.

'A date Tommy?'

He shrugged, 'well yeah, why not? No pressure.'

'No pressure eh?' And they both laughed, she with a little more conviction.

He was holding his breath, slightly nervous.

She let him off the hook quickly.

'Yeah that would be nice Tommy - why not.'

He nodded happily at that - maybe with a little more vigour than he would have liked.

'Great, great - what's the best night for you Donna?'

'Thursday is generally OK for me. I'm out with friends on Friday - you?'

'Hmmm I'm flexible, for you anyway.'

That brought him another smile, she liked the bit of honey and they held each others gaze until she broke it.

'Better get going Tommy, back home to make some lunch.'

She briefly touched his arm and then turned away to make tracks to the tills at the far end of the busy room.

He watched her walk away - hmm she had a gorgeous arse and those long, long legs.

Tommy whistled to himself as he rifled through the shirts.

He even bought himself a change from his usual blues, blacks and greys: a lightish green number with some brown threaded through it - how about that!

That night he hit the Crown and sat down with his old man to listen to the muscular sound of the house blues band, four local blokes, three tradies and an IT guy, who were all competent musicians. The lead guitarist was the star man. He could play alright but, for Tommy's taste, he tended to overdo the string bending solos. Still, Mick was happy enough in the midst of the cacophony, toe tapping and head nodding along. Mick loved the band and the boys in the band loved him. The old bugger was a local icon right enough.

Mick commented on the lightness of his mood in the set break.

'Yeah well- it's spring in't it Dad?' Playing with the old fella a little bit.

'Spring uh?' Mick snorted into his Guinness and took a big swallow of the brew. Mick looked back at him as he licked his lips, his eyes shining in the gloom of the pub's lounge room.

'That's my boy.' Mick told him.

On the Sunday he took the old man for a drive over the tops, they were booked in to have Sunday lunch with Wayne, his missus and the kids. The drive was long enough to feel like a pleasant event but short enough to not be too arduous for the old man. Despite the sunshine and warmth, pockets and slivers of snow still lay in the upper reaches of the north facing hills.

The meal was a gargantuan affair and his old man made a point of eating more than he would have done if it had just been the two of them. His dad was a sucker for a generous hearted woman and Debbie was all that and a little bit more.

Mick even played and interacted with the kids for an hour or so.

After a while, a little look told him that the old man was ready to return to the ranch and Tommy stood up and initiated the farewells. Debbie gave the old man a piece of cheesecake wrapped up in foil and Mick looked for all the world like a kid who'd been given the perfect birthday present.

They listened to the radio for a while on the way back, enjoying the ride and the ease of the silence between them. His old man didn't bother asking him in for a brew and Tommy was fine with it, Mick needed his time alone, that was a long established given.

As he sat in the car he watched the old man juggle the cheesecake over to his right hand as he reached for his keys to open the front door. After he unlocked the door Mick turned and gave him a one figured salute. Tommy gunned the engine and pulled out into the road.

She called him that evening and they confirmed it for Thursday - a pub situated on the leafier side of the city - a smart joint and given the local real estate, inevitably pricey.

Tommy played music until it was time to crash and revelled in the anticipation. He wondered about the boy and how that side of it would go but, what the hell, life couldn't always be gift wrapped with a pretty bow. The kid would have to learn to get along, just like the rest of us.

Darrin was finding that working on the Marshall case was proving to be very frustrating, lots of shoe leather being used kicking up dirt and looking under rocks on the Barrington whereupon all and sundry professed to know fuck all about Matthew and any of his movements - a complete fucking stonewall. Liaison with the cops down where the body had been found had drawn a blank too. It was half a mile from the boy's last resting place to the nearest residencies and a quarter of a mile from the skip to a nearby trading estate. Nobody had anything for them - it looked like the detective work on this one was going to mean somebody leading them to where they had to go by the nose - the Mozzer principle.

It was the crystal meth found in the boy that was keeping the heat on the case but the Drug Squad, according to Moz, were just as bereft of leads as they were.

'Fishing trip this is son - like trying to pin the tail on the bleeding donkey.'

There was overtime going around it though, they had finally put an op post on the Coleshaw. It was located in an empty flat in one of the three God forsaken mid-rises that looked down in their sallow misery over the estate's small shopping precinct, that and the local boozer, The Admiral, and right on down the full length of Oak Road. It was a grand vista that afforded them a bird's eye view of the local, low level bell-end dealers and their impressionable young acolytes who compulsively hung around them in shiftless clusters. Plus, there were a couple of bigger players living up on the estate, mid-level operators who, reputedly, had contacts with the higher end of the city's criminal fraternity. It was a perfect spot really.

So, that was his week sorted, his regular shift then a change of clothes and off to the Coleshaw in his battered but functional Triumph to take up position at the lounge window of flat 18c Windsor House, the Coleshaw.

Big Ged Keegan had popped into the musty dump on the Wednesday of his first week there, his ursine frame filling up the doorway that was between the small hallway and the lounge. As far as he knew Keegan hadn't been co-opted on to the op but he was renowned for having his fingers in lots of pies.

'Neighbours not too noisy for you then young un?'

Keegan had nodded across to the flat next door where-in there lived a permanently ripped, middle-aged Rasta.

Darrin grinned and shook his head, it was company of sorts - a bit of bloody life at least.

Apart from the Rasta man there was only an elderly couple living on this landing, which was the third floor of the block. Home for Fred and Doris was the flat nearest the stairwell. He felt for the poor old buggers, they had to be in their mid-seventies and they were stuck in this crumbling dump, washed up on an unloved, polluted beach surrounded by the jetsam and flotsam of Coleshaw life.

Big Ged had joined him over at the widow, he took up a lot of space did Keegan and Darrin immediately felt that familiar sense of unease in his presence, aware of the ticking of his pulse in his throat.

Keegan jerked his chin over towards the precinct, 'owt doing down there then Dazzer lad?'

'Just the usual shit Sarge – pure scroteville.'

'Any of the older lads been out and about - clocked 'em?'

'Yeah Keiron er.'

'Prendegast?'

'Yeah him and Dwayne, er Dwayne Wilson.'

Ged nodded at that, 'any dealing?'

'Hard to say nothing obvious - they're smoking, weed probably, but…'

'Yeah I know son, it has to be dog balls flagrant to nail

them. Any sign of Chris Johnstone and that meathead brother of his?'

Johnstone was the closest thing the Coleshaw had to a drug baron. And he was a large part of the reason why he was stood in this shitty flat. He lived down off Oak Road, in Linden Avenue. Johnstone was known to regularly hold court at The Admiral - King Chris surrounded by his indolent, hard-nosed, blotch-skinned coterie.

'You collared him once, didn't you Sarge?' It was his turn to ask a question for a fucking change.

Keegan looked at him with an irritating wry amusement.

'Been checking out my scrapbook have yer young Dazzler?'

Darrin smiled a stiff smile back at him, the fucker had to have three inches and eighty pounds on him - he was a definite four be two job.

But Keegan was fucking with him. He laughed and patted Darrin on the shoulder.

'Yeah, over ten years ago now- must be. Prick got off with a slap on the wrist too. A couple of witnesses pulled the pin - shat themselves when they got the hard word. That and that fucking slick Jew lawyer of his.'

Big Ged tutted in disgust at the memory.

'They need to raze this place and start again Darrin.' As he said it the Rasta guy yelled something out and then laughed, maybe he concurred.

'Johnstone connected to the lads in the city?'

Keegan smiled at him again, this time a little patronisingly. They weren't mates yet.

'The lads in the city eh Daz! Well he'd like people to think that he was, but, bottom line, he's a scrote and those particular respectable businessmen - well, let's say they don't break bread at the same table.'

'Fucking needle in a haystack all this then, Sarge?'

'Fraid so young fella, that's why a good snitch is worth more than their weight in gold - right enough. Save you a lot time breathing in mould and listening to jungle bunnies getting stoned through a plasterboard wall.'

Keegan laughed and slapped him, again, on his shoulder.

'How's your dad by the way?'

Darrin failed to hide the surprise.

Keegan flicked his wire brush eyebrows, getting obvious pleasure at Darrin being knocked off balance.

'Known him for years, your old fella, I have. Used to organise some charity nights with him.'

'Shit I didn't know that.'

'Stick around, it's all a learning curve son.'

He let his guard down a little and told Keegan about his old man's present worries.

Keegan rubbed his jaw as he listened and looked down towards the sluggish activity on the Coleshaw.

'Hmmm be a pity to lose it, right enough, been a beacon for a long time your old man's gym. Kept plenty of lads on the straight and narrow has Dougy. Look at those little fuckers.' Ged sprayed a plume of saliva in disgust across the still grimy window.

'They could do with some of that. No discipline, no ambition, no fucking future and no fucking hope.'

Keegan grunted.

'Anyway young fella, that's enough of all that bollocks. Let's leave that crap to those candy arsed social workers eh? I'll get off then, better keep the little lady happy. Later eh young un?'

Big Ged turned away from the window and ambled over to the flat door, Keegan turned at the door and gave him an airy wave goodbye.

Darrin looked out of the window for a few moments then he turned away from what was not going on and went into the kitchen to grab a cloth to wipe the spray of saliva from the window.

On the Monday Pasquale had managed a few moments of clarity and concentration with Tommy but then he'd met up with Junior rather than go on to school. They'd cycled up to the Coleshaw and Junior had scored some smoke from the older black guy Dwayne. Dwayne had given him a brief second or two of the hairy eyeball and then quickly turned his attention back to Junior - a smooth palm slap and presto! The money had turned into a foil.

He had toyed with the idea of going back to his place and smoking it there but she was all fucking born again about that now and she had a nose like a bloodhound so they headed down to the canal instead and found a spot they'd used before. Out around the back then, on inside what had probably been a huge cotton mill. It had three and a half standing walls and a corner with some roof on it - good enough.

Junior talked about moving down to London, he didn't fancy putting up with the disruption when his older brother hit home - no fucking way man. Junior had grown used to being the oldest male in the house too, all that would go out of the window when Wes lobbed up and plenty of shit would be likely to come pouring back in.

'Where do your folks down South live Joon?'

'Haringey bro, why?'

'Fancy a change of scene myself - get out of this shithole like.'

'I could try 'em I guess - pass you off as my adopted brother.'

They had had a good giggle about that.

They chatted for a while about the cage fighting show. Junior had a bit more work with his uncle coming up and pretty much had his ticket sorted.

'You going to go then P?'

'If I can persuade Mum to get it for my birthday I will.'

'Be fucking mint - eight fights the boys said - mad as.'

They settled into silence for a while and it was Junior who eventually brought it up.

'You think the cops will let us be now?'

Pasquale shrugged, 'dunno - maybe.'

Junior nodded, 'wonder where he went - that night like?'

Pasquale looked at Junior, 'don't know, Bazzer…' He shrugged his shoulders. That was as far as he felt like taking the speculation, even with Junior.

Junior looked around the gutted building then he coughed and looked up at the grey sky.

'He told me summat - M like.'

'What?'

'He reckoned that there were these mad parties down at the Quays, Dougan and little Henry had told him about it.'

'Yeah?'

'Yeah, do you reckon he went there?'

Pasquale shook his head - he didn't want to know.

'Hard to believe he's not here eh P?' It was said in a tone he had not heard from Junior before.

Pasquale looked across at him. His friend's eyes were filmed with tears.

Pasquale felt it in his throat, that and something that he normally associated with loneliness, an unmoving lump that constricted his chest.

Junior roughly wiped his eyes with his sleeve and then stood up and walked to the centre of the building looking up at the exposed crossbeams. He stood there for a few moments his back turned towards him.

When he came back he was smiling.

'Got a fiver left P- yer fancy a kebab?'

He did, he was starving - they grabbed their bikes and took off down to the Turkish joint.

Mozzer took over from him just after eight, he still had half an hour to get down to the lesson - plenty of time. Moz had offered him a pastie, which Darrin had declined. Through the wall the juggernaut bass rumbled and rolled on.

'You thinking of putting in a bid for this gaff young fella? As far as I know you've been here every bloody night this week.'

Darrin shrugged, 'how much overtime you claiming on the op then Moz?'

Moz stopped chewing for a moment and then exhaled a couple of pieces of short crust.

'Six hours - they'll cop that.'

'I'll do the same then.'

'Free fucking work Darrin! You must be fucking mad - don't let the union rep find out he'll have your goolies.' Mozzer rolled his eyes at him then glanced towards the grimy window.

'Owt doing down in the pit?'

'Quiet again - pub's a bit busier than usual.'

'Must be pay day for the lazy fuckers - they'll all be out the back there in that piss stinking so called beer garden.'

'Been down there have you Moz?'

'A few times back in the day, had a good snout that drank in there too.'

'Jesus, that would be pushing it a bit wouldn't it?'

'Nah, nah Darrin, bloody hell, I never met her in there. You must be fucking joking - she would a been hanging from a bloody lamp post the next day.'

As they spoke a group of four older men shoulder rolled their way through The Admiral car park.

'Hey up son, I do believe that's Mr Johnstone - our resident King Scrote. See the streak of piss in the blue windcheater?'

Darrin joined Mozzer at the window for a gander.

'Who's the beef with him then Moz?'

'That would be his brother Peter - 'roid rage Pete'. If he had an IQ above fifty he'd be dangerous that twat. Don't recognise the other two though, the usual fucking hangers on probably.'

The four men made their way into the boozer, a pool of light flooded a little way into the car park then snapped quickly off as the door shut behind them.

'You reckon they would clock me in there Moz?'

'In a fucking heartbeat son, if you go in there it will only be as part of a wedge formation. Although I've got a curly blonde wig at home, you can have that if yer like.'

'Goes with your cocktail dress does it Moz?'

The fat fuck liked that one - a couple of walrus laughs,

loud enough to drown out the vibration of the bass for a couple of bars.

'Ah very good Dazzler, very good indeed. Bloody cocktail dress - nice one. Speaking of which aren't you doing your rhumba whatsit tonight?'

Moz executed a couple of surprisingly nimble yet indeterminate steps.

'Salsa Moz, salsa.'

'Hmm, hot and spicy eh son?' This with a lewd rolling of the daft fucker's mid-section.

Darrin glanced pointedly down at Moz's gut.

'Might do you a bit of good Moz, what yer reckon?'

'Oh I'm dancing inside young un - every bloody day me.'

Darrin shook his head with a grin, a waste of fuckin' time that was. He turned and grabbed his coat from the slightly sticky faux leather sofa.

'Enjoy yourself then Moz.'

Moz gave him an airy wave.

'You too son - don't sprain anything.'

Tommy had a training day on the Tuesday, effective contemporary work practises with disaffected urban youth in a multicultural environment, no less. Despite the egg sucking, it made for a break from his normal routine and he did what he always did to make the day go that little bit more quickly, he took a lively part in proceedings. A couple of times he though about chipping in with some personal stuff about Bonnie and her family but he kept it back. It was worlds away from here and experience had taught him how quickly people could be dragged away from their comprehension, interest and comfort zones. He had long preferred to share such things with those that he knew cared to give a fuck.

The group had chatted in the morning session about devising possible strategies for breaking down the gang culture, which was now part of the fabric of life on the local estates. Sometimes the gangs were formed around ethnic groupings but on places like the Coleshaw, where people from a variety of ethnic backgrounds had been thrown together, the boys (and some of the girls) had had no problem in forming a Rainbow Coalition. The kids united through circumstance, shared values and location.

All the usual rationalisations were robustly trotted out by the group; the break down of family, the loosening of community ties, the insidious impact of drugs etc etc. All of it right enough, but, Tommy thought, it was somehow an incomplete picture. He found those explanations a little pat and patronising too, as if the kids on the estates didn't have the capacity to choose to pull themselves out of the mire and that they were somehow inherently blighted - lesser if you like. Tommy knew that it wasn't an easy road when you were starting from the back of the field but he also knew that it was, unequivocally, possible. There were plenty of examples of it in amongst all the cop-out surrender. The older he got the more of an advocate he had become for self help. He now believed that, to a degree, the community sector had, unintentionally, disempowered the community.

It was Sonny's presentation that he'd signed up for, a two hour lecture and discussion about an initiative in Glasgow that had worked wonders on the gangs up there. It was an effective combination of carrot and stick that had given their rough lads the opportunity to pull themselves out of the shit with the caveat that if they chose not to take the opportunity that they would be hit and hit hard by the coppers and the justice system. It had rekindled memories of him chatting about such things with Ralph, Bonnie's lovable rogue truck-driving dad. In truth, Ralph was a proponent of using the stick a lot more than he was of using the carrot. Aboriginal traditional law was strict and unyielding and its enforcement was the responsibility of all members of the community - everybody was the police, in fact no such distinctions were made. Old Ralph eh? Tommy wondered how that rum old sod was going.

Four o'clock and it was school out, he had a bit of paper-work to sort out then he was off to a gym in town.

When he returned to the Centre there were a few mes-sages on the work phone one of which was from Donna. He smiled when he heard her voice but the tone inferred that she wasn't calling him to share any good news. He called her back and she had plenty to feel unhappy about. Last night the kid had gone ballistic over her refusal to buy him a ticket for some cage fighting shit that was to be held in the city. The kid had picked up a chair and threw it through the lounge room window, doing his bit for the local property values - worse still, the little prick had pushed her. He could hear the tears in her smeared voice and as he listened to it unfold he had gripped the receiver, hard, hard enough to make his hand ache. The little fucker had blown the coop, he hadn't come home that night and he still wasn't answering his phone. He'd sent her a terse text just before midnight to say that he was OK but that wouldn't be racking up any brownie points. She said she may have to take a rain check for Thursday and that was all she wrote. Sonny had been informed and they were looking at 'options' for him.

Tommy had called Sonny pretty much straight away and Sonny was palpably keen on the time out option for the kid, especially as there had been more than an intimation of violence.

The kid had shown up at the Centre yesterday and he'd taken that as a sign that he was maybe ready to start getting past the thing with Matthew. He'd been a little more taciturn than usual but he'd warmed up when they'd got into it, they'd even shared a couple of smiles. Pasquale had picked his moment and his target - his mum, then. Understandable, maybe, given what had happened to his friend, but definitely not excusable.

She rang him again on Thursday morning. Sonny had been round to the house and they'd talked about the kid going to the local refuge for time out if things stayed tense at home. She didn't feel ready for that, although it had transpired that the kid was up for it!

'Maybe it would be a good idea Tommy - what do you think?'

Hmm, he thought, he sensed deep waters with enough of an undercurrent to get him quickly caught in the shit and keeping opinions to himself had never been his strong suit.

'Well I can have a chat with him if you like - is he at home now?'

'No he's out - with his mates. That's what he said.'

'What about the Greaves, that's near you, we could meet about - sevenish?'

'OK Tommy,' she sighed, 'that would be nice - see you then.'

He left the Centre about five and let Jimbo know the change of plan, Jimbo wasn't that fussed - that rum turkey always had a plan B up his sleeve.

She was already there when he walked into the quiet bar, nursing a gin and tonic by the looks of it. She was sat gazing quietly at nothing in particular, a little tramline of worry visible between her eyebrows. She gave him a nice smile, which he returned. He signalled another one for her which she knocked back. He hit the bar and came back to her with a Guinness and took the seat opposite her. The table had a tilt and wobble and he lost a bit of the pint when he carelessly plonked it down.

They talked for a couple of hours and this time it was all about her and the kid; the past, the present, options for the future. He tried to just listen but, as she talked, his mind kept returning to Australia. He played with the idea of her being there with him and he managed it. He brought the kid into the picture and it immediately felt like a hell of a reach. Single mums and their single sons, it was a recipe for intense co-dependency. Part of him, a large part of him, felt like edging away - kill it before it grows.

Just before nine she received a text from Pasquale, he was home.

She was half out of her seat as soon as the call was killed.

'Better go Tommy.'

He leaned across the table slightly unsettling his pint of Guinness, again, as he did so and took hold of her hand. She momentarily tensed, then relaxed, she retook her seat and let him keep the contact. He gently stroked the inside of her wrist and forearm, her skin was warm, supple and smooth and, as he did so, some of the tension started to leach from her. Tommy's mum had left him and Mick when he was still in primary school and he knew that Mick still carried a torch for her. It didn't bear to think what Mick would have done if he had ever pushed his mother - there would have been blood and snot on the walls, no preamble, no discussion.

'Listen Donna, why don't we go out this Saturday instead, let's do something nice together?'

She smiled and nodded.

'Be good to live a little eh?' he said.

She looked at him a little sharply this time and he reproached himself for the glib presumption.

She pushed the clouds away again.

'You are right Tommy, let's, why not.'

He walked her back to her place and said goodbye at the front yard gate. He noted the fresh putty around the new window in the lounge and the light that was on in the upstairs bedroom, which confirmed that the kid was home. They said their good-byes and he strolled back for his car, dropping in at a late night mini-mart in order to pick up the daily rag. He quickly flicked through the paper in the shop, nothing at all in there about Matthew Marshall. Fucking fish wrapper, he thought. A cold wind started to pluck at the collar of his jacket. He picked up his pace and grabbed his car from the Greaves car park.

It had been a shit week, one of the worst - she'd knocked him back for the cage fighting night - telling him that no way was she working to pay for things like that and he'd had a moment in which he'd heard only the blood roaring in his head. Pasquale had acted without any recognisable forethought, sweeping his food off the table and onto the floor, the food a heaped steaming mess on her beloved carpet. He couldn't remember much of the details of the next couple of minutes but he did remember the look on her face when he'd pushed her - shock, dismay, hurt and finally anger. This time, his mum had acted purely for her own benefit. Her son had become an adversary. She pushed him with both hands, hard, in the chest. Hard enough to knock him off balance and a salutary reminder to him that his mother was still a strong woman.

She'd got the window sorted straight away, clicking quickly into her fall back efficiency and even that had irritated the shit out of him. Every statement he made quickly swept away, tidied up, dealt with.

Sonny had showed up at the house a couple of days later and the refuge had been mentioned to him as an option and he fancied it just to get away. Matty had spent some time there a couple of years ago but M couldn't handle the rules and the 'faggot youth workers.' It was a mixed joint though, girls too, and that was something. She wasn't for having it though - no fuckin' chance and he relented a bit to the end of Sonny's visit. He'd stay home, wait and see.

On the Friday she'd come to his bedroom and told him that she had a date the next night and it was with Tommy - all very matter of fact and even a little bit fuck you when she said it. He didn't know how he felt about it, maybe like she was somehow gate crashing his world. He liked Tommy though and maybe it would help make things better between them, get her off his case a bit.

Junior was planning a stay down in London in a couple of months and he'd told him that it was cool for him to come down for the ride. He'd let the dust settle first before putting that to her. He felt that familiar wave of anxiety at the thought of leaving home, it was as if the pace of his life was somehow speeding up, taking him downstream with it. All slightly out of his control, fuck did he need a smoke.

She was getting ready to go out - a girls' night. He called out a breezy 'see ya' as she made her usual getting ready to leave noises in the little hallway. She said a flat sounding goodbye then opened and closed the door - gone.

Pasquale still had a tenner left from the money that she had given him last week. If Junior could divvy up the same they would have enough for a foil.

Friday night Darrin had got on the lash with the crew - Trish pressing her leg heavily against his own as they sat at a table in the Lucky Lad wine bar in town. Fuck he'd been tempted but, in a moment of clarity and foresight, he was up and out of his seat for a lengthy chat with Jolika and Stuart instead. They were seated up at the busy bar, all cosied up together with their glasses of red. He'd stayed away from her long enough for Johno to have taken both his seat and Trish's attentions. She'd caught his eye when he'd scoped the new seating arrangements and she'd given him a little reproachful look. Darrin had grinned back at her with a mock raising of his glass, which elicited the response of her raised middle finger. She'd be fine, Trish was as tough as anybody in the station and, to her all was fair in love and war.

He did a late afternoon on the Coleshaw, remotely engaged in more observation of the chav legions and their feckless meanderings. He had the company of a digital radio today and, for once, there was no reggae sledge hammering its bass through the thin wall. Chris Johnstone had hit The Admiral with his crew around about five, probably down there for the game on the box. Then, just after six, something caught his interest, a maroon Jag had pulled into Oak Road and the driver had slowed down and pulled over next to Dwayne and that other toe-rag. The three of them had exchanged pleasantries for a couple of minutes. The binocs had revealed the wide faced mug of a well-dressed middle aged guy with longish wavy hair. He looked a little like Arthur Daley's much tougher brother. After a wee chat the guy zipped up the window then turned into Sycamore. Darrin wrote down the plate, personalised- GYPO1 talk about the dog's bollocks.

He collared Moz the next day about the new face and the fat detective gave him a couple of ruminative nods.

'Hmmm- yeah, I think I know who our man is young Daz, sounds like it'd be Keithy Dalton, Gypsy Keith no less.'

'Yeah go on Moz - more info please.'

Moz snorted at the terse prompting.

'From what I remember, his mum lives on Sycamore. He'd be seeing her Darrin, a good son up to see his mum.'

'But gassing with the young scrotes Moz, why would he be bothering with them?'

'Dunno son - maybe asking them to keep an eye on the car.'

Darrin nodded but he was a long way from convinced by Mozzer's blithe explanation.

Moz noted his disappointment.

'It's good you clocked it son. You're right enough, he is a person of interest. An old school villain connected to Johnny Tibbs and the O'Briens and that's a world away from these scrotes, up to and including blokes like Chris Johnstone. Don't jump to conclusions PC May. Remember, it's patience that makes for a good D.'

He thought about it in the canteen on his break, Moz was probably right; he'd pull Dalton's record though, have a gander and get some background on him.

Trish got the file up for him and she did a print out for him too. He took it over to the corner desk and gave it a long, thorough once over.

There was plenty there but it told him little really other than the fact that the guy was a sleaze bag and a nasty one at that. Dalton had a GBH conviction as a young guy in the late seventies, a procurement of minor's charge which had been dropped, an extortion charge ditto, there were a few lines about whispers re the smuggling of women from the Baltic States for the purpose of prostitution and then the glassing incident, which had seen him do another stretch. So, apart from the two book-end acts of incontestable violence he was the Teflon Man. There was no current address and it was believed that he'd been living down the smoke for the last few years. Next of kin was his mum and a sister who also had form. She'd been busted for dealing in the city clubs nearly twenty years ago now - both of the women presently living at 13 Sycamore Drive.

Darrin folded up the paper and stashed it in his pant's pocket. Trish looked over and gave him a little wave and signalled going out for a bevy. Why not - he felt like he'd earned it.

They had managed a nice evening together, swapping a little bit about their respective pasts, Donna unaware that he had been away from the UK for such a long period of time. She was also very surprised to hear that he'd lived with Aboriginal people for the last ten years of his time in Oz. He told her a little about it and she was a lot better informed than he would have expected. Aware of Australia's assimilation policies, land rights, the Stolen Generation, all the markers of 'modern' Australian Aboriginal history. Most people in England, if they ever thought about it, assumed that Aboriginal people were still walking around in loincloths hunting kangaroos.

She teased him a little about his tastes in women - 'like 'em dark do you Tommy?' He didn't deny it - generally, he did.

They'd also talked about his work at the Centre, he gilded it a little with no mention of his ambivalence with regards to future plans. The 'should I stay or should I go' stuff.

They went onto a nearby pub after the restaurant and did more of the getting to know you. He didn't mind because that was exactly what he wanted to do. The kid had sent her a text at about half past ten and, immediately, a look of ineffable exhaustion had come over her face. She had a quiet moment and then he watched her visibly will the weariness away. She took his hand and squeezed it tightly a few times.

'This is nice Tommy, I'm glad we made the effort.'

'Me too, be nice to do more of it.'

She leaned in and gave him a light kiss on the lips that felt like an electrical charge, a palpable mutual exchange of energy. And, for the briefest of moments, that was all that there was, everything around them fell away - gone.

She pulled away and nodded, more to herself than to him.

'Fancy a nightcap Tommy?' She said it levelly - her eyes alive, maybe even a little hungry.

'Sure, sure, you mean yours?'

She nodded again.

'He's home but a drink would be nice.'

Tommy felt his ardour cool a little at that, but if it was going to be done better sooner than later? Get the kid used to the idea Tommy thought, why not.

'Well as long as…' He didn't finish the sentence, she was opening a door that was hers to open, as simple as.

They finished their drinks and made the short drive over to the house.

Pasquale was sat in the lounge when she ushered him through. The kid was no poker player, surprise plastered all over his face, no obvious resentment though and a pleasant enough hello.

Tommy gave him a smile and took the armchair next to the sofa while Donna went to the kitchen to grab them both a drink.

The kid was quiet, his eyes fixed on some late night chat show on the box.

'You OK Pasquale, been out have yer?'

The kid nodded and briefly looked over at him.

'Yeah - mates.'

Donna returned with the drinks and the kid got up off the sofa with a barely suppressed sigh.

'Stay Pasquale, have a drink and a chat with us.'

'No it's OK Mum,' a nod to the TV, 'fucking bobbins this anyway.' The tone was harsh, the kid engaged in some passive-aggressive chest beating.

Tommy kept his eyes neutral but felt a slight tightening in the shoulders.

Donna didn't let him get away with it.

'OK Pasquale - no need to swear is there love?'

The kid didn't respond to that, he brushed past her and said a terse goodnight to him. Tommy returned the favour, as did his mum. Pasquale trudged off upstairs as morose as fuck, like he'd just found out that somebody had nicked his bicycle.

Donna made off to the bathroom, which gave him the chance to squiz the room. Clean modern furnishings - an expensive leather sofa with two matching chairs and an expensive looking sound system with plenty of neatly placed CD's. She had told him in the restaurant how much she liked her music. Tucked into a corner was a six-seat dining table, which was near the entrance to the kitchen.

The TV was sat in a large mahogany display case the colour of which gave the room plenty of warmth. Its shelves, to his taste, were over filled with framed photographs. He stood up and had a closer look at them, quickly noting that Pasquale's smile seemed to dim with age. She looked great in all of them though. There was only one photograph of her without the kid, what looked like a professional picture of Donna at her graduation, she looked as proud as punch in the mortarboard and gown.

A few minutes later she returned to the lounge room and sat on the sofa next to him, her thigh resting lightly against his and they held hands as they drank. He could hear the kid walking around a bit upstairs and directly above them. A fanfare of sound as the TV went on in his room quickly followed by both silence and stillness.

They made plans for another meet towards the end of the week and Tommy idly speculated about the notion of what it would be like to wake up under her (and the kid's) roof.

They'd see, he thought, nice and easy does it - he could wait.

The next day he hit the local beer garden with his old man

after a tidy Sunday lunch together (a takeaway curry from the Shaheen). It was warm enough for a couple of bumble bees to be busying themselves around an early blooming azalea bush.

His dad had taken a swill of his bitter then he'd let out an unprompted rasping snort.

'Guess what I read yesterday Tom?'

This is why he came, he thought. He nodded to Mick, go on then, give it to me.

'The latest thing for men - fucking cosmetic six packs!'

'What - you mean like boob jobs for blokes?'

'Yeah,' Mick liked that - fodder for him. 'Boob jobs for blokes - fucking la la land, I tell yer. Plastic body parts for plastic people in a plastic fucking age.'

'How much then - did they say?'

'Nah no word on that son - probably cost a lot more than your gym membership though.'

Tommy laughed and shook his head while Mick played out his indignation.

'Times have changed, hey pop?'

'That, my son, is an understatement.'

Fred popped his head out of the pool room door and called Mick to the pool table. Mick would be gone a while, he specialized in grind-a-thons, an uncompromising rake of snookers until his numbed opponent felt like gouging out his own eyes with the cue.

Tommy stretched his legs and picked up the scents of the blooming azaleas - at least everything wasn't fucking plastic.

She'd invited him over for a meal on Thursday and the kid was going to be there too - see if they could get it off to a good start. Life, he thought, never simple and looking like it was about to get more complicated.

He and Junior hung out up the Coleshaw early in the week, edging into Dwayne's group of arse kissing hangers on. They were kids his own age and younger, a few snot nosed pre-teens amongst them. A raggedy arsed bunch and all full of braggart bullshit. One of them, a goofy off white kid named Danny had mentioned M's name loud enough for him to hear it, but not clearly enough for him to make out the context. It was smart arsey though, he could see it on the kid's face. Dwayne had quickly hushed the kid, telling him to shut the fuck up.

A little later on Dwayne had pulled Junior over to the side and, while they talked, he had taken off for a little lap of the estate. He had no wish to engage with the chav numb nuts and he was still pissed off at the mention of M.

On his return Junior was still chatting to an animated Dwayne, Junior called him to come over to join them.

After a few moments of belt tugging and nut hugging Dwayne addressed him directly.

'J here says you're a pretty fuckin' smart young un, that fuckin' right then?'

Pasquale looked at Junior and then at Dwayne, he nodded, 'smart enough.' He told him.

'Fuck me dead right on, smart a fuckin' 'nough eh? Well, that's fuckin' good blood, just been telling J here that we need a couple of new fuckin' lads on the fuckin' team. Shift some smoke around for us - J here is havin' it like and says you and he run close together - that fuckin' right young un?'

Pasquale glanced at Junior again and nodded, again - sure.

'OK then - sorted. I'll have a chat with the crew, check out your fuckin' resume like, I know Junior has the goods, we'll see if you fuckin' do too.'

'All well, you two get back up here on Friday right, and we'll get you fuckin' started then.'

Dwayne reached into his pocket and handed Junior a foil.

'That for fuckin' starters - you can have money or weed if you bring it, either fuckin' way - no fuckin' fuss to me.'

Junior and he exchanged a look and Junior gave Dwayne the smiling thumbs up.

Dwayne got business like again.

'Mouths fuckin' shut though yeah? You stepping up to the fuckin' big boy stuff now?'

And that was that, Dwayne offered a bony palm to the pair of them and with that they rode off to the canal to have a puff down in the lee of the old mill.

As they smoked they excitedly talked business; cash projections, maybe as much as £250 a week each - 'real fuckin' dough for fuckin' once,' said Junior, taking the piss out of that knuckle dragger Dwayne.

During the conversation they reminded each other to be careful and not to blab. If M could keep that part of it quiet then they could too.

The mention of his name took the edge off the giddy high for a little while but still, Pasquale thought, he could do a few more things now - maybe even save up for a flat.

Pasquale and Junior blew their smoke up to the sky as the pigeons roosted on the exposed beams above. The birds cooed, ruffled their feathers and shat on the old mill floor, indifferent to it all.

Jolika had asked him if he was interested in having a weekend away. Next week, she, Stuart and a few of their crew were heading down to Birmingham to a big 'too hot to miss' salsa bash that was happening down there. They checked out the website together during the lunch break, hot shot Cuban instructors would be doing lessons and workshops over the whole of the weekend - you could dance for eighteen fucking hours a day if you wanted to. He was rostered on for the Sunday but, with the approval of Sergeant Thomas, he quickly sorted out a swap out with Johno. The Sarge had looked at him for a few long hard seconds when he had told him why he had wanted the swap and, for a moment, he thought the prick was going to knock him back. The Sarge had finally given him the nod of approval and then went straight back to his Sudoku with a tuneful accompanying whistle of La Bamba.

He did a couple of hours up the Coleshaw, had a lateish work out at the old man's gym and then stuck around to help his dad close the joint up. Numbers were still down, the old man chewing on his bottom lip, which was an old, old sign of worry and stress and, when the old man had been much younger, a warning portent of impending bad temper, a sure fire sign for Darrin to keep well out of the way.

Dougy had a couple of the older boys competing over the weekend down on Humberside. One of the boys was particularly promising, a heavy shouldered kid with a good right hand and reasonable footwork. His old man had hinted more than once as they put away the gloves, mitts and ropes, at him coming for the trip in order to help out. Darrin finally nipped it in the bud, telling the old man about the trip away without telling him exactly why he was going. He'd get a bit more shit than a whistled La Bamba from the old man.

Doug took the knock back pretty well though, confirmation that the space they now had between them was becoming, for him at least, a much more comfortable one.

Thursday and he was back in the Coleshaw flat - there was no booming bass from next door and not much action down below either. He was itching for something to happen and nothing much was, though a kid had been hospitalized through drug use over the weekend and that had reignited all the hoo ha in the press. A photo of Matthew Marshall had been slotted in next to the news story. So, it was all still on, and press bullshit apart it was a real concern. There'd been a bit of talk around the station about pulling in all the known faces just as a matter of course, but that was unlikely given the fact the brass had now committed to the costs of the op.

A movement caught his eye, pulling Darrin out of his slightly morose introspection - aye aye he thought, that car was back again - the wild gypsy rover. This time the Jag' rolled all the way down Oak and pulled into The Admiral car park. Dalton pulled up close to the pub doors and went quickly in to the boozer with a robust, confident vigour - cock of the fucking block. Dalton had half an hour or so in there with the swamp creatures then came briskly back out to drive the couple of hundred yards back to Sycamore.

Be nice to find out where the prick's living, Darrin thought, no current address - that would be a good gap to fill.

Thursday night and his leaky boat had come into port, they'd had a Malay style curry which was delicious and some cake that she'd picked up at Waitrose, helped down with plenty of both ice cream and cream. The kid had been OK if not exactly brimming over with good cheer and all throughout the evening Tommy had felt a tension between them that had never been present at the Community Centre. After the meal, the kid quickly excused himself leaving his plates on the table for his mum to clear up. As Pasquale walked away towards the hallway Tommy noticed how light on his feet the kid was as he left the room - as quick and silent as a cat. He helped her to wash up and, as they did so, they small talked about their respective working weeks. After he'd dried the last dish she thanked him with an arm around the waist and a kiss with some push in it, which sent his mind in a fairly obvious direction. Not here though, there was no way that was going to happen. They quickly compromised with an unplanned trip to the local. She let Pasquale know the plan and they made the walk to the pub, they had a couple of drinks but the hunger of that kiss hung heavily between them. After some relatively meaningless chat about plans for the summer blah, blah, blah, she laid her long fingers on the back of his hand.

'Have you anything to drink at your place then Tommy?'

And that was it - in an instant his body followed his mind out of the door.

She stayed with him until three, where-upon she got up out of his bed with a little sigh. He watched her dress quickly and quietly in the half-light of his bedroom.

Two minutes later and she was ready to go. He rolled out of the bed, tugged on his tracksuit bottoms and walked her to the back door. He watched her move lightly down the wooden stairs and on into the yard. She got to the gate, turned and gave him a wave and then she was gone, as silent as a ripple in a pond.

And that was it for the next few days, the love nest tacitly sorted. He barely slept but he didn't care, it was nice to have something new and alive again. She never mentioned Pasquale whilst they were at his place and that was jake with him. The kid was enough of a ghost at the banquet as it was. They both wanted to bask in the bubble and just let the hassle wash its way around them. She always kept the phone off, turning it back on again just before she made to leave. Messages were waiting for her every time.

Pasquale was a no show again on Monday - Sonny came in, in the afternoon and they talked about him for a while.

'The people who run the refuge have a good programme Tommy.'

'Yeah I know it. Lucy and Tim are the tutors over there - nice people.'

'Yeah, they are - well meaning.'

Tommy raised an eyebrow at him.

'Bit back handed there Sonny - faint praise and all that?'

Sonny shrugged and laughed a little - 'yeah, yeah you're right. Some of the staff there got that Christian thing going though eh?'

'Yep, agreed, it is fucking tedious - but there again, we are a pair of pagans.'

'The lapsed brothers.' Sonny said with a smile

'I reckon you'll be back in the mosque before they get me back to the church.'

Sonny laughed, 'you wanna bet on that altar boy?'

After more chuckles, Sonny changed the topic, he was all business again.

'Did you read about the kid at the weekend - the overdose?'

'Yeah I did, you know him?'

'As it happens no, he's from St Leonards way, not on my patch that.'

'St Leonards - fuck me, the leafy suburbs, he talking yet, the kid?'

'Not heard anything, I might get down the station today, see if Sarge Thomas knows 'owt about it.'

'Ah yeah, you get on with that old bruiser don't yer?'

'That's right Tommy - told him I was a God fearing Methodist.'

'He bought that did he? Ah well Sonny, as long as they always let you leave the station.'

'Speaking of which, I was thinking that maybe I should have a chat with our mutual young pal again, Pasquale. You know about young Matthew, this thing with the new kid might have jogged something with him.'

'You do reckon he knows a bit more than he's letting on then?'

'Probably, he's not street though you know, not like our Junior. He might still see sense and give something up.'

Tommy coughed, 'well the kid has a lot on his plate.'

Sonny nodded at him but he was a little puzzled, 'yeah- why's that then Tom?'

Fuck it, Tommy thought.

'Yeah,' he paused, 'I've just started seeing his mum.'

Sonny shook his head at him and laughed long and hard and Tommy felt himself blush slightly.

'Tommy boy, you slick mover you. Ah well, she is a catch mind, I'll give you that, you bloody rascal. How's the kid with it then?'

'Well I haven't given him a bloody feedback form Sonny. I'm pretty sure he's not ready to call me Dad yet.'

'Hmmm well, Dad's been gone a long time Tommy. You'll be tip toeing through the tulips for a while yet mate.'

He nodded his head and pursed his lips into a thin smile - didn't he fucking know it. Sonny stood up, ready to go.

'Still what's life without a challenge eh Tom?'

'Thanks Sonny, that's very fucking reassuring.'

He and Junior were making plenty of dough and that was a fact.

A couple of days ago, Dwayne had led them up to some alley on a part of the Coleshaw that was a fair distance from the pub and had told them to, 'fuckin' wait there.'

'No fuckin' noise too, right?'

Then off he strolled back onto Oak Street. Five or so minutes later Dwayne suddenly reappeared, stepping a little awkwardly through a gap in a nearby back yard fence, which he'd made by pushing the flimsy looking slats off to one side. The bottoms of Dwayne's jeans were slicked by the wet of the long grass of the house's unkempt garden. He gravely handed them a package each of tidy looking, flatly compressed weed.

'There you go boys, run it down to those fuckin' garages in Epsom Close on the Barrington, you know Johnny Talbot down there, don't yer J?'

Junior nodded, he did.

'He'll be waiting for yers, get back here, fuckin' transactions done fifty each, smooth as fuck.'

And that was it - a forty minute ride, a non-conversation with a lanky dude with bad skin and ta very much. They did two runs the next day and by three o'clock he had a ton thirty nestling in his pocket. He and Junior spent most of the day trying to think of new things to spend the money on. He'd have to be careful - his mum was like Sherlock and Robo Cop rolled into one - she didn't miss a beat. He'd stash it and just buy the things that he could readily consume for the moment; food and smoke probably but he would have to sort something out longer term, maybe one of those cash deposit boxes or something.

She was a lot happier at the moment - humming and singing around the flat when she got home. Leaving him alone more and that was working for him. She'd promised him a meal down Chinatown next weekend on the basis that Tommy would be there too and he'd given her a cool yes, which seemed to please her no end.

He'd do a run in the morning, first up, get over to the Coleshaw about eleven and grab Junior on the way. Planning ahead, he thought, like a businessman. They were going to clean up.

He was back at the flat window on the Monday evening and Delroy was definitely in tonight, sounded like he had a couple of buddies in there with him too. Darrin could hear their low murmuring and volleys of laughter whenever the music shuddered to a halt. There was fuck all happening down the street, just a couple of kids knocking about near the pub, which was obviously quiet after a busy weekend. The pub was bleak and hard looking in the cool drizzle, the antithesis of good cheer.

At change over Darrin asked Johno if he'd seen Dalton's car at all and Johno told him that he had. The guy had rolled up to The Admiral on the Saturday afternoon. He'd had a couple of hours in there this time.

He was still a bit sore from his salsa weekend and, for once, it was in all the right places. The weekend had been a blast, a church hall for the lessons and a nice club for the live band and dancing on the Saturday night. He'd pulled this big blonde from Hastings? Harrow? Darrin couldn't remember which. She'd been a mover in the club and even more so in the hotel room and a couple of hours were spent bouncing each other off the walls. He'd grabbed her mobile number; she was well worth a return visit.

The lessons had been challenging, he'd held his hand up for the intermediates, which were being taken by this tall, athletic looking Cuban guy with a gap toothed grin and business like eyes. After a couple of minutes he had pulled half a dozen of them out of the class and he'd made them sit it out and wait for the next beginners' group. Luis was crystal clear in his assessment of their skill levels.

'You're dancing something,' he had told them, 'but it's not salsa.'

Jolika had given him a little encouraging smile as he'd made his way back to his seat with the other members of the rhythmically challenged posse.

Two hours later Luis had made them do the basic step for a full hour. Luis got the class to clap on the four beat as they rocked backwards and forwards. At least he managed to clap in time with his steps, a couple of the guys in the class were struggling to do that and their failure to do so elicited some amazed head shaking and whistling through the front teeth from Luis. Real fucking confidence booster he was, old Luis.

He'd been sweating like a horse after the hour but he had a few dances after the lesson and yeah, it felt better, Luis quickly proven to be right. He had more flow somehow. It looked like the thirty quid had not been wasted after all.

He'd mentioned the lack of current address for Dalton to Moz and suggested that some kind of tail should be put on him when he drove away from the Coleshaw. Moz had looked at him like he was a fucking loon.

'You think they'll sign off on that PC May, following a guy because he bothers to see his mum on a regular basis?'

Something had broken though, the boy in the hospital had given them a name of the older kid who had fired up the meth for him at the party, 'Dagger' or 'Tagger' the kid had said. The description was hazy but he was definitely a white kid. All the name drew, back at the station, was scratched heads, shrugged shoulders and blank looks - so the info was a hardly a case buster.

Wednesday, he took over from a tall young cop who'd just been transferred to them from down south somewhere. He had a similar kind of accent to the blonde that he'd banged. The bloke was pleasant enough and he didn't even comment about the dancing when they shared a few perfunctory weekend stories, other than to say that he'd had a girlfriend who was into ballroom.

There was bit more action in The Admiral tonight, locals, just the scrag-enders though, no Johnstone, no Dalton.

Then just after nine the maroon Jag' pulled into Oak - Dalton went straight to his mum's place this time.

Fuck it, he thought, it was time to make something happen. He grabbed his coat, made his way out of the flat and the block and went hurriedly across to his Triumph, which he'd parked in a pool of light at the back of the single row of old folks' flats that abutted the midrise.

Darrin was the last man on and he wasn't in the mood for

another hour of nut-scratching and chin pulling, more time wasted revising or not revising his plans for the future whilst staring down at people who had marginally more interesting lives than a fungal infection. He quickly drove round the front of the flats, on past The Admiral, Sycamore and then took a steady right turn into Ivy Close. He turned the car round at the end of the cul-de-sac and waited there just twenty or so yards from Oak Street, he killed the engine and waited.

It was touching eleven before Dalton's car rolled on past his windscreen and he'd nearly missed it. He'd been fighting hard to keep awake after two sedentary hours, amusing himself with thoughts of the blonde and some half-formed, idle speculation, again, about where he was going to go with his career.

He gunned the engine and pulled out to the edge of Ivy waiting for Dalton to turn left into Strickland Road, before he pulled the car out into Oak. He hung well back and got lucky as a taxi picking up a fare from the Farrier's chopped him up - two cars on the street and the fucker couldn't wait ten seconds. It worked for him, though he now had a buffer between him and the Jag'. The Jag' made a couple of turns which led on towards the Orbital and, thankfully, the taxi duly followed Dalton's car. The three of them got onto the slip road and the maroon car had hit the motorway at pretty close to the limit. Darrin kept a reasonable distance back from the taxi which was cruising in the middle lane. The cab was now roughly equidistant between himself and Dalton.

Dalton went past the first three possible turns offs from the Orbital and then there was a quick blink of his left light as he neared the fourth exit, Keithy was off to the Quays then.

The taxi kept on going straight and Darrin gunned it a bit, he didn't know this area that well so it was going to have to be a bit of a wing and a prayer. Thankfully, the turn off proved to be pretty close to Dalton's destination. Five hundred yards or so and Dalton made another left, he could see that the prick was talking on his mobile but maybe that would be distraction enough from the tail. He knew they were somewhere near the canal but he wasn't quite sure where. Up ahead the Jag' had braked and then Dalton made a languid turn into a wide brick archway that led into a complex of newly built town houses and flats.

Darrin drove on past the entrance, tracking the car over his right shoulder as he did so. It looked like Dalton was looking to park up as close as possible to the pool of light, which marked the lobbied entrance of one of the blocks of units. He kept driving for a couple of hundred yards then made a measured turn to pull up fifty or so yards before he got back to the arch. He got out of the car quickly but quietly, just resting the door against the jamb. He stilled himself and listened intently for a minute or two - nothing! The prick must already be inside the building.

He gave it a couple more minutes, leaning against the driver's door and gazing over towards the city lights that lay a couple of miles to the east. Then he made his way over to the lobby nearest to Dalton's car.

There were eight buzzers on the wall plate, no names next to them, just the flat numbers. He started with number one, no answer, there was a woman at home in two, he asked for Irene and she irritably told him no, 'no Irene,' he had the wrong flat, she snarled a parting 'God' in his ear. There was nobody responding in three or four either and then he got a pissed sounding guy in five - who told him with some slur and no little bonhomie that he couldn't help him, 'sorry chief.' He rang six a couple of times and waited again, nothing, he reached for seven and the intercom crackled, number six was home.

'Yeah' - deep voice, local accent.

It was him alright, he could feel it, in an instant he was as alert and erect as a meerkat. He did his Irene spiel.

'She's not here son,' number six responded, 'but if you do catch up with her say goodnight from me.' That was followed by a rich sounding chuckle. A real fucking joker was Keithy Dalton.

Darrin stood in the light for a while nodding to himself, number six. He'd got it, 6/4 Gloucester Mews, the Quays - a current address for Mr. Keith Dalton and a sizeable gap in the op now filled.

MAY

Tommy had planned to meet with the two of them on the edge of Chinatown on what was a lively Saturday afternoon down in the bustling city centre. He'd got down there early giving himself the time to take a walk through the heart of the city for a detour on over to the old red brick Victorian railway station. Just for old time's sake and to look briefly at the commemorated gate that his Grandfather had marched through on his way to Flanders. He was down there a little longer then he had intended and he bumped into Lenny Cole. Lenny was an old work mate of his dad's and was now only a year or so from retirement himself. They chatted for a while about all the changes both on the railways and beyond. Len was a big picture man and as hard-core militant as Mick. Time and old age hadn't softened Len's feelings about what he viewed as a betrayal of the men who had given their time and energy to the British railway industry.

'I remember your old man on the picket line back in the eighties, for that local strike like. The rum bugger had borrowed your steel toecaps han't he? Two sizes too big for him they were, curling up at the front like a pair of bloody bananas!'

They had a good laugh at that.

Tommy had been concreting at the time with an Irish crew that had a hand in motorway maintenance work, hence the work boots.

He remembered that his dad had asked him for a borrow of the boots on the Friday evening, as they were getting ready to go out for what would be a well earned piss up at the end of the working week.

'Sure Dad, what's happening, fancy dress is it?'

'No you daft sod, they reckon the SPG are coming down to the picket line temorra to sort out the picket. If any copper puts their hands on me they're getting one of those in the knackers.'

Tommy had grinned at that but he knew that there was no bluster there - Mick's bite could be a lot worse than his bark.

'They're out there in the kitchen - all yours, with my blessing.'

Mick had only received meagre strike pay during the dispute and as the strike had dragged on he'd bunged his old man whatever surplus he'd had and they'd economised too; more nights in, no benders at the weekend and plenty of scrag end stew for a while.

They had been out on strike for nearly six months Tommy remembered, up until the combined forces of a splintering in the ranks and the privations of a tough winter had forced them back in. The rifts from the strike had created plenty of rancour in the community and there had been more than the odd punch up in the local boozers over it.

He looked at his watch, it was time to shoot off. He wished Lenny well and Lenny clapped him warmly on the back.

'Say hello to the old goat for me.'

'I will Lenny, get your arse up there some time - he'd love it.'

Lenny promised that he would and they made their separate ways. Lenny strolled off to the far end of the station to catch a train home and Tommy made his way back to the bustle and sway of the city centre.

They were waiting for him at the entrance to the restaurant, Donna with a smile but the kid looked as cloudy as a
wet Wednesday.

He felt an inward sigh but kept the smile on his face.

Tommy gave the kid a present, a best of Gil Scott Heron
CD. Hopefully it would help to school the little fucker a bit
beyond the reading and writing lessons he was receiving at
the Centre. At least the kid remembered his manners and
brightened up slightly at the gift and gesture, although Donna seemed to appreciate it more than the kid did.

The place, a Chinese eat as much as you can join, was busy
and the food was better than average and the prices more than
reasonable. They ate in a semi-comfortable silence that Donna regularly punctuated with questions that were directed to
both of them. He'd never been a big talker while eating but
he thought he'd help her share the load a bit. He asked the kid
the right questions and Pasquale came alive for a while, talking about his plans to apply next year to the local art college.
Tommy knew that they would look at school attendance
when considering his admission and, unfortunately, that was
going to make it tough for the kid. Over the last couple of
years he'd been scarcer than the Scarlet Pimpernel.

She asked him if he'd like to come back to their place to
have some cake and a cuppa with them. He didn't particularly want to, he was finding the sub-current brittle, but he said
yes, trying to keep it all on a nice footing, give her the moral
support, show her what a decent cove he was. They had a
little moment at the car, the kid had moved quickly to the
front passenger door but Donna had evenly told him to get
in the back. Tommy wouldn't normally have been that bothered but the kid's rudeness irked him and he made a point of

reaching around him, opening the door and swinging himself robustly into the front seat. As he did so, the kid swore under his breath just loud enough for Tommy to hear it. It wasn't really directed at him but, all the same, he felt the heat rise up in his face.

Donna fired up the engine and immediately turned the radio on, some Hall and Oats spilled out, *Sara Smile*, which led to an almost involuntary shared look between them. Maybe the kid caught it maybe he didn't, maybe Tommy didn't really give too much of a fuck either way. They settled into the journey, she was a good driver, smooth and relaxed and she made it back to base with a slick reverse park just a little downwind from their front door.

The kid made to go straight upstairs but she called him back. She wanted to give him the presents she'd bought him. She went into the lounge and came back with three neatly wrapped parcels. The first one, which the kid opened with no great enthusiasm, was a book on fine art. Thankfully, the kid had brightened at that.

'Might be good for college,' Donna said, Tommy did the right thing and nodded supportively along.

Next up was an expensive looking hooded red top, which got a slightly surly thumbs up although his eyes gave away his pleasure and then, finally, a pair of jeans. He wasn't so happy with those.

'I'm not wearing these things Mum.'

'You don't like them love?'

The kid looked at the ground and truculently shook his head.

'Gay they are Mum, gay as fuck.'

Donna looked at Tommy, wide-eyed with embarrassment,

Tommy felt as neutralised and useful as a marble statue.

'Alright love we can replace them, no need to swear though - is there?'

That set the little fucker off.

'Swearing, what's the matter with fucking swearing! You swear, he fucking swears!'

'Pasquale,' Tommy said, but Donna had already taken a little half step between them.

'Maybe your room is a good idea Pasquale.'

'Right,' the kid said and he threw the jeans at the dining room table. They skidded across the table surface and knocked off a glass, which bounced soundlessly on the carpet.

The kid glared at the unbroken glass then back at Donna.

'I'm going - leave you in fucking peace, with him.'

Then he was gone - Tommy glanced at her, conscious of the rhythm of his breathing, slow and heavy through his nose. He looked at Donna and saw that she was close to tears, angry, embarrassed and maybe even temporarily defeated. They sat together on the sofa for a while and she rested her head on his shoulders while his mind churned.

He looked up at the photos on the fine mahogany cabinet. He was already becoming a little more familiar with their various moods and poses. Donna kitted out as a lady cop with the kid as a pantomime villain - a bag of swag, stripy shirt and painted on moustache, mother and son happily hamming it up for the camera. The two of them in tourist mode standing together against a backdrop of the milling crowds at the St. Peter's Basilica. The centrepiece was a large framed picture of Donna's university graduation, both of them were smiling widely in that one.

After a while, he gently freed himself from her and stood up and stretched, he felt old and more than a little jaded.

'I'll go and have a chat with him Donna.'

'You sure Tommy - you think that's the right thing?'

'I am, be good I think.' He knew that the kid was in the front bedroom over the lounge, she had the en-suite at the back of the house.

After his first gentle knock got no response he realised that the kid was on the headphones and he had to knock hard until he heard the kid spring from the bed.

The kid came to door and stood in the entrance, his long light brown hand resting on the door handle, a brief look up at him then his eyes wandered restlessly over no fixed points.

Tommy felt like chinning him but he took the metaphorical deep breath.

'Listen Pasquale, I know that this is your home and I'm not here to cramp your style or, whatever. But gee mate, talking to your mum like that, it's not on. Have some respect eh? She's a good woman is your mum.'

The kid looked up at him then, the little fucker, angry-eyed, ready to pick up the glove.

'Respect, you don't know her mate, respect, I could tell you things about her.'

He looked at the kid levelly.

'Well, tell me then.'

'You don't know her mate, you don't know.'

'Well tell me and then I'll know, wont I?'

The kid mouthed something unintelligible down at the carpet, then turned back inside the room.

Tommy wanted to say more but, what the hell, it was just pure fucking psychodrama and angst.

She was in the kitchen when he made his way back home, busily unstacking the dishwasher.

He hadn't intended to stay, thankfully, and they said a slightly peremptory goodbye, both of them feeling unbalanced and out of whack.

Fuck did it feel good to get back to his place - sanity.

Darrin asked Trish if she could run the Quay's address through the titles registry and she had the information waiting for him when he returned to the station after three hours of foot patrol. The flat was owned by a company no less - Saltt Shipping, whoever the fuck they were. He didn't know whether that was strange or reasonably commonplace. His mind whirred around it but he couldn't join the dots. He found Moz in the D's office pensively reading the *Daily Star*. He edged up to the desk and sat on the corner at a right angle to him. Moz exhaled slightly and lightly threw the paper down.

Moz gave him the beady eye. His thumbs were rubbing against each other in a kind of podgy mating dance, forearms nestling comfortably on the upper slopes of his big round gut.

'Social call is it Darrin? Moz reached up and rubbed his eyes as he spoke.

'Not quite Moz.' He waited a couple of beats, 'I've got an address for Dalton.'

That snapped him up a fair bit. The fucker even swung his feet off the desk.

'Well, fuck me dead - how?'

Darrin told him how, in detail, he even mentioned the fact that the prick had been talking on his mobile for most of the drive.

Moz chewed on his lower lip and digested the info.

'He definitely didn't see you?'

'Nah - I'm certain.'

'And you even spoke to the prick,' Moz grinned at him. 'Constable May, you intrepid fucker. Not that it proves a damn thing of course, other than the fact that a dishonest living can pay off.'

'You check out that company name yet?' Mozzer asked with a slightly odd, knowing smile.

Darrin shook his head at him, 'I asked Trish but she told me to fuck off this time, too busy, she said.'

'Well young Dazzler, let's have a squiz shall we? Leave it to your Uncle Moz.'

Darrin moved around the desk and stood behind Mozzer as he went into the Companies House Database.

There it was, Saltt Shipping and Imports - four directors named; Cal, Leo and Niall O'Brien and a John Tibbs.

Moz snorted at that, 'hmmm, yes indeedy, the boys eh, you up to speed with this young un?'

He was - four names that were synonymous with the city and its conurbation's organised crime scene.

Mozzer leaned back and sighed, 'well it still doesn't really add anything to the pot, I'm afraid Daz.'

'No, how the fuck not?'

'Nah - he's connected. But he has been for decades now. They'll be shop front legit, the company. It means fuck all really and it means nowt in the context of the drug op.'

'Nowt! You can't see them being involved, even hands off like?'

'Proving it son, proving it! Those fuckers are enmeshed

in this city's tangled web. In fact they are the fucking web. We're better off focusing on the scrotes, believe you me at least then we'll keep our numbers up.'

Darrin nodded but felt underwhelmed and more than a little pissed off.

Mozzer shrugged his shoulders and gave him some avuncular soft soap, 'you'll be surprised how much of life is about appearances Darrin - sad but true that.'

That didn't help much either, in fact he didn't even know what the fat fucker was talking about.

Darrin stood up and walked out of the office, he knew that Barnesy would be looking for him, they should have been out patrolling more than ten minutes ago.

Sarge Thomas called out to him at the dog end of the shift.

'PC May- Chief Inspector Stone wants to see you in his office - right away that's a good lad.'

Barnesy gave him a look and told him that he'd handle his little bit of paperwork. Darrin gave Barnesy his thanks and headed up to the second floor - a little uncertain, a little nervous but feeling energised too.

He knocked on the door and heard a cough and a 'come in'.

He walked into the office and Stone nodded at him to take a seat.

Stone was the top D in the station, a no-nonsense hard-nosed fucker with a jaw line like the prow of a battle cruiser and disconcertingly still eyes. He was also very much the man with a quote when he needed to be and, as such, Stone handled most of the station's media stuff.

'You like detective dramas do you then Constable?'

'Sir?'

'You know the story; lone wolf copper gets his man, screws the hot looking stripper - that kind of thing.'

Darrin shook his head at him. Everybody was talking in fucking riddles today.

Thankfully, the prick cut to the chase.

Stone stood up and had a little wander around the desk - his meaty but manicured hands clasped behind his back.

'Detective Morris has filled me in about your - peregrinations, PC May.'

'Sir?'

Stone coloured, obviously irritated by his obtuseness.

'You and a certain Mr Dalton. Is that simple enough for you son?'

Darrin nodded, 'yes sir.'

'Hmmm, good, better late than never I suppose. You know I've heard a lot of good things about you Constable May. I've heard you're keen, hard working and that you have plenty of bottle too. Those are all good qualities for a go-getting young policeman to have. I've also heard that you don't always favour teamwork and that you regularly need to be pulled pretty hard on the reigns. Would you say that is a fair, balanced assessment?'

'I guess so Chief Inspector.'

'You guess so.'

Stone lasered him with his hard eyes. 'I believe that some of your colleagues refer to you as Dazzler, is that right?'

Darrin ducked his head, feeling a curious mix of pride and embarrassment.

'Well- what I want you to do in the future is dazzle a bit less often and, instead, take directions when you're working on a sensitive operation. I don't want you going off half-cocked in the hope of realising your half-baked theories and speculations. Do I make myself clear, Constable?'

'Very clear Sir.'

'Good, dismissed PC May.'

Darrin stood up to leave the office. He walked a couple of steps towards the door and then turned back to him.

'Am I off it then Sir- the op?'

Stone leaned back and tapped his wide chest for a few beats with an expensive looking pen, just the hint of amusement and maybe even something more playing at the corner of his mouth.

'No son - I want you to stay on it. Just keep what I said firmly at the front of your mind. Life and, hopefully, your career, is not a sprint. Think on, now, get out.'

Darrin gave Stone a curt nod and left the room - what the fuck! Game on.

The kid didn't show on Monday and Tommy was OK with that, the break from him was more than welcome. He busied himself with some paperwork for the first hour of the day then popped in to see Pauline. She still hadn't heard anything about the funding bid but she was excited by an approach from a local advocacy service who'd proposed a working partnership on a project targeting the local Asian community.

Tommy had reservations about the proposal, not because it was a bad idea per-se but because of the fact that the Asian community, other than the odd bit of recurring Pakistani-Bengali tension, particularly amongst the youth, was every bit as cohesive as his own community had once been and were, apart from the obvious social and economic impediments, pretty good at advocating for themselves.

The biggest issue with that community, as far as he could see, was the entrenched disempowerment of its women and girls, victims of cultural values and norms that kept many of them firmly shuttered behind the walls of family and community. He knew that some of the older Asian women, who had been living in England for over forty years, could still barely speak any English. Pauline had ruffled a few feathers about the issue more than once and many of the older Asian guys were outwardly respectful but also very circumspect in their dealings with her.

Tommy had lived as an outsider in another culture and he knew how easy it was to see your ingrained cultural assumptions as a kind of universal truth but, it still rubbed against the grain with him. He didn't like how the women were treated - period.

Pauline thought that such a scheme might be an in to the local Asian community - maybe they could train up some women from the communities themselves to become advocates. Pauline believed that contact and communication was everything and that real change could only happen through it and any subsequent building up of relationships.

'Would you and Sonny be prepared to climb on board with the initiative? If I do decide to go for it Thomas?' she asked.

He made a point of questioning the need for the scheme but he said yes, fuck it he'd be a team player and Pauline needed all the options she could get.

They chewed the fat on things domestic for a while though he didn't tell her about Donna and the kid. Some boundaries didn't need to be blurred.

That night he met with Jimbo for a few welcome pints in the Grapes - a pub that he didn't mind during the week as the joint was always quiet. He avoided it like the pox at the weekends as it was guaranteed to be full of ten bob millionaires slowing down service by blocking up the bar. He didn't enjoy the experience of being surrounded by a rake of vacuous numb nuts jabbering inanely about their golf handicaps and new cars.

Jimbo was stringing two women along at the moment, enjoying the occasionally harried drama and the furtiveness that inevitably entailed. Tommy told him about Donna and the kid.

Jim didn't usually bother with advice, even of an indirect nature but he looked at Tommy for a couple of quiet beats and gave him a shrug of the shoulders.

'Big ask that Tommy boy - does an errant rover like you want to take on that kind of baggage, although if she's as fit as you say she is…..'

That night he lay on his bed and mulled it over. He knew that he'd be awake awhile so he'd left the door to his bedroom and the lounge wide open, chilling out in the dark with some music, Bill Callahan's wry baritone providing the backdrop to his thoughts.

He and Bonnie had tried for a couple of years to have children but it had been to no avail. Tests had showed a battery of reasons why it was unlikely to happen; her inverted womb, her endometriosis and her twisted fallopian tubes, in fact there was more chance of seeing a unicorn galloping down the Barrington shopping precinct.

Tommy couldn't say that was the beginning of their drifting apart but it hadn't helped. What had been a hungry sex life had been reduced to a mere process; a function and they never quite got that side of it back, never getting past the fact that the sex was now a reminder of what could not be.

More so, he had realised, with the time and distance of separation, Bonnie had never fully dealt with the fact that he was a white man. That had never been apparent when they had lived together in the city but once they'd made the decision to leave Sydney and head down to the small coastal town, which was home to her mother and her siblings, it had quickly become an issue for her, though it never was for him. He truly didn't give a rat's arse about it, indeed he enjoyed the difference, thinking that ultimately, it should not matter. Time had shown him which ties were binding and which ones were less so. It had taken two years for them to drift apart. The isthmus that had once connected them was all washed away. He was still looking towards her but she was now looking away from him.

And that was that, a separation and, for him, two more years of being alone. Two hard years of work, study and solitude, two years of not knowing where the fuck he should be until the visit to see his dad had shown him that home always seemed to be wherever the heart was. Tommy was getting older, nearer fifty than forty now and the separation from Bonnie had shown him what it was to be truly on his own. During that period he had often pictured himself as a lonely bird perched on a rock in a rolling ocean swell, an indulgence maybe but one that he had earned.

On Monday Dwayne asked them if they fancied a promotion - up to eighty a run.

'Fuck yeah,' he and J had bitten his hand off.

'Carry more of the same D?' Junior asked.

'More of the fuckin' same and a different fuckin' product too, my man - you boys ever heard of ice?'

Junior nodded and as he did so, Pasquale noted that his friend tightly gripped the handles of his bicycle.

'Up for it then lads, come on, what do yer fuckin' reckon then?' Dwayne grinned wolfishly at them, the prick enjoying dangling the carrot.

They gave each other a little look and it was Pasquale who spoke up for them, 'let's do it.'

Dwayne let out a dramatic and kinda meaningless snort.

'See you boys round the fuckin' back then.'

They waited there for the usual five minutes and Dwayne came through the fence with a pack each for them. Pasquale felt the brittle texture. It looked like a slightly dirty soap - ice.

'Good fuckin' shit that lads, get it down to JT fuckin' pronto like.'

Junior studied his packet then looked across to Dwayne.

'You ever had it then D?'

D took an intake of breath and theatrically widened his eyes.

'What you fuckin' reckon young un? Better than getting your fuckin' end away that fuckin' stuff.'

Junior nodded appreciatively, he had a fair bit more experience in that department than Pasquale, which would help him make the comparison.

'My recommendation though lads,' Dwayne took them both in with a look of disconcerting gravity. 'Uncle Dwayne says leave it the fuck alone - fuckin' alright?'

Pasquale didn't need any telling and he was aware enough

to register the irony of Dwayne's warning. He knew it had killed M and a skip was not where he wanted to end his days.

They took off and Johnny Talbot was waiting for them with that irritating knowing smile on his face, like he wasn't just another raggedy-arsed, tosser estate boy.

They did the business in and out, nice and smooth. Then they went to the movies to see the new Planet of the Apes. They had it right too, Pasquale reckoned, most of the humans in it were pricks.

Pasquale didn't get home till nine. He called out a good night to his mum. She was in the lounge watching the box. He wanted to get right to his room without any kind of mither - chill out with some sounds. But, she came out to catch him. She told him that the school had called her at her work today. He was suspended due to his recurring absences.

'I want you to go and see Sonny tomorrow,' she told him, 'do you know where his office is?'

He nodded at her, 'why's that Mum?'

She swallowed and he saw tears spring into her eyes.

'I want you to leave for the moment Pasquale. I can't put up with this anymore.'

That surprised him, it felt like a slap and, despite himself, he too felt the tears.

She reached out to touch his face but he pulled away and clamped down hard on his emotion.

'It will be for three months love, they have programmes there to help - education, college applications, they can help you with the drugs…' her voice trailed off.

He looked at her with a cold smile, 'Drugs Mum eh, the drugs!'

'Yes Pasquale - the drugs.'

'Going to let the refuge know about your past then, are yer Mum, tell 'em all about that then?'

She shook her head and sighed, 'I can't change the past Pasquale. I did what I had to do to get us here.'

'And look where we are Mum, look where we are. It'll free you up for Tommy though eh?'

She looked at him coldly this time - the big fuckin' freeze and then she turned back to the lounge room - discussion over.

He sat a long time on his bed thinking about it, he was glad in a way but pissed off too. Another decision that she'd made for him - but fuck it, he was ready to go. Pasquale got up from his bed and went over to the tallboy wardrobe and pulled down the large sports bag from the top of it. That and his travel case would do the job.

When Darrin landed at the station, Clive Young, the Sergeant from the Drug Squad was waiting for him at reception. Young was what, mid thirties at the most, he wore a natty pin stripe suit that didn't look off the peg. He had a ready almost ever present smile, offset and not quite matched by bright intelligent eyes that reminded Darrin of an eager rodent. Sarge Thomas gave him a pass for a while and they parked off in the D's office, which was empty apart from a bored looking Sammy Watson who was half-heartedly making some chase up calls on a missing person case.

Young kicked the conversation off, 'heard you showed a bit of initiative then PC May - ruffled a few feathers too, along the way.'

There was amusement in his eyes but Darrin knew that it was best to let that slide past. The station didn't welcome indiscretion and definitely not anything that could be possibly perceived as disloyalty.

He gave Young the straight bat.

'Well you know Sarge - they did keep me on.'

'Well Constable, to cut to the chase, the thing is, thanks to you, we might up it a bit, the op. Check this place out down at the Quays, have a look at this Dalton bloke, might even be some bigger fish to be caught.'

Darrin nodded non-commitally at him, waiting for Young to lay his cards on the table.

'Well we'll see, we'll get down there and canvas a few people, get a feel of the lay of the land. We can sus it out, see if there any unusual comings and goings. There might be some overtime down there for you - a part to play.'

Darrin gave it up and showed Young his appetite for the opportunity. He knew that the relevant gaffers would have to chat with each other before it could be approved. But, his hat was in the ring, CI Stone was cool with it and he was hungry, almost fucking ravenous. It was always better to be a player than a spectator.

Fuck Mozzer, he thought, Mr Play Safe, Mr Careful as you bloody go. He'd been rewarded for taking some initiative. Mozzer could eat and tip toe his way to retirement if that's what he wanted to do.

Tommy had called Donna a couple of days after the incident with the kid and told her that he thought it would be better if they pulled back a bit, that he felt like he was already in heavy waters with something that had barely started. She was OK with it too, more even about it than he had anticipated. On reflection he realised that she had probably been through all of this crap before.

He and Sonny had chatted about the advocacy proposal that Pauline had mentioned. Sonny liked the idea but gave the impression that he wasn't keen on getting involved any more than at arms length. He knew that Sonny was ambivalent about some of the Asian communities' mores and expectations. He had married a white girl a couple of years ago, Estelle. Sonny had met her at university and they had now been together for years. But their relationship had never sat right with his family. They respected him for his hard work and his success but had worried about Sonny's ecumenical approach to life. Sonny had to tightrope walk a fair bit to keep a harmony between the clan and his strong minded wife. Sonny found sanctuary in his work and was currently very focussed on the Glasgow gang initiative. He was travelling up to Glasgow in a couple of week's time for a conference on the subject. It was a biggy according to him, with speakers being flown over from the States.

They talked about the kid for a while. Sonny thought that Pasquale would benefit from the more structured environment of the refuge. School hours were strictly observed there and his education would be part of a personal program designed to get him back to a good place. He would have time to himself in the evenings but had to be back at six if he wanted his grub. Twice a week, he was expected to help cook. Tommy knew that that would be the acquisition of a new skill.

'So', Sonny asked, 'you and Donna, how's that going?'

He told Sonny about the weekend and the fact that he wanted a bit of time out. Sonny didn't think that it was that big a deal.

'Gee not been long has it? Bit of space though, yeah that might work. Give you two the chance to reignite the flames of passion Tommy Boy. You can reweave your magic!'

Tommy rolled his eyes at the silly bastard but, Sonny was right, a little easing of the pressure had to work for all of them. At the moment it was just crap that he didn't really need.

Later that day he popped up to see his old man and they set up a wet the whistle night on Friday and a trip out for Sunday lunch. His dad fancied a walk up to the reservoir now that the days were getting warmer.

Tommy had doubts about his old man making it up there - it was a pretty steep climb in parts but a slow pace and some fair weather should be enough to get the old man up to the top.

His old man was giving him the beady eye - he knew the look, Mick curious about withheld information.

'Thought you'd be introducing me to that new bird of yours soon son, are you hiding me or hiding her?'

'Neither Mick - we're cooling off a bit.'

'Cooling off, cooling off! You've only just started seeing her haven't yer? Bloody hell, cooling off.' The old man cackling to himself and shaking his head, forever amused at the folly of his fellow human beings.

So, with a fair degree of initial reluctance, he reiterated the events of the last few days and wondered, as he told the tale, what the fuck he had ever talked about before the Edward's family had come into his life. His dad was engaged with it though, genuinely interested and once he got past the start it was easy enough to give the old fart the full lowdown.

'Sixteen eh? Old enough to start getting his shit together

- the lad, needs to get off the bloody tit by the sounds of it - I reckon.'

Amen to that, Tommy thought, he turned his mind back to the Saturday and the kid practically throwing those jeans in her face, fucking abysmal that was.

Mick wasn't too impressed with that part of the story either. He didn't buy into the poor Pasquale refrain.

'That's a reason but not a fucking excuse son. Is he going to be thirty and falling back on that shit? No dad, no mum, no fucking family pet - bloody hell! You know I never thought that this lot could make things worse than what those Tory bastards started. But all this poncing about, wiping peoples' arses for them. What fucking good is that for folk? Opportunities with responsibility son, it's not fucking rocket science. These fuckers are like something out of Lewis bloody Carroll, I tell yer.'

Good old Mick, he thought, from the personal to the political in a nano-second. He was bang on the money though and Mick's thoughts echoed what Sonny had been telling him about the work that was being done with the Glasgow gangs. Mick had it nailed, the keys to the asylum needed to be taken back from the lunatics and as time marched on it looked like that was going to be a big, big job.

Tommy called her when he got home. Donna's voice was a little flat, not much coming back his way. The kid was scheduled to go home for the weekend. She was pleased but she was still sad at the way it had gone.

'Ah well,' he said. 'Stay in touch, maybe we could grab a bite some time.'

Hmmm, that didn't exactly get her doing cartwheels either.

'Maybe,' she'd replied.

There you go Sonny, he thought, good old Tommy re-weaving his magic.

He rung off and then fired up the lap top, he wondered if that bird from Watford was still on the site - thankfully she was.

His mum drove him to the refuge early Wednesday morning, two holdalls worth of gear that she had let him pack by himself.

A ten minute drive and they were there, his new home for the next few months.

The refuge itself was a squat, rectangular, one-level yellow brick building that was located on a good size block of land with plenty of space between it and the neighbours.

Pasquale pulled the bags from the back seat and they said a low-key goodbye to each other. Just as she had been since she'd made the decision his mum was calm, almost matter of fact. He leaned in through the driver's window and gave her a peck on the cheek then turned towards the building. He briskly walked up the meandering path to the heavy looking, double locked front door. It swung open on his first knock and he was warmly greeted by a small, middle-aged woman who had dark circles under her eyes and hair the colour of dried out straw. Looming behind her was a tallish guy with big shoulders that were more than offset by a prominent gut.

They smiled at him and the woman did the introductions, they were Wendy and Rob.

The pair shepherded him on through to the office whereupon a fresh-looking Sonny was already there to greet him with a cheery wink.

'Good to see you young un,' Sonny told him. 'Wendy will take you through the paperwork and then I'll be here to sit in while we go through the refuge's programmes, and its expectations.'

Sonny gave him a level look which he softened with a smile then he stood up and left the room. Wendy clucked her way through the paperwork and when that was finished Rob went off to bring back Sonny.

Sonny helped him throw his bags into his new room, two beds in what was a fresh looking, good-sized space. He'd be sharing then. After that they went outside to a paved area at the back of the building. In the right hand far corner of the yard was a large, open corrugated shed that Sonny told him doubled up as the refuge's gym. They sat down at a couple of scratched up round plastic tables, both of which housed ashtrays. One of the ashtrays had three butts mashed up in it, which were coloured at their tips with what looked like Wendy's shade of lipstick - had to be Wendy, he'd smelt the smoke on her.

He sat down and stared into space. Without any preamble or obvious reason Sonny stood up and did a slow 360 of the yard. Satisfied with whatever it was that he saw he returned to take his seat.

'Think you'll be OK here son?'

Pasquale nodded.

'Yeah?'

'Yeah Sonny - I'll be fine.'

'Good, glad to hear it. They're good people here P - Wendy, Rob and the rest of the crew. This would be a good place for you to start pulling it together - know what I mean?'

Pasquale nodded and pulled his right foot up underneath

him. Sonny wasn't finished with him yet.

'Just take your time Pasquale, you're a bright kid, Tommy's told me that. You still fancy going on to Art College?'

'Yeah, I like the idea of, you know doing fine art, sculpture, maybe getting rich and famous like that Damien Hirst guy.'

Sonny raised his eyebrows. He wasn't in the mood for any flippancy.

'Well let's see. Do the work first eh? One step at a time like.'

Pasquale regretted being a bit of a smart arse with him, although he had meant it too in a way, why the fuck not.

Sonny looked at his watch then lightly slapped his thighs and stood up again. He offered Pasquale his hand and said his goodbyes. Pasquale got up too and followed him on through the lounge room. Sonny went back to the office and he turned a right towards what was now his bedroom and spent the next half an hour unpacking his bags and sticking away his gear. When he finished he sent a text to Junior who texted him back straight away.

He wandered back to the office, he'd noticed a bicycle in the gym cum shed and he asked Wendy if he could borrow it.

Wendy shot Rob a quick look then nodded her assent.

'Be careful with it now, wont you dear, it's the only one we've got.'

He gave her his promise then took off. He had twenty minutes to get down to the precinct to meet Junior and he made it in fifteen. Junior was already there, lounging with usual cool just outside Foot Locker, nodding along to his iPod. They did a quick catch up and then took off to the Coleshaw to meet up with Dwayne. He told Dwayne and Junior a little about the ref, reassuring a disinterested Dwayne that he was still up for the afternoons. Dwayne was fuckin' cool with that. He had plenty of other lads ready to step in for the morning run.

Only fifty today, just weed, but that was OK. The other gear still made him think about M too much.

SUMMER

JUNE

It took a fortnight before the Drug boys finally got their shit together to sort out what they were going to do with the observation post in the Coleshaw flat. A tough looking squat Geordie with a pair of Stalinesque eyebrows who had introduced himself as, 'Mac just Mac,' would now be taking up post there on a full time basis. Mac was five six in his boots but he had axe handle wide shoulders and a handshake that could have strangled a drainpipe. He was a little taciturn was Mac but he gave out enough information to let Darrin know that Mac knew who he was.

As the days were now getting longer there were plenty of kids hanging about near the pub and down Oak Road. Some of the kids were hanging with Dwayne and his crew, the others, mostly the younger ones, sticking tight to their own little groups. He'd clocked the pair that he, Moz and Sonny had spoken to about Matthew Marshall a few times, lanky Junior and his sad-eyed olive skinned mate Pasquale. Both of the boys out there on their bicycles, both wearing backpacks, which was a dead set sign that they're probably shifting the shit. They didn't seem to hang around the estate that long but Dwayne would always give them a nod hello and then made the point of engaging with them and he wouldn't be doing that because he was a social butterfly.

The Admiral was getting busier too, plenty of older scrotes emerging into the light, kitted out in muscle vests, seemingly Coleshaw de rigueur for the warmer months. Johnstone and his brother were rolling along to the boozer most evenings now like a couple of fucking low rent kings.

Mozzer hadn't said that much to him of late, despite the initial enthusiasm and kudos, the spontaneous tail job had obviously pissed him off for some reason. Maybe he'd made the lazy fucker look bad or something. Mozzer had told him that Young had been in touch with him about the same gig, the setting up of a parallel observation post down at the Quays - Dalton's pad.

Darrin had asked Moz if Young had mentioned him in dispatches, just to stir the fucker up a bit, help shake him out of the terse, thin lipped, cold as an Eskimo's todger shit. With a sigh and a bit of a grunt Mozzer had reluctantly told him that yes, he had.

He had given Mozzer a shit-eating grin. 'Ta for letting me know Mozzer.'

Moz gave him the raised eyebrows and a begrudging grin but still kept quiet. He'd come around the lazy old fucker. They might even get on the Quays end of it together and share a hanging cheese and pickle butty or two.

Darrin had done a bit of background in prep for the job, digging out some dried out old paperwork on Dalton and his doings.

There was nothing much more there than what was on the up to date computer summary. Although there was one detail that more than grabbed his attention, the name of the arresting officer for the procurement charge that had eventually been dropped, a Detective Constable Gerard Keegan no less. Keegan, who was of a similar vintage to Dalton, Keegan; the station's bona fide, gimlet eyed enforcer. Darrin re-filed the info and stashed that golden nugget into his memory banks.

Mac was down The Admiral tonight, with the view of ingratiating himself with the Johnstone crew. The cover seemed solid enough and Mac was implacably unphased at the thought of swilling Stella with some of the more entrepreneurial end of the underclass. Johno had told Darrin that Mac was ex-army but that fucker was the station gossip and he was surprised that Johno hadn't yet sprouted a pair of tits. Speaking of which, he thought, the big blonde he'd met down Brum was heading up to Leeds for a salsa weekend next week. She'd texted him a couple of days ago and the responding warmth in his loins would provide enough energy to get him easily onto the A62 and over the Pennines.

Later that evening, he stood at the window and watched Mac saunter over to The Admiral with that loose, easy stroll of his. It was a pleasant enough evening; a few of the locals were hanging around outside the pub entrance, smoking fags and bullshitting to each other. Johnstone had been in there for just under an hour and there was a match on the box so he'd be set for the night.

The game finished at nine thirty and Johnstone and his brother left the pub about ten minutes after that. Mac strolled out about twenty minutes later, zipping his coat up against the chill of the wind. A couple of minutes and the key was turning in the lock, Mac came in and heavily dropped down on the sofa. Darrin made him them both a brew and took the other end of the settee.

'How did it go then Mac?'

'All right son - played some pool, talked football with a couple of guys at the bar. Johnstone's brother came over and introduced himself.' Mac laughed softly. 'The older one never took his eyes off us when he did.'

'Bought it, yer reckon?'

'Early days but yeah, I kept it simple. Meathead's not a big conversationalist really and I'm a smallish bloke too, so, as far as he's concerned, I'm no threat. That's the most important thing to a bloke like him.'

They drank their brews in silence for a while.

'How long you been in the service then Mac?'

'Few years now, didn't come in till I was near thirty but I'm ex-army and did a bit in there too.'

'And what works best like - you know – when working undercover?'

'Well like, yer know, keep it simple, like I said, and take your time with it. Good lies have to have a lot of truth in them. When you're dealing with dullards like those across the way it's often better to just shut the fuck up and keep your eyes and ears open. If there is a talker amongst them have a run at him - but don't rush it. But in saying that, and this is important, always be ready for battle stations - it can happen like that.' Mac clicked his fingers for emphasis. 'Bit like you did with that bloody tail job eh?'

Mac grinned at him then bent down to start pulling off his boots.

'Anyway Darrin, I'm getting some shuteye. Up at six and off at six thirty to keep up appearances of the common working man and, as your superior officer, I am ordering you to fuck off home.'

Darrin stood up, took the cups back to the kitchen and rinsed them both out.

Mac thanked him with another grin then looked at him with just one eye open. Maybe he was a little bit pissed after all.

'You're OK you are son, still a colt in some ways, but a

smart one at that.'

Mac saluted him a goodbye and Darrin left him to it - he'd be back on Friday.

Tommy had called her a couple of days after the kid had been parcelled off to the refuge, but the conversation never got out of first gear. He alluded to meeting up but she quickly told him that she needed some time alone. He told her that was probably a good thing but that was the opposite of how he felt. He was missing her but he didn't say it. Lee was coming up for the weekend to catch up with his dear old mum so at least he'd have some company.

Sonny called him the next day to talk about the trip up to Glasgow, on for next week if he fancied it. Sonny's employers had stumped up for him and, if he could get the Centre to do the same, he would bc on the train too. He could do with a change of scene, the thing with Donna and the kid had him feeling more than a little wrung out. He caught Pauline after lunch, it was no problem with her, still plenty in the training budget and she saw the merits of the trip - what a gal.

He sorted it out straight away, switching the diary around, getting Corrine to cover a couple of groups for him - easy peasy.

Tommy had vowed to let the thing with Donna ride. That would be the smartest deal all round really. He didn't trust the kid not too fuck up at the refuge and boomerang back to her doorstep and he wasn't in the mood for another bash at playing the role of Uncle Tommy, a resented back up and back stop for Donna's ongoing domestic drama.

He thought back to Sunday and the gentle stroll that he and Mick had taken up to the reservoir. Plenty of pit stops along the way but the old man had made it. Mick had taken time out to puff contentedly on a well-deserved gasper at the top of the climb. His old man had taken a perch on the grass with his back to the reservoir's perimeter stone wall, chilling out in the peacefulness of all that mellow space.

Tommy took a stroll around the water's edge while his old man stayed put. He rewound his memory further back; to what had to be a decade or so ago now.

A Christmas spent on a friend's bush property down near the area that the Aussies referred to, with their laconic literalness, as the 'Snow'. After a late breakfast, he and the old man had marched up a scrubby brown knob of a hill that was a mile or so from the property. At first, his old man had matched him stride for stride but his breathing became quickly more ragged as the climb went on. Mick pulled the pin three quarters of the way to the top, he was bent over double, raggedly trying to suck in air that his tobacco battered lungs wouldn't let him access. It had jolted Tommy. The experience had been a palpable reminder of the passage of time. His once nimble footed, quick moving father debilitated and hitting such a relatively low wall. Neither of them made any reference to the event but it was indisputable evidence of both Mick's physical decline and of the incremental passing of the torch between them - the old stag and the young one. At the reservoir Tommy had taken time out to look back towards Mick's resting spot and had felt a swell of sad protectiveness for his father. Mick prided himself on his abundant resilience; it was a badge of honour to him. But, nobody beat the clock.

He had pushed the thoughts away and was brought back to the now by the keening peep of the resident kestrel. He immediately looked for it and there it was, circling just a little to the left of where he had seen it before.

The old man looked bright-eyed on his return and Mick managed to get to his pins without any assistance or the offer of it.

They went back to his place and watched a DVD of Chinatown - they were both film noir boys, it was his old man who had introduced him to the genre, both the movies and the books.

It was a great film, a young, slim, hard-edged Jack Nicholson taking on the big boys and losing, the drama played out under the Californian sun.

All in all, he thought, it had been a damned fine day. His dad was off to the races this weekend and Nev had called him to let him know that he'd be keeping an eye on the old bloke - thank God, he thought, for willing, clandestine minders. Lee would be here anyway and Tommy had bought tickets for a hometown band that were on the verge of cracking the big time. They were a decent enough listen although not exactly the Clash at the Apollo. But, Lee rated them, and it would be a nice change of pace from the Crown and the local blues ensemble.

Pasquale was into the swing of it now - enjoying the rhythms of the refuge despite sharing a room and despite the non-negotiable demands that the place made on his time. Five other kids were presently in there with him, which made the joint two shy of being a full house.

He was sharing a room with a big red headed silent kid, Frankie, who the girls and Neil had nicknamed Lurch. In the next room to theirs was Al, a little mouthy jockey of a kid from down in the Midlands somewhere. He was teased mercilessly by the two girls who scathingly and repeatedly referred to him as 'pin dick'. In the single room was Neil, a slightly discomforting, tall, out there, seventeen year old gay kid who provided most of the laughs in the place and finally, the two girls themselves; Jess, a big titted blonde, who loved to prance around the refuge in her underwear and thrived on any melodrama and, finally, the Queen of the joint, Kat, a slightly Goth looking, older girl. She was smart with a whip like wit and she was tough too, a real package. Pasquale had noticed that even the workers were a little circumspect with her. Kat burned brightly most of the time and had, thankfully, taken a shine to him, often referring to him as 'her little cutie'. But, cloud could quickly block out that sun and then Al or even poor Lurch copped it. She had a mouth that could bubble paint.

He'd settled in with the others kids quickly, a couple hours of sussing each other out and that was it, sorted. The staff seemed pretty OK too, Wendy slightly over did the clucking mother hen bit but she knew when to back off and you could have a laugh with her. Rod was a big lazy fucker who spent most of his shift in the office either on the phone or on the computer playing backgammon or chess. There was a younger guy working there too. Colin. He had plenty of energy and always spent the first hour of his shift trying to corral them out of the refuge to do some social or recreational activity - a real pain in the arse. The guy did a lot of flirting with the girls too, which both of them readily lapped up, playing him to the max. Neil had caught his eye a couple of times when Colin was plying his charm with Kat and Jess. Neil made no pretence of the fact that he thought Colin was a wanker and, he had a point.

Pasquale was surprised at how cool he was with Neil but maybe that was because Neil himself was cool. His mum had had a couple of gay male friends who had come to the house when they still had dinner parties and, for that matter, when she'd had a few wilder parties too. It was Kim who had shown him the paper folding and, at the weekends, he'd taken him and his mum out to galleries. He'd liked Kim - he was upbeat and chill, the best boyfriend his mum had never had. He'd been sure that she had been a little in love with him too.

Still, that was years ago now.

The staff had done this goals thing with him and they were trying to set down an education programme that would get him into a local sixth form college, specialising in art and maybe history. Wendy had explained that it was do-able, if he committed himself. He needed some qual's though and he knew that he still had a lot of catching up to do.

He invariably met up with Junior in the late afternoons and they rode the packages to the Barrington, regular and as smooth as. He had the money stashed in the refuge but it was risky and vulnerable there, he could have asked the staff to keep it for him maybe but they would ask questions - £500 plus. No way would they take that at face value, not even that dopy bleeder Rod.

He'd decided to stash it at his mum's, his room had access to the attic, it would be right enough there. Not this weekend though he was having a break from her - let her think about that a little bit too.

She'd called him on the Friday asking him if he still wanted to stay over but there wasn't much coming back when he said no and that stayed with him for a while. He did a run with Junior on the Saturday morning and then he went out with the refuge crew for ten-pin bowling and pizza. Two more runs on the Sunday and he nearly had seven hundred in the bin.

Junior had been back with him to the ref' a couple of times and had been much more impressed with Jess's curves than he had been with Neil's arch confidence. Neil spun Junior out and, both times, had quickly bailed, rolling his eyes at Neil's prancing and preening. Jess had asked him if Junior was single and he had told her that he wasn't. He didn't want her knowing any of their business. Neil lamented Junior's fake relationship.

'Hung like a horse too I bet,' Neil had said.

Jess then mimed some fellatio and both the girls and Neil had fallen about with laughter. Pasquale had felt himself blush, which had brought out another volley of laughter till Kat chided the other two to leave him alone. Neil answered, 'yes Mum' then gracefully stood up, executed a pirouette and flounced off into the kitchen to make him self another coffee - the fucker was a caffeine addict and seemed to get by on six hours sleep a night.

Pasquale spent the next hour in their company relaxed and inert, watching transfixed as Kat braided Jess's hair. It was as if he had been given the keys to a strange, strange land.

Darrin had struggled to stay put at the op post on the Friday, Mac had left about seven to enjoy the delights of The Admiral and that was it really. Another three hours watching deadbeats of different ages killing time refining the art of doing fuck all. He knew that a few of the crew were hitting town tonight and he'd promised to catch up with them later on but they'd be pie-eyed by the time that he landed. Besides, it was Leeds tomorrow and he was definitely up for that, some dancing and a very uninhibited larger woman - spot on. He felt the stirrings of an erection and briefly kneaded his cock a couple of times as the light and the sound of some music spilled out of The Admiral. Despite Mac's advice he could feel his interest in this start to ebb - too much of the same thing and too many hours on the job. Twelve hour days, four times a week plus a straight shift on top. His old man had always stressed the need for rest, albeit in the context of training. But, he'd never listened to him, as far as he was concerned, the body was an instrument to be bent to his will.

His mobile rang and it was Young, the smooth sergeant who'd liked his attitude.

'Got the number off your desk sergeant, he said you probably wouldn't mind when I told him what it was about.'

Darrin immediately felt the buzz and yeah yeahed him along.

'I know you've been up there in the flat a fair bit and now Mac's embedded, we can do with your energies elsewhere.'

Darrin struggled to hold in his impatience.

'Seeing that you brought it in, I wonder if you fancy a couple of shifts down at Dalton's flat. I'm fine tuning that with my guv' next week and we could do with somebody with keen eyes down there. You in then Constable?'

'I'm in Sarge…in like Flynn.'

Young laughed, 'good man - I'll be in touch and soon.'

He resumed his post and the next two hours flew by, Mac unlocking the door a little after ten.

Darrin told Mac about Young's call and Mac nodded along

with that little half smile of his.

'Maybe they want you as a new recruit, fancy it like?'

'With fucking bells on.'

'Might mean a move away though son - hard to work undercover where every dealer knows yer first name and yer star sign.'

Hmm, moving away didn't sound too bad, must be plenty of places for a near intermediate, salsa dancing undercover cop to ply his trade. He laughed a little at himself and Mac smiled at him with his eyes.

Darrin jerked his head to the widow. 'How did you go then - owt doing?'

'Yeah, not too bad - loyalties were lightly made and no doubt would be quickly taken away too.' Mac saw that Darrin was puzzled, so he filled in the gaps for him.

'A couple of the regulars wanted me to stay and do some after time. I had to plead an early shift. The wankers could just about get their heads around that, the idea of somebody having to bail out cause they got to get up early for work.'

'You have a chat with Johnstone too?'

'Yeah - only with Pete though, not with Chris. We had a game of pool, mostly grunts from him but he slipped in a couple of questions about my workplace. Subtle as a kick in the nuts he is. Dwayne was in there too, of course.'

He was? Fuck, Darrin had missed it - maybe during the call or when he had gone for a piss.

Mac didn't comment on the omission, 'yeah, he had a bit of a lengthy chat with the Johnstone inner circle, plenty of meaningful nods and no smiling faces. It looked like it was all business to me - scrawny fucker was drinking orange juice! Dedicated to his craft is that lad.'

Darrin took that in but had nothing to add, his mind drifting back to Young's call and the prospect of bouncing around the luscious blonde. He said his goodbyes and headed home not even bothering with the boozer. The call had given him enough buzz and he'd save it up for tomorrow. Trish had been giving him that look again. He reckoned Barnesy was up for a turn and, if so, that would have his full blessing.

Nev had called him the day after the old man had rocked back home from the horse-racing weekend. Mick had had a dizzy spell on the Sunday morning when they were strolling through the town centre. Nev said that the old man had been a little out of it, incoherent and disoriented for a little while. Tommy had felt real concern at the news, Nev was not the kind of guy to overstate it.

He'd gone up to see the old man on the Sunday evening taking Lee round for a catch up chat. The old man seemed as right as rain and even a little jaunty, although that could have been down to seeing Lee. His old man liked Lee because he was the only one of the gang that Tommy had grown up with who had any whiff of the alternative about him.

They'd shot the breeze for a couple of hours - music and politics with minimum nostalgia, it was always all now and tomorrow with the old man. His dad never got misty eyed about the past even with a slew of malt whiskeys inside him. There had been no renditions of *Danny Boy* in the Cochrane household. The old man had declined his suggestion of going out to the pub, both Mick and Lee were not particularly enticed by the fact that it was crib night at the Bull.

He had thought about popping round again today but that would be two nights on the bounce and the old boy needed his space to recharge the batteries. He gave him a quick call to let him know about Glasgow. When he did, Mick reminded him that he'd already told him about it yesterday and that was that.

Tommy called Donna from work the next day and they agreed to a spot of lunch on the Friday. After he hung up he thought that maybe he was giving her mixed messages. But, what the hell, she was worth testing the water with and, according to both Donna and Sonny, the kid was as happy as Larry at the refuge. In his mind that was confirmation that he was more than ready to leave the bloody nest. The next morning he met Sonny at a bleary eyed pre-dawn at the City's refurbished, dog's bollocks railway station and they caught the speed train up north. The train got them up to Glasgow bang on the timetable and they took a taxi across the City and made it to the venue just after the 9.30 kick off. Luckily, the first speaker was still wrestling with the Power Point and nobody took any notice of their slightly rushed entrance.

Tommy enjoyed all of the speakers but the stand out for him was a tough looking runt who had a near impenetrable local accent that was as harsh as a sack of broken bottles being thrown down a stairwell. He had lively eyes and a scar that ran from under his chin to the half-lobe of his left ear. Kenny Lawson was the poster boy for his home city's Community Initiative to Reduce Violence scheme and his was a very convincing and inspirational story arc. Years of agro riddled bullshit with a reserved bunk bed at the local big house. Up until the time that Kenny, who was leader of one of city's bigger gangs, had been introduced to the option of the scheme and had been given the choice of that carrot or the stick. Kenny had had an epiphany of sorts, he'd embraced the opportunity and was now employed as a street based youth worker. He was now reborn as a slightly ravaged apostle on the coal-face, spreading the message to the younger lads. Tommy imagined the movie, a young Robert Carlyle as the lead.

Before the lunch break a big bluff American cop talked about the American pilot scheme. He had showed a short DVD bolstered with some dead pan, hard-arsed anecdotes and some encouraging statistics re the scheme's impact on re-cidivism. The Jock cops picked up the baton after lunch with a film of more gang members from the north and the east of the city, the lads talking about what it meant for them to get opportunities for work and training. Interestingly, the scheme ran with the notion of it being natural to be in a gang but it reached out to give individual members alternative path options that could lead away from the cycle of bore-dom, exclusion, turf wars and hard earned reps. Coppers, youth workers, local government, teachers, social workers had all pitched in.

As one of the speakers noted it was about the whole of the community being prepared to commit to cultural and at-titudinal change. As Kenny had succinctly said, 'it's ahl of urs prahblem.'

They hung around and schmoozed a little after the last speaker had brought it to a close. Both of them felt more than a little inspired by the day and they were keen to make the time and effort to swap cards with other professionals, chatting between themselves all the while about dragging a version down South. They could both taste the challenge and the possibilities.

On the journey home Sonny's head was hitting his chest before they crossed the border and Tommy was only a few minutes behind him. Estelle picked them up at the station and they dropped him off at the flat. Despite the late night, he was up at six the next morning, wide-awake and feeling energised. He had an early morning workout at the Bodyworks gym and he was at his desk before nine. Pauline dropped in and asked him about the day and she was in good spirits too. They'd made it through to the final round for the buckets of cash Community Lottery grant. Tommy speculated about whether he could/would stay at the Centre if the work with Sonny got off the ground, but he'd keep that up his sleeve for the moment. He didn't want Pauline to think that he was contemplating pissing off and maybe there was a way of juggling the both. He knew that Corrine wouldn't mind taking on some of his hours.

It was a warm day, up in the seventies, more like summer than spring, and the warmth of the day mirrored and fed the bounce that he felt in his step.

That night he had fun cutting a rug with the old man. Mick was on good form, lacerating the banks and their role in placing private property out of the reach of the common man, scorning the idea of the self regulating, organic market. He had hammered it a fair bit, half a dozen Guinness's or so meant a crash in the old man's spare room. The early morning traffic woke him up before seven, much heavier now than it had been when they had first moved in here some thirty odd years ago.

Ch, ch, changes alright and guaranteed to keep on coming.

Tommy had the literacy/employment group this morning and Bones had scored himself an interview for a store man position at a warehouse, which was located near the old docks next to the gentrified Quays. So they would have a chat about interview techniques, see if he could get the cheeky little prick to focus for more than a minute. Bones was keen though and it was good to help him get a shot. Maybe this would be a significant step away from the dross. His mind went back to King Kenny of the Northside, he'd turned it around and Bones could too.

He nicked some of the old man's smokey bacon and had a quick fry up. Mick was no longer an early riser, very early into his retirement he'd given reign to his night owl patterns. Tommy picked up the car and headed straight to the Centre, he was slightly on the nose in the clothes department. But, he'd do, Donna would have to put up with Tommy au naturelle for their lunch date.

He met her in a burger bar, which was located on the ground floor of a new office block just around the corner from the older part of the city centre. The joint was doing a roaring trade with the shirt and tie brigade. She'd scored a corner table at the street window, which offered them both a view and a modest amount of privacy. She looked a lot better than he felt. The hour with Bones had reminded him how little sleep he'd had over the last couple of nights.

Tommy got his order in and they talked, slipping into it with a comforting ease. She was adjusting to the kid being away and even starting to enjoy it, she said. They chatted about work and it was all amiable enough in a detached kind of way. They'd put the breaks on and it looked like that would be the holding pattern until…until, well he didn't know. Single life felt OK at the moment, maybe he'd reached a point where he knew what he didn't want and maybe what he wouldn't put up with too, it was about fucking time. So that was that - all amiable enough. Open ended, take care, call you soon and bye bye.

Later he trained at old man Mays and sweated out what was still left of the Guinness. Dougy's son, Daz, was there and they'd had a spar together. The young bloke was quick and busy but he'd still managed to drop it on him a couple of times, spinning him into the ropes with a short left hook and sending him across the ring with a straight right hand. The young bloke was like a raw boned Terminator though, and the belts had only led to Darrin coming back even harder at him. Tommy peek-a-booed and wrestled him for a couple of minutes but was thankful when Dougy called time - he was fucked.

Jimbo called him just after eight see if he fancied a swill but he was too tired, there was nothing on his mind but rest and sleep.

Pasquale and his mum had had the weekend together and it was OK between them; a couple of DVD's, some clothes shopping and a takeaway, it was all right enough. Pasquale felt like there was space between them now, a space that he had never known before, which was awkward in a way, but it was kind of better too, he was starting to feel more like his own man now not just her little boy. It was nice to have his old room for the weekend though. Lurch was noisier in his sleep than he was in his waking hours. Lots of bad dreams and nightly three a.m journeys to the kitchen for a soothing hot chocolate.

Pasquale had taken the opportunity of the weekend visit to stash his money up in the rafters above his bedroom, just an easy arm's grab from the hatch. He'd moved the chest of drawers across to get up there, it was all done nice and quietly - his movements masked by the sounds of her ever present Motown.

He had well over a grand saved up now - fucking mind boggling! He and Junior had talked about going into business together, maybe a recording studio or something, Jess had a great voice and though he wasn't that big on chicks rapping she was pretty good at that too. They often bounced rhymes off each other at the ref much to Neil and Kats' delight. Their free styling promptly and predictably followed by Neil snatching back the spotlight with a campy version of a show stopping tune that some wannabe had been chirping on the previous weekend's X-factor. He was as funny as fuck though and he and the girls were planning to give Britain's Got Talent a shot - pin dick Al had scoffed at that but a few words to the wiser from Kat quickly had Al singing from the same page.

His mum had dropped him off on the Sunday evening and it was a warmer goodbye between them this time. All the crew were in their usual places; Kat, Neil and Jess were out the back of the ref, Rob was blobbing out in the office, Lurch and Al were in the lounge watching some action film on the telly. The three of them had asked him about his weekend and he asked them the same about the ref. It had been quiet they told him, they'd had a one nighter in yesterday, some girl that Sonny had brought in for an emergency bed. Neil had partied a little bit down the Quarter but had pulled the pin early - saving it for next weekend.

Pasquale asked him what he had on.

Neil feigned coyness, 'a little private party next weekend

P, a night with my daddy or daddies to be accurate.' He pumped his eyebrows and pursed his lips at the girls.

'Hmmm I'll be a little saddle sore but flush with goodies – a girl has to make a living after all.'

Neil gave Pasquale a little once over.

'Pity you're straight P, they'd love you.'

'No fucking chance pal.'

'Alright, alright, chill. We all know how butch you are.'

'Tell him how much you got last time,' Jess prompted.

Neil feigned deliberation, '500 for the night – not bad eh P?'

Pasquale nodded, not bad at all, but he was working overtime trying to keep his thoughts away from what Neil had to do to make the money.

'Down the Quarter is it then – the party? Pasquale asking him just for the sake of saying something.

'Oh no P, it's all much more upmarket than the fuckin' Quarter. The Quays no less, we have a gorgeous flat to play in; city views, a spa, cock-tails on the terrace.' Neil did a little shimmy of his head – very pleased with himself.

'And that, dear boy, is all you need to know – Neil doesn't kiss and tell.'

'Kiss and tell,' Kat said, 'more like suck and tell, you slag.'

And that was much more than Pasquale wanted to know. He made his excuses and dropped his bag off in his room stopping at the office to let Rod know he was back. He went out to the lounge and joined Lurch and Al for the tail end of a Van Diesel movie.

Darrin had just done a few days of plod, teamed up this time with Johno, both of them out on the manor wearing short sleeves in the bright sunshine. The Summer was well on its way. Nothing much had happened during the week - all was quiet in Dodge. They'd chatted their shifts away with shop-keepers and local faces, helped a couple of Japanese tourists with directions to the cathedral and had kept an eye on the kids in the shopping mall and the precinct. An old Ukranian lady had been knocked over in the High Street. Her bag had been nicked and the poor old bird had dislocated her shoulder in the fall but, in a surprising, and increasingly rare show of community spirit, a couple of builders who were on their butty break had given chase and actually nabbed the fucker. He turned out to be, surprise surprise, some toe-rag from the Barrington. Go to jail son and don't pass go! Next day the builders were on the front page of the local paper looking well and deservedly chuffed with themselves. The pair of them pictured giving it the thumbs up with matching cheesy grins.

Young had called him up on Wednesday afternoon and had asked him to come down to their squad's office late afternoon the next day. He had cleared it with Sarge Thomas then hurriedly changed into his civvies at the end of his shift. He made tracks and hopped on board the light-rail across to the twin city. He knew where to find him, Young and his crew where housed in an ugly, utilitarian concrete block, which was half a dozen storeys high. The building was the nerve centre of all of the conurbation's major crime ops.

At the ground floor reception he showed his ID to the alert middle-aged cop behind the desk. Darrin got a measured nod from him and made his way on up to the fourth floor.

When he exited from the lift he couldn't see any signs to

lead him to where he needed to go. He approached a couple of fast moving, file carrying coppers who, when he asked them the way, looked at him like he was some kind of a plonker before giving him, with an overt reluctance, brusque final directions.

Young and his team were housed in a largish, corner office that Young appeared to be sharing with three other detectives. All the desks were currently occupied and everybody looked busy. Young stood up and waved him over with an easy smile and made him the offer of a brew. He said yes and Young went off to do the honours.

He took the time out to gaze through the large window that was situated behind Young's comfortable looking padded office chair. Darrin could make out the tall white columns and propellers of the wind farm up on the distant moors. A look to his left gave him a wide scope panorama of the city centre. Very fucking nice indeed.

Young quickly came back and handed him the tea, he cleared his throat and introduced him to the other men in the room. He received a smile, a couple of nods and a one-fingered salute hello.

Young took his seat and pushed a moderately thick file over the desk to him.

'Some background in there for you to peruse Darrin.'

He flicked it open, an old photo of Dalton and some personal info paperwork; his record, briefings on an Operation Holland that had taken place back in the eighties, more photos of guys who all looked vaguely familiar. They were capable, tough looking men one and all. They were the O'Brien boys and Johnny, 'they call me Mister' Tibbs.

'Yep, our very own and very infamous Saltt crew,' Young

said.

Darrin looked at the file again, 'I'm curious like Sarge, why the two t's- you know Saltt?'

'Well it's a pun PC May.'

That didn't help him and he showed it - definitely none the fucking wiser.

Young explained it to him with a slightly irksome grin on his mug.

'Well, here's one for your detective skills PC May. You've got the O'Brien boys,' Young counted them off on his fingers; 'Niall, the dearly departed Ambrose, Callum and Leo plus the one and only Mr Tibbs.'

'No, I'm still in the dark there Sarge.'

Young smiled at him again - gee the fucker loved stringing things out.

'It's the initials of their first names constable, N.A.C.L-Sodium Chloride, Salt - a t tacked on the end to account for Mr Tibbs.'

Darrin nodded, vaguely impressed, he guessed, and Young gave him another pleased looking grin like he'd thought of it all by himself.

'Cute bastards eh, and this manor's top criminals for more than thirty years now. Let me count the ways; drug smuggling, people smuggling, money laundering, prostitution and drugs. Links in the Middle East, Africa and of course, plenty of contacts in dear old Ireland.'

'Fuck!'

'Yes, fuck indeed and they are obviously, a very, very tough nut to crack.'

Young was stating the bleeding obvious there. According to the Saltt file there was barely a conviction between the main players. In fact, there was nothing at all on any of them since the late seventies. Talk about hiding in plain sight.

'So, these guys are Dalton's employers then?'

'Undoubtedly, now, speaking of which, that is where you come in. Observation of the flat - you'll be logging all the incomings and outgoings. It's all grunt work but you never know, PC May, stranger things have happened. We have a list of residents' cars and we want to know of anybody parking up there whose car is not on that list. Any taxi drop-offs that may be related to Keith Dalton etc. We'll be using a Portakabin on that bit of waste ground opposite and diagonal to the block, close enough to the entrance for a nice clear view. Our team will be looking out and nobody will be seeing in. We're going to get some boys inside when we get the go ahead too, set up some mikes in there. You never know he might get sloppy, talk some business.'

'And that, PC May, is that, I'll let you know when we know. Should all be sorted in the next few days, you never know, we might crack these cocky bastards yet.'

Darrin nodded at him. DS Young, he thought, patronising, irritating but somehow impressive too, only a little older than he was and already swimming amongst the big fishes, showing Darrin where he could be in a few years time. He wouldn't be top of Darrin's role mode list but, fair play to the guy, he was bang square in the middle of the real action.

Pasquale had had a good week at the refuge, Wendy had got him on this learning programme, which meant that he would be able to do his assignments and his exams away from school even if he was to go back home. He would still be able to access the ref's services for tutors and go to the college to use their facilities.

Up at the Coleshaw, Dwayne had been keeping them busy too. On the Thursday Johnny Talbot hadn't been there to meet them, instead it was an older guy weighed down with plenty of jewellery, putridly ponging from yards away of too much Brut cologne. The dude had thick, moist lips that reminded him of a picture he had once seen in a magazine of a large tropical fish. Much more disconcertingly, the guy had mad eyes. He was an obvious barm-pot, the nutter instantly let on that he knew who Junior was too and had front up asked him all the usual shit about his brother Wes.

'Did some bird together me and your kid like,' the dude told them. 'Used to run together back in the day we did, just like you and your quiet pal here.'

Junior smiled disinterestedly but politely at the new guy, reaching over as he did so to grab Pasquale's pack from him. Junior handed both packages over to the stranger, who, on receipt, yawned widely showing off a mouthful of gold whilst ostentatiously tugging on his tackle with an unencumbered left hand. As he did so, he exposed a scripted tattoo that started just below his ribs and ran on under his shiny red boxers.

Fishlips turned and left them without any further comment, just a desultory wave goodbye like he had much better places to be and things to do. He and Junior rode back down to the mill to have a leisurely puff. He had a few hours up his sleeve before he had to get back to the refuge, nine o'clock he'd promised them.

They parked up and Junior nimbly rolled a couple of three paper jobs.

Pasquale took a pull and they sat quietly in the warm

stillness, half listening to the muffled sound of traffic on the nearby Platt Road.

He had to ask.

'Who was that then Junior?'

Junior kept a few moments of silence and rubbed on what were the makings of a goatee.

'That, my friend, was the one and only Bazzer Dougan. Old Mad Dog himself.'

'Fuck really - wacked looking bastard in't he?'

Junior nodded, 'truly - hope it was a one off, I prefer Johnny T's pizza faced acne to that loopy fucker's ugly mug.'

'That's true man - not too pretty down the Barrington - are they?'

They had a good laugh at that and then they chilled out with their smokes for a nice stretch, neither of them mentioned M's phone call but Pasquale spent the next half an hour or so thinking about it. No degrees of separation now.

Neil came back to the refuge late on the Sunday afternoon. He was dressed head to toe in new gear with his old stuff folded up in a plastic Primark bag. He was also sporting a new earring, a diamond stud that the girls cooed over.

Neil reckoned it was worth a grand. Pasquale doubted that but it didn't look cheap either.

'New admirer then sugar boy?' Kat asked.

'New-ish pet, Daddy D introduced him to yours truly a couple of months ago - he made good on his promises this weekend.'

'Good party then?' Jess asked.

'Yes lover girl - boys only this one but Daddy D does like to mix and match sometimes. I told him about you, told him you were hot and he seemed interested. Maybe I'll get you along for the next one, if I decide to go. My new daddy might want me all to himself of course.'

Jess nodded along, ever the eager pup. She had a boyfriend of sorts - Sean, a middle class kid who came to see her at the ref now and again. Sean's Mum didn't approve of the teenage romance though and Sean didn't like hanging around at the ref for too long. He was intimidated by Kat and more than a little freaked out by Neil who flirted outrageously with him.

The others made their way inside to watch the repeat of X-Factor. He heard them laughing and squealing, telling Al to shut the fuck up when he plucked up enough bottle to ask them to be quiet.

Pasquale thought about Neil's ball squirming story for a little while. Despite the new clobber and the earring, Neil was looking rough, like he hadn't slept for a week. He was slightly wild eyed and continuously licking his lips as if he'd been stumbling through the desert for a few days. Neil was cool right enough but there was something a little bit creepy about it all.

Pasquale stretched back in the chair, he was feeling good, he had two months left here and, at the moment, he didn't want it to end. He looked up at the stone wall gable end of the building that loomed over the backyard of the refuge and thought about his mate, the owl.

A couple of mornings ago he had glanced up and there, sitting in the space left by the missing half stone at the apex of the wall, was a large, silent barn owl. It must have been there when he'd slid the backdoor open to come outside to eat his breakfast cereal but it hadn't flown away, which was cool too. At that time of the day it was always quiet inside the refuge, only Rod had been up and about when he'd got up out of his bed. Rod was bumbling around the lounge room tidying up last night's disarray. Pasquale didn't mind the early mornings and it gave him the chance to get some time alone.

He'd sat as still as he could and kept his eye on the bird as he'd hungrily spooned up the food making sure that the spoon didn't click against the side of the bowl. He pictured himself as the owl looking down at him eating the cereal and that was nice and trippy. When he turned in his chair to look at the noise Rod made when heading into the kitchen the bird picked that moment to leave its perch. In his peripheral vision Pasquale caught the blur of its silent leaving. He watched the powerful down thrust of the bird's wings as it disappeared over the next-door neighbour's slate roof. Majestic, he thought.

They'd had a meeting about the op earlier in the week. Amongst the team there was a feeling of uncertainty about the best direction for them to take. Ideally, they wanted to start making some undercover buys but, apart from a bit of weed, all the buying and selling was being done away from the shops and the pub. Probably down in the warren of the cul-de-sacs, laneways and ginnels that came off Oak Road. That meant they couldn't get anything incriminating on film and they had to be careful with anything like a direct approach, as strangers were treated with hostile suspicion on the Coleshaw and were more likely to get a kicking rather than be welcomed on board to the party that never ends. The only ray of light was the fact that Mac was ingratiating himself with the locals, largely due to his pool skills and his indefatigable ability to listen. He'd even had a couple of tokes out the back of the boozer with the Johnstones. After some moments of collective head scratching it was Mac himself who came up with a possible next move.

'I got one for yers all like, how about you lot giving me a bloody girlfriend!'

That elicited a few half-laughs, though nobody was quite sure what the fuck he was on about.

Mac fleshed out his idea.

'They probably wouldn't buy me being interested in anything beyond the weed, that's the problem with our working man thing - got me pegged as too straight for that but me with a scrubber girlfriend in tow with a taste for the heavy gear. That might work.'

Young liked it and so did DI Bowden.

'Hmmm what about Judy Crouch? She'd scrub up well.' Bowden said.

Mac nodded along to the suggestion, 'aye, she'd be good for the job our Jude.'

Bowden delegated Young to make the necessary calls and they moved on briefly to the Quays.

'Our lads are in there tomorrow,' Bowden told them, 'ready to go in there as soon as the prick makes his tracks to the warehouse. There's no land-line so we'll have to use a general voice and movement activated mike. Not ideal, but the tapes will be ready to run in the Portakabin.'

Bowden nodded over towards a lugubrious sergeant by the name of Lumb who was overseeing the technical side of the operation.

'Tapes will be picked up, replaced and then transcripted on a daily basis,' Lumb said, which was almost a speech for him. Mozzer referred to him as 'the embalmed one.'

Darrin was on duty at the Quays on the Friday and back

on with Mac on Saturday, which would be the night that the 'girlfriend' would be introduced. Apparently, Judy was a jock from up Aberdeen way so that would pre-empt the problem of any local association.

Bowden wrapped it up and, before he left, he had a brief chat with Mozzer who'd gotten past his shittiness and was even starting to be a little enthused by the energy of the team. He would have to be, because Bowden and Young wouldn't be prepared to carry a plump middle-aged rooster that no longer crowed. Moz would have to piss or get off the pot.

Anyway, they were paired up on the Friday - him on camera, Moz on headphones.

'Butch and Sundance,' according to Young, which brought a few laughs.

'Stan and Olly more like,' said Mac, which got a lot more.

The ribbing didn't bother him - Darrin was part of the team and that, for the moment, was enough.

He'd left the car at home and walked home via the old man's gym. Maybe Tommy Cochrane would be in again and they'd have another spar. He owed him one for the bruised right temple that was still a little tender to the touch. He'd jab his fucking head off this time.

Well, so much for celibacy and single life. Donna had called him late on a Thursday and invited him over for a drink and a chat at her place. They managed to kill the bottle without once mentioning the passion killer that was the kid. She had given him a look then reached over and stroked his thigh and then kept on reaching. They had fucked in the lounge - hungry and hi-energy, even on the dining room table - a work out.

Satiated they'd dragged themselves up to her pristine double bed and lay there and talked at length in the balmy night. He had one ear on the insistent sound of an owl in the nearby park - she'd never heard that before, she told him, maybe it was an omen, she said without saying of what. That made him think briefly of Bonnie. She loved her signs and portents did Bonnie, to her everything was personally relevant and everything was interconnected. He smiled at the memory and realised that he missed her a little. Donna caught the smile and mirrored it, her hand languidly stroking his abdomen.

'Feeling good babe?'

'Hmm, it's hard not to be.'

Her hand circled a little lower.

'Tired?'

'I was, but maybe not so tired now,' she laughed and bit him gently on his ear.

He woke to the sound of her in the en-suite, showering and singing softly to herself. He'd have to get moving and, this time, he definitely needed a change of clothes.

Tommy went in the bathroom and spoke to her through the fog of the shower unit, she popped her head out and they kissed then made some tentative plans for the next few days.

Weekend was off, the kid would be there and he'd let her tell him what he wanted to hear about that one. That, for her, it was best if they kept it separate, the two of them. That was more than jake with him. It meant he could put Uncle Tommy back in the cupboard. He said he'd call her and then he made tracks home - a body wash, a change of clothes and back out to work.

There was a staff meeting on today, Pauline bringing to the table the possible scenarios if they didn't get the grant. Pretty much everybody would have to go part-time including herself. He didn't mind really, he had the thing with Sonny up his sleeve and enough in the bank if he had to carry it for a while. Besides, it looked like the summer was kicking off early this year. Hot, slightly humid days and a storm predicted for the upcoming Sunday.

Sonny popped into the meeting to let them know about a couple of incidents that had happened over the weekend, it was the usual litany of urban woe. A female Asian shopkeeper abused and pushed over by a couple of white teenage girls and a school kid attacked and given a - possibly retaliatory - kicking by a group of Asian boys. Hmmm, Tommy thought, long days, school holidays and, according to the media in the irritating parlance of the day, the prospect of a barbecue summer. All of which could be a recipe for a lot of shit going down over the next couple of months. Sonny had had a chat, again, with the Asian community leaders who were confident they could keep a lid on it from their end.

Tommy's mind left the room for a while. He and Jimbo were planning a trip to York for a bit of culture leavened with a night on the turps. Jimbo reckoned there were easy pickings to be had over there, 'even for old farts like us.' Divorcee Central according to Jim, although how he gathered his data was a mystery, Tommy was pretty sure that Google didn't stretch that far. Anyway, it would be a change of pace and a visit to a town that he had always enjoyed. Summer was usually his favourite season.

Pasquale had planned to go to his Mum's but he had put it

off for another week. She'd given him a couple of chances to change his mind but he'd knocked it back both times. He could tell that the second refusal had irked her a little but she kept it to herself. The predicted storm had hit hard late Sunday evening and Jess and Neil had made a right fucking meal of it - egged on by the fact that Wendy was genuinely shit scared. He'd loved it though - it was a feast for the senses, he'd sat out the back of the refuge in the wild clamour of the noise and the flashes of light only being forced back inside when the rain had arrowed in under the awning that covered the tables and chairs. Five seconds of that and he was pissed wet through. Wendy had chided him for being 'a dill' and she'd told him to dry off and get changed.

He didn't have to accommodate Lurch any more as he had gone off to live with an Aunty, pin dick Al had moved out just a couple of days after Lurch, fostered out to a couple over near Liverpool somewhere. So, it was just the four of them now and that felt great, good company when he wanted it and the luxury of his own space too.

Pasquale took his time with the shower then joined the others for a rake of left over butties, remnants of Wendy and Neil's traditional Sunday lunch with all the bollocks thrown in - delicious. It was X-Factor night and for once he didn't mind watching the drama unfold. As he watched the box he kept one ear on the now receding storm, which was moving eastwards away towards the tops.

His mum rang the following evening, just after eight. They had talked about his day, he was doing well with his work even his maths and science was picking up a bit and they had chatted a little about the storm too. It had done some damage to the house, she'd found a leak in her bedroom and bathroom, it looked like the winds may have shifted a couple of slates. He feigned interest, but he was focussed on the upcoming days, he'd seen the weather forecast for the next few days, fine and sunny, perfect for him and Junior to crack on with it.

Later in the week Pasquale saw the flash car again cruising through the Coleshaw. Dwayne had turned to give the driver a wave. The guy had nodded in return but hadn't stopped, turning straight into Sycamore. Dwayne had watched the car for a couple of beats but had made no comment and Pasquale didn't pay it too much attention either, the car's novelty was starting to wear off a little. Dwayne gave them the five-minute mark, off to the alley and two packs each, weed and the heavy stuff, £130 in the bin. That meant he'd have £600 or more for the tin.

They pulled out of the alley just as the car was pulling out of Sycamore, the Jag swung out to the middle of Oak and the guy kept it slow, cruising on besides them. He slid down the passenger window to give him a quick look and a smile. Pasquale dredged up a smile in return and the guy turned his attention back to the road. He put his head down and picked up his pedalling - for once leaving Junior in his wake. His heart was pumping hard in his chest but not through the exertion. Junior reeled him in, quickly catching up with him at the intersection and they turned left together down towards the Barrington. The car was in a line of traffic already a couple of hundred yards ahead of them. Pasquale realised that its engine had barely made a sound.

On their first night together down the Quays, Darrin and Moz had spent fours hours in the Portakabin - ten till two a.m. It was a warm evening that had slowly turned into a cool night. They had to put the blow heater on to take the chill off.

There was no sign of Dalton until just after one. Tonight, Dalton was home alone with only some takeaway food as company. The flat door opening had activated the mike and Moz didn't bother with the headphones so that they could both listen in to the show.

It was just kitchen sounds at first, the tap being run, cupboards opened and closed, the chink of plates and then a microwave being kick started.

The mike was good alright, they could pick up his heavy breathing and the odd sigh and fart. He'd made a call on a mobile that was both brief and perfunctory - to family by the sounds of it. There were a couple of questions about his mum to his sister and a whinge about some cousins who were coming 'across the pond,' in the next month or so. From his tone it sounded like Dalton was looking forward to that event as much as a dose of the crabs.

They could hear Keithy tucking into his food, sounds of lip smacking contentment that made him aware of his own hunger - they'd killed the last of the butties over an hour ago. There was plenty of accompanying squeaks and creaks as Keith moved his bulk around on the leather sofa. Ten minutes later, the sound of the sliding of the balcony door and then the single click of a lighter. Dalton making a few self-satisfied there you go then Emperor of the Universe noises out on the balcony. A few minutes silence then a loud snort and Dalton's rasping bark of a laugh. Dalton had then stepped back into the lounge and busied himself clicking off the lights. There was the sound of a door closing then a few seconds of nothing and then another click and the bug in the bedroom picked him up. Dalton caught on tape pissing like a horse on a rock in the en-suite bog and then, after some brief ablutions, heavily hitting the hay. A prolonged silence, a couple of chow-mein farts, a little bit of tossing and turning and Keithy was out like a light, his shallow breathing becoming slow and heavy. Then they heard a light snore, Keith Dalton lying peacefully in the arms of the Sandman.

He and Moz gave each other a look - quarter to two and that was it, all wrapped up. They were both suitably impressed by the clarity of the mikes, both hungry and starting to get tired. They agreed on a late night kebab and a bit of a debrief. Mozzer was still a little sceptical as to the value of it all.

'Too fucking smart he is Darrin, no land-line see. No names on the mobile, unless he brings somebody back there, and then they start talking business. What the fuck are we going to get from it, apart from the soundtrack of him enjoying the good life?'

Moz shrugged irritably at it all.

Darrin focused on his kebab and let Mozzer wind down.

'Remember what you told me Moz - patience, patience.'

For once Moz offered no riposte and then he nodded at him with a rueful smile.

'You're right son, taught you well then, din't I Dazzle boy?'

Darrin saluted him with the remainder of his kebab, 'that you did Moz that you did - now eat yer bloody grub.' No harm in keeping the prick happy now was there?

York had been a blast and Jimbo had been right, Quasimodo

would have pulled in that town. They had pulled two women as light and easy as the Artful Dodger picking a pocket or two. The four of them had finished the evening cosied up in a smart little semi somewhere on the edge of town and they'd had a little private party. After the consensuals they had a couple of hours sleep and then a taxi back to the B and B to make sure that they didn't miss the fry up.

The weekend had satiated him, he didn't feel in any rush to call Donna and he didn't feel any guilt about it either. He would give some time to catching up with the old man instead. In fact it felt good to be more measured with her, after all, steady as it goes had not been his normal modus operandi and he'd too often had to repent his haste at leisure. For most of his adult life he had oscillated between the two ends of the spectrum, plenty of meaningless but usually enjoyable sex, interspersed with longish, monogamous relationships in which the possibility of marriage, settling down and kids had always been there, shimmering somewhere in the mid-distance but, ultimately, proving to be just a trick of the light. He'd felt that familiar compulsion with Donna, to love and be loved, get in there boots and all. The old, old pattern but the enforced time out because of dramas with the kid and her subsequent pulling away had established parameters that he was happy enough with.

She called him on the Thursday at the Centre. She'd had a bit of roof damage from the weekend's storm and had suffered a leak that had slightly stained her en-suite wall. She'd booked a roofer to come around tomorrow morning, a friend of a friend, she said.

That evening they went out for a meal and he boxed smart and brought a change of clothes, which meant there would no rushing around before work and it would also give him the opportunity to find out if her en-suite shower unit could comfortably accommodate two adults.

His mum had called him on Friday to say that she couldn't pick him up and could he get a cab over to her place tomorrow morning. Pasquale arrived there at about eleven and knocked briskly on the door. She opened up, well grim faced. No hello, no embrace, no kiss. He followed her into the lounge and saw the issue in hand before she had to refer to it. His money tin was on the dining room table - lid off and conspicuously empty.

Pasquale looked at her and waited and she did the same. He was conscious of the click of the kitchen wall clock and the fact that he couldn't keep his right foot still - it silently percussioned out a jittery tattoo on her beloved carpet.

The fucking storm! He thought, cursing his luck.

Her eyes gestured towards the tin, 'well Pasquale?'

He didn't know what to say, he was caught inertly between offence and defence.

He shrugged his shoulders.

'Where did you get the money - tell me?'

'Ermmm, me and Junior we been…'

She raised her eyebrows, no prompts to help him get there, no gap filling.

'Working,' he finished.

'Working! Working doing what exactly Pasquale?'

The game was up but he stayed quiet - silence seemed to be the best fall back position.

There was no way off the hook though he knew that he was fucked.

'You and Junior are doing what, to make that kind of money Pasquale?'

He shook his head at her, his eyes filling slightly with the frustration.

She did a little half turn and swept the tin off the table. It bounced off the sofa and hit the radiator under the lounge room window - she was as mad as hell.

'Tell me, or I'll call the police and you can tell them instead.'

That snapped him out of it.

'OK, OK we were doing errands.'

'Errands?'

'Yeah, moving weed around on our bikes from the Coleshaw to the Barrington.'

He shrugged his shoulders - what's the big deal?

Her eyes went inward slightly.

'Who for?'

He shook his head.

'Who for Pasquale? It's me or the police - choose.'

'Alright, alright. A guy called Dwayne, Junior knows him. For fucks sake!'

'For fucks sake!' She yelled back. She slapped him, hard, across the side of the head. The blow knocked him off balance and it dizzied him too.

Pasquale steadied himself, his arms rigid at his side his fists curled and pulsing.

The tears came then and the anger.

'You can fuckin' talk!' He shouted.

'What do you mean?' she hissed. Her eyes flicking towards the nearest neighbouring wall.

'You, you did it for years. How did we get that first house

eh? You only ever did cleaning work. You think I'm daft you do. You made it that way, why not me?'

She sighed and took a step towards him but he backed away.

Her face had softened, slightly.

'Listen love, listen. You are putting yourself at risk Pasquale. You are putting everything at risk, your future love, your future.' She looked down and shook her head. 'I'm not proud of what I did Pasquale but I had less choice than you do now, you understand that don't you?'

He nodded, 'where's my money Mum?'

'In the bank Pasquale, I opened an account for you.'

He looked at her quizzically - what was she on.

'Two signatures till you are eighteen and then it's yours.'

He nodded, mollified a little.

'No more though Pasquale, if I get a whiff of it again I go to the police, in a flash. No more chances, this is it. Are you sure it's just weed Pasquale?'

'Yes Mum, just weed,' fixing his will on holding her gaze.

'You do remember Matthew, don't you?'

'Of course I do - fucking hell Mum!'

'Well keep that in mind eh Pasquale, Matthew - sixteen and all gone.'

She held her hand out and softly touched his face - he flinched but he let her do it and then he let her keep it there.

'You have all the talent in the world son, please don't throw it away.'

She turned and went through to the kitchen. He stayed in the lounge, stock-still and silent. He wondered if he could continue to keep the rest of it from her, no Dwayne this weekend, he thought, that would be more than pushing it, it would be dumb. He'd give Junior a bell on Monday maybe announce his retirement. Fuck, he thought, three, four hundred a week down the shitter. He went up to his room and stayed there until she called him down for lunch.

JULY

Keith Dalton had thrown them a curve ball, Tuesday night he'd rocked up in the Jag with a young blonde couple in tow, possibly siblings, according to the boys on the watch. They'd had drinks together in the lounge and on the terrace and then Keith had proceeded to 'entertain' the pair of them in his bedroom. Mozzer had happily given him all the unnecessary details when they had taken their turn in the Portakabin on the Friday. By Mozzer's account, it had been a cavalcade of sucking, fucking, moaning and grunting. Plus, and opinion was mixed as to whether this was a good thing or a bad thing, they had lost the mike in the bedroom. A few minutes into the cavorting there had been a loud crash and then nothing. Silent, up until a spent Keithy's heavy tread had activated the mike in the lounge, Dalton hoarsely calling out to the young ones, asking them if they wanted more drinks.

So that was that - they could try and get back in there but, as yet, the young couple had hardly left the joint since the bounce around. Keithy had come back home with bags of food and plenty of booze on the Thursday. It looked like his friends would be staying for a while.

Still, they had the lounge room mike - Dalton was regularly on the mobile, still only nicknames and initials with no obvious point of reference in the conversations. He was as cute and careful as a shithouse rat.

Saltt had an office and warehouse down on the freight yards and a car breaker's business near the edge of the city but both businesses had night watchmen and there had not

223

yet been a safe opportunity to get their tech' boys into either place without raising suspicion. Plus, DI Bowden was pretty sure that the O'Briens would sweep both premises on a regular basis - the O'Briens and Tibbs had not stayed at the top of their tree through incaution. The bottom line was that the cops had been trying to put it on that band of brothers for more than thirty years and the Saltt crew had been and were still at least a couple of steps ahead of the law and its agents. There had been whispers, of course, of there being a hidden, helping hand from within. But there had never even been a sniff of evidence, never mind any concrete proof, of a source or sources from within the ranks of the thin blue line. It was just the usual urban paranoia.

Mac had introduced June, his 'missus', to the regulars at The Admiral and had scored a bit of puff for the pair of them. Johnstone's beef head brother had given him the smoke and Mac had casually dropped in how 'her indoors' liked a bit of the heavier stuff. Pete Johnstone had laughed at that and advised that Mac get her on the game, as he'd need the brass - sound advice.

One recent development had pricked their interest on the Friday shift. Dalton had been caught talking to Blair and Cass, his houseguests, about a party that he would be throwing at the flat in a couple of week's time. Dalton had purringly reassured the pair that they would be 'the stars of the show' and chances were that the two of them were not being booked in to perform magic tricks.

So, at least there was now the feeling of things moving forward and that sense of momentum was helping Darrin deal with the mundane part of the job. This month had seen a continuation of the fine May weather, long warm days and evenings - fine enough to put the spring in anybody's step, and there had been plenty of street activity too for them to deal with. They'd had a small scale stand off at the precinct between some Leeside Asian lads and a group over from the Barrington. They'd nipped that in the bud before it had got out of hand - both camps given the bum's rush whilst swaggeringly keeping face.

He was up for another weekend away too, this time to see to a top, big-name Cuban band that would be playing at the Roundhouse in London. After the gig there was a big salsa party, which was happening in a nearby club. Jolika had sorted some digs out for them in Camden, which seemed to be ridiculously expensive. Still, fuck it, he was on the overtime with plenty more to come. Maybe Keithy Dalton would string them along till Christmas and keep him quids in. Darrin laughed that off, he was turning into Mozzer fucking junior.

Tommy had seen her for lunch and throughout the meal she had looked a little strained and the kid had been conspicuous by his absence from the conversation. He had mooted the idea of a trip down to London to stay with Lee and Bernie for the weekend and she'd brightened a little at the thought of that, but she had ended the discussion with an even, 'we'll see.'

It was looking like one of those days. When he got to work, Pauline had told him about an overdose that had taken place over the weekend. The body was found in the stairwell of one of the Coleshaw mid-rises and it had turned out to be the uncle of one of the boys who usually came down for the basketball on Thursday nights. The kid was a good little

soccer player too and had even played a bit for one of the local team's first eleven, which was no mean achievement for
a sixteen year old. Pauline had known the guy when he was
on the straight, a tradesman who had done some work on her
place years ago, she'd lost track of him and now she knew
why.

'Sad, sad, sad,' she'd told him at his office door, 'thirty
bloody six.' She was off to the funeral on Friday.

Donna had called him the next day and inveigled an in-
vite to his for some food. He didn't mind, it would be nice
to cook for somebody else. He hadn't done it for years apart
from helping Mick with a Sunday roast when they couldn't
be bothered with the pub. He'd been subsisting for a long
time on a rotating menu of his repertoire of six old favourite
dishes and variations there-of.

They'd had a good evening, he'd cooked a seafood lasagne,
which was as about as complicated as it got for him in the
kitchen. After the food they watched an easily digested rom-
com for sexy seniors with Jack Nicholson and Diane Ke-
aton. After that they had explored each other's bodies in the
long twilight. She was horny, even a little frenzied - pressing down vigorously on him with her eyes closed, her head
slightly turned away from him. Not that he minded, she had
a great body, which he examined with a pleasurable detach-
ment as he felt the heat in his loins inevitably swell and burst.

They lay quietly together for a while as she was turned
towards the bedroom wall. Tommy was slowly running his
fingers from her ribs to her hip.

'London,' she said.

'London?'

'Yeah, those friends of yours, it sounds like fun Tommy.

I'd like that, be good for us to get away.'

Nice one, he thought, he'd call Lee tomorrow. Be interesting to see what they think of her.

Tommy continued to hold her and was just starting to drift off when she started to press back into him. This time it was languid and gentle and she called out his name when he rubbed her to climax.

He gave Lee a bell that morning from work. Lee said he'd run it by Bernie but he was sure it would be fine. They were playing a gig that Saturday, a reggae cover band, Mash it Up, mostly Marley and Peter Tosh. It was a nice earner for the two of them.

Sonny had rained on the parade slightly, calling him to let him know that a group of young guys had steamed into one of the local Asian green-grocers yesterday and had pushed a customer to the floor and damaged some of the shelving and stock. They had taken off for the Coleshaw and a group of older Asian guys had given chase. Some of the locals had got into it with the posse when the Asian crew had skidded to a halt near The Admiral. Just verbals at first with a few of the local kids and then some bozos had spilled out of the boozer, enough of them for the Asian guys to hit reverse and get the fuck out of Dodge. Sonny was a little worried, tensions on the rise and all that - he was heading up to the Coleshaw today to chat to some of the young-uns and he'd also asked the cops for a bit more street presence but they were already stretched too thin to cover more bases. Sonny had been philosophical about it as per.

'If it is to go off Tommy, then it is in the lap of the one true God.'

'Gods Sonny, shouldn't that be Gods?'

'What are you then Tommy, a bloody Hindu fella?'

'Not really Sunil, don't mind the Madras though.'

Sonny laughed, 'pagan you are Tommy, a bloody devil.'

'And gonna stay that way Sonny.'

'Amen to that brother.'

He had a few quiet moments after the call and he thought about Donna for a while. It was moving forward between them but he'd fallen into love before at the first hint of tenderness and he was more than a little tired of that old, sad pattern. His life as a serial monogamist, stumbling in and out of relationships, wounded but none the wiser. Too often he'd been in love with the euphoria of falling in love. He'd had more than a decade of it - setting up the love nest, experiencing the slings and arrows of life together, reality inevitably reasserting itself, then the hitting of the wall and the packing of the bags. A change of address, a little time alone, then he'd be out looking for it again. Good for developing resilience but compulsively dumb too. That had been the pattern right up until meeting and losing Bonnie. But, he'd come through that too and here he was, back in the place that he'd thought he'd left behind. Home, he thought, where the fuck is it and what the fuck is it? He still wasn't sure.

Pasquale mulled it over and then he'd texted Junior to tell him that he wouldn't be doing a run the following day. Instead, he'd hung around the refuge. More changes were on the way here too. There was now a supported living arrangement in place for Kat, which included ongoing educational support for her too. Kat was pleased with it but he could tell that she was apprehensive, she was having a lot more quiet moments and she was a little more snappy than usual with both Neil and Jess. Thank god Al wasn't still at the ref. She would have bitten his head off.

There was a new kid coming in tonight and he'd be sharing the room with him, a younger one this time, which should be OK. The staff had had a meeting about the admission this morning. He was from down south somewhere and that didn't augur well for the amount of shit that he was likely to take. Neil and Jess had been chatting excitedly about Daddy D's upcoming party and Neil had teasingly insinuated an invitation to him, which he had blanked completely.

Junior had called him the next day - no pressure, he said. He had some smoke if he fancied it, meet up at the mill. Junior was there before him, a smoke rolled and already blasting. He looked up and smiled and tossed its twin to Pasquale. They chatted around a few things. Junior was still intent on going down to Haringey before his brother got out.

Pasquale didn't offer much comment, he was OK up here at the moment, Haringey had lost its lustre for him. It was chill being at the ref.

'Dwayne asked where you were yesterday. I told him you'd pulled the plug.'

'He OK with it?'

'Yeah suppose, kind of. He reckons we were his best boys like, more reliable than the raggedy arses up there on the Coleshaw - the top boys us P, he knows it too.'

Pasquale liked that right enough but he feigned indifference to the compliment.

'Said he'd up the money for us too if we decide to come back to it.'

That got his interest.

'Yeah - 60 for the smoke he said and a fucking ton for the

ice! Can't turn it over fast enough he reckons, there were more cops up there at the weekend though, he's bugging about that. We had to pull away from the shop to talk. You know, get down to those lanes. Bit boring it was like, hanging about down there.' Junior shrugged his shoulders.

Fucking hell, Pasquale thought, a ton for the ice!

'I'd have to find a new stash,' he said to Junior.

Junior nodded towards the corner of the mill.

'Look down there, down there, next to yer,' Junior straightened his long arm and pointed just to the right of him with his boney index finger. Pasquale got it, a loose brick with most of its mortar gone, positioned almost right in the corner of the building.

'That'll move easy enough P.'

Pasquale tried it and it did, there was a few inches of space behind the brick and the outer wall of the building.

'Your mum's not going to find that, is she?'

Pasquale stood up and grabbed his bicycle.

'Where you off to bro'?'

'Pound shop J, get myself a new tin.'

Junior laughed, sprang to his feet and wiped the dust from the arse of his jeans.

'Top man - we back in business then?'

Pasquale laughed, 'never really left it bro'.'

Junior sent a text to Dwayne from outside the pound shop, thirty seconds later and the reply came through. He'd have a bag each for them, now.

A hundred smackers, Pasquale thought, like shelling fuckin' peas.

Darrin had worked overtime every evening apart from the

Friday, two days on the Coleshaw and a couple of shifts down at the Quays, the first with Mozzer and a few pleasant hours with Jolika who was binning the readies for the London weekend.

Mac had been down The Admiral on both nights, one with June one without and he'd managed to get into Dwayne for some crystal meth for his 'old lady'. Dwayne hadn't said yes but he hadn't said no either, maybe he was waiting to run it past Johnstone, covering his arse before he took the plunge with a new customer.

Somewhat embarrassingly, both for him and Jolika, randy old Keith and his house guests had chosen their shift to use the lounge for some gymnastics. The fucker was insatiable and all the permutations had appeared to have been tried. The girl was particularly loud and he and Jolika had laughed, awkwardly, at her protracted yodellings. Thankfully, Dalton had a bit of mood music on, maybe as a safeguard against startling the neighbours.

In regards to his movements there was nothing doing, Dalton was as predictable as the lunar cycle. He was out of there most mornings around about eight, they'd done a little tail on him from the flat but there was no meat on that bone. He was clocking on down at the Saltt warehouse in the nearby freight yards - just like a regular working Joe. The young-uns seemed to spend most of the day in the pit, rousing themselves in the late afternoons. They often went out in the evenings and always came back shit faced. The upshot of it all was that the flat was rarely empty and that there was no way that they could get another mike in there. Not that the mike was bringing any great reward, only more chat about the upcoming party. Dalton was always cagey, still only using names on the mobile when he spoke to either his mum or his sister.

Young had called him up on Thursday. The night before June had gone into The Admiral wearing a wire and they now had Dwayne firmly by the bollocks - product and price clearly caught on the tape. After a brief discussion with June and Mac, Dwayne had told her to meet him in the lane that backed up between Linden and Sycamore. Dwayne had handed June a ton's worth of ice, Dwayne's fingerprints were all over the package, bang to fucking rights indeed.

However, Young and Bowden didn't want to pull him in just yet. They wanted to hold back on it, banking on Dwayne still being an in to Johnstone and the possibility of a bust higher up the food chain. The team were happy with that, nobody was of the opinion that Dwayne was going anywhere, it was a just a matter of turning the calendar pages before Dwayne would meet his destiny.

During the days, he was foot patrolling around the precinct, the new shopping mall and the High Street. Patrols had been upped for the summer months as some of the natives had been getting restless. Things hadn't really kicked off up here for over twenty years and the Chief and the Super had made it crystal that they wanted it to stay that way.

Friday he'd had a session with the old man; circuits, some weights, pad and bags. He was revved alright - work busy - social life buzzing.

The weekend was over before he knew it - the band was a blast although he found the Roundhouse a little too crowded for his taste. He'd quickly tired of the pull and sway of the crowd so, half an hour into the set, he'd made his way over to the margins of the audience. He had quickly been pounced upon by a group of youngish Latina women, one of whom was drop dead gorgeous, edible in a backless, gravity defying dress and four inch heels. They played pass the parcel with him for the rest of the set and by the end of the gig he was drenched in sweat. The girls were off to some party in Archway and the stunner had given him the address. Darrin was tempted, but they'd already shelled out for the after gig party and he knew that there would be plenty of talent there too. He couldn't see Jolika, Stuart or any of the crew that had made the trip down amongst the exiting crowd but, when he stumbled outside into the busy Camden streets, Jolika and Stu were already out there, chatting to some short, good looking salsero. According to the fliers he had in his hand he was a dance teacher down in Brighton - using the gig to tout for business. The three of them were talking about a festival in France that was coming up in August, three days of bands and dancing. It looked like supply was matching demand in the salsa world.

They got to the party at about two and left it in the light of the early morning. He'd scored, not scored, scored and not scored again and, in the end, he just didn't care, happy to let himself be carried away by the buzz. Three hours kip, up to pack, breakfast and back to Euston. Darrin was out for the count before they passed Wembley Stadium and he awoke to the announcement that the train was pulling into Macclesfield.

Donna had called him to say that the kid was going to be home for the next two nights but that she was still definitely on for the London trip. Tommy organised the next Friday afternoon off, the Centre owed him some hours for the unpaid overtime that he'd racked up through working at the monthly safe raves.

Pauline was still palpably sweating it on the Centre getting the big money. The Lottery had contacted her to let her know that the funding decisions were to be made in the next few days.

Pauline had learned to develop stoicism and patience in her role but it was obvious that the uncertainty was plaguing her. She had tuned out immediately after giving him the update, absently scratching her head for a few seconds as she looked out through her office window, the view from which was probably her only concession to her status at the Centre, a wide angle vista of the wild and lonely moors.

Tommy coughed and she came back to the room turning away from the window with a wan smile.

'We can plan ahead then, when we find out,' she told him, 'you know Tommy, twenty five years hard work and we still have to bloody wing it.'

'It's not that bad Pauline, it will all still be here long after we're gone.'

'Hmmm, it would be nice to share your optimism Tommy, but there are plenty of others, just as good as we are, that have folded love. The bloody funding tap switched off, making do with volunteers rather than paid staff…hmmm.' Another look out of the window and another strained 'what can you do?' smile.

'Hey - worst option, like you said, we all go to part time. That's OK eh? it's not ideal but it's not the end of the world either. We can keep looking for other sources of dough, you know, use more volunteers ourselves if we have to, keep the programmes going - no problem.'

'Ah well Thomas, I guess at least we will soon know - thanks for the support though love - appreciate it.'

He nodded and smiled but he didn't have any pep talk left. Some shit was just out of your hands.

Thursday he had run over to Donna's after an hour or so chewing the fat with the old man. Mick had been venting about free schools this time, brandishing *The Observer* as he did so. Corporate capitalism by stealth was Mick's take on it. 'Everything is about a quid with these fuckers - you watch. It'll be bloody hi-jacked by big business and the bloody holy rollers. If I were younger Tommy I tell yer, I'd be gone from here in a flash and fuck the lot of them.'

When a little of the steam had boiled off, he managed to steer his old man on to cricket and they'd talked about taking a trip on the train up to Durham. Catch a one dayer up there somewhere near the end of the season - the old man was up for it, train travel and cricket - two of Mick's staples.

Donna had warmed up some curry that was left over from the previous day for tea and they had chilled out for a while after the food, watching a show about four soft English kids who had been shooed off to some retirement joint in California to test their comparative fitness levels with the resident oldies. The show was a classic example of the body following the mind. The relentless 'can do' spirit of the American retirees and the embarrassment of the kids at getting their arses kicked by people fifty years their senior had, eventually, whipped the young ones out of their affectations and torpor. He'd found it surprisingly inspirational and the show had left him feeling positive about what a little bit of will, support and good attitude could achieve. Tommy had made to share his thoughts with Donna but it didn't look as if the show had

had the same impact on her. Maybe she had a steeper hill to climb before she touched down in the Promised Land.

There was a look on her face that he hadn't seen before - dark was the word that came to mind.

He asked her if she was OK and she told him no, he asked her why and she told him.

There it was; the kid, the roof, the tin, the money, the fucking drugs.

At first he was surprised, then, with a little reflection, not surprised at all. She had found over a grand in there - fuck.

He asked her if she wanted him to speak to Sonny and she gave him an emphatic no, even looking a little annoyed with the suggestion.

'I'll do it if I have to Tommy - he's my son.'

That pierced him a bit but he bit down on any words that he may soon live to regret. Shut the fuck up, he told himself, willing himself, with no little effort, into a neutral space.

'What are you going to do then Donna?'

'Give him a chance Tommy, I'll call the refuge, see what he's been up to after school and then if he lets me down…'

'Hmm, well lets hope he doesn't,' thinking that maybe the kid needed the fall. He'd had a lifetime of being given chances - the little twat.

'Just weed eh?'

'That's what he says Tommy.'

He breathed out heavily, reluctantly climbing into the back seat and letting her stay in charge of it. He wondered how long he would be able to keep his mouth shut.

'You're still sure about coming down to London?' he asked.

She nodded and put her hand on his shoulder.

'Yes, do me good - stop me moping about all this nonsense for a while.'

Tommy nodded at her although he wasn't convinced that 200 miles and some quality reggae covers would be enough for that job. Jimbo had called him earlier in the week, asking if he was interested in taking a package trip to Thailand in November. He'd been lukewarm in response although he hadn't binned it either. Maybe he'd green light it. He could feel the pressure dropping all around him with the prospect of a bumpy ride ahead. Tommy looked around the room and he made the inventory: Donna, the overkill photo collection, the delicately tasteful origami and her stupid little prick of a son.

This week was to be the last regular week of lessons, just a few group tutorials and then the summer break. Plenty of leisure activities had been put forward by the refuge staff with input and feedback from the residents but they were all optional. That left him with plenty of time to hang out and chill. The ref now had a leaving date for Kat and she'd already been to her new flat with a female worker for a try-out sleep-over.

Neil and Jess were revving up for the party at the weekend. Jess had given Sean the arse, again, and was now 'young, free and single.'

'Maybe not free pet,' Neil reminded her.

The new kid, Liam, was kind of OK, quite self contained and pretty sharp and the others didn't seem to mind him either. He smoked like a chimney but shared his fags out and that kept him in brownie points. He made a point of taking the piss out of the workers, particularly Rob, who took his shit with a slightly disconcerting good humour. Pasquale didn't trust the little fucker as far as he could throw him. Liam had asked him a couple of times if he could come along for the ride in the afternoon and he'd abruptly palmed him off. He'd appeared unperturbed by the rebuff and it hadn't stopped the fucker from asking again. Dwayne was keeping them busy; regular runs and now some smaller packs direct to the customer. He'd done a run on the Coleshaw itself, a short ride over to one of the piss stinking mid rises near The Admiral pub. Some lank haired bird had answered the door. Her old man had given him a casual glance and a half-smile from the dump of the lounge/kitchen. The guy was a short, tough looking old dude and Pasquale had found his gaze a little disconcerting, he didn't look like a user-loser either, definitely not.

He'd had a couple of pangs about his mum as he peddled it but he reckoned he could keep it separate if he was smart. She was away this weekend too - friends she'd told him - probably Tommy from her look but he didn't give a flying fuck.

On Friday the Jag had pulled up next to them as they were chatting with one of Dwayne's boys, the three of them were hanging out down between Linden and Sycamore - Junior didn't like it down there, he preferred the shops and the pub, to him it was all the same, just part of the same fucking dump - no difference at all.

The guy had given them a warm hello, his eyes flicking over Junior and Bailey but finally coming to a rest on him, as he instinctively knew that they would.

'Hope you boys are behaving yourselves.' No context, no build up to the words. He was a jarring fucker.

They all nodded but remained mute, Pasquale felt his

heart race again, his gaze held by the man's smiling, watery, blue eyes.

'How old are you son?' he asked Pasquale.

'Sixteen.' he managed, pleased at sounding level with it.

'Sixteen eh…good age that - sixteen.'

The guy gave him a wink then a raspy laugh.

'Later boys,' and then he pulled away to make the turn into Sycamore.

Pasquale looked at Junior who grimaced and spat on the floor.

'Creepy fucker he is,' Junior said.

Pasquale nodded but Bailey said nothing and if he had bothered to speak he still would have said nothing. A shrill whistle told them that Dwayne was ready for them down in the alley. Bailey took up post whilst they made their way to the rendezvous point.

'New batch this fuckin' lot boys,' Dwayne had told them on meet up, 'better quality for the same fuckin' price, tell Johnny to pass that onto the fuckin' crew down there. Sell the product and the fuckin' product sells itself. Off you fuckin' go then lads.'

They wheeled away and this time they made the trip by a different route. Dwayne had told them that they needed to mix it up a bit, warning them against predictability, this from a guy who never left the fucking estate!

Pasquale looked over his shoulder and saw that Dwayne was heading back down Oak towards the shops. He felt a momentary anxiety pass through him that didn't really make any sense. He kick-started his bike and did a slingshot around the corner, already trailing in Junior's wake.

The following week was even busier than the previous one. Darrin had alternated the nights between the Quays and the Coleshaw. There had been no sign of Keithy Dalton up on the estate but he'd been keeping up the family contact with brief nightly chats with the mum and the sister. There was also plenty of talk around Saturday's soiree - Dalton doing plenty of thinking with his dick.

Young and Mac had chatted about the possibility of pulling Dwayne in to put some pressure on, see how far up the food chain he might go. Young wasn't confident that Dwayne would fold though and he was advocating keeping it slow and steady like he was a fucking oil tanker captain, eyes to be kept on the bigger prizes down the line. Mac was a little pissed off with the holding pattern though, the kid coming to the door had rankled him.

'Little fucker, well dressed and cold eyed, all fucking business he was the little shit - Jesus.' But Mac saw the merit in Young's argument. Johnstone the Elder was still keeping his distance from him; no drug talk, no money talk - nothing. Johnstone had done a few years stir though and that tended to keep a thinking man cautious. Mac was starting to see how bigger fish like the Saltt crew might be happy to have a man like him on board.

'Ignore the shell suit and you've possibly got a three figure IQ,' was Mac's reassessment.

Darrin regularly spotted the two kids that he and Moz had interviewed about Matthew Marshall, the lad in the skip. They were fixtures up on the Coleshaw appearing or already present whenever he was on. The pair of them were now hanging out well away from the pub, usually about three-quarters of the way down Oak. He was starting to pay particular attention to them, clocking them this evening as they chatted with Dwayne and a couple of the younger boys. A simple pattern to their movements quickly emerged, a meet up and chat with Dwayne and whichever of his cohorts happened to be hanging around, then the two of them disappearing down the lane whenever Dwayne made tracks, the pair reappearing five or so minutes later on Oak then hitting it away from the estate and a left turn into Strickland. Darrin wondered if a tail would be feasible on the up-to-no-good little fuckers. He couldn't see how they could nab them on the estate, there were too many people around to alert the pair to their presence. In transit would be better but that was manpower and they were stretched as it was. Darrin sighed, logistics - what a fucking headache.

He'd pulled up at the Portakabin after salsa on Thursday, too revved up to just go home and he took a pew in there with Young and Lumb. Tonight, there was just the young couple in the flat, occasionally shouting at each other over the sound of the blaring TV. No sign of Keithy himself, maybe he was out getting the party hats and condoms for this Saturday night.

Darrin pulled the pin about midnight, nodding off at the table whilst reluctantly listening to some dance music shit on Dalton's sound system. The inconsiderate fuckers had been whooping it up a little bit to the music, the pair not paying much heed to Dalton's daily instructions for them to keep it down. Dalton must have tolerant neighbours, he thought, they wouldn't be getting away with that shit next door to his gaff.

Friday and it was plod time around the centre on yet another beautiful warm day. The pubs, inevitably, were doing a lively trade. Last night there had been another dust up near the precinct, an argument in the kebab shop had escalated out of control and some little fucker had pulled a knife and chivved another customer, a young Asian guy. The shop owners had chased the protagonist off, but Sarge Thomas had stressed again the need to be proactive, 'nip it in the bud boys and girls - Mount Olympus,' a theatrical raising of his bushy eyebrows to the heavens, 'is getting nervous and that means they start giving me shit and that means' - he sardonically looked around the room, 'you know the rest.'

Darrin asked Jolika if she fancied some of his overtime and thankfully she stepped in to pick it up. He'd be down the Quays on Saturday and he would be staying there until Dalton's party wound up and that would make it a very long day. He went over to his folk's place and let his mum feed him. After the grub, the old man pulled the pin to head off to the gym for a few hours and he sat down with his mum on the sofa watching the box and answering her mildly probing questions with an abridged version of that which constituted his life and his career.

She liked the fact that he was dancing salsa. Back in the day she'd been nifty on her pins herself but the old man had to be put into a half-nelson to get up and shake his stuff. He marvelled at her loyalty to his father, thirty years living in his shadow and the day in day out accommodation of the old man's restless truculence.

He asked her how she would feel if he was to transfer away.

She gave him her gentle appraisal, 'thinking of it, are you then Darrin love?'

'Not yet Mum, let's see how things pan out first.'

She laughed, 'always looking to the next thing eh our Darrin? It's alright love, as long as you still come home and see us.'

And that was that - she was OK with it. Not that it would have made any difference if she wasn't. In that regard he knew that he was his father's son.

Friday night he and Junior had heeded Dwayne's advice and taken a different route to the Barrington, they'd headed down through Leeside this time. Junior had pulled over for a pit stop at the offie on Prince Street. He'd promised his mum he'd pick her up a packet of fags. They would do the drop then run the smokes over to his mum on their way back to Dwayne. The offie was a Paki shop that he and Junior scored cans in from time to time. On making their way back out of the shop they found that this time they had company. An older Asian guy with a fair bit of facial fuzz was sat on Junior's bike bigging it up to his mates. They were a crew of five or six lads, mid to late teens, all of them would be locals - the Leeside boys never strayed that far apart from the area with its grid of uniform redbrick terraces. Junior took a breath and implacably told the dickhead to get off the bike. The guy smirked at his mates - not for having it was he.

'Nah, I fancy a ride chap - Az! Grab the other one. Let's take 'em for a spin.'

The guy turned the wheel to move off as the tallest of his mates stepped forward to grab Pasquale's bicycle. Pasquale already had his hands on the handles and frame, no fucking way. As the tall guy came forward, Junior shot out his right arm and caught the ringleader in the shoulder, the blow as fast as fuck. The guy hit the shop wall but just about managed to stay on board the bike - his cheeks now flush with colour. A ripple of unease ran round the group and they held their positions. Az had backed off about half a step from Pasquale, a little uncertain now. Behind them they heard some bustle followed by a loud bellow from the door of the shop, Mr Shamir, as angry as a wild hog and as loud as a banshee.

'You little bastards - you bring bloody trouble here, leave these boys alone you bloody bastards.'

Mr Shamir took a surprisingly quick step forward past Pasquale and grabbed hold of Az by a handful of his hair pulling him up onto his toes.

'And what did I tell you before, that I go and talk to your bloody parents, tell them what little bastards you are.'

Aziz was in a lot of pain but was keeping his mouth shut. The other guy quickly hopped off Junior's bike and held up his hands placatingly to Mr Shamir. Telling him with little conviction that they were just having fun.

Mr Shamir was not a taker.

'Bullshit and cobblers boy! You, you are a little bastard Mansoor, always the bloody trouble maker round here, better that you get a bloody job, you lazy bastard.'

He threw Aziz into a couple of his mates who stumbled a little as they broke his trajectory. The group took that as their cue to beat it, all of them were going in the same direction now, quickly away from a still pissed off Mr. Shamir.

Mr Shamir huffed and snorted a couple of times, his hands on his hips, glaring after their retreat. The boys took a right into nearby Thomas Street, getting out of his sight as quickly as possible.

Mr Shamir turned his attention to them - becalmed now by the back down.

'OK boys you can go now, that way.' He had nodded in the opposite direction to Thomas Street, 'is probably the best for you.'

Pasquale and Junior voiced their thanks and Mr Shamir went back into his shop. They'd have to get a leg on now, late already, which was not a good habit to get into. Leeside would be avoided in the future though - fuck Dwayne and his alternate routes.

Despite the little dark cloud that was hanging around up north, they had managed to have a good weekend together. Tommy wasn't sure how she would hit it off with his mates but he needn't have worried. Donna and Bernie talked their way through most of the Friday and it was all a breeze to Lee, the happily self-contained sod. Another little dark cloud had manifested itself before he had left his work at the Centre. Pauline had announced at the staff meeting that they had only received a quarter of the money they had asked for from the Lottery. So, it meant hours would have to be cut across the board and, in just a couple of month's time Pauline herself would be going down to four days a week. She was giving those who wanted it the opportunity to reduce their hours on a voluntary basis and then she and the treasurer would sit down and make the necessary adjustments.

But, she promised, nobody will be losing their job. This, she said, with a little pugnacious jut of the jaw and a lift of the head that, perhaps a little ungraciously, put him in mind of a diminutive red headed Mussolini.

Tommy had chatted to Pauline after the meeting, patiently taking his turn behind Helen, the rather comely young manager of the pre-school kid's service. Helen had been a narrowly averted near miss. He'd almost made a bid for her affections at a staff piss up some time just before Christmas. They had briefly been left in a one to one moment and she had let it slip that she had a 'thing' for older guys. He feigned surprise at the news but his instant tumescence had him feeling fifteen years younger. He still patted himself on the back for having the judgement not to go through with it and now she had a nice young bloke in tow. Word on the street, was that he was a surveyor, working for a city based firm - wedding bells were already being mentioned by the Centre's cognoscenti.

When Helen finally made tracks, he told Pauline that he was willing to drop a couple of days if that would help her and if that would keep Corrine in her present hours. Pauline looked at him with a gratitude that he found almost frightening in its sincerity. But, he took the plaudits in good faith - this was not the time for him to be a hard arse.

They had blasted their way through the Saturday; Greenwich, Cutty Sark, the market, an early curry then back to the flat so Lee and Bernie could get ready for their gig. The band's bass player had picked them up in a battered but colourfully decked out transit van and he had ferried the four of them to the gig. Tommy and Lee had sat in the back with the gear - the girls were up the front, riding shotgun with Wendell.

He asked Lee what she thought about Donna. After a couple of beats Lee gave him that shy smile of his.

'Well, she's definitely a looker Tommy.'

He waited for a little more but Lee didn't add to it and Tommy didn't prompt his friend for any more. He had a distinct sense of faint praise, which puzzled him slightly. He left it; he'd known Lee for forty years and that was the only maths that mattered.

Wendell was playing some Steel Pulse up front and it looked very much like he and the girls were sharing a spliff, the party had started.

The gig was a blast, the pub was packed, the band had been playing regular gigs there for over a year and they had built up an appreciative following. Two songs in and the front half of the audience was grooving to Lee's chopping guitar and Wendell's rumbling bass, with Bernie and a tasty mate funking out on backing vocals. The combo was fronted by a singer with one metre dreads and a voice that, if you closed your eyes....

They pulled outside for the interval, taking in the cooling air and the busy streets and Wendell and Bernie had joined them. According to Bernie, Lee was still inside checking out a problem with the keyboard mike. Wendell laughed, 'man's a perfectionist,' he said. Wendell had a quick shufty up and down the street and pulled out a twin of the earlier joint that the girls had shared with him in the van. The four of them passed it around like naughty teenagers. Tommy noticed that there was a half moon slowly rising to the rooftops over in the east and just the faintest twinkling of a few stars up there too. He had the thought that he hadn't seen the Milky Way ever since he'd been back in England. Donna shook him out of the reverie, nonchalantly nestling her gorgeous backside into his groin and then passing the joint over her shoulder. He took a long hit then turned her chin towards him leaned into her and blew the smoke into her mouth. Wendell laughed at that too, 'good to share eh man?'

The second half was even better than the first; *Stepping*

Razor, Four Hundred Years, Legalize It and *Three Little Birds.*
Get up, Stand Up finished it off.

They waited while Lee and the singer sorted out the dough
with the landlord and Wendell offered them a lift home, but
they were all in the mood to kick on a bit.

Tommy woke up early the next day and, as was always
the case when he had a hangover, he couldn't stay in bed.
Donna was out of it, silent and still and there was no stirring
yet from either Lee or Bernie. He went into the kitchen and
made himself a coffee and then another, turning over in his
mind about what to do about one of those little black clouds
up north. A phone call to Sonny would be all that it would
take and then it would be dealing with the aftermath with
Donna. He tried out a few permutations but couldn't seem
to make it avoid ending in tears. Tommy mused briefly on
what the old man would have done but that would be easy
enough to answer, the kid would already be in juvie cooling
his heels and looking nervously over at his larger roommates.
Lord knows that the two of them had had their darker days
together. At the age of sixteen, Mick, after one of their more
incendiary dust ups, had bounced him down the road for a
year's enforced sabbatical with family and friends.

Mick, just like Bonnie's old man, didn't believe in the
softly softly approach. Give them the stick first and, maybe,
if they behaved themselves, a bit of carrot down the track.
Whatever, he thought. He couldn't just let it slide on by.

Despite the quiet Friday Darrin was knackered all day Saturday, tired enough to crash in bed for a couple of hours after
lunch. The last time he had kipped during the day he'd had
a four-day flu, which had absolutely battered him. That was

years ago now; just a few months after he had started working at the warehouse and he hadn't been sick since.

He was out of the door at five and down the Quays in less than twenty minutes, more than half an hour early for his rostered shift. Lumb was parked up in there, on the headset as always, this time he was partnered up with a youngish DC by the name of Frankie Walker. Frankie was all boy-scout; alert at his post, eagerly scanning the entrance of the flats like a human periscope. A couple of cars had already pulled in and Keithy was busy entertaining in the lounge room, engaging in chit chat and the passing round of the hors d'ouveres.

Dalton left the flat half-fivish and returned just after six. Just about the same time that Young was nestling down into Lumb's warmed up chair. Darrin had grabbed the camera from Frankie.

Dalton had returned with a couple of late teens in tow, a tall skinny young bloke and a bright young thing who was a sight to behold, a mini dress that was just about warming her arse matched up with a mid-riff top that was struggling to hold back her plentiful boobs.

Dalton dropped the two young ones off then turned the car out into the street and then came back twenty minutes or so later with a car full of revellers. Three more youngsters this time, a girl and two young guys, and a po-faced older guy who was sat ram rod straight in the front passenger seat. He was a handsome looking jasper, late thirties, probably. He exuded money, a proper education and maybe even good breeding, definitely slumming it with the under classes.

At a little past eight o'clock, a souped up shit box announced its oncoming presence with some vibrating bass and a fishtailed turn into the car park. Looky there, he thought, a known face. A gangly streak of piss, mid-twenties or so, had sprung out of the driving seat as if a firecracker had been dropped down his shorts. The face gestured impatiently for the remaining occupants of the car to get out, pronto. It was the one and only Bazzer Dougan, the half legendary scumbag dealer from the Barrington. Bazzer would make a fair dent in the parties' collective social standing. With him were two younger males and a couple of brassy young birds who could be heard from a hundred yards away. They spilled out of the car and trailed Bazzer to the lobby, the neighbours duly alerted to their presence by their cacophony. Darrin let Young know that Bazzer had joined the celebrations and a moment later Dalton's intercom picked up Bazzer's scally tones.

A few more cars pulled in over the next couple of hours, mostly older guys, all of them arriving alone, giving the environs a cursory once over before they walked over towards the entrance and its buzzers - hard-ons and guilty minds alright. By ten the joint was jumping but there was too much babble and not enough clarity on the tapes to pick up anything up of consequence. Dalton had told Bazzer to calm it down- 'once and once only' was the caveat he gave him. A little later than that and the music was dimmed to a quiet murmur and then there was a vacuum in the hub-hub, which slowly began to be punctuated by some moaning and groaning from amongst the ensemble, probably a bit of a cabaret on Keith's shag pile. Half an hour of that and then somebody put the music up again but not as loud as it had been before the screwing had started. The party itself sounded a little more subdued too, a few voices, some doors opening and closing, a brief reprise of the squelching noises, which was underscored by a volley of lewd female laughter. That was pretty much it for the next couple of hours. People intermittently broke away for some banal slightly surreal post coital chit-chats - that and the irritation of the balcony door being repeatedly opened and closed. They had picked up a few names; a Tony, a Neil, a Claudia, a Stuart, a Chad, a Nicky, a Paula, and a Jess and then the rest were all initials, the older guys. Mr's B, F, G, J, P, S and T. That would account for all of the older guys who were there, not including Dalton and Bazzer.

By two o'clock the fuck fest was starting to wind down, Keithy still the loud, jovial mein host holding court and dispensing good cheer and funnies in the lounge room. Darrin pictured him in a silk kimono, stretched tight by the barrel chest and hard gut, a cigar and a malt, everything fucking hunky-dory in Keithy's world.

Then there was a bit of a commotion, a crying girl - Paula. A man's voice came into the lounge room just a few seconds behind her. The guy was pissed off, calling the girl a slag and he complained loudly to Keithy reiterating his assessment of her, telling Dalton that he was dissatisfied with the 'service'. Keith shushed the girl and told the guy to take a powder - he was level with him but he put a bit of steel in there too. After he dealt with the guy, Dalton went straight back to the girl with some soothing counsel.

'Don't worry love,' Dalton cooed with an unnerving gentleness. 'He didn't mean it. Here have a taste of this, that'll sort you out. That's a good girl, don't worry I'll keep him away. I think Mr G. might have his eye on you and why not, you're such a gorgeous thing - aren't yer?'

A few sniffles and a snort and that was it, the drama was

over. By three most of the well-heeled gents were pulling away from the forecourt, back from whence they came. One of the men left with the tall young guy that had turned up with the voluptuous honey in the mini skirt, a pair up by the looks of things. Bazzer and Dalton ferried the non-driving youth home in a couple of runs. Dalton was back at the ranch before four.

Darrin looked at Young, ready for the post mortem.

'Well Sarge what does all that get us apart from fading hard ons?'

Young didn't laugh.

'Well - it's all intel' for us Constable, the devil is in the detail son, although I shouldn't have to point that out to you really. We'll look up the names and the registrations, try and make sense of the web later. Drugs on the premises obviously, I don't think the kids were under agers and that would be a bloody minefield anyway.'

'Yeah but are we any closer to nailing this fucker to drugs, prostitution, anything?'

Young became irritated with him.

'It's not that easy Darrin, as I'm sure you've already been told. Beyond reasonable doubt - remember? Or do you think we should pull him in because you don't like the sleazy fucker?'

Darrin sighed, he knew Young was right, Mozzer or Mac would have told him the same thing.

'Maybe grab Dwayne, or Bazzer Dougan then - a body, any fucking body?'

Young shook his head and laughed.

'You're a piece of work you are Dazzler, Wyatt bloody Earp indeed, Mac's on that fucker Dwayne. Don't worry he'll be nailed soon enough.'

Young laughed again and leant over to give him a comradely pat on the shoulder, 'come on let's get the fuck home to our beds.'

Darrin stood up and stretched and looked out of the tinted window that faced the car park - all was quiet now. The birds were already hitting their straps when they walked back to their cars and he felt tired enough to sleep for a week.

Sonny had called round for lunch during the week and they had chatted about the Glasgow gang's project for a while. Sonny was of the opinion that the money would probably be through early in the new year. Four days a week, fifty-fifty split of the workload if he wanted it that way. He told Sonny about Pauline's Lottery disappointment.

'That might work out alright for you Tommy, if you can carry the shortfall for a couple of months.'

He could, there was no doubt about that, though it might mean a bit of frugality for a while.

'Old Mick wouldn't see you starve would he?'

That he wouldn't, they had made do with scrag end and dumplings plenty enough in the past and that was fuck all to what the old man had endured in his youth. As a youngster Mick had had a bad enough diet to see him rendered toothless by the age of seventeen.

There was a moment, a lull in the conversation where he almost spilled Donna's news about the kid to Sonny. Sonny had let him know earlier that Dougy's boy, Darrin May, had told him that he'd seen Pasquale and his mate regularly hanging around the Coleshaw.

'Recently was it?' Tommy had asked him, keeping his

253

voice as neutral as possible.

Sonny, thankfully, was not blessed with supernatural powers of intuition and he hadn't noted his veiled concern. But he gave him some info, which stayed with him for the rest of the day and beyond.

'PC May said he was up there farting around only last week. He has him down as a possible courier, no proof though - just speculation...reasonable speculation.'

That evening he'd raised it with her with what he hoped was a tactful deftness as they laid into the fried beans and guacamole that she'd cooked up for them.

'I have to trust him Tommy.'

'But you know Donna, the tin in the attic - the lies.'

'You don't have kids, Tommy, you don't know what it's like.'

He let that through to the keeper - there was plenty he could have said but, as it was, the taste of the nachos was already dying in his mouth.

Tommy didn't mention the conversation with Sonny and he wondered, again, who or what he was trying to protect.

The rest of the meal was an exercise in uncomfortable silence. TV maintained the barrier for the rest of the evening. He thought about skipping out but he didn't. That night, for the first time, they slept together without having sex.

Breakfast was a bit more of a cheery affair. Donna told him that Bernie had mentioned that she and Lee were thinking about moving to Brighton.

'Really!' He exclaimed. That was out of the fucking blue.

She nodded, Lee hadn't mentioned or hinted at a move but Lee was a cagey prick, he told you about most things in his life well after the bloody event.

'Bernie said we should go down for a weekend with them. It would be a sus out for them and a break for us.'

'Hmm,' he said, 'that sounds like an idea.' Giving it a lot more enthusiasm than he actually felt.

She dropped him off at his place and he did an in and out, grabbing some paperwork that he would need to help him put the youth service newsletter together.

Us, he thought - was starting to feel like a distant shore.

AUGUST

Monday and he was back at the window chatting to Mac about the party and his attendant frustrations with the operation.

Mac only gave him more cold comfort - toeing the party line.

'Info gathering Darrin, it's like a big fucking jigsaw and you need every piece to get the full picture. You got those registrations and tied in that scrote from the Barrington to Dalton too, that's a result.' Without pause Mac did a quick change of gear, 'what do you reckon to working with Young then?'

Darrin turned and looked at Mac who was giving him that steady, slightly unnerving look of his.

'OK, I guess, yeah, why?'

'Just be careful with him son, that is all I'm saying to yers. Don't look to be jumping on his coat tails. He doesn't count higher than the number one the smooth bastard, know what I mean?'

Darrin did, he nodded and turned back to the window, plenty of kids were out hanging around the shops and scattered on further down the road. Dwayne regularly grabbing his crotch while holding court, gape mouthed laughter at his own jokes.

Mac came over and joined him at the window. Mac was gearing up to make his nightly pilgrimage to The Admiral. He was flying solo tonight, no June on the arm, which Mac didn't mind at all. As far as he was concerned that was easier in a lot of ways. Recently, a couple of the regulars had made less than gentlemanly remarks about June. Pushing him a little bit, seeing how much he'd take from them. He'd considered asking one of them to step outside to give him a touch up but the guy was fairly tight with Johnstone and he had let it pass. Mac was keeping it in his back pocket. A bit of hard man stuff could be another way in for him with Johnstone. Apart from his brother, Johnstone did look a little light on muscle.

A couple of kids were cycling down Oak towards the court of Dwayne - again, it was the two little pricks that Sonny had brought in.

Mac tapped his index finger a few times against the window.

'See that kid in the red top?'

'Sure, what about him?'

'That's the little fucker who knocked on the door with the gear for June.'

'You sure?'

That got him a look that made him regret the question.

'We can bag him - see what gives.'

Mac clapped him gently on the shoulder.

'Too early yet young un, we'll end up with just the sprat. If we get lucky he'd cough up Dwayne at the most and that will be that - it doesn't justify all the time and the expense son.'

He told Mac that the two kids had been friends of the boy in the skip.

Mac nodded and chewed on his bottom lip.

'See what I mean Daz, it's a fucking jigsaw with lots of missing pieces. As my friend the Buddhist monk would say

- everything is connected, or was that CI Stone? I do get the two of them confused.'

Mac laughed to himself.

'I think I need a holiday Darrin, not another night of drinking more piss in that fucking dump of a pub. That's good intel' though son - well done. We can use it when it's time to give the box a shake, let's see what pops out then eh?'

Mac gave the vista one more look and then turned away from the window.

'Anyway, I'd better get it together.'

Darrin stayed at his post and gazed into the far distance. He'd have a chat with Sonny, see if he can get something from the kid. It was time to start putting the pressure on.

Jess had got back to the refuge around lunch - Rob was on that shift and he'd called her into the office to give her the obligatory bollocking. She was meant to be back at ten last night. Her absence had created a fair old flap, the coppers had been called and informed that she hadn't come home. Rob read the riot act in that strangely subdued, flat way of his, like he was reiterating a shopping list; not honouring the terms of her contract; sanctions, duty of care, grounded, last warning…blah, blah, blah. Jess had relayed a lengthy gist of it to a vaguely interested Kat, whilst he'd chilled out playing a game on his mobile. Jess looked tired and quickly headed off for a shower and a lie down. She didn't re-emerge until teatime, which pretty much coincided with the arrival of an equally jaded looking but clearly happy Neil.

'Good news pets,' Neil told them. 'Looks like the romance is hotting up for yours truly, he wants me to move in with him and be his little wife - bless. The two of us are going to build a love nest together.'

Kat and Jess looked swept away by the notion but he didn't know what the fuck to say. According to Neil the guy was some businessman and he sounded well loaded.

'Yes dears, no more sharing for this little bunny - Neil and Tony for ever.'

Neil trilled at the thought of domestic bliss and Pasquale couldn't help but smile.

Neil leaned over and patted Jess on her shapely thigh, 'and you girlfriend, did Daddy D see you right?'

Jess nodded, 'he did, well and truly - fun weren't it Neil?'

'Hmm, it was, glad you enjoyed it love, gorgeous pad eh? That view and that spa - wonderful.' He gave her an arch look, 'fanny sore then love?'

'Bout as sore as your arsehole, you slut.'

Neil feigned outrage, 'well no more of that naughty stuff for me lover girl - it's just Mister and Mister from now on.'

Rob called them from the lounge, 'X-Factor kids.'

'Oh that's right,' Neil said, 'the recovering ice addict is auditioning tonight - can't miss that.'

And off they went. Fuck, Pasquale thought, they could all move when they wanted to - fags scooped up and the three of them inside in a flash to claim their favourite seats.

Kat stopped at the slide doors and asked him if he was coming in, he thought about it, recovering ice addict? Why not - that might be summat worth looking at.

Tuesday lunch and Wendy told him that Sonny was coming round to see him about three for a catch up - she didn't know what for but she gave him that reassuring smile of hers, 'not to worry pet - I'm sure it's just a catch up call.'

Pasquale wasn't worried but it meant he'd have to knock back an afternoon run. He told Junior who said he do a solo and then he'd meet up with him after tea down at the mill. They could run up the Coleshaw later and get one in, no problem.

Sonny came in pretty much on time and Wendy called Pasquale into the office. Sonny was in there waiting for him, slightly rocking back on one of the office chairs - looking at him but without that usual easy, chilled out grin of his.

Sonny nodded to the nearest chair. Then he looked at him silently for a couple of beats.

'I'm going to cut to the chase here Pasquale because the time to be fannying about is over. I've been hearing some worrying whispers about you lad.'

Pasquale rubbed his hands across his eyes just to give them something to do and looked away out of the window.

'Yeah?' he replied.

Sonny reached over and turned Pasquale's chair until it was square with his.

'Yeah. Look at me son, not out of the fucking window please. I'm taking the time to come here and talk to you, so do me the courtesy of listening, all right. You're up the Coleshaw I hear, running with the crowd, keeping bad company the usual shit. You've been seen and been noted by people who can give you a lot of grief - trust me on that one.'

Pasquale managed to keep the eye contact but he could feel himself rapidly retreating inwards.

'You've used up a fair bit of good will already mate. I'll list it for you; the Centre, your school, getting you in here. It's all work you know, other peoples' that is. Bottom line - you don't have any cards left to play. Next step a rehab order -

maybe even juvie down the line. Does that sound like that would be a good path for you, eh Pasquale?'

Pasquale dropped his eyes and mumbled a no.

Sonny looked at him silently.

'No, well that means you do know the bottom line then. Ultimately, it's your call young fella. Stay away from the Coleshaw, keep your nose clean and make your mum proud of you, she deserves it.'

He bit his tongue at that one - Sonny knew fuck all about his mum - and him too for that matter.

Later that evening, he lay on his bed and thought it over. He'd call Junior tell him he would take a break and advise Junior to maybe do the same thing.

The next day they met at the mill and talked it through. Junior had told Dwayne yesterday straight off after his phone call. Dwayne was pissed off but savvy enough, he knew that it was better for him to get the word early. Maybe they could ship down the Barrington and, with the necessary introductions, get on to Bazzer's crew, get something going there. But that didn't appeal to either of them, the thought of working for that mad bastard - no way. They were fucked then, unemployed, null and void, he'd just lost his first job. Junior talked about Haringey, maybe relocating - that would be something. He wondered who'd told Sonny, maybe his mum but he doubted it.

Sonny had caught up with him on Thursday. There was another conference coming up on the gang initiative. This one was likely to be held in a couple of month's time but that would be a likely clash with the possible Thailand trip with Jimbo.

Sonny finished off his steak pie and threw the wrapper into the bin. He made to stand up then sat back down.

'Planning to stay are yer Sonny?'

'Love to - you've got such a nice place, nah, joking apart I nearly forgot Tom, I had a chat with Donna's boy a couple a days ago. I'd had confirmation, and this is from the coppers mind you, which is a bloody worry, that he and his mate are involved on the scene up on the Coleshaw, hopefully I've put enough of a scare into the stupid little sod to make him see sense.'

'What - you say he's been seen dealing?'

'Yep, up there most days according to that young copper er Darrin, Darrin May. Tommy raised his eyebrows at that - not many fucking degrees of separation there.

'He reckons the kid dropped off some crack to an undercover cop up the Coleshaw. Well and truly playing with bloody fire he is. He'll get swept up when they are ready - they've got him in their bloody sights.'

'He's been up there the last few days - yeah?'

'According to our friendly plod, yeah, regular as fucking clockwork,' Sonny looked at him quizzically. 'Why Tom?'

Tommy exhaled, fuck it.

'Donna - she told me that she found a big wad of cash in his room. He admitted to her that he'd been running gear down to the Barrington.'

Sonny looked at him a lot harder than he usually did. 'Tommy! You covered for that little prick?'

'Yeah - I guess I did.'

'Fuck me, Tommy!'

'Yeah, yeah Sonny, I know, I know.'

This time Sonny did stand up and then he stayed on his

feet, pacing the room for a full minute, imperceptibly nodding to himself as he did, working it all through.

'Well good thing for the kid I warned him off then - if he pays heed to it that is.'

'Sorry Sonny, I know that this puts us in an invidious position.'

'Don't know Tommy, the cops were holding back on it because of some op they're running. This could be another way of sorting it out. Pull the kid and his mate - maybe their supplier too. I'll have another chat with Darrin.'

Tommy asked him the question with his eyes.

'Don't worry Tommy. I'll say I got an anonymous phone call from a concerned citizen.'

Tommy thanked him and Sonny clapped him on the shoulder.

'The things we do for love eh bro?'

'Love!' Tommy snorted, 'more like a fucking bouquet of barbed wire.'

Sonny looked at him, more than a little surprised at the invective.

'Ah come on Tommy, it's nothing that can't be fixed.'

Tommy nodded at him but he wasn't too sure.

He was seeing Donna that night. He already knew that the refuge had called and had told her about Sonny's chat with Pasquale.

She had seemed resolved to it all. He needed to learn, she had said, maybe it would be better if he took the fall. But, truth was he didn't buy it, he knew that she was probably just talking the talk and he decided that he would keep the conversation with Sonny to himself.

He'd entered the maze, he thought, passively complicit

and compromised to the point of shame and, unlike Pasquale, he didn't even have the excuse of youth.

Darrin had taken a little time off from the Quays although Young had called to let him know that they now had all the names from the car registrations. Pillars of the community one and all; a building company owner, a textiles importer who had rumoured connections with the Saltt crew, a guy who owned a chain of hair dressing salons, a couple of money boys and a well known lawyer - wife and kids at home and firmly ensconced in the closet.

Sonny had told him about the chat with the kid and Darrin had mixed feelings about the way it was being handled. In his opinion it was more of a break than the kid deserved, but Mac had reassured him that the kid would be nailed.

'He'll fuck up soon enough and then he'll have to learn the hard way, do him good too, he's an arrogant little fucker, kid or no kid. He looked at June like she was a piece of shit.'

He was rostered on with Johno for foot patrol on the Thursday late shift. It was a warm evening and it was pretty busy around the precinct and the High Street. The pedestrianised strip was full of swarming late night shoppers and plenty of 'get it in yer' revellers. Then a call came through at about eight o'clock that there had been an incident down near the Barrington. Some kid had swiped a woman's handbag just as a patrol car had turned into the street. The patrol had given chase and a house painter's Transit, which was coming in the opposite direction had side swiped him. He was put out for the count with a shattered left leg - both the major bones well and truly fucked up.

The kid was known to them and was thought to be one of

a network of two-wheeled couriers and look outs that were operating on the Barrington. Word was quickly out about the incident and a mob of hooded youths had gathered near the Barrington shops, setting a couple of wheelie bins on fire. All units were called back quickly to the station and within half an hour there were a couple of dozen coppers up there facing them off.

The order was to go in hard, nip it in the bud and the mob had scattered when they'd charged at them with their batons drawn. But they were up for the fight and there had been a steady return of the mob to both flanks of the assembled coppers. A few of the crowd had grabbed the wheelie bin from behind the estate's much-loved off-licence, had tipped all the bottles out and then missiled them at the police cordon. Darrin was close to the middle of the line with Johno on his left and big Chev to his right. Most of the bottles fell short and, in the lull, Sergeant Proctor gave them the word to steam in to the bottle throwers. The Barrington lads scattered again and fell back towards the little park in front of the twin high rises. This time Proctor gave them the word to hold their position, they put the vans at both ends of the tatty shopping strip and that was pretty much that for the next three or so hours. Three hours of tension and curdled adrenaline listening to the baying profanities and threats echoing out from the park. The pricks had taken time out to mindlessly set the park's swings on fire. A couple of community leaders and a church Minister were called up to the estate to try and calm it down. Sonny was also brought in as he had the Barrington as part of his patch as well as the Coleshaw.

Darrin clocked Sonny in action - well and truly earning his money was our Sunil, he was up there at the playground trying to talk some reason into the young fellas. By two o'clock it had all died down, the mob had retreated into the shadows and Sonny and the responsible few had wearily beaten a track to wherever their cars were parked up. He watched the colours of the fire engine's lights sweep and arc around the tower blocks as the fire boys did a precautionary dousing down of the melted, smouldering set of swings. It was just what the place needed - less facilities.

Saturday and Darrin was back in for the afternoon shift, the station was busy, absolutely broiling with activity and tension. As a precaution extra bodies had been pulled in, just in case they had to deal with any more flare-ups.

It wasn't good news on the kid, he was still out of it and it looked like he might even lose the leg. There had been a couple of roaming packs on both of the big estates during the late morning and the early shift had already moved on groups of bad intentioned young lads from the High Street area and the Mall. Throughout the day various pillars of the community had been coming in and out of the station and the brass had had a meeting with a group of them round about noon. Sonny and his crew were out there again, trying to douse it all down but it was tense and everybody's fingers were tightly crossed hoping that it would eventually prove to be the storm that would not find landfall.

Within ten minutes of arriving at the station, he was back out on the streets teamed up with Johno, no time for a brew a catch up or a bull shit with his crew. They were on patrol on the High Street and before they left the station Sarge Thomas told them that, once they were out they were out. Riot teams were on stand by and it was all hands on deck.

Sarge Thomas was out on the pavement too, involved in the coordination, busily keeping in contact with the teams assigned to the Coleshaw, the Barrington and the Mall. They were keeping an eye on Leeside too just in case a race element crept into it. There were still a few grudges to be settled down there.

They had cleared away a little would be mob in the late afternoon and, according to the Sarge, it was still fairly quiet on both the Coleshaw and the Barrington. Plenty of the community were knocking about on Leeside, being seen in order to keep the peace - so nothing up there yet either. By the late afternoon, the tension had begun ratcheting down slightly. Maybe the pricks had got it out of their systems the night before.

Then the news came through about six - the kid had died. Sarge Thomas taking the call and relaying it on, the Sarge as grim as fuck, the implications etched on his face. The kid had never woken up, internal injuries too much bleeding - and gone.

Within an hour the crowds up on the Coleshaw and the Barrington had re-gathered. A few burning bins and the usual goading - the lads stationed up there were holding back this time, they were worried that they didn't have the numbers to take them front on.

The centre seemed OK, though they had taken the precaution of getting the riot gear on, but the mob they'd cleared away hadn't returned and it was now just the usual Friday night piss up crowd. Families, shoppers, business owners and their staff were all out of there as per usual by teatime. Then, in the blink of an eye, there they were. Darrin scoped fifty or so of the fuckers coming south from the top end of the by-pass. They were holding back, animatedly gathered at the top of end of the High Street, malevolently marking time about three hundreds yards away from their positions.

The Friday night crowd were now glancing nervously up the street - that mob looked like nobody's idea of a good time. Darrin saw the owners of Piccolos approaching Sergeant Thomas for a quick word, both men looking anxious. After a briefing from the Sarge they quickly headed off to their bar and a minute later they were pulling the shutters down over the bar windows and shooing out their compliant early bird customers.

Reports were coming in that the Coleshaw and the Barrington were both quiet, nothing doing at all, which seemed a little strange. Within the next half-hour it became obvious why that was the case. The gang of fifty that had gathered at the top of the end of the street had suddenly swollen in the space of twenty minutes to become the gang of a few hundred. It looked like this was where it was going to go down. Reinforcements were called in and Darrin and the boys had taken up position near the two vans that were parked nose to nose across the High Street, strategically placed between the precinct and the mob.

A few more minutes of the stand off and then the gang broke. A dozen or so lads came through the middle of the throng pushing two big wheelie bins. They had probably corralled them from the back of the shopping mall, which was a half a mile or so back up the by-pass. The bins were ablaze and being pushed with a reasonable velocity down towards their line. Darrin felt the blast of adrenalin, the muscles in his legs, arms and shoulders beginning to twitch, the sweat cooling as it ran down from his face to his collar.

Then it was on, fettered anticipation boiling over into action - bottles and pieces of masonry arcing through the air towards them, a few of the missiles hitting the side of the vans with crashing blows. A minute of that passed, their line was kept tight pretty much shoulder-to-shoulder and the shields were kept up for maximum protection. Through his helmet he could hear the muted, heavy thuds of the bricks and the cracking explosions of the glass. He was ready to go now, aching to fucking move. DI Kendrick raised his arm and signalled the first charge - up they went, six abreast. Darrin was in the second row running hard, not feeling the weight of his gear, oblivious to the sweat that was coursing down his back.

The mob scattered and headed back towards the by-pass, some of them breaking off into the High Street's side streets, one little fucker falling over as he turned to get away. As he ran past him Darrin wacked the kid hard across the top of his back bringing out a scream of pain. He knew that the kid would be swept up by the snatch team and he kept on running right at the heart of the fuckers. There was a demolition site at the top left end of the High Street and about fifty of them were waiting for them there, primed with rubble, masonry and bottles. Their charging lines came to a stuttering halt and they quickly raised their shields as the volley of missiles came down upon them. He was hit on the left shoulder and big Chev went down with his visor shattered, his lower face a mask of blood. Another bottle smashed just behind them, exploding into flames and, as it did so, Darrin heard the fuckers on the demolition site hoot and holler, delighted at the sight of the coppers hurriedly dancing away from the fire. He grabbed the still prone and now targetted Chev and he held his shield over him. With the help of Barnesy, they got him back onto his feet and made a slow, clumsy retreat back to the wagons, Chev sandwiched between him and Barnesy, Darrin walking backwards his left arm gripping Chev's waistband, his right keeping his battered shield aloft. The mob had flowed back into the vacuum, emboldened by the coppers' retreat and Kendrick ordered them back to the second line down near the pedestrian mall. They had the shops covered there, both ends of the mall were sealed up and they had the numbers to protect it.

The High Street belonged to the rioters now and they quickly turned their pitiless attention to ransacking the shops; an electrical store that had been there since he was a kid; an Asian mini-market, a florist, a pound shop, Ridgeleys menswear, Footlocker - all of them smashed, trashed and burned. Scores of the little fuckers making off with various goods - shopping trolleys commandeered from the mall to help them haul it away. News crews and media were now in the thick of it marking it all down for posterity and wider consumption. Some of the fuckers had filmed themselves on their mobiles and Blackberries and mugged for the cameras - their YouTube moment.

His shoulder was hurting like fuck but he was told to wait and watch - Kendrick said they didn't have the numbers to engage again with the looters, so the local businesses had to be sacrificed on the altar of expediency. As he watched the looters his stomach churned with anger and a sense of futility and helplessness. It felt like surrender, a capitulation to the scumbags.

It was six a.m before the fire brigade could get in to douse what was left of the High Street. Word had come through via Sarge Thomas that the Community Centre on Barker

Street had been torched too.

Darrin was stood down at eight as reinforcements from neighbouring forces had allowed them to completely cordon the centre off. Before he turned to leave he took in the vista for one last time and Sergeant Thomas, who now looked at least a decade older in the bright morning light after the long night before, tapped him on his sore shoulder and told him to shake a leg. Thomas saw him wince at the touch and the Sarge quickly called over the medics and organised a ride down to A and E for him. Two hours later and he was being patched up by a pretty nurse. There was nothing broken, just deep bruising and he was given painkillers to take the edge off.

Darrin rang the station and told them about the shoulder, he was told to stand down and to take a couple of days off. They now had the numbers to cover. He went to his mum's for his lunch, she clucked and fussed over him and, for once, he was grateful for it.

He was knackered in body and in mind and he went for a lie down in his old room and slept through until almost midnight.

When he returned downstairs his old man was still up listening to the radio, which was always Doug's preference whenever he was alone. It was tuned into a local station with only one topic being discussed.

His dad looked at him with a rare show of concern.

'You alright then son?'

Darrin nodded and tried to mask a wince, it was definitely time for more painkillers. His dad offered him a brew and he listened to the radio as his dad busied himself in the kitchen. According to the radio it was all quiet tonight - too fucking late that, he thought.

Pasquale had heard about the agro from Junior who had been hanging out up on the Coleshaw when it was all kicking off and Kat and Jess had also received texts about what was going down in the centre - sounded like arma-fuckin'-geddon. They had a lockdown, nobody was allowed out of the refuge and Wendy had popped around mid evening to nervously check on her charges and to offer Rod a bit of moral support.

He went to bed early, which raised a few comments from the others. He lay on his bed for an hour or so then got up and slipped out through the bedroom window. He made his way to the back shed putting enough distance between himself and the back door of the refuge to ensure that he didn't trip the sensor light and quietly slid open the lightweight corrugated door. He grabbed the petrol can that held the juice for the lawnmower and poured a pint or so of fuel into one of the lidded glass jars that housed some screws and nails. Satisfied that he had enough, he put the jar, along with a cleanish rag, into his backpack and then grabbed the bicycle.

Junior was waiting for him at the Centre, stepping out of the shadows at the sound of his whistle from around the side of the long part of the T-shaped building. It was a moonless night and there were only a few lights around the front of the Centre - nice and dark for their purpose. Pasquale led Junior around to the back office window. He grabbed the hammer from him and smashed in the window as completely as he could. The alarm was immediately triggered, grating and dramatically insistent but it barely pierced his grim intent. He stuffed the rag in the jar of petrol leaving just a few inches of it dry. He lit the rag then he threw the bottle at the far wall of the office where it smashed and spectacularly exploded into flames - arma-fuckin'-geddon.

They cycled a quarter a mile or so away to a little park from where they had a clear view of the Centre. Junior had rolled them a couple of joints and they smoked and waited. After a few minutes they could smell the smoke and after five more they could see the flames rolling up the back of the Centre, dramatically eating away at the large part of the building that held the basketball court where they held the monthly raves.

It took half an hour before they heard the siren. According to Junior's phone there was mega-mayhem in the Centre and bins and a few cars were still ablaze on both the Coleshaw and the Barrington. There was a 'copter buzzing the High Street and plenty of flame coming from over that way too. They hung around for another hour and then took off, splitting up immediately as they did so. When he climbed back in the window his room was still empty, Liam was still up watching the late movie probably with Rob and night bird Kat.

Pasquale went through to the bathroom, cleaned himself up and stashed his clothes in the wash basket.

He lay in the dark for a while and listened to the blare of sirens in the distance, a sense of grim satisfaction turning his mouth into a bleak thin line. What was that Sonny had told him? Yeah, that was it. There are always consequences to your actions.

Pauline rang Tommy just after nine - the sirens and the circling chopper had delayed his sleep for a couple of hours until he'd remembered that he had some ear plugs at the back of his sock drawer. Her news had jolted him awake. He ate some toast, showered and got down there a little after ten. She was round the back of the building near what was left of his office, animatedly chatting with a middle-aged fireman and Jeannie, her office administrator. He called out her name and she called back and gave him the briefest of smiles, her face blotchy and tired. The emergency services had taped out a perimeter some twenty yards from the back and side-walls of the building. The roof had buckled but was still intact. The wall of his office was a blackened shell, his desk and the computer now a fused lumpen mess. When she had finished chatting with the fire guy she turned in his direction, they walked up to each other and embraced. He held her for a few moments but she'd done with any crying. She stepped back and looked at him, her hands tightly clenching his upper arms.

'Anybody see anything Pauline?'

She shook her head, 'it was called in just after half eleven, by the time they got here it was well ablaze.'

He stepped half a pace to the side and took in the mess again.

'Who would want to do this Pauline?'

She shook her head, 'don't know love, doesn't make sense does it? But, given last night, who knows.'

He wasn't convinced by the connection, the town centre and the estates had been orchestrated but that had been somehow organic too and predictable. He could see the cause and effect in it. The riot was a curdled reaction arising from the interminable status quo of disaffection, struggle and unhappiness, which had fed the mob mentality. Finally erupting into battle stations, the 'let's get into it' with the coppers and the jackal like ransacking of the shops. But, to his mind, this seemed odd, an anomaly that was out of whack with the rest of the fucked up night.

'Anyway Thomas, it looks like you'll be sharing an office for a while. The front of the building's still usable apparently and the reception should be big enough for the groups. Maybe the council might have a room or two for us to use.'

Typical Pauline, he thought, the Phoenix rising whilst the place is still smouldering. She was always looking for a way to keep going, as redoubtable as the people of London in the Blitz.

'Yeah, yeah we can do all that - everything is covered.'

He looked around to his left, smoke still spiralling over there too, the High Street in fucking tatters.

'Looks like we're still waiting for that Great Leap Forward eh Pauline?'

She smiled and touched him lightly on the cheek, 'that fight never stops Tommy, that's why they put people like you and me down here.'

Tommy nodded grimly - she was half-right in her assertion, he was starting to feel battle fatigue though. Let them have their shit heap, he thought.

Tommy met the old man in the Farriers for lunch and he set his stall out early with Guinness and a malt chaser. Mick raised an eyebrow but didn't comment. Nev dropped in and Drink Gorman was already there, half-lit and already starting to burble. Mick's old sparring partner, Jimmy Buck came in too, which meant that there would be some guaranteed laughs to leaven the disbelief and the anger.

Today he was in the mood for it and he matched the old man for spleen. He'd even shared his spiritual sickness theory with them during the lengthy, slightly circular conversation about last night's events, the youth as the spawn of a culture of rampant vacuous commercialism. His dad liked it - nodding along furiously, getting off on his son's bristling anger at least as much as the details of his argument. The old man had always enjoyed seeing his fighting side, the displays of the chip off the old block.

'Aye right on son, right you bloody well are, there's no excuse for the little fuckers' behaviour but they've been doled out a diet of false idols for decades now. If we want any kind of fucking enlightenment let's get rid of the TV for fucking starters.' That comment caused Drink to burpingly giggle in slight alarm. Nev broke the silence, 'there are some decent shows on though Mick, yer know, National Geographic and that.'

The old man rolled his eyes to the heavens but gave Nev a pass.

'Let them eat fucking cake,' Mick said and JB laughed and then chimed in.

'Get the little cunts in the army and kick the mums' and dads' arses too. Fucking nanny state has killed us, soft as shit this lot, good job Adolf wasn't born in the nineteen fifties.'

Tommy agreed, he disagreed, they were right, they were wrong, he was certain, he was uncertain and he was, pound to a penny, as pissed as a fart. He drank all the way through the day. Mick had temporarily bailed out in the late afternoon, off home for tea and a nap. The old man returning a few hours later, fresh faced for his weekly dose of the blues band.

The band's industrial noise levels always made any attempt at conversation a complete waste of time, beefed up bass and drum underpinning toe curling string bending guitar, just the way Mick liked it. The old man nodding along to the rolling four-four beat, that percussive motion of his punctuated with the occasional 'get it up yer' punch of the air. Tommy up and dancing with Lil, the comely barmaid, to Dr. Feelgood's *Back in the Night*. Tonight they were temporarily in seventh heaven - rolling back the years.

Tommy woke up to the sunlight pouring in through the window of his old man's front bedroom. He looked at his watch and groaned, it was nine o'clock, his mouth and throat were as dry as a march through the Gobi and he had a crushing headache that painfully pulsed with every breath. He forced himself to dress and just about kept it all down. He drank as much water as he could bear and had a futile look for some aspirin. He didn't know why he'd bothered as the old man regarded using tablets as a sure fire sign of weak willed degeneracy. He climbed back up the stairs to wash his face and had a quick clean of the teeth with his old man's spare toothbrush, finally wincing his way on out of Mick's pad just before ten. It was a long walk home, it would be nearly two hours by the time he arrived at his own flat. Tommy went via the High Street and felt a genuine sadness as he looked at the fucking mess that was the aftermath of the riot. They hadn't fucking missed, that was for sure. He knew the young couple who'd had the florists and, Jesus, poor old Harry Pritchard and his electrical goods joint! He'd bought loads of second-hand albums from Harry when he was still in his teens.

There was a high police presence down there and both ends of the High Street remained sealed off. The clean up crews were already in, bolstered by some of the shopkeepers sorting through the crap in the areas where the buildings were deemed to be safe.

Tommy turned away from the mess and walked the rest of the way home. He spent the afternoon laid up inertly on the couch like a beached sea elephant that was saving his energy for the mating season. Thankfully, his supply of aspirin was kicking in to do the trick. He was grateful for the company of the muted pictures of the TV. The stereo was fully loaded up with CD's so he wouldn't have to move for hours if he didn't want to.

Donna hadn't called, which irritated him a little even though he hadn't called her. Later on in the evening he eventually plucked up the energy and resolve to get through to her. He apologised, he was meant to be cooking her dinner last night. She gave him exculpation but in a cool neutral way which, although understandable, irritated him again.

And that was it for the next few days, the aftermath; local politicians, visiting national politicians, every man and his dog pitching in with their ten cents worth. The left banged their drum, blaming poverty, lack of opportunity and social exclusion. The right rat a tatted back with criminality, family breakdown, the gang and drug culture, one parent and no parent families and the nanny state absolving people from individual responsibility. The local Archbishop even had a poke at the false idols of consumerism and celebrity and the growth of reality TV. The kids blamed the coppers, lack of jobs, things to do and places to go. The shopkeepers were gutted and angry and wondered why they had bothered putting in the time and effort for a local community that was so ready to cannibalise them. Little old ladies were frightened and he was missing his life in Australia and the sunny tolerant relaxed hedonism of inner city Sydney. He had a few days off while they sorted out the building although he checked in on

Pauline and the gang every day. He felt he at least owed her, and the rest of the staff that.

He met up with Donna on the Wednesday, her place this time and he told her about the conversation with Sonny.

'You told him what I told you, about Pasquale?'

He looked at her levelly and nodded, trying to read her face and failing miserably.

'And what made you think that was OK Tommy?'

Fucking hell - he was being chastised!

'Sonny knew Donna - he told me. He'd had the word from a reliable source. Pasquale was lucky not to have been pulled in.'

'Why did they leave him alone then - if he is still... dealing?'

Tommy caught the hesitation and just like that he'd felt something start to take shape in his mind; the talk that he'd had with the kid at his bedroom doorway, the fact that her time-line was a little out, a house bought in a reasonable part of the city before she took up her university studies. Sure, he thought, the city was cheap then, still pulling out of its post-industrial wasteland rep of the eighties. But, a single mum doing what was semi-skilled work at best. It just didn't add up - period.

She was looking at him for an answer, 'Well Tommy?'

'Don't know Donna, I don't know. He's fortunate though, I know that.'

Looking at her face was not any great source of comfort to him but, fuck it, he was tired of tiptoeing around, trying to compartmentalise everything in his fucking life.

She laid her knife and fork down at the side of her plate and calmly asked him to leave the house.

Tommy had a dumb moment, not a hundred percent sure if she was being serious. She noted his uncertainty and she repeated it for him.

He hadn't finished his curry but maybe it wasn't time to point that out.

He stood up, walked past her and let himself out, a little embarrassed, a little angry and more than a little relieved.

He went back home and lay on the couch and flicked on the TV and watched a wildlife documentary. Nev was right, TV can be pretty good. He was still a little tired from the all dayer on Saturday. What a fucking weekend, he thought, shit sprayed all over the walls.

Tommy thought about his own youth - the punk rock years and good ole Maggie Thatcher. He agreed with Mick, that you could draw a line of consequence from that blighted era. It had been a tipping point in the nation's history, one that had seen so many of the working class start to slide into membership of a burgeoning underclass. There and then so much of the self-identification of the community had started to erode. The bridge between youth and adulthood was now even more fraught and uncertain. Back in the day that difficult part of the journey had been made easier by the learning of a trade and the pride and certainty that that brought. A life of substance and meaning had been replaced by a rancid gruel of drugs, daytime TV, mindless computer games, the worship of baubles and trinkets and the celebrity fuck fest.

He loathed the actions of the little fuckers but he understood it, it hadn't risen out of a vacuum and that generation were now the product and the proponents of a nihilism that had not been there when he was a kid. Everybody, to different degrees, was copping the consequences, the only question was, where to from here?

Tommy half rolled off the couch with a groan feeling stiff and creaky - old, old, old, he thought and turned off the box. He put on the first Clash album and listened to the bristling energy and the band's vehement calls for action and awareness. Still ringing like a bell after all those years. He felt restless but didn't know where to take it - that was an old feeling but one that he hadn't had in a long time. He turned the music off and did some breathing exercises for ten minutes or so and that seemed to do the trick, his thoughts no longer tumbling and disjointed. Becalmed, he flicked the TV back on and surfed for a few minutes finding nothing on that he wanted to watch. His dad was right, he thought, TV is shit.

He phoned Lee and asked if it was cool if he headed back down in a couple of weeks time. They chatted about the riot for a while and Lee asked if Donna would be coming down too but didn't offer any comment when he'd told him no. Lee mentioned a trip to Brighton as a reccie for Bernie and himself. Tommy liked the sound of that, a day by the seaside would be just the ticket to blow away some of the urban angst.

They said their goodbyes and he sat in the quiet for a while, turning off the lamp and looking at the night sky noting, again, the lack of starlight. He awoke an hour or so later. Feeling stiff and more than a little cold he made his way to his bed.

Darrin had let his mum feed him for a few more days, the shoulder was still tender and sore enough to make a lot of doing the basics a drag. He didn't mind being fussed over for a little while, dealing with the riot seemed to have worked wonders for his patience. He'd popped into work on Tuesday and sat in the canteen for half an hour with a few of his colleagues picking over the bones of Saturday night. Chev was still in the hospital; jaw wired up, some missing teeth and concussion - twenty or so of the crew had picked up injuries. A dozen or so of the crew were now off work.

Sarge Thomas stuck his head in the canteen door and told him that a call had come through for him from DS Young. He said his goodbyes to his colleagues and made his way to the desk. Sarge Thomas gave him the phone with a little wriggle-lifting of the eyebrows, which spoke volumes about what he thought about the young detective. Young was his usual effervescent self. 'I've been told you did well on Saturday Dazzer boy, regular hero is the word in dispatches. Take all the time off you need son, we want you back but only when you're hundred percent.'

Darrin noted, again, the oft-used 'son' but let it slide. He reassured Young that he was OK and would probably be able to get back to the operation whenever they needed him. He was already getting a little bored, missing the action and even the inaction of station life. Again, Young told him to take his time and fed his appetite with a brief update. Dalton was now planning a little 'naughtyical' (Young's expression) holiday away in the South of France with his two young friends. Apparently, the Saltt crew had a yacht down on the Cote d'Azure. 'If you're right for Friday,' Young told him, 'climb back on board with Mac - let me know the day before though.'

Darrin said he would and he knew that he would be more than ready for it. Standing at the flat window wasn't going to worry his shoulder any. He looked at his watch, it was getting on for one and his mum had promised him rag pudding and mushy peas for dinner. Time to hit the road, he gave the Sarge a goodbye and Thomas shooed him on his way. 'You need a life you do son - a few more hobbies on top of that bloody dancing of yours.'

Darrin didn't give that any thought, he was OK with the way it all was. He gingerly wind-milled his shoulder as he walked out of the station doors, thinking about Friday up at the Coleshaw

AUTUMN

SEPTEMBER

Monday evening and he and Junior had met down at the mill - the light was starting to drop away conspicuously earlier now, though at least it was still warm. They chatted about the riots. Junior had heard they'd pulled in at least fifty of the lads and that the coppers were using Blackberry, Twitter and Facebook to try to nail the ones that they did have and to track down those that they didn't. Junior had cycled past the Community Centre just that morning, 'we fucked that place up good and proper.' he told him.

Pasquale was reassured by the 'we'- realising that he and Junior were sharing a lot of secrets these days. Junior asked him if was sure about pulling out. 'Good, good money blood. You know it.' Pasquale nodded along - he didn't need reminding about that. He had more than two grand stashed in the tin in the wall and he wasn't sure what to do with it other than keep it there. He'd only use it when he was ready to make a move. They spent the next half hour talking it through, leading to the conclusion that he'd formed before they had started talking, that he wasn't yet ready to give it away.

Junior called Dwayne and asked if he would meet them in the park from which they had watched the Centre burn, Dwayne hummed and hawed a bit but they knew that they were his top lads. Dwayne couldn't trust those dopey bleeders up the Coleshaw. He agreed to meet them in one hour, Junior strolled off and scored some pizza slices to take the edge off the hunger, at least they now had a plan.

Dwayne took his time mulling it over, his head bobbing up and down while he stroked on his sizeable Adam's apple. As he did so, his slightly bulbous eyes scoured the nearby tree line of the park like he was on the look out for bleeding snipers. Junior reckoned that Dwayne rarely left the Coleshaw, 'like a bleeding old man he is.'

He and Junior had worked it all out. There was a narrow walkway that doglegged off Strickland. It went on through to meet the lane, way at the back of Linden. Dwayne could meet them there for the pick up instead; it would be well away from any prying eyes. They would fix a definite time before they arrived at the estate, they didn't want to be hanging around the Coleshaw for fucking ages before they got down to business. 'In and out,' Pasquale told him, 'we'll cycle down the lane way to Oak, fifty yards back up to Strickland and off we go - sorted.'

Dwayne managed to get his head around it, speculating with them for a while as to who had put the word out to Sonny. He made a show of staunchly standing up for his boys but it was obvious that he wasn't sure about their loyalty. 'Anyway the other boys needn't to fuckin' know,' Dwayne said, 'well away from the fuckin' shops, keep it between the fuckin' three of us.'

Junior and Pasquale stayed quiet, letting him own the idea. Dwayne did a bit more head bobbing, 'alright fellas, I'll run it past the fuckin' gaffer.' He looked at his chunky wristwatch, which dwarfed his fine boned wrist and forearm, 'talk to to yer tomorra.' Dwayne split for the Coleshaw and he and Junior headed back to the mill. He had an hour to kill and a little smoke before returning to the ref' would help seal the deal.

The next day Junior called him before lunch, they were on designated time, six o'clock and they'd keep that flexible, change up, if necessary, on a day to day basis. That evening they were up there two minutes before the appointed time and Dwayne only kept them waiting for five minutes, they did the exchange with no fuss and a minimum of chat and then they were down the lane and off, gone before any fucker knew that they were even there.

Thursday evening and Darrin was back at the window listening to Mac whistle a few bars of Black Velvet Band something that he'd heard his mum belt out a few times when he was a kid, during her couple of gins in at the Sunday gatherings of the clan. Daylight was starting to ebb away and he'd only have a couple of hours before the watch would be pointless. Mac had had a development though. Last night his podgy tormentor had had another go at him, loudly asking Mac, for the benefit of his mates, if June was up for a little spit roast action. Mac had put down his pool cue and dropped him with a palm heel strike to the solar plexus, effective enough for the guy to deposit the night's festivities and his daily carb' intake into a retching pile, right next to the pool table. As Mac told it, a few beats after the damage had been done, Pete 'Biffo' Johnson had done his best enforcer impression, rumbling across the room like he was about to bench press somebody, stolidly and superfluously placing himself between the severely chastened, supine silver medallist and the calm but still battle ready Mac. 'To be fair to the dim fucker he did enough to make sure that nobody else joined in for which I was truly thankful and, I got the money prize too. A bit later on big bro' Chris called me over for a chin-wag and plied me for a bit more background info. I slipped him the military stuff and, sure enough, that caught his attention. We can flesh that out if needs be.' 'He liked the cut of your jib, eh Mac?'

'He did that young Daz - everybody is either of use or not of use to a fucker like him. We'll see if he runs something past me, I might be sitting on his sofa in a week checking out the home cinema.' Darrin laughed, 'watching *Scarface* no doubt.'

'You got it bucko - wont be bloody *Toy Story* that's for sure.'

Darrin turned his attention back to the window, Dwayne had broken off from the mob twenty or so minutes ago and now was strolling back to them with that slightly comical bow legged roll of his, idly scratching his balls as he did so - pure fucking bonobo that lad.

He and Mac chewed the fat for a while longer and then Mac headed off to The Admiral just before eight. Tonight was the pool competition, earlier this year the pub had been allowed back in the local league after a three year ban for a disagreement that had got out of hand at the Bull's Head, which was another rough hole down on the Hill. Darrin wasn't sure about the pool but the stoush would have been a fair match up.

He left the flat five minutes after Mac left for The Admiral. He thought about heading to the Quays then binned it. Darrin was bored with Dalton and his empty headed lovebirds, sharing inanities and getting off on their porno films. South of France! That drop-kick, living the fucking high life, taking everything and putting in nowt.

Darrin called Young from his car and he'd been right in his assessment, fuck all was moving down there too. Keithy was off at the weekend but they were holding back on going into the flat. It look liked Dalton might have arranged a house sitter. Some bloke and his bird would be in there, they had no name as yet but Dalton had been a little deferential during the calls, so, one of the party crew maybe. He'd get down there and check it out, if not Saturday then the Sunday. He was back on the plod on Monday - desk duties, he'd been ordered to ease his way back in. He drove home via the High Street, which was open again to the public although some of the shop fronts remained boarded up and were still taped off. A couple of bored looking coppers had been posted to make sure that people respected the exclusion zones. He'd heard about it on the radio a few days after the riot. The estimated cost to the community; the damage to property, the business lost, the insurance costs, overtime for the boys, all in all it added up to well over a million quid. There had been an organised clean up on Wednesday, which was both symbolic and practical; shopkeepers, local community leaders and Mr and Mrs Joe Public coming together to take the time to show that they gave a fuck. Maybe all was not lost after all, he thought, Darrin gunned the engine and, this time, headed back to his own gaff. He'd had enough nurture - it was big boy time again.

Tommy called Sonny at the end of the week after the lengthy, emergency staff meeting that was held in the temporarily closed to the public reception area of the Centre. There had been a few tears amongst the staff but nobody was bailing out, Pauline referred to them all as her 'second family' and that was like a sunburst around the room, he had nearly teared up a little himself at that. He told Sonny about the chat with Donna. Sonny thought he was doing the right thing to walk and stay away. 'It's too big a fucking elephant to ignore that one Tom - he'll always be her boy - know what I mean?'

That he did, Sonny was right and he was feeling a sense of relief around the decision to let it go, it was a clean slate of sorts. He also shared with Sonny his suspicions about the community centre fire. The investigators had confirmed that it had started at his office window, smashed in from the outside - petrol used to kick it off. Sonny told him to keep that under his hat, 'I reckon that boy is on borrowed time, thinks he knows everything and knows fuck all.' close

'Yeah you're right. You know Sonny, Mick used to tell me that all the time when I was a spotty teenager, trying to give him all of my adolescent shit. He'd give me that and the fact that he'd already forgotten more than I knew. I used to hate it when he said that to me.'

'Well you didn't forget that though, did you Tom?'

Tommy laughed, good old mercurial Sonny, 'nah mate - he was right though - of course.'

'It's a tough one eh? We can't expect them to behave like forty year olds when they're fifteen but…'

'There has to be consequences.'

'Undoubtedly.'

Speaking of Mick, he was now freed up for the weekend, if the weather was fine they could have another run up to the ressie whilst the warmth was still around.

Young had been right about Dalton's houseguest, he turned out to be a middle-aged dude, who Darrin thought he recognised but couldn't quite place. The guy had arrived in a new model BMW pulling into Keith's parking space only an hour or so after Dalton and his friends had pulled away in the Jag. Enough bags had been thrown in the boot of the car to keep the three of them away for a month.

The stranger had light footed it around the front of the car in order to open the passenger door for a drop-dead leggy blonde. He then gathered up a couple of night bags from the back seat, pulling in his midriff as he made his way on over to her. She waited for him at the lobby entrance exuding all the entitlement of glamour and beauty, her hand idly twisting a strand of her golden locks as she did so. Darrin had called Young up to the observation window.

'Know him Sarge?'

Darrin gave a curt nod towards the couple and that was followed by a protracted silence as Young, the stupid prick, made one of his theatrical shows of considering the implications.

'Well?' Darrin asked again, this time a little sharper than he intended but, what the fuck.

Young gave him a little peeved look, which was quickly replaced by his ventriloquist dummy, high beam smile.

'That Constable May is an underworld celebrity. Mr Niall O'Brien, the eldest brother of the brothers O'Brien. Chairman of the Saltt board of directors.'

It clicked for him then, the photo in the file that Young had shown him had to be at least twenty years old. He mentioned that and let its implications sink in, that got rid of Young's fucking smile for a while.

Lumb let him listen in to the couple's conversation but, again, there was nothing of interest, just lots of sugars, honeys and babes, the tinkling of glasses, the slide and close of the balcony door and Sade crooning her smooth as molasses torch songs. Niall was indeed old school.

Bottom line it was another snooze fest unless you were into jacking off on other peoples' trysts. He bottomed out around about ten and called up Trish, the crew were in Piccolos and it sounded like it was rocking. Just ten minutes away, he'd leave the car in the theatre car park. Darrin gave Lumb and Young a curt farewell and hit the night air. There was still plenty of time to get a glow on.

Dwayne was bang on reliable for the first few days and he and Junior were in and out like clockwork. Sunday afternoon and they'd arranged it for five this time. It was drizzling slightly and he'd thrown up the hood of the red top that she'd bought him for his birthday. He'd spent last night with her but she had barely said a word to him and after tea he'd spent the time up in his room on the Xbox - enjoying the solitude and the feeling of being in the zone with the game.

Twenty minutes waiting in the alley and the fucker still hadn't showed up. Junior fished out his mobile and rang him - it went straight to answer. They looked at each other and agreed on five more minutes then split. Junior strolled down the alley, stuck his head around the corner and looked down Oak towards the shops for a few seconds. He sauntered back up towards Pasquale shaking his head as he did so - not impressed.

'Any sign of him Joon?'

'He's down there, chatting with a couple of fit looking birds, boom box going. Showing off to 'em he is, the fucking dickhead.'

Pasquale breathed heavily through his nose, some businessman Dwayne was proving to be. Junior irritatedly picked up his bike, 'I'll go and get him - for fucks sake.'

Junior took off and turned right into the street. He watched the gap for a few moments then leaned back against the fence and looked up at the grey sky. It was a little chill today, a good job that the hoodie was fleece lined - that was his mum, always thinking ahead. He felt a warmth towards her that he hadn't felt for quite a while, maybe he'd get her something nice for her birthday. He looked at his watch, ten more minutes had gone and Junior was not yet back. He walked down the alley and briefly stood in Oak. Junior was pointing his bike back up to the alley and Pasquale could see his impatience, his wave returned with an exasperated shrug. At last, Dwayne broke away from the chicks, all three of them laughing as he did so - Mr fucking big bollocks. Junior was already pushing the pedals, all business. The two of them had to wait another five minutes for Dwayne to climb through the fence with the packages tucked away in his shoulder bag.

Dwayne handed the gear over and Pasquale reminded him of the agreement, 'quick in and quick out, we agreed.'

'Ease up young un, for fucks sake. All work and no fuckin' play you are,' Dwayne tut-tutted his exasperation at him. Junior had turned his bicycle and was already headed off down the alley, not interested in any discussion.

'Some pussy would fuckin' sort you out P,' Dwayne told him, 'the fuckin' cheddar's not fuckin' everything son.'

Pasquale turned his bike to see that Junior was making a skidding left towards Strickland. He stood in the saddle and hit it.

Darrin had gone over to the folks' place for Sunday lunch

and, for the first time in a long time there was a full house of uncles, aunties and cousins, all of them eager to ask him about his role in the riot. All of them, even his hard-eyed, begrudging Aunty Beryl cooing over him and treating him like a hero. He had two hours of 'our Darrin' this and 'our Darrin' fucking that. His mum couldn't stop beaming and his dad was twinkle-eyed proud over the pages of the *Sunday Mirror*.

The old fella even got into the back and forth. 'Tell them about the recommendation son - go on.'

He did, he'd been put forward for recognition for his actions from both Sarge Thomas and DI Kendrick for shielding big Chev, helping him back up to his feet and then on back to the line. Just doing the job, he modestly told the clan but it felt nice to be king for a day.

He had plenty of work to do though and the doing of it was predominantly occupying his mind and after lapping it all up he had made his excuses. It was already half past three and he was full as, truly roast dinnered and apple pied up to the fucking gills. Darrin touched his tight stomach and reminded himself to get his arse back to the gym as soon as possible.

Mac was lying on the sofa when he got to the flat, a couple of Sunday rags on his chest, nodding along to the sounds on his iPod - probably that appalling folky shite that he was into - all that swirling mist enveloping the magic isle bollocks. He was slightly startled when Darrin walked into the room, although, to be fair, he had told Mac that he'd be there nearer five.

Mac hadn't seen Chris Johnstone since 'the incident' as Mac now called it. His brother had been in last night, out with some reasonably tasty if downmarket bird who was taking up most of his attention by fervently chewing on his earlobes as if they were a packet of pork scratchings. Biffo Pete had surprised Mac by asking him how June was going when they had briefly been stood side by side at the bar, a tacit recognition of Mac's definitive actions near the pool table.

As it happened June was sidelined from the op at the moment. She was working on allegations of abuse in one of the city's many old folks' homes, working shifts undercover in the guise of a nursing auxiliary. Mac laughed at that, 'poor cow, adult diapers and one mile an hour walks down to the local park to feed the ducks. Must be bad, she reckoned she was even missing being in the bloody Admiral.'

They chatted about Dalton's new guest for a while. Mac had heard about the Saltt crew in relation to organised crime even when he was up there in Geordie land. 'Criminal royalty they are son, if that is the right fuckin word, living proof that, for some anyways, crime can and does pay.' Mac shook his head; the mere thought of that being the case pissed him off.

Just before five, Darrin stood up and went to the window with Mac's lightweight but powerful binoculars in hand. Quiet down there, no surprise that, it was a pretty shitty day weather wise, heavy, impenetrable, low cloud with on and off again rain. Dwayne was up there at his post, chatting with a couple of big breasted young wenches, music system at his feet, more of the bonobo crotch grabbing and plenty of shared laughter.

Mac told him he was up for some fish fingers and did he want some? He blew that off, he was just over the crest of the mountain that was the digestion of his mum's Sunday dinner.

A youngish black kid was cycling towards Dwayne and his fan club. The kid came to a skidding halt right in front of Dwayne waving his arms around a bit. Darrin had seen him plenty of times before - it was young Junior. The two of them chatted for a little while and then Dwayne turned his attention back to the girls. Junior wasn't interested in the flirt fest, turning his back on the group and facing the bike back up towards Strickland Road.

A couple of minutes later Darrin caught a little flash of red at the top of his vision. Some kid was out on the street standing down towards the bottom of Oak near that little alley down there that backed on to Linden. He lifted the glasses and caught a clear view of Junior's other half, Pasquale, the good looking mixed race kid. Pasquale animatedly waved to his mate who gave him a little return shrug of the shoulders. A few minutes passed then Dwayne broke away and said something to Junior who took off up to Oak with the other kid disappearing into the alley.

He grabbed his coat and told Mac that he was hitting the street.

'Got something son?'

'Maybe,' he said, Darrin was quickly out of the door with no looking back. He took the stairs in bounding strides of threes and fours, he went on out the back of the mid-rise then with a measured haste around the right hand side of the sad looking terraced houses, which abutted The Admiral car park. A couple of hundred yards at a fast paced walk and he was moving past the two girls who gave him a little look and a giggle. On past Sycamore, and his shoulder was now giving him shit every step of the way but he kept up the long striding pace. He reckoned he had a minute, at the most, to get there. Thirty yards on and he was now past Linden, only ten more yards to the alley. Junior shot out of the narrow gap pedalling hard with a grim faced focus. As close as he was, Junior hadn't registered his approach, taking a skidding left and shooting off to Strickland, fast as the fucking wind. He turned into the alley to see the other kid barrelling towards him, only three yards away at the most. The kid yelled and hit the breaks but he took Darrin out anyway, he went down on his arse and the kid hit the wall just to his left. The kid was dazed and looked in slightly worse shape than he felt. Darrin thought he heard a bit of noise further down the alley but a quick look confirmed that there was nobody to be seen. The kid was groaning, his nose bloodied, the darker red staining the bright red of his hooded top. Darrin pushed himself up with his decent arm and collared him, as he did so he reached behind the kid's back with his sore arm and unzipped his backpack. He picked the kid up to his feet by his collar and put the package in his face. 'Gotcha you little bastard,' he told him. The kid was pale and in shock, he didn't look so fucking arrogant now.

Darrin phoned it in and a squad car was up there in five minutes flat, the girls were looking down in their direction when the car pulled up and they gave him the finger when he cheerily waved at them with the package. Ten minutes later and he was booking the kid in at the station desk and then Sarge Thomas led him down to the pen and Pasquale Edwards was duly processed.

Darrin got the mother's home phone number from the kid but there was nobody home. The kid had given him her mobile too and he got the same deal with that. Sonny was on call that day and he arrived at the station less than half an hour after Pasquale's paperwork had been sorted out. Sonny had caught up with him in the quiet canteen as he was nursing his second cup of tea. A sore left shin and a grazed elbow was the only damage from the collision.

Sonny was his usual upbeat self, asking him about his old injury and then his new ones when Darrin had told him the circumstances of the arrest. Darrin finished briefing him, then he and Sonny went to the desk and asked Sarge Thomas to get the kid from the holding cell so that they could take him into the interrogation room.

He quizzed the kid about the package but got fuck all. The kid was stupidly stoic, playing street tough, his disdain at Darrin's questions not in sync with his eyes, which betrayed his anxiety and alarm. His gaze was darting constantly between Sonny and himself - as flighty and restless as a box full of kittens.

After Darrin had finished, Sonny had a crack at him.

'Do yourself a favour Pasquale, answer the constable's questions, let's make it easy for yourself. You could be looking at juvie here even though it's your first offence. You won't like it in there son, trust me. The refuge is Butlins in comparison.'

But still the kid held his silence. Sonny sighed and stood up, 'I'll try his mum again.'

The kid watched Sonny leave and Darrin gave him the beady once over. 'Well, are you going to be smart Pasquale or are you just going to be another little smart arse?'

The kid looked briefly over his shoulder over towards the door and then he met Darrin's gaze.

'I have something for you, maybe.'

'OK then, wait till Sonny gets back and say it in front of

him too – right?' The kid nodded, he was up for it.

Sonny returned in a couple of minutes, he'd gone straight through to her answer phone.

Sonny sat back down, Darrin gave him a little 'it's on' look and pushed his chin at the kid, 'Go on then son, let's have it.'

The kid looked at Sonny then back to him, he gulped a couple of times then took a deep breath, 'remember me mate M - Matthew Marshall.' They did, and both men unconsciously edged forward on their chairs. 'Well, I remembered a little while ago, that the day before he died he'd mentioned going to a party on the Saturday, down at the Quays,' he said. At that Darrin felt a surge of adrenalin boot up his heart rate. He could feel the pulse in his legs. In fact, it was all he could do to stay in the fucking chair.

'Go on,' he told him.

'He said a name too, yer know on the phone. Bazzer, I think it was, Bazzer Dougan. He was talking to him I think - straight up.'

Darrin nodded to himself and looked at Sonny. He turned his attention back to the kid who was staring at the floor again.

This time it was Sonny that broke the silence.

'Why didn't you tell us this before Pasquale? For fucks sake! He was your friend - supposedly.'

The kid nodded and his shoulders started to shake a little, a tear running down his cheek down to his jaw line.

Sonny curled his mouth at him.

'Who is that for then pal, for Matty or for you?'

Darrin let the kid cry, fuck him, his mum could deal with that shit. He'd call Young, kick it upstairs see how this affected the overall picture. He voiced a silent prayer of thanks to a god that he had stopped believing in years ago and somewhere in his mind a still blurred face began to take on a little more definition.

He got up and asked Sonny if he was OK to stay with the kid for a few minutes. Sonny nodded, well pissed off and as stony faced as an Easter Island statue, there would be no succour for the kid there either.

Pasquale was stuck in the room for at least two more hours. Sonny and the cop had relentlessly taken it in turns, tag-teaming him with their bullshit questions. Sonny was still striving to persuade him to give it up about the package. He was trying to scare him with talk about the local juvie prison - Bolton Wood. Sonny cranked it up telling him that he had heard that a couple of local lads who'd been thrown in there for taking part in the riots had been nailed within a couples of days of being locked up. They'd had the wrong allegiance to the wrong crew and were in the wrong place at the wrong time. Both of them had been leathered and both had ended up in hospital. Sonny told him it didn't have to be that way for him and, at that, the copper told him that maybe a leathering might do him some good. The door opened and the big sergeant had ushered his mum into the room. Sonny stood up and grabbed a chair from the corner of the room. He gave her the chair and the two men made room so that she could place herself in between Sonny and the copper. She didn't say a word to him but her eyes never left his face. The copper took the time to outline the charge to her and all of the possible outcomes. She raised her eyebrows and nodded at him but that was it. As soon as he finished giving her the lowdown she lasered him with her eyes.

'Good time to talk to us Pasquale,' Sonny said, 'I know you're scared but don't worry we can still work it out.'

He pulled his eyes up from the scarred table and looked at her and then back to the cop who pointed to the tape.

'For the record Pasquale – official.'

And that was it he let it go - part of it anyway. He told them about Dwayne and the arrangement, he kept Junior out of it, saying he had never carried just him, which pissed off the copper and drew a snort of disbelief from his mum. Fifteen minutes or so later and that was it, all wrapped up.

He'd be bailed to the refuge who had already been briefed about his arrest. His mum would get the summons with the date for his court appearance, which was likely to be sooner rather than later. He was given a bail notice, which explained the conditions of the bail. Sonny or one of his team would pick him up at the refuge and they would take him to report at the police station every day up until the court appearance. The copper had had a chat with his superiors and the prick had told them that he was of the opinion that Pasquale was at risk of re-offending. Therefore, he would be tagged and put under curfew. He almost launched a protest at that but kept it zipped - Sonny and his mum were ready to eat him alive. His mum left the station after signing some paperwork and Sonny was co-opted to take him back to the refuge.

The copper led him off to get tagged and that took another hour of fucking around, which gave Sonny an excuse to leave too. Sonny took three hours to come back to the station and without any explanation or even cursory engagement walked him out to his car. The cop who collared him and the Sergeant farewelled him with a brace of stony stares that could have frozen water.

Sonny turned to him as they walked across the car park.
'Welcome to the system Pasquale.'

They rode back to the refuge in a thick silence. No matter which way he turned, he had a sense of doors being closed in his face.

Darrin had alerted Young and his team about the arrest and the info that the kid had spilled. The package he had grabbed from the kid had been dusted and that fucking idiot Dwayne was all over that one too. Young had hummed and hawed a little then kicked it upstairs for a decision. Word quickly came back down to bust him, pronto. It transpired that Dwayne had skipped after the kid's arrest but there was no need for the deerstalker and pipe as the crotch grabbing plonker was found with a minimum of detective work. He was holed up at his auntie's place in Bridgewater, which was less than five miles away from the Coleshaw. A couple of cruising past bobbies had seen him strolling away from the local Chinese takeaway and had phoned it in. Detectives had picked him up at his aunts on the Monday - no mither, no fuss. He was brought to the central nick, charged and remanded in custody, no chance of Dwayne receiving bail given the charge and his priors.

Young had licked his lips when he'd heard the kid's drop on Bazzer. When Darrin had discussed it with him, he too, just like Mac before him, had used the word 'jigsaw' as a metaphor for the job. Maybe that was part of the drug squad training course. It was tenuous of course. As yet, there was no proof, only hearsay blah, blah, blah. But, given the fact that Dougan had turned up with a few barely legal lads and lasses at Dalton's last bash, they could not avoid looking at it. Alerting Keithy Dalton to an imminent grab though, that was the team's cause of concern, the noose was beginning to tighten on that prick and they didn't want to fuck it up now.

After some hastily arranged debate and no little angst the team agreed that he and Moz would have a friendly knock on Bazzer's door. They'd bring up the specific intel' about Matthew Marshall but not mention the parties at the Quays. The consensus was that a sniff of that and Bazzer, and probably Dalton, would fly.

So that was it, they had a plan - Mozzer to lead in and him to ride shotgun. On the ride over Mozzer's motor was still ponging but no better or worse than it had been a few months ago, at least Moz had a go at a clean out, only a couple of wrappers and paper cups in evidence on the back seat.

As they meandered, dog-legged and right-angled their way close to the centre of the estate Darrin was assailed by the usual feeling of him entering a sub-world, one of a terminal dreary torpor. The estate was full of people whose lives were either in abeyance or deterioration, only upwardly mobile whenever they stepped into the Job Centre lift. Darrin had to pay due to a few outposts of tenacious citizenry, homes with well kept gardens, boxes full of flowers proudly displayed on a couple of window sills but these were anomalies and very fucking infrequent ones at that.

A cursory glance at Bazzer's front yard told him that Mr. Dougan was obviously not a keen gardener. On display; a couple of rusting bikes, an engine block, a punctured football and three randomly scattered, small wellington boots, such was Bazzer-boy's tilt at the Barrington's garden of the year contest.

Darrin walloped the door a few times and immediately

heard some yelling inside. Bazzer was definitely home, loudly entreating his missus to do the honours -'bitch'. She did as she was told and opened up. Mrs. Bazzer was a small malnourished looking pregnant girl/woman who pulled the door open with the energy and zest of a brown bear waking up from a six-month kip. Darrin noted the fading bruising underneath her left eye. He did the introductions and, as he did so, she looked at him with an apathy that bordered on the pathological. Bazzer came busying up quickly behind her when he heard it was the feds, plenty of energy from that twat. As per his rep and Mozzer's pencil sketch briefings he was full of 'fuck you' piss and vinegar, his pale, blue eyes glittering with malevolent thoughts and bad intentions.

Baz was surly but locked into remaining scrote polite. He knew Moz and gave him a begrudging nod of recognition. He looked at Darrin as if he didn't particularly care for his presence or for his existence. Darrin smiled evenly at him but kept his eyes hard, giving Baz the silent message that he didn't give a fuck about that, either way.

'Can we come in Mr. Dougan have a chat?' Darrin asked, after the pleasantries were over.

'What's it about like? I'm busy at the mo.'

Darrin looked down at the slightly stained pyjama bottoms and smirked straight into his face.

'Oh yeah, busy eh? Brushing up on a bit of Open University are we then Bazzer? We can do it down the station if you like, must be a warrant we can dredge up from somewhere, what do you reckon Detective Morris?'

Bazzer scowled and motioned for them to get the fuck in.

The garden was picture postcard tidy compared to the lounge room. Bazzer told his missus to shift out of the room, 'men's business', he growled at her, punctuating the assertion by throwing a pile of clothes and some kiddies' jigsaws and board games off the sofa and onto the floor.

She shared her unhappiness with Bazzer with a snarled but slightly muted 'prick' and reluctantly marched off a couple of narked and protesting X-boxing mud larks. As the three of them crocodile walked past them out into the kitchen the youngest, a red head of five or so, gave Darrin a glance and the ghost of a shy smile. He had his dad's piercing baby blues and a solid little build which suggested that he'd outweigh his old man by a good fifty pounds when he hit maturity, maybe in him would be the ghost of Bazzer's ultimate Christmas future, one could only hope.

Moz led off on the kid's story, it had been agreed by the team that he would be the mouthpiece with Darrin watching on. Bazzer listened to him with a facsimile of polite interest whilst scratching various parts of his body. Baz continuously switched his gaze between them and the frozen TV screen, all the while licking his bright full lips with a slightly obscene regularity.

Dougan let Mozzer talk it all out before he made any response, he knew nothing, of course, never spoke to the kid, never seen him, didn't know who he was. A complete stone-wall job - he was a good fucking liar, Darrin had to give him that. 'Love to help you officers but yer know sorry like…' all the predictable bollocks.

Darrin heard Moz sigh and start to move his arse forward on the sticky sofa.

Darrin looked intently at Bazzer's profile, his eyes were back on the frozen screen again and Darrin felt the urge to smash him and keep on smashing him.

Fuck it, he thought.

He snatched the baton from his 'where do we go to from here' partner.

'We've heard that the lad might have gone down to some party like, just before he disappeared Baz. Know anything about that then do yer?'

That got the fucker's attention right enough, he couldn't hide the gulp in his throat. Moz moved uncomfortably on the sofa letting out a little whistle of breath at Darrin's break from the script.

'P-party?' Bazzer's head twitched a couple of times in a little two-step left-right, left-right reflex. There was no eye contact at all now and he had a sudden interest in what was not going on in the back yard.

Darrin leant in a little and pushed away Mozzer's attempt to grab his forearm.

'Yeah that's right, we've been told it were somewhere down at the Quays.'

At that Bazzer turned his head looked right into his eyes and vigorously shook his head.

'No officer. Know nothing about any party. OK, nah, nothing, nowt like.'

Darrin looked at him in silence for a few moments, conscious of a slight twitch beneath his own left eye, all of his will was focussed on being still, steady, in the moment.

Dougan reiterated with a shrug, 'help you if I could officers but, like I said.'

Ah well, that was that then, for the moment.

Darrin stood up to go and Mozzer was up half a beat behind him. Darrin turned to the lounge room door then did a little half turn back, which brought Dougan back into his eye line.

Bazzer looked up at him with a malevolence that actually made the hair stand up on the back of Darrin's neck. A half sneer curling back his upper lip far enough to show his gold spotted left incisor.

'Hang on a minute though cuntstable. Yeah, I heard summat on the grapevine like. Bloke in a pub, don't know him like, chatting about that he were. He'd heard tell some important folk like to pork them young uns, yeah. Yeah, important folk, he reckoned.' And this time he looked at both Mozzer and Darrin, 'important protected folk like - maybe you might know what I mean Mr Morris?'

Darrin turned to Moz who had his eyes fixed on Bazzer.

'No, I can't say I do Dougan,' Moz said, his voice as cold as an Arctic blast. 'You got any more bullshit to want to tell us, boy?'

Bazzer snorted, his lips twisting into another sneer.

'No Mr Morris, I've got nothing for you at all.'

When they got back to the car, Darrin had expected a roasting but it didn't come, just wave upon wave of heavy, static filled silence. But it was Moz who spoke first as they pulled away from Dougan's home and on out of the Barrington.

'Be nice to nail that prick, eh Daz?'

Darrin mutely nodded and glanced over at his colleague's profile.

'Yeah, sounds like he might be able to give us plenty if he cracked. Be like pulling back a rock that would. What do you reckon Moz?'

Mozzer tapped his meaty left thigh a few times before he answered, then he did a little double index fingered tattoo on the steering wheel. 'He'd lie to God that slack jawed fucker would and shit on his mum while he did so. And, well, you let the cat out of bag din't you Dazzle - going to be ramifications about that, fucking hell.'

Darrin glanced at him, 'fuck it Moz, let's shake the tree for a change, where the fuck are we going with all this?'

Moz made as if to reply but didn't. Instead, he turned to look out the driver's seat window as mute and pissed off as Marley's ghost.

They made the rest of the journey with no further reference to it. Ramifications, Darrin thought, good, let's fucking hope so.

OCTOBER

Tommy called Sonny on Tuesday, the kid was now on bail, tagged, and, given the amount of weed that he was found with, lucky not to be held in custody. Sonny said that there was some solid evidence that the kid had been ferrying around the hard stuff too but the cops were choosing to sit on that nugget at the moment. So, maybe the little prick had been a little lucky again.

Sonny thought the kid would probably end up in a secure training centre rather than juvie. Apparently, he'd spilled enough info to them to get him out of those particular woods. He considered calling Donna to chat it through but he decided against it. He was ready to close the book on the kid, let him take the hard medicine and if he was binning Pasquale that probably meant he'd be binning her too.

More importantly, it had been a few days without contact with Mick so he called round to see the old man. Mick was home, obviously content in his chair, reading the newspaper with a half finished brew at his side. His bar ashtray was two thirds full and rising with a ragged pyramid of dimps. There had to be enough tar in Mick's lungs to do a fair patch up job on the M62.

They sat in silence for a few minutes then his old man tapped the paper, 'one in here for you today son, you'll like this.'

'Oh yeah, go on then?'

'Yeah, bout these bloody chimps, taken away from their mothers in infancy then kept in labs for thirty years just to be tested. They were let out for the first time yesterday. Poor fuckers had never seen the sun, never! Fucking disgraceful I reckon, and they reckon we are at the apex of the fucking pyramid of evolution. Fuckin' Jaffas.'

His old man rested his paper in his lap and peered at him over his reading glasses.

'You know son, I've been giving what you said a lot of thought.'

'Oh yeah what's that then Dad?'

'You know that spiritual sickness stuff? I read that and I can't get my head around the cruelty of it. I don't know whether to get mad or to fucking cry, truly I don't.'

Tommy looked intently at his old man. He could count on two fingers the number of times that he'd seen Mick shed any tears.

He smiled at Mick.

'Well, there is a belief that next year, on the day after your birthday as it happens, there will be an event that will eventually lead to the collective enlightenment of mankind.'

Mick nodded, 'oh yeah I've read about that, that Mayan calendar thing right?'

Tommy nodded at him, 'yeah you got it Mick, the Mayan calendar.'

'Well, if I'm still around son, I'll raise a birthday malt to it. But I don't think you'll be seeing a day of collective enlightenment Tommy, never mind me.'

'Yeah think you might be right Dad but…you never know.'

His dad looked at him and laughed, 'bloody barm pot you are lad, bloody Mayans - bloody jaffas.'

Tommy laughed with him till it tapered out into another easy silence, Mick reading, him listening to, who was it? John Martyn? Had to be, John doing his soulful thang on Mick's relatively new and much used DAB radio.

He looked at his watch - time to make tracks.

'Fancy the pub tomorra - me and Jimbo are having it?'

Mick rubbed his chin for a couple of moments and then gave a thumbs down with an emphatic nod of his noggin.

'I would but it's the bloody football tomorra in't it. That bloody TV will be on in every room in the fuckin' pub. Blokes gawping transfixed at the screen, no thanks son, I'll pass.'

Mick gave out a few of his patented rueful pissing in the wind chortles.

'OK Mick, I'm away at Lee's this weekend. I'm going to check out Brighton with him and Bern.

That sparked the old fella up again. He put his paper down and took off his specs.

'Brighton. I remember that bloody town well. Me, your Uncle Tom, Uncle Fred and Richard went down there, had a bucks' weekend fer Richard's wedding.'

Mick laughed at the relished memory.

'Bloody hell, we did some fine misbehaving.' Mick gave him his mischievous leprechaun grin and a knowing wink.

'You'll like it down there son, your kind of place I reckon, not like this bloody dump - have a good 'un if I don't see yer before yer go.'

'Thanks Dad, I will. I'll have a look. See if they erected a plaque in memory of your visit. I'll give you a bell when I get back.' He stood up to go and patted his dad gently on the shoulder before he made his way to the front door.

'Leave the door son,' Mick told him, 'I'll lock it up behind yer.'

Tommy walked out into the surprisingly cool air and quickly turned up the collar of his jacket.

He was with his dad about the football, imagine a world without soccer, he thought. That would be fucking fine.

So, his routine was tightly locked in, right up to the court case. A visit by Sonny or another member of the Youth Visiting Team in the morning and then another one of the team would come back to take him to the station to report to the cops in the afternoon. The other kids in the ref told him that they thought the tag was cool but he didn't think so, it wasn't even remotely cool and he was pissed off enough to not even pretend to buy into their bullshit about it. Junior had sent him a text telling him that his loot was safe. He had over two grand in that tin and, as yet, no fucking idea of how he was going to get to it.

Things were changing all around him right enough, Kat would be gone in a couple of weeks, off to her own flat and Neil was making his plans for a move out with his sugar-daddy. When away from Neil, Kat and Jess told him that they thought it was all likely to fall through quickly. They couldn't imagine anybody living one-on-one with Neil on a 24/7 basis, they weren't wrong about that, Neil was a fucking roman candle of incessant drama.

Despite all that shit - the refuge felt like exactly that to him at the moment - a place where he felt both accepted and safe. Dwayne would have been busted for sure unless he'd been smart enough to get away and he didn't feel safe with any of his old haunts, apart from his mum's. The thought of being caught up on the Coleshaw or the Barrington filled him with dread, they would fuck him up for sure. His mum had visited him a couple of times during the week but she hadn't talked to him about the possibility of him going to hers for the weekend. The punishment had started as far as she was concerned.

A week on Thursday then and he'd know for sure where his next home would be. The others had reassured him that the training centres were OK, if that was where he was to be going. None of the others had mentioned juvie in his presence apart from his prick of a roommate who had been leapt on by the gang and venomously told to shut the fuck up. Kat said she'd stay in touch and he thought that she probably would, Neil and Jess had parroted the same thing but he knew that they were both as fickle as fuck and he doubted that they would come through for him. Be nice to see a bit more of Jess, she'd been looking at him a little differently since he was charged and, let's face it, she was as hot as fuck.

He hated the uncertainty but, what the fuck could he do? If he bolted it would only make things worse for him. His mum and the rest of them were right, it was time to take the medicine. Pasquale put his feet up on one of the plastic chairs at the back of the ref and looked, for the zillionth time, at his tag and thought unresolved thoughts about the two grand with his name on it resting in that cavity mill wall.

The ops team had met up a couple of days after their chat with Bazzer. Dwayne was banged up in the nearest big house but keeping resolutely schtum about his gaffers. The consensus was that the operation hadn't been compromised by the arrest and that they were still OK to go on both up at the Coleshaw and down at the Quays. The scrotes would put down Darrin's bust to bad timing and bad luck although they had decided to pull him out of the estate just to be safe. Dalton would be back early next week according to a call that he'd made to O'Brien's mobile. O'Brien sounded indifferent to that bit of news, he'd been in and out of the fuck-pad with his piece pretty much every day since Keithy had taken off and the girlfriend had stayed in the apartment whenever O'Brien had been away - long evenings on her tod singing flatly to herself in the spa. Aching love ballads mostly, she was missing her tarnished knight.

Interestingly and surprisingly, Moz hadn't mentioned his slip to Young, Bowden or, as far as he knew, anybody else on the team. So, if the coppers' knowledge of the parties had somehow got back to anybody in the Saltt crew thus far, the O'Briens were keeping that bit of information to themselves.

As far as Darrin was concerned it was all still a long bow, they would have to get leverage from Bazzer himself to get anywhere near the higher echelons and, although Dougan was as daft as a brush, he had strong self preservation instincts and was likely to remain loyal to the Saltt crew. Darrin reckoned that the chance of Bazzer spilling was negligible.

Mac had been invited to a piss up at Biffo Johnstone's place over the weekend; a few cans, a huge bowl of weed, mixed nuts and raisins and a DVD on the flat screen, 'one of the fucking *Die Hards* no less' and he'd had the misfortune to be shown Pete's competition bodybuilding photos. 'Came third in the regional finals' according to Mac, which got the biggest laugh of the meeting.

The following day Darrin was back on the plod, ambling round the battered Centre with Johno. The clean up was pretty much finished now, the florist shop was still boarded up but old Harry was already back in business- as hardy as a desert rose that old fella - and the Asian mini market had its doors open too. His shoulder was pretty much OK although it was still a little stiff if he tried a straight-arm lift. They clocked off the shift at eight, he was a little weary but not ready to go back to the flat so he hit the canteen for a snack, a brew and a read of the paper. At this time of the day it was guaranteed to be quiet and that would suit him fine. He felt like he'd been talking all day and, inevitably with Johno for company, he'd had to use or at least pretend to use his listening skills a fair bit.

He was just about to wrap it all up and get ready to make his way home when he heard the familiar gravelly baritone call out his name from the doorway.

'P.C. Darrin May - a local hero and a young gun on the rise.'

He could have done without it, in fact he needed Keegan at the moment like he needed a dose of crabs, but he kept the irritation from his face and managed to drag up the riposte of a mirroring smile.

Keegan ambled over to the table in his heavy, bow legged gait. He grabbed a chair turned it around and straddled it. He folded his meaty arms akimbo over the chair's back.

'How you been then lad?'

'Fine thanks Sarge not too bad at all, and you?'

'Not bad lad - keeping the streets safe and all that cobblers. How's that shoulder of yours? Heard about what you did with young Chev, you showed some ticker there son.'

Despite himself, Darrin felt a surge of pride at the big man's thumbs up - Keegan was not renowned for giving out the bouquets.

'Thanks Sarge - I appreciate it.'

'Still enjoying the D stuff are yer? How's that all going? Heard you had a possible lead on the lad that was found in the skip.'

Keegan's grin remained on his face but the eyes were scoping him now, steel plate hard and very intense. Fuck knows what Keegan would be like in the interrogation room - scary.

Darrin shifted around in his seat a little, he folded his arms and then willed himself to unfold them.

'Yeah, well yer know how it is Sarge, the kid might have just been covering his arse, yer know fishing for a break. We had him bang to rights for the weed. He was fucked on that one.'

Keegan nodded a few times in solemn appraisal then he lifted the big bison head and resumed the optical work out. Not fucking finished by any means.

'Heard you rattled that dumb ass nutter Bazzer Dougan's cage too - how's he fit in with it all yer reckon?' Keegan took a casual little look at his thumbnail.

Darrin didn't miss a beat.

'Not sure really Sarge, the kid I collared reckoned the dead lad made a call to somebody called Bazzer and that he'd talked about a party, down the Quays somewhere like. Bazzer gave us fuck all though, he was tighter lipped than the pharaohs, that mad-eyed gob-shite.'

That got Keegan rubbing his jaw - the big man looking inwards now.

Darrin ploughed on like a boat slipping irrevocably from its moorings and out to the rough open sea - fuck it. 'Yeah spouting shite he were, talking a load of crap about the top end of town and about him being protected.'

Keegan snorted at that, spraying a light plume of saliva over the table and onto Darrin's sleeveless left arm, 'who'd protect that no mark arsehole - not even his fuckin mum would protect that scrawny cum stain.'

Yeah, yeah, he'd got the message - Dougan was a cunt - unanimous.

'Yeah right enough Sarge, I think he was trying to lay a false trail. You know, puffing himself up a bit. I know a bloke who knows a bloke, the usual bollocks.'

Keegan leaned across the table and patted him lightly on his forearm, Darrin didn't move and he smiled right back into those hard eyes.

'Getting a name for yourself you are young Darrin, fair enough too. You've come a long way for a guy who was riding a forklift a couple of years back.'

Darrin continued looking into the eyes, Darrin smiled again, matching Keegan's shit eating grin with one of his own.

'Yeah, right, thanks Sarge. I guess you're right about that. Of course there is always the exhumation angle too.'

'Exhumation - what you mean?' a little quick in his response maybe - for Keegan.

Keegan leaned forward, lifting the back legs of the chair off the ground as he did so, his heavy brow now some six inches or so closer to his own.

'Yeah you know Sarge, if he did go to a party at the Quays just before he ended up in that skip. It might be worthwhile, you know to check him out, for any foreign DNA like. They might have missed something, you know in his clacker, stomach contents and that. You know how they are Sarge, they can be a bit rushed and sloppy without a prod in the right direction and before the new info, well, there was no possible sex angle then, was there?'

Keegan shook his head at him and gave out a mirthless harsh laugh that bounced off the canteen walls.

'Nah Constable nah, you're jumping way ahead there son. They'll only usually do that around cause of death and I thought they'd nailed it with the toxicology reports, overdose, that new crap they're all smoking and sticking into their veins.'

There was a few moments of silence between them, Keegan pushed out his lower lip and looked towards the drinks machine, which was over to the left of Darrin's shoulder - his face was impassive and impossible to read.

'Well it's an interesting thought young Daz. Run it by the brass, you never know, they might be up for it.'

Darrin nodded into Keegan's face, aware of his raised pulse and the adrenalin that was making his legs tremble under the table.

Keegan heavily pushed himself up - the fucker had to be knocking eighteen stone and apart from a mid-size paunch little of it was excess.

Keegan put the twinkle back in his eye and the hale and hearty back in his voice.

'Alright then son take it easy - keep up the good work-very impressive.'

Darrin held the big man's gaze again, as benign as a light breeze.

'Thanks for that Sarge, I will.'

Keegan rolled away and Darrin watched him turn right into the corridor, heading off towards the lifts.

Darrin folded the paper up and put it under his arm. He'd

finish it off when he got home. He had a fair bit of thinking to do.

Junior had texted him asking him if it was cool that he come up to the ref. Pasquale told him to contact the office first and try and make an appointment for just after lunch. That would give them some time before whichever one of the youth team arrived to take him to the cop station, if he was lucky it would be Leah - she was fit for an older bird and just sitting in the car with her was enough to give him a raging hard on. Luckily, Rob was on shift and he agreed to Junior visiting, but only with plenty of fucking conditions attached. He had to let Rob know that Junior had arrived as soon as he got there, there was to be no leaving the grounds of the refuge during the visit, and the visit was to be capped at half an hour max, after that Junior had to be on his way.

Junior showed about two, right on the dot - he was on foot, no bike, wearing his back pack and he had a folded soft grey cap held tight in his right mitt. The three others were sat outside at the tables and they showed no inclination to move away - so he and Junior stayed put in the lounge room. Rob silently checked it out and then went back to the office to finish off playing his computer chess. Before he left, Rob reminded him of the ground rules, as if he would have fuckin' forgotten them, particularly emphasising the thirty minutes tops.

The TV was on low, some daytime drivel that even Neil and Jess couldn't be bothered to watch. Junior was quiet, but, there again, he usually was. He did a couple of laps of the lounge room with his eyes then casually handed the cap to him.

'Here you go P. You might want to stash that in your room - right away like.'

Pasquale glanced at him, stood up and made his way through the kitchen and into the corridor that led past the office. He could hear Rob, not so busy on the office phone murmuring to somebody, probably that porky bird of his. Pasquale went quickly into his room and he unfolded the cap with his back pressed hard against the closed door. It was all there, a nice thick wad of twenties and tens, just under two and a half grand. Junior had even put a plastic band around it. He stashed the money in his kit bag in the wardrobe then returned to Junior in the lounge.

He sat down and extended his palm and Junior touched hands with him.

'Ta bro.'

'No worries P - you earned it.'

Junior looked at him levelly for a moment.

'They took Dwayne in - nobody's saying it were down to you though.'

'Yet.'

Junior nodded, 'yeah, yeah you're right, yet.'

'It's all quiet up there - nobody's stepped up either.'

Junior dipped his head then glanced up at him.

'Thanks too P for - yer know.'

'It's all right man, we're partners.'

Junior smiled at that.

Pasquale decided to tell him, it was weighing heavily and not letting it out was not making it go away.

'I told them about Bazzer though Junior.'

'What, you mean the gear?' Junior looked startled.

'No, no man not that, the phone call that M made to the

prick - the party and that.'

Junior looked at him quietly then gave him the nod.

'Shit, no shit, fair enough I suppose. He ain't gone no-where though, still kicking on the Barrington, as far as I know anyways.'

Pasquale thought about that for a while, 'maybe they thought I was shitting them.'

Junior shrugged, 'yeah maybe - they ain't talked to me again either.'

Pasquale thought it prudent to remind him why that was, he knew that Junior would be a little ambivalent about letting the coppers know about the call.

'Well you weren't mentioned were you? You got to pull back though, that copper that nabbed me must have seen yer.'

Junior leaned back into the sofa and breathed out heavily towards the ceiling. Pasquale could hear Junior's cogs whirring, trying to process all the angles.

Pasquale kept quiet and looked at the TV for a while, some bloke with plenty of jowl was rapidly chopping up a cabbage whilst talking to the camera.

'Next Thursday eh?' Junior said.

'Yeah, pretty soon.'

'They told you what you're likely to get?'

'Yeah, kind of, Sonny reckons it'll be one of those secure units - it'll be fucking miles away from here. Like a big ref he reckons, but stricter; no smoking, bed early, up early. You get your own room but.'

Junior nodded, 'hmmm, that part of it don't sound too bad.'

'Lessons every day though, most of the time you got to

stay locked up in there and the workers always go outside with yer for any excursions, appointments and that.'

Junior smiled, 'might be some fit birds in there mind, eh blood.'

Pasquale shook his head and grimaced, 'I think it's all lads.'

'Shit,' Junior said, 'don't want you coming out a there a turd burglar P.' Junior had an involuntary glance in Neil's direction, he and the girls still busy back there, doing nowt.

Pasquale looked at him and Junior softened it up with a laugh, 'kidding man, kidding.'

'What you decided then Junior, hanging around or what?'

'Dunno P, spoke to my mum bout Haringey again. She reckons they're OK with me going down there to stay.'

'Go for it man, get out of this fucking dump.'

There was a volley of raucous laughter from the back of the building, which momentarily distracted them. They both looked outside to see Neil shimmying along to some tune in his head, the girls lapping it up.

Pasquale looked over and smiled and then he had a pang of impending loss. He was going to be saying a lot of goodbyes.

Rob walked into the lounge and gave them the final bell.

'Ty is here in ten Pasquale - take you to the police station.'

Even Rob was making a point of spelling it out - how he'd fucked up.

They stood up and looked at each other with shy half smiles and then Junior stepped forward and embraced him - something that they'd never done before.

They stepped apart and Junior promptly made for the back door, he slid it open and then half turned back into the room.

He saluted him with a nod and a little wave from the hip.

324

'Later then bro.'

'Later Junior.' Junior turned away and, with a few long strides, he was gone.

Tommy had taken a half-day off at the Centre in preparation for the trip to Brighton, Mick's words still replaying in his head about the need for him to leave the nest. On balance he knew that Mick was right but it was a compromise that he was willing to make while the old man was still sunny side up. He was intrigued at the prospect of visiting a place that had only really registered on his radar whenever he had listened to the Who's *Quadrophenia* and he hadn't listened to that odyssey of teenage angst for at least twenty years. He knew fuck all about the place but Lee had waxed lyrical about it during their last phone call, which had pricked his interest a little. He hadn't heard such enthusiasm from his friend since he and Bern had first set up their own recording studio back in the late eighties.

He made Euston just after eight and an hour or so later he was ensconced in Lee's kitchen with some red wine, pizza, an animated Bern and a chilled out Lee. Bernie was right into the Brighton thing, non-stop jabber from her about both the trip and their probable plans for moving down there in the future. He got it out of the way and talked a little about Donna and the kid. Bernie said that she liked her - but just couldn't see it somehow, the two of them as a couple.

'Any reason why Bern?'

'Don't know really - maybe just coming from a different place somehow - in some ways she's just too straight for you Tommy - you have that wandering gypsy soul.'

Lee smiled at that and Tommy laughed, 'gee whiz, I guess

coming from you that would be a compliment eh Bern?'

She nodded at him, earnestly straight faced and sincere, 'definitely.'

They killed two bottles of the plonk but they had an earlyish night as the plan was to be down at Victoria by eleven at the latest. Then it would be straight to the hotel, off out for lunch and a meet up with a couple of friends of theirs, a pair of fellow musicians who had made the break to the south coast a couple of years ago.

Tommy woke up in the charcoal grey of the pre-dawn. It was just after six according to his mobile. On checking the time he remembered that he'd left his fucking charger at home, again, and the battery was nearly gone so he clicked the phone off. Ah well, he thought, it would be good to be out of range for a day or two, make it feel like more of a break. Anyway, he had a couple of hours up his sleeve and the lounge room was nice and warm - more kip was the order of the day.

He went to change position slightly but found that when he went to move his legs they wouldn't respond at all. He tried again but no, nothing. He could still feel the limbs but they were dead weight, lifeless. He didn't feel panicked at all, more like he was strangely detached from the experience somehow, both the observer and the observed. Tommy heard a voice in his head, his own but, there again, not quite his own. It was separate somehow, outside of him. A male voice though and it was very calm, sonorous and measured.

'This is what it feels like to die,' the voice said.

Clear as a bell and, again, a second time.

'This is what it feels like to die.'

He lay there bemused, he couldn't equate the words with

the experience, as freaky as the experience was, because he knew he wasn't dying - it was all so fucking odd. He waited twenty seconds or so, still calm, still unpanicked, with no more incoming messages from James Earl Jones either. He tried once again and, this time, his legs responded, normal service resumed; there was no ache in them, no pins and needles, no cramping and, yeah, he supposed, no worries. Tommy thought about it for a little while - it should have been alarming but that wasn't how he felt, maybe he'd get alarmed about it later. The experience had felt matter of fact, and that residue, that feeling of acceptance and inevitability was somehow consonant with the tone of that voice.

Bernie came in and roused him just after eight and he mentioned the experience to her as they sat in the kitchen together drinking coffee. But his lack of alarm at the experience elicited a muted response from her, just a quizzical look and a cocked eyebrow.

They arrived at Brighton Station pretty much on midday. A half full train had got a bit of a lick on and had made the trip in just over an hour. He liked the town's station. It was an elegant throwback to the age of steam that reminded him of Mick's old workplace but without the patina and ambience of grit.

The place was packed with loads of young and not so young people milling around the cavernous forecourt. The three of them made their way to the taxi rank, swerving and zig-zagging through clusters of foreign students as they did so. Groups of French, Italian and Spanish youngsters notably relaxed yet with the natural animation and liveliness of youth. They were fresh faced and had none of the wary, watchful swagger of many of the home grown younger end.

They jumped in a cab near the wide station entrance. He took the front and Lee gave the driver the destination, which was a two mile drive down to the hotel in Hove. The driver was a ruddy-faced middle-aged Saxon whose sedentary work had had a marked impact on his girth. He immediately took a right turn off the main road, which looked as though it ran south all the way down to the sea, and drove on west, staying parallel to the Channel, the blue of which Tommy could glimpse through the narrow street vistas that led down to the seashore. A mile or so later the driver took a left and then turned right into what was another busy main road; plenty of cyclists of all ages, posses of double-decker buses and cars and, unlike the now relatively empty streets of his home town chock full of pedestrians too. Lee and Bern had enthused about that the fact that Brighton was a 'walk anywhere' city. Less than a mile later they took another right-angled left hand turn, which gave them a clear vista of the glass like water. They drove slowly down a wide street that was buttressed by two lengthy rows of four storey, big windowed brick town houses, all of which looked to have been broken up into flats.

The hotel was right down at the bottom of the street, its architecture consonant with the sentinel town houses - Regency according to Lee. In itself the hotel was nothing grand but it was pleasant enough. It had a bar which doubled up as a reception and a large restaurant area off to the left of that which was opened for business but empty. The three of them checked in and agreed to meet back in the bar in half an hour so that then they could take off for a stroll down to the nearby seafront.

His room was small but clean, the only view from it that

of the neighbouring building's large side wall - so it would be for sleeping purposes only. Tommy took his time getting ready as he knew that Bern would surely be taking hers. He was down the bar nursing a beer for nearly twenty minutes before Lee came in through the room's double swing doors with a raising of his eyebrows and a grimace of apology. Bern came bustling in a few strides behind him, head down and looking for something in her large handbag. She was always rushed that girl, yet never on time - amazing.

Anyway, no fuss, he was on the clock plenty enough back oop north and he was determined to let the weekend pass by in a laissez-faire state of mind. They made their way out, chucked a left and with a hop skip and a jump, which was slightly stalled by the number of cars rolling down the seafront road, they hit the wide promenade and strolled on eastwards down towards the pier. It was a bright warm day and the Hove end of the seafront was busy, but you still had plenty of space to move and, apart from the odd jogger, people were very much taking their time with it. However, as soon as they walked past the striking angel statue, which marked the Brighton-Hove border, the promenade got much narrower and a hell of a lot busier. It was still a chill vibe though, plenty of folk languishing on the pebbled beach on deck chairs and towels; family groups, some oldies and plenty of younger people too, a real mix of ages and very, very relaxed - people happy at just being were they were.

Lee asked him what his first impressions were as they strolled past the little outdoor market that was situated near the remarkable enduring skeleton of the west pier. Impressed, he told him 'pleasantly surprised.'

Inland just past the little market were the city's landmark

hotels, the Hilton and the Grand, it was the latter that the IRA had lit up in their attempt to off the Blessed Margaret all those years ago.

Two drag queens passed them down near the beach volleyball sand pit, glammed up to the max, both of them well over six foot in their heels, arm in arm and deep in conversation. Seemingly oblivious and impervious to any rubber necked stares and, Tommy noted interestingly enough, most people didn't seem to give a rat's arse about their presence. In fact, the townsfolk appeared to be conspicuously indifferent. That was something else he hadn't experienced for a long time, not since walking down Oxford Street and Darlinghurst Road in Sydney. Fucking hell, he thought, here all these years and he'd never known that such a place existed in the UK.

They had a leisurely nosh of some chips on the Palace Pier, stuffing their faces as they leaned against the pier's rails. Tommy took in the distant view to the east, the resonant shimmering drama of the south coast's iconic white cliffs, striking despite or maybe because of their familiarity and then he turned to take in the western view with its long sweep of fine Regency buildings. All that slightly faded glamour. Inland to the north up behind the urban spill there was a glimpse of the lush soft green roll of the Sussex Downs.

Stomachs satisfied, they made a slow paced return trip towards the hotel and, as they did so, it struck him that, for him, Hove was the place to be if you were living here. It was close to the action, everything was in easy walking distance but not too mad either - much more the pace of life for a middle-aged codger like himself.

They had a late lunch/early tea at a place just over the road from the hotel. The restaurant/bar was a bamboo decorated, cocooned throwback to some time in the seventies, which was a little incongruously located in the ground floor of a largish block of flats. The place was owned by a Javanese family who worked both the bar and the in-house Indonesian restaurant. There was little natural light in the joint and a flyer cello-taped to one of the bar's large supporting columns told him it was karaoke night tonight. Bernie wouldn't be having that with a barge pole, she could be a little elitist when it came to try-hard amateur warblers could our Bern.

Her friends, who had been waiting for them in the bar area were right enough, a pair of hippies for the new millennium kinda folk, which, he ruminated, would be pretty much the same as hippies of the old millennium kinda folk. Both disarmingly gentle with the guy, the talker of the two. As they sipped the first round of drinks he gave them the lowdown on the town, they loved it down here, the guy said it was a haven of 'relative tolerance' and he theorised that its 'specialness' was down to the fact that it was situated on a ley-line, which ran under some park in Hove and then on out into the Channel. This got Bernie's juices flowing, sending her off into one of her white witch, Wicca reveries, inspiring her enough to put the idea to Lee that they should come back down on the shortest day of the year to join their friends and others for a little solstice ceremony. Lee didn't miss a beat, Mr. Straight Bat keeping it in neutral with a couple of half-hearted maybes followed by a well timed visit to the bar. Tommy had to hide his grin at his friend's retreat with some superfluous use of his napkin.

Another round and then they fare-welled the couple, with a time arranged to meet up later in Kemptown. The guy was playing keyboards in a local Latin American combo, the Three Wise Monkeys, so that was the evening sorted.

The guy told Tommy that that was the gay part of town. Tommy felt an irritation at the unnecessary information, which he knew was being given for his benefit alone. To him it was an example of how even the right on can be hobbled by their own misperceptions, but in the spirit of the weekend and as a nod to his ever obliging friends he let it pass.

They had a crash at the hotel for a couple of hours. He checked his mobile, which was drained now so he turned it back off and stuck it back in his travel bag. He slept heavily for a couple of hours - no problems with his legs this time and no Jovian voices in his head either - that was a fucking bizarre experience!

After a stroll through the heart of the city, they were at the pub by nine and it was packed and already buzzing with anticipation. The band did a little cursory sound check then ripped into it. The Three Wise Monkeys were four white boys fronted by an older South American guy dressed in an immaculate white suit and matching Panama hat. He had an ageless look and a good voice. His baritone pipes were augmented with a judicious leathering of the cowbell, mercurial feet and a twinkle eyed regard for the pretty chicas who were busting their moves just a yard away from his mike stand. The band was fucking fab' and Bernie didn't need any urging to get him to dance and when he got up he stayed up. Lee usually only danced internally but, yeah, it looked like he was dancing, a bit Flock of Seagulls maybe but borderline exuberance for him.

The Monkeys played until half ten and then had a little break, which allowed half of the pub to pour outside and take the time to cool down in both the busy main street and the side street that led on to the sea. Tommy wiped his face with his shirt then looked up at a flat across the street, wherein sat a guy in his lounge room engrossed in whatever was on his computer while a beefy seagull patrolled the window sill of his flat.

They went back inside to bounce around for another sweat-soaked hour. After the gig they walked all the way back to the hotel and it was still well busy down on the seafront; a few drunks, plenty of kids but nothing to get alarmed about, there was no need for him to reach for the brass knuckles. Yeah, he thought, he could live down here, no problem- Jaysus, he felt young again.

On the Sunday, they caught the late afternoon train back to London after a day walking the city centre and the seafront. They had parked off at a promenade café for some people watching, washed down with coffee and some good quality carrot cake. Lee had brought down his travel set backgammon with him and they had a best of five whilst Bern went off for a bit of a wander - la Dolce fucking Vita alright.

Tommy had said goodbye to Lee and Bern at Victoria and then made the tube trip across to Euston. When he got back to his flat, he put the phone on charge but left it turned off. He needed some time out and an early night, he'd let his life back in tomorrow. He was meeting up with Pauline in the morning to try and get a bit of a clearer structure together for the temporary locations of the activities that were on the youth service's programme for the rest of the calendar year. The youth service, the young mothers' programme and the oldies would have to be sharing the reception area for a while and it all needed sorting asap. He thought about firing up the lap top to see what the Brighton singles scene had to offer, lord knows he'd seen plenty of attractive women down there but he decided against it and went for sofa surfing with some golden era Bowie instead. Two hours of contentment that culminated in the pleasure of climbing back into his own bed.

Pasquale's Mum had come to see him the day before his court appearance and they had chatted for a while in the privacy of his room, which was her idea not his. He'd given her the money before they'd taken a seat. She'd given him a look and pursed her lips as if she was about to bollock him but then she let it go and accepted it without any comment. Front up, she told him that she was considering a move away, looking at a transfer through her present job. She thought that this would give 'them a fresh start'. He noted the 'them' but this time it was his turn to keep it zipped.

She left after half an hour or so and he spent the rest of the evening getting his gear together then he went outside to join the others out the back of the ref and chilled out for a while, half listening to their comforting, familiar babble.

He set his alarm early so he could get some time alone before he left. He looked for the owl as he always did at that time of the day but he hadn't seen the bird for a little while now. Sonny picked him up just after eight and a pyjama-ed trio of Kat, Jess and Neil made a little guard of honour to farewell him. Tight hugs and kisses from the girls and he even gave a slightly tearful Neil a warm embrace. Wendy had dropped in on her day off to say goodbye to him and he had to bite down hard on his emotions to keep it all in check.

As it transpired Sonny was on the money - they gave him

one year in a secure unit down in Oxford.

The female magistrate had given him a lengthy bollock-ing, peering at him as she did so over her wanky half-moon glasses. Telling him, as she did so, that she was not giving him the soft option, it was all the usual predictable shite. She had noted that he had been 'cooperative with the authorities,' which caused him to look nervously around the room - no Dwayne or Bazzer Dougan to be seen in the gallery though, only an impassive Sonny, his slightly anxious looking mum and some indifferent stone-faced officials.

He had half an hour of being forced to listen to what he already knew. The magistrate gave him the opportunity to talk, he had plenty to say but he wasn't going to do that here. He stumbled out a 'no' and as he did so his legs jumped and twitched uncontrollably under the table. The magistrate gave him a stern nod and then turned to his mum and gave her the chance to comment. Thankfully she kept it brief and without any 'he's a good boy my Pasquale' shit either.

She told the court of her plans to relocate and of her concerns for his academic prospects. She was all very business-like, her voice clear and steady - quite impressive, he thought - nice one.

And then it was done - Sonny was to make the drive and she was heading back to work.

Sonny gave them a moment alone.

She rested her hand on his shoulders and he noted again that they were almost eye-to-eye now.

She looked at him unwaveringly for a few moments then her chin wobbled slightly when she made to speak and her mouth seemed to move a couple of times of its own volition but she breathed deeply and sucked it on down. 'Well son -

it's not how I saw it going for us, but…'

He stepped in, he'd have plenty of time to think about it all.

'It will be OK Mum - I'll be right, don't worry…you worry too much some times, you do.'

She nodded and breathed in sharply and gulped in a little more air.

Then she kissed him on the forehead and turned quickly away, her heels clipping past Sonny who was stood a few strides away, leaning against the bonnet of his car, his hands folded across his chest, slowly chewing his bottom lip with a look on his mug that said he would rather be somewhere else.

Pasquale picked up his two bags and threw them in the boot of Sonny's car.

They jumped in and Sonny turned to him to tell him to strap up, making no comment about the tear that was sliding down his right cheek.

'OK then Pasquale, let's go - hope you like your new home.'

Darrin approached Young on Tuesday about getting an order to dig up the kid but Young brushed it off, not for giving it any play at all.

'Don't know about that Darrin, why? No new evidence is there and, if I remember, it was clearly an overdose, right?'

He shrugged a half hearted agreement at Young but he didn't want it to be bounced away that easily.

'Thought, you know Sarge, if the kid had been to the party we might find some DNA on him. Those kids are going there to be fucked after all - not to play games of Boggle.'

Young looked at him then down at his pressed, knife-edge slacks and proceeded to brush something away that, to Darrin's eye, clearly wasn't there. Mutual irritation was becoming their normal mode of communication. Darrin realised that he didn't have a lot left to play in his hand.

Young gave him a compromise of sorts.

'I'll kick it up stairs to the gaffers, we'll see what they have to say about it. You're on for tonight at Dalton's aren't you?' He was, Dalton was now back from France, this time without his houseguests.

'Anything been going down yet?' Darrin asked.

'Usual shit - back and forward to the warehouse, up to the Coleshaw to see his mum and sister - presents for them both from his holiday on the Med'.'

'Yeah, OK then, I'm on it, I'll be there by six. Anything been happening up the Coleshaw after Dwayne's collar?'

'Yeah it's looking promising up there. Mac noticed a bit of tension between Chris Johnstone and his brother, a bit of finger pointing and raised voices in The Admiral. No doubt they'll find some bozo to step in to replace Dwayne but there's been nothing on the street. It looks like the sweet shop has temporarily closed for business - maybe the pressure is getting to them.'

'Nothing falling back on Mac though, is there?' It was a dumb question really, just gap filling trying to get Young back on an even keel with him.

'No he's sweet - canny bastard he is.'

He gave a half smile at Young's cod Geordie. Young was impossible to like even when the prick made the effort.

Young gathered up his folders making ready to go and Darrin turned towards the door.

Young called out to his back, 'oh yeah, one thing has come in, from the Barrington. I almost forgot to tell you.'

Darrin felt some electricity run from the small of his back to his shoulders, he turned back to face him.

'Yeah?'

'Yeah - well, maybe.'

Young continued.

'That scrote you and Moz chatted to - Baz, Bazzer Dougan.'

'Yeah,' nodding at him to get to it - his breathing now slightly quickened and shallow.

'Disappeared…his missus called up the station this morning.'

'Really, fuck! That is news.'

'We'll see, like I said, maybe it could prove to be nothing.'

Darrin turned back towards the door ignoring Young's blandishments, feeling slightly giddy with the implications of it.

It turned out there was no maybe about it and Bazzer Dougan didn't stay missing for very long. The call came in before he'd even made it down to the Quays. Dougan had been found by a dog walker in some bushes in Rosetta Park - his pants pulled down, his cock hanging out of his boxers and a stab wound to the heart. Crystal meth, a fair bit of it too, was found in his pant's pocket.

The park was a well-known beat and that was the picture that quickly became the party line around the station. Bazzer quickly pigeon holed as a closet shirt lifter, which tied in nicely with the possible procurement of kids and Dalton's party scene. It was convincing but not, Darrin thought, that convincing, all a bit too convenient and too pat, like there was a big fucking neon sign pointing the way for them. He thought of talking to Mozzer about it but dismissed that option without giving any real consideration as to why all that shit with Moz had left things not feeling right. It was uncomfortable between them now and it was well beyond the occasional bout of irritation that they had had with each other. He'd have to wait, Darrin thought, take his time.

When Tommy turned his mobile back on a series of alerts told him that he had a lot more messages than he would have anticipated after just a weekend away; Jimbo, Johnny Buck, Nev and Linda, Mick's next door neighbour, had all contacted him to say variations of the same thing. His dad was decamped in the local hospital. Cobbled together, the messages had given him a composite sketch of what happened with his old man while he was away in Brighton. Mick hadn't been seen by anybody on the Thursday and Friday and his lounge room curtains had remained drawn throughout both of those days, which was an unusual event in itself. Linda, a little concerned, had knocked on his door Saturday morning but left it late as she knew that Mick enjoyed a lie in. She thought that she could hear the murmur of his radio but there was no answer and the curtains remained closed again throughout that day too. Saturday evening, now worried, she'd called Johnny Buck and Johnny came over, JB knocking hard and long at both the back and the front doors. The two of them had speculated that Mick might have gone away for a few days but he usually told Linda if that was to be the case. Sunday lunch time Johnny Buck had grabbed Nev from the boozer and they had gone back up to Mick's house. Johnny had made an executive decision when they had, again, received no answer - quickly smashing in the front door to find Mick slumped in his recliner - immobile, dehydrated, soiled, out of it and barely conscious.

Tommy was down at the hospital within fifteen minutes of listening to the calls, he quickly ascertained Mick's ward and the nurses on the ward desk let him straight in to see him, although it was still out of the visiting hours. The old man was asleep; gaunt, parchment pale and parchment frail. But, all up, he didn't look too worse for wear and the old fucker was still kicking. Tommy felt a wave of relief, it looked like it had been a close call.

He came back in the evening and Jimbo and Johnny Buck were already there at the bedside, chatting with the old man who was propped up in bed, listening to JB talk with that amused, indulgent look in his eyes, which he often reserved for Buck.

'Ten percent truth, ninety percent bullshit and hundred percent entertaining,' was Mick's assessment of Buck's meandering tails of mischief and derring do. Jimbo stood back to let him in and he bowed down to give the old man a quick, gentle embrace.

The old man gave him a soft 'hi,' and a little 'what can you do,' raising of the eyebrows.

'How you feeling then Dad?'

Another shrug, 'Alright I guess - not as good as you I reckon,' Mick gave him a wintery smile/grimace - an unusually fatalistic one at that.

Johnny Buck filled in some clinical details, 'they've got fluids in him Tom - he's looking a lot bloody better than he was.'

Tommy turned to JB and motioned with a flick of the

head that they go outside to chat.

JB's good cheer disappeared as soon as he knew that they were out of the old man's eye line.

'He were a fucking mess Tommy, musta been there a few days the doctors reckon. They think he may have had a fall somewhere in the house, made it to his chair then just sat there, couldn't move his legs at all the poor bastard.'

Tommy pictured, not for the first time in the last hour or so the phone on the coffee table that would have been within easy reach of his dad's right elbow. Again, he was thinking squarely about the fact, and the implications of the fact that the old man had made no attempt to alert anyone to his predicament. He was sure that Mick had made a conscious decision to let it all go and he, hundreds of miles away in bloody Brighton had clearly heard that decision, 'this is what it feels like to die,' sent to him through the fucking ether - no degree of separation.

Tommy patted JB on his wide bony shoulder, 'thanks John, he'll be right, you know what he's like, a tough old sod he is.'

'Aye, yer right son, yer right enough. He had us worried though, a fucking mess he were.'

'They X-rayed him yet?'

'Don't think so, I asked him but he said he didn't know - probably a bit out of it with the drugs and that.'

They turned and went back in to the ward and for the next hour they chatted like four old mates propping up the bar. Mick warming up to it a little bit, not talking that much and, at times, a little halting and mixed up in his speech. Tommy had never heard that before from Mick.

His dad had slivers of brown lodged under the fingernails

on both of his hands - Tommy popped back to the nurses' desk and commented on that, asking them what the story was.

The young nurse on duty told him that he'd been soiled when they brought him in. He pointed out that, to a degree, he still was and they told him that due to Health and Safety issues/regs/fucking concerns, she no longer provided that kind of care for the patients.

Tommy had a 'have I slipped into a parallel universe' moment but left it alone - he needed his energy for other things. He'd bring some clippers and a nailbrush in the next day and get the old man sorted out. The nurses told him that they would be onto the X-rays tomorrow and they would give him a blood transfusion too, after that they'd know more about what was going on with him.

When he got back to the bed Mick had nodded off and they quietly left him to it.

For the next few days Tommy did a run over to see him at lunch, Pauline had no issue with the need for the extra time off. He stayed at the Centre till six then he was straight back to the hospital for the evening visiting hours. The old man had noticeably perked up with the series of blood transfusions and was looking fresh and in the pink. Mick had people with him every time he visited - a rotating roster of Nev, Jimbo, JB, old Lenny from the railway, the boys from the blues band, Drink Gorman and an assortment of other regulars from his various watering holes. Linda, her daughter and even Di, Mick's many years past old flame had shown up, she was still fetchingly tasty too - much closer to his age than Mick's.

During the visits Mick was listening a lot more than he

was talking, there were no displays of recalcitrance from him and he was ever the gent with the nurses. Mick always did put women on a pedestal. The old man was rallying the troops the best that he could, lots of winks and thumbs ups - trying to minimise the fuss around him in as much of an energy saving way as possible.

Tommy saw the specialist on Thursday. He was a slightly diffident Asian guy, maybe his age, maybe a bit younger. They parked off in a non-descript room, which was located just around the corridor from ward's reception area. The small windowless room housed a half dozen or so reasonably comfortable newish looking battleship grey chairs. The walls were filled with the usual NHS paraphernalia promoting health awareness, handy hints and vigilance. Without any fanfare or pre-amble the doctor told him that the X-rays had shown that Mick had brain cancer - secondaries, he said. They hadn't found the primary and there was a suspicion that there was some internal bleeding too, probably as a result of a fall. They were reluctant to perform any invasive surgery on a frail seventy six year old. The guy gave him a grave, unreadable look though there was not much need for a postscript after that.

Deep down he'd already known it, known it ever since Mick had opened the door to him some eighteen months ago, and Tommy absorbed the impact of the news relatively lightly as if somebody had just flicked him across the chops.

'How long,' he asked, 'are we talking – months? A year?'

'In my estimation six months would be the maximum Mr Cochrane. It's hard to say though and we don't like to speculate about such matters. It might only be weeks even but it's impossible to say.' He shrugged a kind of sorry at him but there was no way to gild it.

Weeks!

He thanked the doctor who stood, came over to his chair to shake his hand with a light cool grip whilst placing his left hand for a few moments on his right shoulder - the guy told him that he was sorry, very sorry.

After a few moments alone he made the short walk back to the ward. Linda was at Mick's bedside fussing over him in her low-key good-natured way.

Tommy took the chair between Mick's bed and the long ward window that looked out to the north-eastern fringes of the town and on up to the moors. He leaned over the bed rails and rested his hand on his father's forearm. Mick looked at him a little quizzically but he was OK with it.

He told Linda the bottom line when they left the ward and she immediately burst into tears, he held her and they lightly rocked together for a while, impervious towards and uncaring about the flow of activity that swept on around them.

He went home but he didn't eat. He put on some music that he didn't hear then went to his bed to lay down and, finally, in the dark and in the silence he wept hard and long for his old man. Mick was on his final journey.

Tommy was the first one in to see him on the Saturday. The ward was busy today with lots of family milling around the beds. He'd had an update from the nurses - yesterday they had tried some light physio' on him and the old man couldn't use his pins at all and the prognosis for mobility was not good. Mick was a realist - he would know what that meant - no going home.

They sat quietly together for a while; after all they had

had half a lifetime of shared silences. Tommy was sat again with his back to the wall-length window taking in the movements and postures of those attending to their ailing loved ones.

His old man was awake and he'd managed a bit of food this morning - some pale scrambled eggs washed down with a red jelly for afters.

Tommy leaned in over the bed rail feeling the weight of all those soon to be shed tears pressing against his eyes and tapped his old man on the shoulder. Mick turned his head and looked at him and Tommy delivered the words that he had incessantly replayed in his mind for the last twenty-four hours.

'You know Dad, you can let go if that is what you want to do. You don't have to stick around mate - it's OK, you don't have to, not for me or for anybody else you don't.'

Mick looked levelly at him and, for a moment, Tommy wasn't sure that it had registered with him. Then Mick gave him a brief nod and turned his head back to look briefly over at the guy in the opposite bed to his, and then he looked up at the ceiling and kept his gaze there. A few moments lapsed and then Mick reached over with his right hand to pat the back of Tommy's and then Mick kept the hand there.

Drink and Nev showed up some ten minutes or so later. Nev with a couple of books for Mick, one of which was a biography of George Best, Mick rolled his eyes at that but thanked Nev for it anyway. They shot the shit for a while and Tommy left a few minutes before visiting time was over. He turned in the doorway to the ward to look at the tableaux of the three friends - then he went straight home, empty, spent - yet somehow unburdened too. He'd said what had needed to be said.

Tommy saw the change in him the next day. It was amazing really, powerful testimony to how the body followed the mind. Death was now clearly showing on the old man's face. Mick had started to incrementally step away, drawing back from this mortal coil. Over the next few days there was little talk from him, just the odd nod and a cheery thumbs up. The conversation of his visitors flowed over, across and around the old man as he serenely lay there in his bed, the ailing King as still and calm as a rock in an eddying stream.

Every night, as soon Tommy lay down in his bed he asked for his old man to let go - in fact he willed it. He couldn't bear the thought of a protracted struggle both for Mick's sake and, perhaps selfishly for his own sake too. He embraced the overwhelming helplessness. No matter what he wanted he could not do a fucking thing to prevent it. It was all beyond his wishes and well beyond the force of his will. After another week in the ward they transferred Mick over to the hospice, which was located a couple of miles away from the hospital, Mick was obviously beyond their care now. On the day of the transfer Tommy had taken the afternoon off work and made the fifteen minute drive over there from his flat. The hospice was located on a large block of landscaped grounds, a single storey building flooded with lots of light and suffused with a feeling of space and tranquillity, everything that took place in there felt calm and unhurried.

The hospice reception directed him to Mick's room and he spent an hour or so sat in a big comfy chair next to the high bed listening to the old man's shallow breathing. Mick's digital radio was playing softly next to the bed. He got up and double-checked that it was tuned into Mick's favourite station.

He felt himself start to nod off briefly and when he woke the old man was awake and stirring slightly.

He said, a 'hello Dad' and Mick's eyes turned towards him and he blinked a hello back.

A nurse had a left a beaker of tea on the tray next to Mick's bed and Tommy stood up, walked around to the tray and asked the old man if he would like a drink. Mick blinked another yes, this time emphasised with the shadow of a nod.

He went to the head of the bed, put his hand between the pillows and lifted Mick's head up and brought the beaker carefully to his lips.

He tipped the beaker gently and Mick took in a taste.

Tommy put the beaker back down, still holding Mick up with his right arm behind the pillow.

'How was that then Dad?'

Mick gulped a couple of times and, after a few seconds his voice came to him from a long, long way off. It was no more than a dry rustle but, all the same, it was distinctively Mick.

'Just right son, just right.'

Tommy nodded and smiled at him. He gently let Mick's head down and returned back to his chair.

His old man was back asleep within a couple of breaths.

Tommy got up and left the room.

Linda called him at home the next morning just as he was busy gathering up all his work gear in his little kitchen space.

Her voice was wobbly and smeared. Mick had gone just fifteen, twenty minutes ago. She'd been there in the room with him - he hadn't been alone.

As he tried to absorb the news it felt as if, albeit briefly, his mind and body had splintered as if he was dimensionless - nowhere and fucking everywhere - ego, sense of self completely gone. The room grew, then shrank and then grew again. He felt himself sway and he had put his hands on the kitchen table to stop himself from falling.

He willed himself into autopilot, jumped in the car and was at the hospice in the usual fifteen minutes drive. The girl on the reception told him that the nurses were laying him out and he could see him as soon as they finished, which, she reassured him with a sympathetic smile, wouldn't be too much longer. He phoned Jimbo as he waited and gave him the news. Jimbo told him he was leaving work right away and would be there in ten.

A nurse called him in through to a wicker chaired anteroom, it was a warm, sunny, light filled space, which had lots of pot plants, cane furniture and some magazines that were neatly placed into a pile on a low level glassed table. He opened the mid-brown door at the end of the anteroom and there he was. Laid out on a high single bed almost unrecognisable in death as the man he'd always known, a desiccated husk, his face frozen into the rictus of a hollow-cheeked death-mask grimace. They'd dressed him in one of his signature check shirts and track suit bottoms and someone had placed a flower on the pillow just to the right side of his head - a very un-Mick like touch but, still…

Linda got up from a chair in the corner of the room and gave him a kiss and a long hug.

Tommy went over to Mick and stood next to him, nodding to himself without any real meaning in the gesture. He leant down and kissed his dad softly on his forehead and, as the tears rolled down his face, he told Mick that he loved him. Then he stood there for a long, long while, his hand resting lightly on Mick's bony chest.

NOVEMBER

Pasquale had adjusted pretty quickly to life in the unit. He was assigned a key worker as soon as he arrived, this huge bloke from New Zealand, Steve, whose gentle voice belied his mammoth muscles and cool as fuck tattoos. The kids were a mixed bag, some in there because of family problems or because they had nowhere else to go, others like him, inside doing their bird because of criminal offences.

Everything was on a fucking timetable though and there was a privileges system too. If you kept your nose clean, the more brownie points they gave you - fuck up and they were all taken away and you were right back down at the bottom of the ladder.

The place had a good gym that pissed all over that sad ass shed at the ref and there was an expectation that he use it. He didn't mind the exercise bikes but Steve had got him doing some weights too - all smiles and easy prompts as he busted his bollocks.

It was a little touchy feely at times, inmates were given the opportunity to discuss their issues with each other as they sat in a big, surly, self conscious circle with the staff gawping on.

There was no free access to any room in the joint, staff had to lock and unlock nearly every room apart from the large communal area and that was all a fucking drag. It was a full day of lessons too and there would be no break for what would have normally been the school holidays either.

The kids quickly found out that he was a criminal placement and that gave him a cache of sorts although he made the point of keeping that in his back pocket. He was towards the older end of the residents so it wasn't difficult to sort out what was, for him, a comfortable place on the pecking order. His mum came down south every second weekend to see him, she'd banked the dough for him and she had a job transfer in the pipeline, possibly down in the smoke. Junior had sent him an email. He was already down in Haringey. So, maybe, they would hook up again.

Wendy had been in weekly contact from the ref and he was surprised at how much that communication and gesture meant to him. Kat was doing well in her new place and they hadn't heard anything from Neil since he'd moved out.

A lot of the kids whinged about the place, it was too big, too small, too many rules, too many restrictions, can't smoke, can't do this, can't do fucking that.

But, he liked the rhythm of the place and the regular workouts with Steve and some of the other boys. It was making him feel stronger and cleaner somehow. He felt good about not smoking weed too.

He was doing well at his lessons - knocking them dead in art with his paintings and he'd even done some sculptures, working hard with Rosie the art teacher, proudly keeping the pieces he'd made on display in his room.

He had to see a shrink once a week and she was a smart one too. She was getting him to think about what had brought him to this point in his life, probing around about his mum and his dad and, at first, that had pissed him off a bit. She was like water though, lapping at his shore, forwards and then backwards but always coming.

They told him that, if all went well, towards the end of the year he'd get more supervised time away from the unit -

mobilities they called it.

As Steve said, repeatedly, it was all up to him and if you fuck up it's because you've fucked up. Growing pains, Steve called it.

Pasquale had always known it. In fact, it was like they were holding a mirror up to him. Maybe the time for bullshit was over. His mum had often alluded to the fact that he had no men in his (and her) life and now they were fucking everywhere. Steve was right, he had choices and they were his to make. That had to be a kind of freedom, he supposed.

The station had buzzed for a few days with the Bazzer killing - everybody on the same page that it was a gay-boy tryst gone wrong. They had no leads and no suspects. Mozzer had been pulled onto the investigation team and nobody had approached him about the chat he'd had with Baz, that stone remaining left unturned and he was happy to keep it that way, although it stayed as a sort of wary tension within him, he wasn't comfortable with the implications of it and his mind regularly wandered through a maze of possible meanings, none of which unburdened him. He was tired of feeling like the lone voice in the wilderness, seeing what nobody else appeared to see.

With regard to Bazzer Dougan they had no leads and no witnesses. They picked up a few guys who were known cottagers in the area but had drawn a blank with them. There was nobody amongst them with that kind of violence on their sheet and Bazzer would have been no easy mark either. Bazzer's missus was sounding off a fair bit, reckoning that a rival had offed him. According to her, people were envious of Bazzer and his success!

Darrin dropped in to see Mac towards the end of the week but the Coleshaw was still in limbo - kids milling around, the usual crew in and out of The Admiral. Mac had brought June in again to see if they could get another tickle on what was happening with the ice but he was told by steroid Johnstone that he'd heard from big bro that there was nothing doing. This time Pete had recommended rehab to Mac as an option for June. Mac thought that the guy was joking at first but then a look into those slightly frenetic teddy bear button eyes told him that the bozo was speaking in earnest, mate to mate like - Johnstone was fucking nuts.

Mac had been told that they may have to pull the plug on the op - a couple more weeks of nothing and that would be it. There had been word of bottom squeaking sounds being made by the brass about the drain on their angst-ridden budgets.

Friday night he was down at the Quays, leg weary after back-to-back daily workouts with the old man and the hours spent on the pavement with Johno. They'd been working down on the High Street today - the florists and the Foot-locker store next door were being pulled down. The buildings had been deemed unsafe. The youngish couple who owned the flower shop were planning a move to Spain. She had family somewhere near Barcelona and was eager to make a fresh start. That news had brought his restlessness back to the surface and he'd resolved to stop fucking about and give SOCA a go this weekend. He'd check out the website again, maybe get the application going at least.

There was a new Detective in the portakabin when he arrived, a young guy with an open face, a straw neck and jug ears who bounded over to shake his hand - a Constable Dave Kingston.

Darrin took over from Lumb on the cans, happy to get off his aching feet for a while. Keithy Dalton was at home watching TV, only moving to refresh his glass and giving out plenty of contented yawns as the evening wore on.

Darrin was frustrated with it all. He had that feeling of important things falling just outside his understanding and well outside his control, a sense of impotence with the whole fucking shebang. He was sure that he had most of the pieces in the jigsaw but he had no way of putting them together, as Mac had said to him, 'suspicion ain't knowing and knowing ain't proving.'

It was just before eleven and he and Dave were killing time swapping resumes when Keith's mobile rang. Keith said a muffled hello then killed the volume on the box.

'Gee man, been a while big fella. How's tricks then chief?'

Then there was a lengthy silence, which was broken intermittently by Keith mouthing, 'right right.'

'No man.' Dalton further responded. 'It's all sorted, come on G, it's tidied up in't it? Nothing to worry about fella.'

The other party didn't appear to be mollified.

'Yeah, yeah that's fine. Come on boss, let's let it all calm down. They're running in circles aren't they?' A little urgency in the voice now, the first time in the last few months that Darrin had heard Dalton sound out of kilter.

More silence, nearly a minute of it this time, Keith breathing heavily through his mouth, the tinkling of ice on glass then a slurp.

'OK, OK, no problem. I'll be up there in half an hour for fucks sake.'

That was it, the click of the phone, a heavy sigh of exasperation from Dalton then he was quickly out of the lounge.

He was back in there in two minutes tops and then straight out of the flat door.

Kingston looked over at Darrin.

'Interesting?'

'Maybe - don't hold your breath though. Up there with watching Eastenders this shit.'

Dalton hurriedly came out into the pool of light that illuminated the lobby of the block, buttoning up his car coat as he did so. He put his hat on and hunched his shoulders against the cold.

Dalton climbed into the car and he was gone - turning left, maybe heading towards the orbital.

Darrin felt the frustration again, the op was feeling half arsed, too many gaps and the surveillance on the flat was giving them nothing. Mac looked like the best bet but that window might get snapped closed too and then they would just have to pack it all up and for fucking what?

Kingston asked him if he fancied a pint, he did, he was well in the mood. In fact he felt like getting hammered and if they got a shufty on he could still do it.

It was a clear sunny day for Mick's funeral, almost shirtsleeve warm in the late morning sun. The hearse arrived just before eleven and he, Johnny Buck, Nev, Jimbo and his cousin Dale - Uncle John's boy who he hadn't seen for nearly twenty years all climbed into the following car. A funeral director with a top hat and the necessary solemn bearing and gait walked the cortege down the road for a hundred yards or so, stopping, probably not by design, just next to the Farriers. After a brief pause and a nod to Mick's coffin he climbed in to the leading hearse to ride shotgun with his pal taking off his top hat as he climbed into the seat. As soon as he buckled up, the cortege smoothly made tracks to the crematorium.

Predictably, there was a good turn out for the old man; friends, drinking buddies, plenty of old work mates. A number of his own friends were there too, including Lee and Bernie up from London. Pauline and some of the Centre staff were there and Sonny and Estelle had made it, she with a little bairn in her arms. It was a full house inside the chapel.

Drink Gorman was press-ganged in and the six of them lifted the box that housed the old man's body onto their shoulders, he and Johnny Buck at the back, as they were the two tallest. Steely Dan's *Do It Again* played as they walked the coffin down in between the pews, his left hand gripping Johnny's right shoulder tightly as they made their way to the front of the chapel.

It was a nice enough service, JB got up and spoke until he no longer could, his twinkle eyed anecdote about him and Mick afloat on the Norfolk Broads truncated and terminated with an unbridled, choking emotion. Nev said a few words too, simple but affecting. Nev told the congregation that Mick was the straightest bloke he'd ever known and a bloody true mate too. They had asked him if he wanted to say something, read out a poem or do a eulogy but he didn't think that there was any way that he would have kept it together and he wasn't going to break down in front of all those people - he'd continue his crying when he was alone.

Half an hour and it was done and dusted. They filed out past the coffin and turned left out of the building. The next lot of mourners were already crowding the entrance ready to take their turn at the heartfelt goodbyes.

The wake was held at the Crown - butties, pies and booze,

there were some tears but plenty more smiles. Everybody was easily slipping into the dictates of the familiar environment. Within a couple of hours it was wrapped up, he thanked Paul the landlord and told him that he'd see him soon, maybe band night. On leaving the pub, he walked the few hundred yards up the slope to his old man's place and let himself in through the now boarded up front door, a few shards of broken glass still littered the vestibule. He'd come back and clean them up in a couple of days time.

Tommy had a little look around the front room but there wasn't that much to take in, his old man had been a minimalist. Just his recliner, a sofa that kind of matched the chair and an open display cabinet that was home to some dusty nicotine stained bric a brac - the moraine of family and personal history. He would take the set of Caxton encyclopaedias and, something with a lot more emotional clout to it, a small clog that Mick and his two brothers had worn as infants. The clog had three distinct holes punched into the stiff leather, which denoted the brothers' different foot sizes.

Linda had been in from next door to do a bit of a clean up. She'd emptied the ashtray and given the chair a good wipe down, he could still smell the disinfectant. There was a betting slip on Mick's side table just next to the telephone. He'd had a couple of bets on for races that had been run over a fortnight ago now. Tommy put the slip into his pocket and walked the couple of hundred yards back towards the Crown to drop into the nearby bookies. Mick had won thirty-five quid! He folded the winnings put them in his pocket and went straight to his car. He'd come back at the weekend to see what else needed sorting out. He was done for this day.

Darrin had taken the weekend off and he took a long deliberate walk on the Saturday, all the way out to Rosetta Park in order to make the point of checking out the final resting place of Bazzer Dougan. He'd been found by a golden retriever in a little copse of bushes and trees that were some thirty odd yards from the gent's toilet block. He still didn't buy the consensus, it was still too pat and still too fucking convenient in its timing. There had been ramifications all right. Moz had been bang on about that.

He had looked at the SOCA website when he'd returned home, taking his time to wade his way through the Personal Qualities Framework. After he'd done that he downloaded the application form. There were no vacancies at the moment but he'd decided to throw his hat into the ring, he filled it out and emailed it on.

Sunday he spent with his folks, Sunday lunch followed by the taking in of a game of amateur rugby league up at the local park with the old man. Tommy Cochrane was up there with that mate of his, Jimbo, and his dad had wandered over at half-time to have a brief chat with him. The old man had gone to Mick's funeral and whilst they had talked his dad had gripped Tommy by the upper arm and Darrin could see how much Mick's death had meant to Dougy. There was no lightweight intent behind the exchange. Darrin mused with a palpable sadness that men like Mick and his old man were fast becoming yesterday's warriors, a slowly eroding bridge to a past that was inevitably becoming more and more remote. Not particularly in terms of the time that had passed, he thought, but all the fucking changes and the speed of that change. He was still in his twenties and he could feel that. God knows what it must be like for people of their generation.

Monday at the station and there was a message waiting, given to him by the new desk sergeant, the newly promoted and uniformly respected Tina Clough - he was to call DS Young as soon as possible, please.

He did, before he did anything else in fact. Young was revved up all right, breathy and animated, struggling to maintain his standard Teflon composure.

'Big news Darrin, big news.'

'Yeah?'

No fucking around with him this time, straight to it.

'Yeah Dalton - he's gone, disappeared!'

'Disappeared! Fuck. You're kidding, when?'

'Never came back after Friday night. They found his car up at Stanedge, it had been there all day Saturday. It was called in by the guy with the food van, early on Sunday morning.'

'Fuck!'

'Yeah - and he's not in it either, the mobiles off - he's gone into fucking thin air.'

'The tapes, Sarge, the tapes. Are there any indication of what may have happened on them?'

'Yeah - well you heard his last conversation Darrin, he sounds a little strained, maybe even a bit agitated, but there's not much there, is there? Usual shit, no names, no concrete information, sweet fuck-all – bloody hell.'

'Come on in tomorrow,' Young told him. 'I've already cleared it with your gaffers and we'll get everybody together - brainstorm it a bit.'

Fucking hell, Darrin thought, for all of his permutations and musings he hadn't seen this one coming. The next day they commandeered the detectives' room and played the tape back and forth for nearly a tension filled frustrating hour, trying to pull something, anything, out of the ether that would help them make sense of it.

But, the playing back and forth repeatedly served to tell them exactly fuck all, apart from what they already knew. In reality, their brainstorming meant nothing apart from a fair bit of staring into space, muttered expletives and synchronized head scratching.

'Another gang?' Lumb had theorized.

'More likely the Saltt boys themselves, I reckon,' said Mac. That sounded better to Darrin and to most of the others too, judging by the echoing group nods and mutterings.

'Back to the South of France, said Mozzer, 'missing the warm weather.'

That one hit the ground like a lead balloon and got Mozzer nothing but a few seconds of silence and a rake of looks that confirmed he was now the office plank.

Darrin asked for the tape to be played one more time and listened to it, again, intently, even calling for shush when Lumb and Young started yapping over the top of it.

Darrin circled his hand when the taped hissed to a halt. 'Again', he said, but the others were over it. Darrin stepped up from his perch and hit the play button.

He wasn't sure, but, maybe, maybe there was something in the rhythm of Dalton's sentences, a name in there maybe. 'Gee man' was not an expression he had ever heard Dalton use before. Perhaps it was G-Man, he thought, the fuckers loved their initials. Fucking hell, G-Man - he was sure of it.

Darrin looked around the room - Bowden, Young, Lumb, Mac, Moz, June, Walsh and the new guy Kingston and he bit down, literally tasting blood in the inside of his mouth on the revelation of his insight

Mac brought it to a close with a heavy shrug of his shoulders.

'Ah well, if he has fucking gone, no great loss eh? It's one for the good guys far as I'm concerned.'

Nobody demurred on that one. Bowden looked at his watch, 'OK then gents and good lady once more unto the breach - let's wrap it up for today.'

They stayed on the flat for a few more days. Nearly a week after the disappearance Niall O'Brien turned up and spent an hour or so in the joint, they could hear some cupboards and drawers being opened and closed but he came out of the flat apparently empty handed. That was followed by a few days of nothing and Young told the team one more week and that was it, the Quays side of it would be finished.

Friday and he was planning for the weekend, up to Glasgow this time, for a bit of tartan salsa with Jolika and Stuart. He hadn't danced much since he'd done his shoulder. With the injury it had been much too painful to do the lead and he was looking forward to getting back into it.

Darrin went into the canteen at the end of the shift and the large room was surprisingly full and rowdy. Keegan and a couple of his buddies appeared to be at the focal point of the tumult. There was an empty table in the corner of the room a couple of strides away from the till and when he grabbed his tea and a pie he made his way straight to it. Trish came over to see him after a couple of minutes of his 'Darrin no mates' solitude and she gave him a little thrust of the hip and an arched eyebrow.

'Not joining us then Dazzler?'

He waved at his plate, 'in and out Trish.'

'Hmmm, that doesn't sound like you.' She gave him a smile that he could feel in his pant's pocket.

He nodded over at the noise, 'what's happening then?' Mozzer was over there now, his arm draped around Keegan's beefy shoulder, comrades in arms enjoying a hearty laugh together.

'You not heard then?'

Fuck, she was getting as bad as Young.

He intimated a give it to me.

'DS Keegan - he's retiring, taking his pension, over thirty years in, the lucky sod.'

He kept his face neutral and looked at the back of Keegan's big head.

Mozzer had broken off from the jollies for a moment or two and he caught Darrin's glance and motioned for him to come over and join them.

Darrin leaned back in his chair, he looked straight at Mozzer dead-eyed and didn't respond.

Mozzer gave him a shrug and Trish stepped to his right to block his view of Keegan's table.

'Well?' she asked.

He shook his head, 'things to do and places to go me, Trish.'

She tutted, exasperated with him, 'fair enough misery guts - later, maybe.'

Darrin finished what was left of his tea, returned his tray to the counter and walked out of there. He thought about turning around to give Keegan the eye but he didn't. Out into the corridor and on past Sergeant Clough who gave him a cheery wave, his stomach churning with sour distaste and frustration. The following Tuesday, he was running late for the midday shift and had to jog from his car into the building. Sarge Thomas made a show of pointedly looking at his watch then tapped it as Darrin moved quickly past the charge desk. He went with haste down to the lift's doors, which opened just as he arrived there. Keegan stepped out into the corridor, his frame filling up two thirds of the lift's entrance. There was less than a metre between them but he didn't step back to give Keegan any space and if Keegan had done so he would have been back in the lift.

Darrin leaned in towards him. He could smell the mints, the tobacco and the clear vodka spirit. He noted the broken capillaries that leeched from the big man's nose on across his broad cheeks.

Keegan gave him a 'how do' and made to go past - Darrin touched him lightly on the arm and plastered a smile across his face.

'Off I heard then Sarge, congrats, end of the month eh?'

Keegan rocked a little on his heels, stifled something and smiled back at him. 'That's right Constable, more than thirty years of ball ache given to this lot, more than enough I reckon.'

Darrin didn't allow any gap in the conversation to develop.

'Where are you off to then Sarge? Somewhere nice I hope.'

Keegan nodded along at that, he was a little bit more engaged now - back in balance, back in control. The fucking big man.

'Yeah, missus has persuaded me to open a B and B down in Bournemouth, I'll be on fried egg duty,' he chuckled.

Darrin clapped him hard on the shoulder, 'ah well, best of luck with that, G Man. Hope it all works out well for you.'

Keegan absorbed it with a slight widening of his eyes and a pulling back, by at least an inch, of the big heavy head, his smile slipping from his face like a landslide.

Sarge Thomas called out from the desk, 'move your arse PC May - now like!'

Keegan stood to one side to give him access the lift - Darrin stepped in and hit the button for the top floor.

Keegan turned and looked at him. The mask was gone now, all those years of corruption and the accumulation of barely hidden contempt in plain sight on that big hard face. Darrin held the look, his own mouth pulling back into a carnivorous smile.

Keegan leaned back slightly and hooked his thumbs in his pant's pockets.

'You be careful out there son - it's a dangerous world we live in.'

Darrin winked mockingly at him. 'Good advice that and back at yer Keegan, you too. Unfinished business.' He took his finger off the open button and the lift doors came noisily together.

Bournemouth eh! Darrin thought, as the lift started to climb. Maybe the prick wasn't out of reach yet. After all, time was on his fucking side.

WINTER

DECEMBER

Sonny had called him with confirmation of an end of January kick off date for a local version of the gangs' initiative. Tommy had been silently grateful that Sonny had decided not to let what had happened with Donna and Pasquale fuck that up for him. Boy did he owe him one.

The rear of the building had been rebuilt at the Centre and business would be back to normal by the end of the month. He'd reduce his hours and that would go a little way to give Pauline and her strained finances some breathing space.

Tommy had taken time out in order to stuff Mick's clothes into half a dozen or so plastic bags and had taken the drive over to couple of charity shops. He donated Mick's last lot of winnings to Mick's favourite charity, Save the Children. He'd picked up the clog and the encyclopaedias and a bag of photos which showed Mick as a boy with his mum, dad and brothers. All of them having fun at a family holiday on the beach at Filey - the photos, old and slightly faded, had been taken just a couple of years before the start of the Second World War.

He'd wait to put the house on the market, maybe do it early in the New Year, there was no rush. In the early evening that he'd picked up Mick's gear he'd stood in the back yard for a while. The yard was a suntrap, south-west facing and away from the noise of the traffic. In the warm afternoons and evenings Mick used to love to sit out there with his paper, his brew and a fag chewing over politics and the current affairs, lightening up the experience with the sports and his picks for the next day's racing.

He had heard a rustle in the big tree that loomed over Linda's backyard wall. He'd looked up and saw a big white barn owl sitting up there in the bald branches. It was looking down towards him, occasionally turning its head to the left and to the right. Tommy stood there for at least twenty minutes and watched the silent bird, thinking of Mick as he did so. He had the realisation that Mick was now a gap in his life that would never be filled.

Finally the owl took off, on over his head and flying east towards the low moor. He immediately went back inside the kitchen, locked the house up and drove back home.

On his return Tommy fired up the computer and had a look at this dating website that he'd joined just a couple of weeks ago. He'd taken a gander at the gals down in Brighton and had added as one of his new 'friends' an attractive African woman who was living down there, somewhere in Hove. He'd had a strange instant moment of recognition when he'd seen one of her additional photos, he was certain that they'd crossed paths, although, despite racking his memory, he couldn't remember when. Anyway, she'd reciprocated his interest and added him as a 'friend' too, which meant that they could now correspond directly with each other. He looked again at the oddly affecting picture. He still had no memory of where they might have met - strange.

Ah well, Tommy thought, 'friends!' Maybe that was something he could build upon.